THE NEXT TO DIE

"What's wrong, Larry?" Joyce asked.

"Did you hear something?" He quickly glanced around, but the car windows were opaque with vapor.

"Nothing. Come on, Larry," she urged. "Let's do it."

Twigs snapped just outside the car and Larry's back stiffened beneath her hands. "It's probably just a deer," she whispered. "It'll go away in a minute."

"Yeah," Larry whispered. "Let's make love, babe."

Something thumped against the car door.

Larry pulled away, fumbling at his zipper. He rolled off Joyce, back into the driver's seat. She straightened her skirt and flipped the lever controlling the seat back. It flung her upright and she saw Larry's hand on the door handle.

"No, don't!" she hissed.

He hesitated, then removed his hand. An instant passed, then a dull glow showed through the steamy windows. A flashlight.

Someone tapped on the glass.

"It's a cop." Larry sighed with relief and put his hand on the window crank.

"No, wait!" Joyce cried as she watched the window go down.

A black-gloved hand snaked through the open window and grabbed Larry by the collar, yanking him halfway out. A millisecond passed. There was a clicking sound, then a muted blast and something whizzed past Joyce's face, followed by a spray of hot, salty liquid . . .

Books by Tamara Thorne

HAUNTED

MOONFALL

ETERNITY

Published by Pinnacle Books

ETERNITY

Tamara Thorne

PINNACLE BOOKS
KENSINGTON PUBLISHING CORP.

http://www.pinnaclebooks.com

PINNACLE BOOKS are published by

Kensington Publishing Corp.
850 Third Avenue
New York, NY 10022

All Kensington Titles, Imprints and Distributed Lines are available at special quantity discounts for bulk purchases for sales promotions premiums, fund-raising, and educational or institutional use. Special book excerpts or customized printings can also be created to fit specific needs. For details, write or phone the office of the Kensington special sales manager: Kensington Publishing Corp., 850 Third Avenue, New York, NY 10022, attn: Special Sales Department, Phone: 1-800-221-2647.

PINNACLE and the P logo Reg. U.S. Pat. & TM Off.

First Printing: February 2001
10 9 8 7 6 5 4 3 2 1

Printed in the United States of America

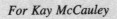
For Kay McCauley

One

> The soul, like the body, lives by what it feeds
> on . . .
>   —Josiah Gilbert Holland

He had always been fond of the ax and he wielded it with the skill of a lumberjack, though he was hardly that.

The standing stones cast afternoon shadows over the corpse as Jack surveyed his work. Frank Lawson's head, cleanly severed, the bullet hole a neat dark pit in the center of his forehead, lay precisely in line with his neck. Arms were detached from the torso at the shoulders and separated again at elbows and wrists. He considered separating the fingers from the palms as well, then decided against it because his own thinly gloved hands already ached from exposure to the frigid air shrouding Icehouse Mountain.

He had sliced the legs, flesh and bone, cleanly at the groin, then divided the right one again at knee and ankle, each precise cut obvious only by the sluggish ooze of thickening blood. Even that, camouflaged by the sheriff's dark brown uniform, was not too telling from a distance.

Kneeling, Jack raised the ax once more, aiming carefully at the left knee. He let the blade fall, and smiled at the simple pleasure of another perfect cut. It had been too long since he'd taken pride in his work, had taken the time to do it right. Far too long.

As he prepared to make the final cut, the growl of an engine toiling up the mountain road above the meadow made him pause. Irritated, he rose, glancing at his watch. Two o'clock. Another tour wasn't due for ninety minutes. Perhaps the vehicle was carrying hikers to the trailhead at the end of the road, another thousand feet up. More likely, it contained tourists coming here, to Icehouse Circle, the most popular destination on the mountain.

A Jeep. He recognized the timbre of the engine as the driver shifted to a lower gear to climb the last hairpin before the turnout where Lawson's black and white Ford Explorer was parked. Jack stepped behind one of the ancient stone megaliths and waited, listening to the crunch of gravel as the vehicle pulled off the road. A moment later the engine cut out.

Damn it. Directly before him, the body lay in the center of Icehouse Circle—Little Stonehenge, the tourists insipidly called it. Beyond, the steep stone trail led up to the roadside parking area.

He glanced around the meadow as doors slammed above. Patches of old snow lay cloaked in shadows, and ragged gray lichen clung tenuously to rocks and ancient tree stumps, while summer flowers, profusions of lavenders, blues, pinks, and yellows, thrived in the crystalline sunlight. The alpine grassland extended a hundred yards to the southerly stairs and two hundred feet to the east, north, and west where it ended abruptly in a rough semicircle of treacherous glacial drops. There was no avenue of escape and few places to hide.

A feminine voice drifted down, quickly followed by a child's laughter. Jack trotted fifty feet to a fallen redwood not far from the northern rim of the stone circle. Rotting bark crumbled as he scrambled over it. Blind white grubs squirmed obscenely within a nest in the hollow. Crouching near the twist of gnarled, dead roots, he pulled off his bright red windbreaker and stuffed it down under the log. Shivering in a black T-shirt, he silently cursed his uncharacteristic lack of foresight. He gulped in the crisp air and suddenly adrenaline burst inside him, fire in his veins, a rare treasure, easily forgotten.

Dizzy with the sensation, he nearly laughed. His actions were not a curse but a gift to relieve boredom, his own and others'. Without a few indulgences, the occasional surprise, there was no challenge, no *joie de vivre*.

A smile twitched across his lips as two figures appeared on the path. One was a woman wearing a garish purple parka that marked her an employee of Bigfoot Tours, the other, a boy of nine or ten in a sky-blue jacket.

The child spoke. "Is that it, Mom?" Jack felt a fresh burst of fire as the boy pointed across the meadow toward the circle of stones. Toward his hiding place.

"That's it, Josh," the woman said as they reached the bottom of the trail. "Little Stonehenge. What do you think?"

"Cool." He took his mother's hand and yanked, but she stood her ground.

"It looks a lot like the real Stonehenge in England," she said, taking a few slow steps onto the rock-lined meadow path, her gaze unwaveringly fixed on the stone circle. "It's smaller and there's no henge, but it's probably just as old. Some people say it's a fake, though."

"If it's old, how can it be a fake?"

She laughed, the sound clear and not altogether unpleasant. "I guess it's because some so-called experts claim the same people—*exactly* the same people—who built Stonehenge came here and built this one, too, which is impossible since it took more than a thousand years to build Stonehenge. Of course, they also think Merlin was the chief engineer—"

The words hung in the air as her hands came down firmly on the boy's shoulders and pulled him back against her body.

Jack smiled, realizing she had spotted the corpse. "Jeez, Mom, what's the matter?"

"Stay put."

"Why?"

She shushed the boy then called out, "Sheriff Lawson?"

Lawson, of course, made no reply.

"Sheriff?" she called again. After a brief pause, she bent and spoke softly in the child's ear. As she straightened, the boy crossed his arms over his chest in a display of annoyance, but stayed put while his mother approached the megaliths alone. She hesitated at the Circle's edge, peering apprehensively at the body twenty feet farther in. "Sheriff?"

You already know he's dead, my dear woman. Now step up and admire my handiwork.

A cold gust of wind made the wildflowers tremble, then blew the purple hood from the woman's head, revealing attractive features and wheat-colored hair falling in waves about her shoulders. He recognized her.

She hesitated an instant, then turned to remind the child to remain stationary. Returning her gaze to Lawson's body, she slowly, very slowly, stepped into the Circle.

Jack's calf muscle spasmed, twisting into an agonizing knot, but he held his breath and willed the pain away. After a few seconds, it began to loosen and he exhaled, glad that the wind immediately carried away the vapor of his breath.

She stopped three steps short of the corpse, staring, her breath coming in small white puffs. He watched the color drain from her face, wishing he could experience her thoughts and emotions as her mind assimilated what lay before her.

"Mom?" the boy called.

"Stay where you are," the woman commanded, her voice surprisingly strong. Slowly, she looked up, her scanning eyes and flared nostrils betraying incipient panic. She reminded him of a fox scenting the hounds. He held his breath until she at last looked back down at what remained of the sheriff of Eternity County.

He had expected her to scream, run, or both, and was pleasantly surprised by her display of backbone as she slowly edged around the body, taking it all in.

Every bit. Every piece. Amused, Jack watched as she turned her back to him and looked at the sheriff's legs. "Oh dear God," she gasped. Perhaps, he thought, she was smart enough to recognize the meaning of the ankle that remained attached to the lower leg.

Suddenly she whirled, eyes narrowing as she searched her surroundings once more. She spotted the ax at the same moment he did, the blade glinting as it caught a ray of sunlight. It had been sloppy of him to forget it, but he was too fascinated now to care.

Briefly he thought she was going to disappoint him, to lose her nerve, but her paralysis ended in a heartbeat. Pleased, he watched as she pivoted, her eyes tracing over every rock and flower. Silently, she raised her hand in a firm halt gesture as she rechecked her son.

As she faced the body again, he considered taking her purely for sport. This one would fight.

Abruptly, she stepped past the body, tentatively approaching his deadfall. He poised to spring, but she halted at the ax. Silently, he opened his mouth and inhaled deeply, scenting her fear as she looked at the bloody blade. Her black-gloved hand started to reach down, then stopped. She surveyed the landscape once more.

A smart woman, Jack thought with admiration, a rarity because she understood that she'd interrupted the artist at his work. She didn't move this time, didn't turn away from him and he wondered if she might sense his gaze and unconsciously know not to turn her back on a predator.

For a minute and a half—he counted each second—she stood there, her eyes roaming and roving, her fingers held slightly curled, but stiff with tension. Her nostrils flared with each exhalation.

Suddenly, she stepped past the ax and the nearest outer megalith, straight toward him. He held his breath as she scanned to the west, the east, and then, finally, north, gazing directly at him. She squinted down at the massive deadfall and he felt her eyes boring through the trunk, seeing him, *knowing* him.

He tensed for attack as she took one more step, but then she halted and stared at something on the ground by the trunk.

Glancing down, he saw his red windbreaker, the sleeve cuff just beyond the trunk's edge. *Now she knows I'm here.* He readied for action, excited, impatient.

But she came no closer. Instead, she turned and sprinted across the meadow toward her son. Jack watched as she hurried the boy up the trail and disappeared over the hill's crest. A moment later, the Jeep roared to life. The screech of burning rubber as she peeled out pleased him.

Quickly, he retrieved the ax and finished the job on Lawson. After, he took the blade to northern cliffs beyond the deadfall and flung it into the deep glacial crevasse. He leaned over the old wooden railing, watching as the hatchet cartwheeled down into the icy shadows, the steel ringing belltones in the charged atmosphere. In a moment it was gone. Forever. For eternity.

PART ONE

PART ONE

Two

August 16

> *kill, v.t.* To create a vacancy without nominating a
> successor.
>
> —Ambrose Bierce

Zach Tully had wanted out of the department and out of Los Angeles and now, after more than three frustrating years spent trying to flush out the Backdoor Man, he told himself he wasn't giving up the search, just leaving the city and the force. *And good riddance.*

He had begun the last leg of the journey only minutes before and now he saw Shasta Lake and the summer-brown mountains surrounding the long-fingered reservoir. Interstate 5 north from LA had been an easy, if hot and boring, drive that made him wonder how grueling it must have been in the sweaty old days before air conditioning. The highway ribboned through long dry stretches of oil fields, tumbleweeds, and phone lines, desolate land dotted with gas stations, truck stops, and McDonald's. When he passed into the northern half of the state, the business loops turned into towns with trees and finally gave way to the vast suburban sprawl of Sacramento.

He'd gotten a late start the previous day and was thoroughly sick of driving by the time he hit the state capital, but he pushed on. Two hours later he stopped in Redding where he treated himself to a room in a historic but drafty western-style hotel dating back to gold rush times. Among the points of interest were bullet holes in the dining room's ornate pressed-tin ceiling and, in his tiny room, an allegedly famous brass bed. The desk clerk proudly told him that Wild Bill Hickok had once spent the night in that very room and very bed and after waking with an aching back, Tully figured that Hickok must have slept on the same mattress, too.

Now, still enjoying the view of the lake, he was beginning to look forward to seeing his new home for the first time. Ever since accepting the position of sheriff for Eternity County, he'd been more apprehensive than pleased. While he'd pictured himself moving to a small city, something with a population under twenty thousand, it hadn't occurred to him that he might end up in a village of fewer than five hundred permanent residents. Pretty extreme for a city boy.

He had spent sleepless nights wondering if he had done something he'd regret. He still wondered. After all, he hadn't even sent a résumé to the place. The mayor, a well-spoken man who identified himself as Ambrose Abbott, told him someone at the CHP office at Horse Junction, eighty miles southeast of Eternity, spoke very highly of Tully's abilities. He'd never even heard of Horse Junction, let alone Eternity. He tried to inquire further, but Abbott didn't give him a chance. Instead, he launched into a sales pitch, saying that Eternity—town and county—needed a new sheriff, someone experienced and capable of autonomous action and excellent judgment. The last sheriff, Abbott said, met with a fatal accident recently, and the town council hoped Tully would accept the offer.

Eternity, the mayor claimed, was a charming and quiet tourist town, the only inhabited area in the tiny county. He would find life good there. Abbott continued to extol the perks of the position, and Tully found it harder and harder to resist as he heard about the competitive salary, the three full-time deputies, and the fully furnished 2,000-square-foot log cabin that came with the job. But it was the fishing hole behind the cabin that made the position impossible to turn down.

Even so, the worrying began the moment he announced he was leaving the department. Had he acted too quickly? Could he stand the isolation? Was it really a good idea to give up his senior status in homicide, to leave his friends and his partner? He didn't know the answers to his questions, but he didn't retract his notice, either. Soon it was too late to back out. Not only would it be dishonorable, the guys would have ribbed him without mercy.

The previous Friday had been his final day at Rampart Division. After work, his buddies threw him a going-away party, a bittersweet affair that he had dreaded because, as he expected, one of the guys, his judgment impaired by a pitcher of beer, nostalgically brought up Tully's near-catch of the Backdoor Killer three years back. John Mendoza, his partner, shut the drunk up, but Tully's tenuous good spirits were shot down.

He'd put on a good front and finished the evening with only Mendoza aware of his brooding. The detectives remained in the bar after the others had departed. "The only thing I'm going to miss is your ugly face," Tully had told Mendoza with beery affection. He meant it. After his family was murdered, Mendoza had kept him going. Without him, he might have crawled into a bottle or maybe even eaten a bullet. He hoped he could get along without John.

"Yeah," Mendoza had said as he twisted a lime slice down into his Corona bottle. "I envy you, buddy. No pollution, no gangs. Hell, probably no graffiti. And you're the goddamned *sheriff* for Christ's sake. Nobody's gonna be telling you what to do."

"Say the word and I'll get you a spot on the force."

"What?" Mendoza snorted. "You want me to be Barney Fife to your Sheriff Taylor?"

"Badass Barney." Tully chuckled. "You want it, you got it."

"Tully, I don't want it. I'd go nuts if I had to stay in a place like that. I like the city—scum and all.'' He shook his dark head. ''And I couldn't live in snow.''

''Oh hell, Mendoza, don't be a wimp. There's no snow from late June until September.'' His own joking words depressed him. ''October in a good year.''

His partner eyed him. ''Seriously, man, aren't you gonna go stir crazy in a place like that?''

''Maybe. Won't know until I try.''

''How far's the big city?''

''Three hours to a little city. It's not so far, but the road into Eternity County is one of those sidewinder jobs. The place is pretty much on its own in the winter.''

''Jesus Christ, you mean you can't get out at all for six months at a stretch?''

''Six months?'' That possibility hadn't even occurred to him; he'd assumed they'd be snowed in during storms only. Visions of Jack Nicholson cavorting with an ax danced through his head. ''Well, could happen, I guess.'' He paused, feeling foolish for his lack of research then added lamely, ''The fishing's supposed to be great.''

''Good. If you make it through your first winter and still like it, I'll come up and go fishing with you next summer.''

''I'd like that.'' He felt a goofy grin attach itself to his mouth. It made him glad he hadn't had more to drink.

''So, tell me something, partner.''

Tully raised his eyebrows and waited.

''Are you really sure you want to do this?''

''You don't think I should?''

''It's time,'' Mendoza said gently. ''I hate to see you go, but I think you should. I'm just a little surprised you're willing.''

''I'll never give up the search for the Backdoor Man.'' Soberness returned, a hard, heavy brick. ''I promised myself I'd get that son of a bitch. But he hasn't signatured another killing since . . . since Linda and Kevin.'' It was still hard to say their names aloud.

''He's probably dead or out of the state,'' Mendoza told

him. "Out of the country, even. In jail for something else, maybe."

"Could be. But I don't think so." The hairs on his arms bumped up and he felt a sudden surge of the old anger, the old drive. "He's still out there, John. I can feel him. Someday, he's going to be all mine."

"I know." Mendoza studied him over the top of his beer bottle. "But I'm glad you've got enough sense to start a new life. You've been obsessed, man."

"I know, I know." Tully waved him off. Mendoza had read him this act pretty regularly for the last two years.

"Your guilt eats you alive. There was nothing you—"

"Could do," Tully finished, irritated. "I'm getting out, so you don't need to lecture me, Mother."

"Okay, sorry. I guess you've got a handle on it."

But do I, really? Traffic on I-5 thinned as Tully passed the exit for a tiny town called La Moine and followed the interstate into the tree-dotted hills. After the murders he'd never spent another night in his house in Santo Verde. Instead, he put it on the market and moved into a one-bedroom apartment in Echo Park. Once the house sold, he never even visited again. Not until last week, when he'd forced himself to drive by one last time. The bungalow had a fresh coat of paint and a blue bicycle lay carelessly on the lawn. The sight nearly tore his heart out.

He'd returned to his apartment, worrying that once again he was failing Linda and Kevin by leaving LA without catching their murderer. That night, the old nightmares returned with a vengeance. He had relived that night so many times in his dreams; nightly for the first year, then weekly, finally no more than once a month. The hell of it was, the dreams wore him out and terrified him with the images of bodies and blood, the untouched birthday cake and unseen eyes watching him. The echo of laughter in his ears.

Every time he had the dream, he awoke trembling and covered in sweat, nagged by the feeling he had missed something important. To this day, he wondered if it was true—God knew he hadn't behaved like a cop that night.

The miles flew by. HORSE JUNCTION, he read. NEXT EXIT. A blue California Highway Patrol sign was mounted beneath the sign. He took the off-ramp, momentarily gliding into the CHP's lot. He stepped out of the cool confines of his dark blue Camaro and stretched.

The summer sun beat down on him as he straightened his clothing and ran a comb quickly through his hair. Refreshingly cool air assailed him as he walked inside and introduced himself to the receptionist.

She knew who he was. "We thought we'd be seeing you, Sheriff Tully. Let me tell Chief Ladd you're here."

She busied herself with the comm line while Tully marveled at being called "Sheriff." Mendoza had been right about Tully's fantasies: beneath the hard-boiled, jaded exterior beat the heart of Sheriff Taylor, longing for his own personal Mayberry. His mood lifted another notch.

"Chief Ladd will see you now," the receptionist told him with a sweet smile. "Down the hall to the right, first door."

The designated door opened and a heavyset man with graying blond hair stepped out. "Come on in, Tully." He extended his hand. "Howard Ladd."

The man had a grip like a steel trap but Tully met it solidly. "Good to meet you, Chief."

Ladd sat down in his padded desk chair and gestured at the seat across from him. "What can I do for you?" He picked up a briar pipe and tamped it.

"I have a few questions."

Ladd lit up and gazed at him from under his unruly eyebrows. "Thought you might. Shoot."

"Ambrose Abbott, the mayor of Eternity, told me that someone here recommended me."

"That would be me."

"Why? You don't know me."

"I know *of* you."

"I don't recall sending a résumé here."

"You didn't." Ladd wasn't the forthcoming type.

Tully had scattered a mere dozen résumés among various law enforcement agencies in northern California so it was a good bet some might have been sent on to other offices. He cocked an eyebrow. "Was a copy forwarded to you?"

"No. Ambrose Abbott didn't hear about you from me." Ladd relit his pipe. "He already had your résumé. You'll have to ask him how he got it."

Tully nodded then leaned back in his chair. "I'll do that. How is it you've heard of me?"

"Everyone in law enforcement's heard of you. You're famous for solving the El Niño murders. That took a good bit of policework," he added. "Maybe you can tell me more about it sometime."

"Be glad to." Tully paused. "I didn't realize the El Nino case was such big news outside of LA."

"Sure. That and the Delmonico case really established your reputation. I'll tell you, those were some nasty antics those Delmonicos pulled. Incest, cannibalism, everything in between." He rubbed his chin, eyeing Tully. "You were the only one who ever came close to solving the Backdoor killings. Losing that bastard must've really frosted your balls." Ladd hesitated, obviously remembering who the killer's last victims were. "Hell of a thing to lose your family like that. Sorry."

"Yeah." Tully shifted uncomfortably in his chair then cleared his throat. "Ambrose Abbott told me that Eternity's last sheriff met with a fatal accident."

"Accident?" Ladd guffawed. "That's a good one."

Tully leaned forward. "What?"

"Accident, my ass. Lawson was butchered like a side of beef." The bushy brows arched. "Maybe the town council was afraid the truth would scare you off."

"It's hard to believe they'd lie about something like that. What the hell am I getting into?"

"Eternity, son. You *know* about Eternity, don't you?"

"Tourism is its main source of income," Tully recited, embarrassed as a schoolboy. He'd looked the town up in a few travel guides before he said yes. After, he never got around to a detailed check. *Stupid. Stupid.* "Icehouse Mountain is renowned for its height, its spas, and resorts, not to mention its great skiing." He paused, allowing his lips to curl into a smirk. "And Bigfoot lives there."

"There's more, Tully. Lots more." Howard Ladd laughed heartily. "Caught you with your pants down, didn't I?"

Tully took a deep breath. "Maybe you'd better tell me."

"They're all nuts up there."

" 'Nuts' as in they believe in Bigfoot?"

"Tully, that Bigfoot crap is just the tip of the iceberg. So to speak." The chief cleared his throat. "You're going to be dealing with drunken tourists, a high crime rate, religious nuts, New Agers, and Shady Pines." He chuckled. "You'll have your hands full, that's for sure."

"Shady Pines?"

The glint in Ladd's eye belied his sympathetic voice. "The Shady Pines Sanitarium. Security's a little lax."

"Christ." Tully's mind was reeling. "I suppose it's for the criminally insane?"

"Lord, no. With a name like Shady Pines?" The chief didn't bother to hide his amusement. "It's where rich folks stick their Uncle Napoleons and Aunt Mata Haris. Your criminals are out on the streets."

"You're serious about the high crime rate?"

"Damn straight I'm serious."

"What kind of crime are you referring to? Robberies? Bar brawls? Car theft?"

"You'll get some of those, sure, but mostly I'm talking about homicide." Ladd spoke almost offhandedly, though his eyes narrowed and bored into Tully's, waiting for a reaction.

"You're kidding!"

"Why do you think they're willing to pay for a hotshot like you? People are always disappearing. A lot of them turn up dead." Ladd shook his head. "Tully, with the reputation you've got for cracking homicide cases, I thought you took this gig because you were looking for a challenge. I'm surprised you didn't do your homework."

Tully nodded, unable to argue. "I didn't want any reason to talk myself out of coming. *Caveat emptor,* huh?"

"Betcher ass," Ladd said, a little too enthusiastically. "But you're going to love it. It's your kind of bailiwick."

So long, Mayberry. "Is your department handling the investigation of the sheriff's murder?"

"Hell, no. We steer clear of Eternity County. I lost a man up there six years ago after the sheriff before last was murdered. Sent Jack Murphy up to help out until Sheriff Lawson arrived. Murphy climbed in his vehicle one morning and drove up Eternity Highway, you know, on rounds. When he started back down, his brakes failed. Murder. Squashed him like a bug smack dab in the middle of Icehouse Gorge. Heard of it?"

"No."

"Vicious stretch of road. You'll pass through it on your way up."

"Your man, Murphy. No chance it was an accident?"

"No chance. His brake lines were cut. Nobody ever caught the bastard. Whoever did it most likely lives up there. You'll probably shake hands with him and never know it."

"Wait a minute, Chief. In addition to your officer, two sheriffs have been murdered up there? Two in a row?"

"Yeah, but Stan Henry was shot during a bank robbery. We've got that perp behind bars. Anyway, as far as I know, your deputies are working the Lawson case and that other murder from a couple months back. The town council kept it out of the papers. The council's in charge. Abbott's the head honcho, and he's okay but cranky. Regular Grade A prick, to be honest, but only if you take it lying down. Stand up to him, he'll respect you."

"Wait a minute. Hold it." Tully put his hand up like a traffic cop. "Back up. You're saying the town council covered up a homicide?"

"Not exactly." Ladd fiddled with his pipe, then looked up at Tully from beneath his bushy brows. He spoke in a wry tone. "It was kept quiet. They buried it. Bad for the tourist trade." He paused then added almost defensively, "That's important up there. Tourism is Eternity's lifeblood." He gave Tully a twisted little grin.

"Tell me about the murder," Tully said bluntly.

"Not much to tell. The victim was a former Shady Pines resident. Family died off, so they turned him loose in town. That happens a lot. Eternity's pretty freethinking about indigents and lunatics. They put them up, put them to work, if they're able. Guess they don't mind the loonies since most of the working population are half crazy anyway—"

"The murder?" Tully prompted.

"They found him in the picnic area near the trailhead at the top of Icehouse Road, up on the mountain. He was in the men's room. And the ladies' room. And a couple of trash cans."

"The indigent and the sheriff were both mutilated?"

"Didn't see any of it myself. Abbott told me the job on the indigent was messier than the one done on Sheriff Lawson, but it sounds like you've got yourself a single perp." He sucked the pipe. "Serial killer. Right up your alley."

Tully decided to change the subject. "Tell me about the town council. Sounds like Eternity's big on politics."

"Sure. Lots of that." Ladd knocked the ashes out of the pipe and leaned forward. "You want my opinion, the council covers up all sorts of things. The lifers cover up for one another."

"Lifers?"

"That's what they call themselves, the ones who've been there forever. And I do mean forever. You ever hear of Icehouse Circle? Little Stonehenge?"

"That's where the megaliths are located?"

"You familiar with the hocus-pocus part of the place?"

"I'm afraid not."

"Well, you get a book on it, or go on the tour up the mountain to learn about it. I can't do the story justice—it's the biggest load of horseshit I've ever heard, but the lifers all claim it's gospel."

The intercom buzzed and Ladd picked up. "Yeah, Loretta?" He glanced at his watch. "Have him cool his heels for just a minute." Ladd hung up. "Got an appointment waiting on me." He stood up, Tully following suit. "You'll do fine up there, Sheriff, as long as you don't let them get to you with their tall tales. With your track record, you'll have everything square in no time."

Tully endured another bone-crunching handshake. "Thanks."

"Anytime. Don't go getting yourself killed, now."

Three

It was Kate McPherson's day off and she had promised herself she would make the most of it. She opened her eyes and stretched luxuriously, relishing the warm water and bubbles of her decadent afternoon bath. Inhaling the fresh rain fragrance of mineral salts wafting from the steamy tub, she sighed happily. Josh wouldn't be home from school for another hour, and that left her free to do anything she wanted. Or nothing at all.

She closed her eyes and let her thoughts drift, seeing her son's smile, still uncertain but real in a way it had never been in the years before she left Carl. Kate's stomach still tightened at the merest thought of her ex-husband.

She had met psychologist Carl Leland when she was a junior at NYU. He was a decade older, handsome and self-assured, with a thriving private practice. Kate found him even more interesting because he was a writer at work on his first book, a feel-good pop psychology tome that seemed immensely important at the time.

She stretched, feeling the bubbles caress her skin. Carl had been a manipulator, not wanting her to work for the same reason he smoothly discouraged her few friends; he simply didn't want to share her. It wasn't enough to make her leave, or even admit the truth.

But when Josh began kindergarten, Carl discouraged his son

from making friends. He went so far as to tell him that his classmates only invited him to parties, to spend the night, or play after school because of his status as son of a famous author and psychologist.

There was no talking to Carl, so months later, she fled with Josh on a bright Monday morning as soon as Carl left for his office.

Kate lifted one leg above the bubbles and soaped it. The first months had been tough while she waited for Carl's reactions to the divorce papers. She had communicated through a lawyer so that her almost-ex and his silver tongue couldn't convince her to return to the easy, luxurious life.

To her surprise, Carl hadn't not contested the divorce—probably because she refused to ask for alimony or even child support—and he hadn't challenged her request for sole guardianship of their son. He had only asked for nonspecific visiting rights.

It was all wonderful. Too wonderful. Kate hadn't bought his agreeability back then and she didn't buy it now. Anyone as possessive as Carl Leland would never be willing to give up his chattel without a fight. Unless he had a mistress . . . or was planning a Machiavellian trap. To this day, she didn't know which it was, but she still hoped for the former and feared the latter.

The bathwater was warm, but she shivered. She had found her way to Eternity eighteen months previously, choosing it because it was so remote that Carl would be unlikely to visit. She'd been correct about that; he sometimes called Josh and promised to visit soon, but he never did.

She soaped the other leg. It had been nearly two years since she'd seen Carl, but time hadn't eased her concern. Despite appearances, Carl was not a man who would let go. And he possessed vast amounts of patience. He'd try to claim his "property" sooner or later. *I can handle him now.*

Before the incident at Icehouse Circle, she hadn't been so sure, but that day had given her self-confidence.

Even in that awful instant when she realized she'd interrupted the killer at work, she had found the extra strength she needed because she knew that Josh depended on her.

At first, she hadn't thought the experience had much of an effect on her life, but she had to admit that she had become attuned to every little sound, every creak of the house. It was hard to sleep these days and difficult not to obsess on the killer, to wonder whether or not he knew who she was.

Stop thinking about it! She pulled the drain on the tub then stepped out and put on a long blue bathrobe. After knotting the belt she unclipped her dark blond hair and brushed it out. It haloed with static electricity, even in the humid bathroom. One of the oddities of Eternity, she thought. A dash of Little Stonehenge might be found anywhere in the region of the strange town.

Eternity suited her with its not-quite-right geology and friendly, though not-quite-right citizens. She had privacy, a small but excellent school for Josh, and a job that suited her interests in western history and folklore and kept her physically fit. Being a tour guide might not be a worthy position as far as her horrified ex-husband was concerned, but Kate truly enjoyed it.

She padded across the hall to her bedroom. Small, it was light and airy with white walls, a braided rug on the golden oak floor, and a thrift store brass bed covered with a cabbage-rose-printed comforter.

Kate pulled on a clean pair of jeans then pawed through a bright jumble of sweaters in her bureau, enjoying the disorganization because it was another sign of freedom from Carl's rules and regulations. Choosing a turquoise cowlneck, she slipped it over her head—*Braless, Carl. Yes, braless!*

After putting on her sneakers, she went downstairs. The first floor consisted of a combined living and dining area, a half bath, and a kitchen with two doors, one opening to the stairs that led to the garage beneath the cabin, the other to a small back porch/utility room which, in turn, led to a fenceless backyard of sorts.

She crossed the living room and went out the sliding glass

doors onto the broad front deck, which overlooked the forests of fir, spruce, and pine. At night, when the wind was up, she caught brief glimpses of the twinkling lights of downtown Eternity.

The redwood deck was her favorite place. She had furnished it with white wrought-iron furniture and pots of herbs and flowers that spent most of the year crowded on the kitchen counters and lining all the windows in the cabin. She felt the soil around a lush basil plant, then turned to fetch her watering can.

Out of the corner of her eye, she caught a glimpse of an envelope on the welcome mat at the front door, just visible from the deck. Curious, she went in and opened the entryway.

Picking up the envelope, she retreated inside. Her first name was scrawled in an unfamiliar spiky hand on the envelope, which bore no address or stamp.

A party invitation? Curiously, she turned it over, found no clue. She opened the envelope and pulled out a folded piece of paper.

> *My dear,*
> *You have a charming son. I shall enjoy getting to know him better.*
>
> *Jacky*

She read the scrawl once, twice, her stomach knotting, the skin on her scalp tightening. *What kind of sick joke is this?*

Something rattled behind her.

Kate whirled. Forgotten, the note drifted to the floor. Another rattle. From the kitchen. The back door? Or the door to the garage? She couldn't remember if she'd locked it or not.

Her revolver was upstairs, the nearest phone across the living room, past the open drapes. She edged to the fireplace and grabbed the poker, then tiptoed past the dining area to the kitchen threshold. She waited, heard nothing, then peeked around the corner. The kitchen appeared undisturbed and no one was visible through the window over the sink.

Lowering the poker, she entered the room, her heart thumping wildly. A vision of herself at Josh's age rose, a terrified, over-imaginative child peering out her bedroom window, certain that her personal monster, a faceless bogeyman, prowled outside, sniffing and tapping and scraping his sharp nails against the glass, seeking entry.

You didn't imagine this. She crossed the kitchen, checked the heavy back door. Locked up tight. Nothing was disturbed; no one was in the backyard.

She moved to the flimsier door that led to the garage. Her heart jumped. Unlocked, not quite latched, it pulled open in her hand, revealing stairs shadowed in darkness, stippled by sunlight.

A sudden rustling below startled her and she slammed the door and locked it. Breathing hard, she cursed herself for leaving the garage door below wide open.

Raccoons? she thought hopefully. Trash pickup was tomorrow; her can was full to overflowing. Yes, raccoons. She relaxed slightly. Maybe her bogeyman was a deer.

Another rattle in the garage. Nervously, she glanced toward the telephone, wondering if she should call the sheriff's office. No, she decided, it would be too humiliating when all the deputy found was the garbage can tipped over.

What if someone's really down there? The killer?

Reluctantly she went to the telephone and jumped back in horror when it shrilled just as she closed her fingers around the handset. It clattered to the floor.

"Katherine?" asked a tinny voice. "Joshua? Hello?"

Carl. Just what I need. She snagged up the handset along with the note she had let fall on the floor. She counted to five, the garage forgotten. "Hello, Carl. What do you want?"

"Katherine? Is something wrong?"

"No," she said stonily. "I just have my hands full."

"You're out of breath," he pressed, all concern and sympathy. "Are you *sure* you're all right?"

"I'm fine." Realizing she was balling up the note, crushing it in her hand, she forced herself to stop. "Why are you calling?"

"I wanted you to know I'm leaving on a book tour next week, so I might be hard to reach for a while."

"That's not a problem," she said, her mind racing. Carl sometimes sent little notes, handwritten clichés, tucked in with the checks for Josh. He still sent valentines, birthday cards. Could he be responsible for the note? The handwriting didn't look like his, but that meant little. "I didn't know you had published a new book. Congratulations."

"Six weeks on the *New York Times* best-seller list." He chuckled paternally. "You must be really isolated up there. No newspaper?"

"Just the local."

"No TV? You didn't see me on Oprah?"

The last was bait, but she didn't take it. "Sorry, I never watch talk shows," she said sweetly. "I work. Is there anything else?"

"Do you need anything? Money for Josh? For yourself?"

"We're getting along fine." She added grudgingly, "Thanks for asking."

"I don't understand what it is I've done that has made you reject me like this. I'd like to explore your anger, Katherine. I'd like to work things out."

"Carl, I don't have time to talk. School's letting out soon and Josh expects me to pick him up today. Is there anything else?"

"Now, now, Katherine, it's August." He chuckled. "Please don't lie to me. Josh is on vacation."

"Not in Eternity. We have winter vacation here. Because of the snow." His ignorance made her think Carl wasn't in town, wasn't responsible for the note.

"Why would you want to live in such a horrible backward place when you can have everything you want?"

"I have everything I want. Good-bye—"

"Wait."

Reluctantly, she put the handset back to her ear. "What is it, Carl?"

"I'll be up for a visit soon."

"Why?" She couldn't hide her sarcasm. "You're not doing a signing in this backwater, are you?"

"Oh, Katherine. I wish you could hear the unresolved conflicts in your voice. I could help you reach your inner child, if only you'd allow me—"

"Blow it out your ass," she said. Delighted by the silence on Carl's end, she felt herself blush. She'd never used profanity in front of him before. It had just popped out.

"Katherine, you must be ill—"

"No. I'm better than I've ever been in my life. Don't talk to me like I'm a patient or one of your fans, Carl. Speak English, not pop psych. Can you do that?"

"I'm sorry, darling. I didn't realize . . ."

She didn't reply.

"I've sent you a copy of my new book. I think you'll enjoy it."

She said nothing.

"It's called *Healing Through Manipulation.*"

"The book you were born to write," she said dryly.

It was lost on him. "Yes. It is. And I think you'll benefit from reading it."

"Did you send it already?"

"Yes. This morning."

"Have you sent anything else lately? Any notes?"

"No. I'm sorry. I've been very busy and I've neglected you and Joshua terribly. You wouldn't believe the pressure I'm under."

She didn't ask, but said, "I hope you have a successful book tour. Don't worry about us. We have everything we need."

"Except me."

God, the man was a snake. Before she could summon up an appropriate comeback, he spoke again. "My tour will end in Oregon around Labor Day. I'm going to rent a car and drive down to visit you and Josh."

"You are?" she asked, knowing she shouldn't show any negative reaction. That would only encourage him.

"Yes, I am. I promise. Katherine, do you have a guest room?"

"No. If you want, I'll arrange a cabin rental for you." *On the other side of town.*

"That would be wonderful. I'll arrive Labor Day weekend and stay a week. Can you arrange it all?"

"Yes. I'll call your secretary so that she can send your deposit in for you."

He hesitated, then agreed. After a few more bits of unnecessary advice on how to run her life, he hung up. He hadn't even asked about Josh. *Typical.*

She would book him a cabin—what better way to keep him at a distance—and she would call his secretary. It was unlikely the man would show up, judging by the hesitancy in his voice when she agreed to find him a place to stay. He'd wanted her to protest his visit. Or invite him to stay with her. He wanted a reaction.

Pleased with the way she'd handled him, she glanced at the note wadded in her hand. *Kids, maybe. A prank. A joke.*

Her heart stuttered as someone rapped on the front door. Sticking the note in her pocket, she took a deep breath and went to peer out the viewer. The mayor stood outside, bushy mustache hiding his upper lip, polished walking stick in hand.

Ambrose Abbott was almost frightfully fit for a man who had to be on the far side of seventy, and his personality was intriguingly odd and decidedly acerbic. He was a steamroller of a man who spoke his mind whether anyone wanted him to or not, but he was utterly mum about his personal life. Kate enjoyed his brief visits, perhaps because of his refreshing refusal to mince words, perhaps because she felt perversely honored to be sought out as company by such a notorious misanthrope.

She opened the door. "Mayor Abbott, come in!"

He nodded his head of thick gray hair and walked purposefully into the kitchen. "Any chance you have some of that lemonade on hand?"

She followed him and opened the refrigerator. "I made some last night. Have a seat," she added, but he already had.

She carried the pitcher and glasses to the table. "Out for a walk?"

"Appears so." He drained half the glass. "Damned people all over the place. Eternity's too crowded these days. Hard to find a place to think anymore."

"Crowded?" she asked, surprised. "Did a busload of tourists arrive early?" She knew he saw the vacation business as an unavoidable necessity.

"No, no. And thank whatever gods are spying on us for that. Just a lot of politics, settling things for the new sheriff. Deputy Settles is sulking more than usual since he doesn't want to give up being acting sheriff and our singing councilman is again hinting broadly that he himself would make a fine sheriff if our new man doesn't fit in. I had to get out for a stroll before my mind snapped from all the bickering and dickering." He shook his head. "People. Can't live with them, can't shoot them all and drop them in a bottomless pit."

"The new sheriff is coming?"

"Hell, he's here, my dear. He hasn't checked in yet, but he's been spotted prowling around like a wolf looking to mark his territory." He finished the lemonade.

Kate refilled his glass. "I read the article about him in the *Herald.* What a terrible thing, finding your family murdered."

"Not terrible. It's just life. It's a joke. A huge practical joke." He shook his head. "I'd better get back to my constitutional. I thought I'd visit Alpine Meadow this afternoon."

"That's an eight-mile hike. Aren't you afraid you'll miss the sheriff?"

Abbott showed square teeth in a wicked grin. "He's wandering around with no regard for *my* time. Let him wait while I do my own bit of wandering."

"Maybe I should talk to him."

"Why?" Abbott stood and pushed his chair in.

"Because I found the body."

"I'm sure you'll encounter our new sheriff at some point." He moved to the front door and grabbed his walking stick. "You're not still concerned for your safety, are you? Enough time has passed . . . If the murderer were going to do something to you, he would have acted by now.''

"I'm still concerned."

Abbott turned, eyed her. "Why is that?"

She pulled the note from her pocket and handed it to him. "I found this on the doorstep shortly before you arrived."

Donning a pair of wire-rimmed reading glasses, he smoothed the paper and read it. "May I keep this?"

"Shouldn't I give it to the new sheriff?"

"I'll take care of it." He put the paper in his pocket as if she had agreed. "You're concerned?"

"It's a note threatening my son . . ." Kate began, her irritation growing. "And there were noises in my garage just after I found it. Yes. I think it's safe to say I'm concerned."

Abbott nearly smiled. "You left the garage door open. Invitation to a feast. I'll take a look, though."

Kate followed him out, not completely convinced she'd left the big door open; she rarely did. But Josh might have. She wished she could be sure, but a moment later it didn't matter: she saw that the garbage can was toppled, its contents strewn around and under her car. There was even a banana peel on the Sentra's hood.

Abbott nodded at the garbage. "Best be careful. You don't need bears in here."

"I will." She paused. "About the note."

"The law will have it in a short time. Don't waste time worrying. As you are well aware, we have more than our share of eccentrics. Shady Pines is just over the hill from here. You know how often some of the residents visit us . . . and how imaginative they are in their attempts to gain attention."

He turned and started up the side of the mountain before she could protest. Abbott meant well, but his theory about Shady Pines was ludicrous. A cold breeze stabbed through the sun's thin warmth, making goose bumps rise beneath her sweater.

Four

When Tully left Horse Junction, he'd been strongly tempted to turn the car around and head back to Los Angeles, tail between his legs. He pulled onto the northbound I-5. Chief Ladd had to be pulling his leg or at least exaggerating about Eternity. When everything was said and done, the basic truth was that Tully still needed a change and he had made his choice.

In the distance, he could already make out the bluish snow-capped peak of Icehouse Mountain, and after ten more miles of rolling hills, he came to the exit that would lead him there. Turning onto the narrow Eternity Highway, he began traveling northwest on the last longish leg of his journey.

Soon he was surrounded by pine forest that hid the mountain from view. The road began a mild twisting climb. He rolled down the Camaro's window, turned off the air conditioner and enjoyed the fact that although the outside air was still on the warm side, it no longer felt like the seventh circle of hell on an August afternoon. The heady fresh scent of pine renewed his hopes and expectations.

The going was slow, giving him time to think, and by the time he was nearing the Eternity County line almost two hours later, he felt he had finally come to terms with the knowledge that he hadn't done any research on his prospective home because he really didn't want to find a reason to back out. He'd been unrealistic about the whole move. But how realistic could he be about something that seemed so unreal?

When he crossed into Eternity County, the road grew even narrower, more pot-holed and twisted. Its condition made him wonder if Eternity really was the thriving tourist town Abbott had claimed. The road seemed too quiet, too deserted and forlorn.

It was only two in the afternoon, but it seemed much later because the lodgepole pines and burgeoning redwood groves had closed in around him, blocking most of the sun, leaving it to dapple the road and forest floor with muted light. For the last twenty miles, the elevation had been holding fairly steady at around three thousand feet, but as Tully took a hairpin turn, the road started climbing again.

He slowed, seeing a doe and fawn walking among the trees. Tully felt himself grinning like a fool at the sight; he'd never seen a live deer outside of a petting zoo despite several fishing trips with Kevin in the San Bernardino Mountains. His heart hitched at the thought of his son, and he shoved the memories roughly away.

The road began to curve northward and he caught another glimpse of Icehouse Mountain through a rare break in the trees. He pulled to the side of the road and killed the engine then stepped out and stretched his stiff muscles. Staring up through the pines, he could see the icebound peak, thousands of feet above.

The afternoon sun reflected crystalline prisms that seemed to dance upon the ancient glaciers, and he suddenly understood why this mountain had engendered so much myth and superstition. Icehouse was not only majestic, but very nearly magical. It was the stuff of fairy tales, disturbingly familiar. A snatch of a song from his childhood floated back to him—*Oh, the birds and the bees and the lemonade streams on the Big Rock Candy Mountain*—and he realized that he must have seen photos of Icehouse when he was very young because this was the place he'd pictured when he'd sung the song.

After a while, he returned to the car. Soon the rutted highway began to round the southwest base of the mountain. An elevation marker indicated six thousand feet and shortly after that a sign announced that Eternity was only five miles distant.

Something moved in the woods to his right. Startled, he peered at a shadowed creature nearly invisible among the trees. It wasn't a deer; it stood upright. *Maybe a man or a bear.* He smiled to himself, wondering if this was the sort of thing that qualified as a Bigfoot sighting. Something deep within the woods howled, an unearthly wail that prickled the hairs up on the back of his neck. An instant later, a bird screeched obscenities, breaking the spell. The hulking figure disappeared.

A small sign announced Icehouse Gorge just before the road began a treacherous climb through a precariously tall, narrow ravine. On the right, blasted granite snugged against the road's edge. To the left, there were no guardrails or even shoulders, only beat-up orange snow markers lining the sheer drop at the asphalt's crumbly edge. Twenty feet beyond the crevasse, stunted pines clung tenaciously to whatever soil they could find between vertical slabs and flows of volcanic rock. It was a deathtrap; he wondered how many rusted-out wrecks lay at the bottom of the ravine.

The gorge ended at the 7000-foot marker. Around the next bend was a redwood sign with carved white letters reading, WELCOME TO ETERNITY. Painted in fading script below that were two messages: POPULATION 498 and A LITTLE BIT OF HEAVEN ON EARTH. Just past that was a seven-foot-tall die-cut sign depicting a hulking brown-furred creature holding a placard that read, SEE BIGFOOT AT SNAKES ALIVE! CURIOSITY SHOPPE!!

The woods thinned slightly and Tully began to spot dirt roads and small cabins among the trees. Along the roadside, sign after sign advertised spas, ski resorts, shops, and eateries. He drove up one more hill and when he gained the 8000-foot summit, he saw the village below. Tully tapped the brake, unconsciously holding his breath as he stared down at the town. *His* town.

Abbott had told the truth about one thing: Eternity really

was a charming sight. The downtown area was surprisingly flat and built around a large tree-filled town square. Chalet-style buildings with steeply pitched roofs lined the square all around for several blocks before giving way to the forest. Beyond, between the trees, he could just make out hilly roads winding every which way and lined with clusters of cabins, crowded together near the downtown area, and progressively more isolated farther out.

A horn blared behind him and Tully stepped on the gas just in time to keep a yellow Mustang from rear-ending him. Brakes squealed, then the car careened around him, double yellow lines be damned. Instantly, it zipped back in front of him, barely missing an oncoming beer truck. The truck driver leaned on his horn and shook his fist at the speeder. After it passed, the Mustang's driver decided to irritate Tully by slowing to a crawl, but all the unseen driver really did was give him plenty of time to memorize the license plate. The driver soon tired of his game and accelerated. Charming, Tully thought, hoping he would eventually have the pleasure of pulling the speeder over.

He cruised down to the square then decided to explore more of the town before checking in with Ambrose Abbott. The central square—a rectangle, really—was good-sized, filled with green grass, flowers, aspens, and oaks already turning fall reds and yellows. Tall pine trees dotted the lawns. At one end of the park, benches lined a large pond. At the other, they stood sentinel around brightly painted slides, swings, and other playground equipment. Several women sat watching children play and an elderly couple holding hands strolled along a winding path that led past more graceful wrought-iron benches. Picnic tables were scattered beneath the trees and a white bandshell rose in a clearing near a three-tiered fountain.

Old-fashioned three-globe streetlamps lining the sidewalks combined with the quaint storefronts and the park to make Tully feel as if he'd stepped back in time. The modern vehicles parked on the business side of the street barely dampened the effect.

Across from the short west end of the park, he could see a

drugstore, small market, hardware store, and several gift shops. He turned on Main Street East, and found a dry cleaners, several restaurants, bookstores, an antique shop, and a German tavern called Oktober Fest. Across from the pond, were the courthouse, a post office, tourist information center, firehouse, and library.

Turning left, he saw another bar, Shalimar's, which had a 1960s-style red-quilted door and fake snow and icicles dripping off its eaves. Next came an old playhouse turned duplex movie theater, an Italian restaurant called Carlo's, a real estate office, a delicatessen, the Lemurian Society, and the King's Tart, a bakery wafting sweet fragrances that made Tully's stomach growl. He nearly stopped, then decided to finish his tour before satisfying his rampant sweet tooth.

He continued on, passing the last building on the block. It housed the *Eternity Weekly Herald*. On the next block, he spotted a small sign directing him toward the sheriff's station. He followed the arrow and cruised slowly past his new office. It looked more like a log-cabin-style ranger post than a sheriff's station but Tully saw nothing wrong with that.

United States and California flags waved from a pole in front, and low brick flower beds held a profusion of brilliant orange and red flowers. He pulled into the postage-stamp parking lot just past the station. There was a red Nissan pickup and two black-and-whites in the lot, one a Crown Vic, the other a hulking four-wheel-drive Ford Explorer. He nearly pulled into a slot between the black and whites, but again changed his mind, reminding himself that once he made his presence known, his time wouldn't be his own.

Back onto the road, he cruised the rest of the downtown streets then headed north again on Eternity Highway to see what was on the far side of town. He passed two faded court-style motels before spotting a small burger stand. He pulled through and was soon on the road again, munching a bad burger, soggy fries, and sipping a rather uncarbonated Coke. He'd never thought he'd miss McDonald's or Taco Bell, but with every greasy bite, his craving for what he couldn't have grew stronger.

The road curved broadly before leading past a huge old stone resort named Eternity Hot Springs. Expensive vehicles of all makes dotted the parking lot. Passing it, he drove another half mile without seeing any more signs of life, then just when he decided to turn around and head back into town, he spotted another die-cut Bigfoot holding a placard that read, SNAKES ALIVE! CURIOSITY SHOPPE! ! SEE BIGFOOT. 1000 FT. He couldn't pass that up.

Snakes Alive! was the tackiest tourist trap Tully had ever seen, and he'd seen plenty. In fact, he had a great nostalgia for such places because they reminded him of family vacations when he was little. For two weeks every year, he, his older brother, and parents would travel at breakneck speed across the country and back again. The alligator farms and trading posts were practically their only stops because his otherwise gung-ho dad couldn't resist them, even if it required driving ten miles down a dirt road to see *The World's Most Horrifying Mutant Discovery,* or *Authentic Indian Fossils, Dinosaur Bones—Cheap,* or even a simple mound of *Martian Mystery Rocks.* Guiltily, Tully reminded himself that he had never made the time to take Linda and Kevin on a cross-country trip, had never treated his own son to fake mummies or constipated-looking crocodiles.

There's nothing you can do about that now. The knowledge didn't help and as he pulled into the empty dirt lot in front of the ramshackle building, his mood darkened. He turned off the ignition and stared at the steering wheel.

"Howdy, mister. You coming in?"

Startled, Tully looked up into the bright eyes of a bewhiskered old man, small and spry in bib overalls and a faded checkered shirt. He looked like he should have a corncob pipe in his mouth and a pickax in his hand.

"Come to see Bigfoot, have you?"

"No," he replied. "I don't think so."

"Whatever's eating on you, Mister, it'll stop once you see my Bigfoot diorama. Come on in. My treat."

From long experience, Tully knew he would only become more depressed if he didn't pull himself out of the funk quickly.

It was hard to stop the feelings, even after all this time, because he still felt that he didn't deserve any pleasure after letting his family die. He'd been all through it with the police shrink, who kept talking about guilt and self-punishment. The whole episode had been an exercise in futility because nothing the shrink could say made light bulbs go off or the pain go away. Tully knew it all, right down to the fact that he had to get on with his life and stop wallowing in guilt. It was either that, or take a gun and put himself out of his misery. Sometimes that bullet still sounded pretty damn good.

"You're a woolgathering youngster," the old geezer said, opening a bag of chewing tobacco and inserting a wad between stained teeth.

Tully forced himself to smile. "Thanks, I'll come in." He climbed out of the car.

The old man extended his hand. "Jackson Coop," he said, shaking Tully's with surprising strength, "Proprietor of *Snakes Alive!* I added that 'Curiosity Shoppe' stuff because people'd come here thinking all I had was a snake farm, nothing else. You ever seen a two-headed snake?"

Tully had, at an alligator farm, but he knew Coop didn't want to hear that. He shook his head. "No, I haven't."

"Well, you're about to. You picked a good time to stop in—there's not much business today. You passing through?"

Tully hesitated. "No, I'm not."

Jackson Coop cocked an eyebrow and peered up into Tully's face. "You mean you live here? Never seen you around before."

"I just arrived, Mr. Coop."

"Plain old Coop is what they call me. Always liked it better than my given. My momma had a crush on Old Hickory himself, so she called me Jackson, but it always seemed to me Jackson and Coop oughta be reversed."

"Your mother had a crush on *Andrew* Jackson?" Tully asked, squelching a smile.

"Ain't that what I just told'ja, son?"

Tully nodded, wondering if the man was a few bricks short.

Coop spat, just missing the Camaro's tire. "What do they call you?"

"My name is Zach Tully—" he began.

"Zach Tully." The old man rolled the name around on his tongue. "Tully. Zach Tully. I know that name." He scratched his beard. "One of them hooligans that ran around with Hank Antrim's gang was a Tully. You any relation?"

Senile? "Not to my knowledge."

Coop cackled gleefully, wiping tobacco juice away with the back of his sleeve. "Damn chaw'll be the death of me, but it's the only thing that keeps my landlady from trying to kiss on me." He spat out the wad and wagged his finger in the vicinity of Tully's nose. "You're the new sheriff. You're *that* Tully, aren'tcha?"

Tully smiled and met a second handshake. "That's me."

"Well, Sheriff, you don't never hav'ta pay to get in the museum. That ain't a bribe, just a fact."

"Thanks."

"Anybody know you're here?"

"I thought I'd see the town first."

"Smart fella. Well, come on in. You're likely to see a Bigfoot or two up here and you better be able to tell it from bear. Where you from?"

"Los Angeles."

"You big city lawmen really eat as many donuts as the TV makes out?"

Tully laughed. "Of course not." That was a general statement: he himself was a sugar junkie, and he hadn't forgotten the fragrant promises wafting from the downtown bakery.

"Ever seen a bear?" Coop abruptly asked.

"Sure." *In a zoo.*

"Well, it's easy to mix 'em up with Bigfoot if they rear up. I better show you what you're looking for." He started walking. Tully trailed behind, wondering what he'd gotten himself into.

"Me," Coop said over his shoulder, "I seen plenty of both. Bears are more dangerous, though if a Bigfoot gets a whiff of a woman who's cycling, he can cause real problems. One of

my critters, I shot after he'd broken into a lady's house, trying
to get at her.''

"You shot a Bigfoot?"

"Sure. Stuffed the biggest one, got the skins of the rest
hanging on the walls.'' They reached the door. Coop turned,
his hand on the latch. ''There ain't no law against shooting
them, is there? I got my hunting license here somewheres.''
He started digging in his pocket.

Tully held up his hand. ''No, no, that's okay. It's—it's just
that there've been so few sightings reported that I'm amazed
you've killed any.'' *Please let me sound sincere.* ''You could
be a rich man, with all those skins,'' he added lamely.

"Goddamned government cover-ups.'' Coop squinched his
face up until he looked like Popeye. ''Word's leaked out that
I'm nothing but an eccentric kook. Agents spread that around
so's the TV shows won't touch me, least not the ones that
count. I think maybe the government threatened 'em.'' He
paused, then lowered his voice conspiratorially. ''Once, near
twenty years ago, half a dozen TV people came out. One of
'em was murdered and the rest skedaddled.'' He shook his
head. ''Haven't been back since.''

"Murdered?"

"Well, officially, a bear got 'er.'' He chuckled. ''Maybe
she was cycling and Bigfoot took her.'' His expression turned
serious and he added. ''Nah, I'm joshing about Bigfoot. I seen
that woman's body and I think it was murder. The government
probably did it.'' He scratched his chin thoughtfully. '' 'Course
it coulda been one of the killers that live hereabouts, but who's
to say? Me, I think it was a government cover-up.''

Tully nodded. *The first person I meet in my new home is a
senile old codger who shoots Bigfoots. Bigfeet?* In his mind,
he could hear John Mendoza's gleeful laughter. ''Maybe we
can discuss her death when I'm not so short on time,'' he told
Coop, hoping he sounded diplomatic.

Coop nodded. ''Frank Lawson always was gonna do that,
but he didn't live long enough.'' He smiled yellowly. ''I hope

you got better luck.'' He held the door open and gestured Tully inside. ''Here we go.''

Snakes Alive! was tacky-tourist from its racks of dusty post-cards to foot-shaped mugs and Bigfoot salt and pepper shakers to buttons emblazoned with slogans like *Icehouse Mountain!*, *I Visited the Vortex and Lived!*, *Bigfoot Lives!* and *Little Stone-henge Rocks!* Coop apparently loved exclamation marks.

''There's one of my skins,'' Coop pointed to a moth-eaten fur on the rear wall. ''That there's the littlest skin. Just a tease. Come on back this way.'' He led him toward a door by the skin, past another die-cut Bigfoot placard reading BIGFOOT MUSEUM! SEE THE REAL THING! ONLY $4 .50! Tully followed Coop past a terrarium full of tarantulas, then they paused in front of another holding a small two-headed king snake. After admiring the reptile, they crossed to the museum door and Tully checked out the alleged Bigfoot pelt. It had to be a bearskin. A rank smell clung to it.

Coop opened the door onto darkness. The rank odor was stronger within, mixed with the cloying tang of mothballs and mildew. The old man disappeared, then dusty yellow light bloomed inside the museum.

Glass display cases in need of polishing lined three walls of the twenty-by-twenty-foot area, and there were two more running across the center of the room as well. Three walls displayed hand-drawn Ripleyesque posters as well as one ''Bigfoot'' skin apiece. The fourth wall was hidden behind a faded green curtain.

''Here we go.'' Jackson Coop pulled the cord and the drapes opened, revealing the diorama. The wall was amateurishly painted, a landscape of pines and a bright blue stream with Icehouse Mountain looming in the background, ominous storm clouds behind its peak. Bigfoot himself stood before the paint-ing between several fake Christmas trees on a bed of pine needles. Tully had to admit it: the creature was impressive. It stood about eight feet tall, legs splayed, arms extended over-head, hands menacingly half clenched. The monkeyish face was set in a cruel snarl.

''So that's Bigfoot,'' Tully said. He figured the monster

was mostly bear—the fur appeared to be real—with a little chimpanzee mixed in, along with a whole lot of creative needle-work worthy of Barnum and Bailey.

"That's him." Cackling, Coop eyed Tully. "Caught him right where it shows in the picture. I painted the background myself, so it'd be exactly right. Got him nearly thirty years ago. You know what a Bigfoot really is?"

"Missing link?"

Coop chuckled. "Everybody thinks that, but it ain't so. He's the remains of the lost race of Lemuria."

"Lemuria," Tully said, buying time. Coop was looking at him like he was supposed to know what he was talking about. "Wasn't that some place like Atlantis?"

Coop pulled out his pouch of chewing tobacco and inserted a fresh wad. "Atlantis was founded by Lemurians," he explained patiently. "See, Sheriff, Lemuria was this big old island off the California coast about fifteen thousand years ago. Maybe even thirty thousand. The Lemurians had it all. They built houses out of gold and they had spaceships, and telepathy, and were way more advanced than us. But they got kind of full of themselves, probably because they didn't have anything to do but levitate each other and read books." Coop scratched his chin thoughtfully. "Not having to work for nothing no more, they started doing all kinds of perverted stuff, and their gods told the lot of 'em to shape up or they was gonna be sorry because their island would blow up.

"Well, they just kept messing up, indulging in all the deadly sins, which were pretty much the same ones as we have. You know, adultery, greed, orgies, sloth, sacrificing virgins to the local volcano, things of that nature. And then it got worse. First they started practicing incest." Coop's eyes twinkled. "And I guess they got pretty damn good at it. Then they got bored and went on to havin' sexual relations with animals."

"Is that a fact?" Tully asked to fill the sudden silence.

"It sure is, Sheriff. And bestiality caught on better than incest ever did. Pretty soon, they were all doing it with animals—and then you know what happened . . ." Coop peered at Tully from beneath his frizzy eyebrows.

The old man was expecting an answer, but Tully didn't have one. "I don't know. What happened?"

Coop gave him a boy-are-you-dense look. "Mutant babies," he said darkly. "Half human, half beast." He poked his thumb toward the Bigfoot. "Like him."

"I see." Tully glanced meaningfully at his watch, but Jackson Coop didn't take the hint.

"Well, that was the last straw, and the gods set off the volcano. Destroyed the whole dang island, and it started sinking. There was a little group of chosen ones, Lemurians who were still a hundred percent human, who didn't believe in bestiality or incest and they escaped, sorta like in Noah's ark, only their ship flew, and they went off and founded Atlantis. Most of the rest of 'em died. But a few escaped and took their half-breed children with them. They came here."

"That's quite a story." Tully checked his watch again. "Did the Lemurians build Little Stonehenge?"

"Sure. Who else would? Why, I can tell you—"

"Another day?" Tully interrupted. "It's getting late and the mayor will be wondering where I am."

" 'Course he will, if he's not off on one of his tramps. He loves a good tramp, old Ambrose does. Not much for people, you know." Coop pulled the curtain closed. "One thing to remember about those damn Bigfoot; they're slippery. Some folks believe they can dematerialize, but personally, I think that's a load of bull."

Jackson Coop's expression was unreadable and as Tully followed him back through the store, he wondered what the old man was up to—if anything. As he listened to his ramblings, he'd grown less certain that the man was senile. The eyes held too much intelligence, there was too much humor in the curl of his lip. Probably a Shady Pines alumni, he thought, though he didn't quite believe it. More likely, the new kid in town had just been through some sort of initiation. Maybe an invitation to go snipe hunting was in the wings.

"Thanks again," he said as he shook Coop's hand at the door. He turned to leave.

"Hey, Tully."

He turned back, surprised at the sharpness of Coop's voice.

"I like you."

Tully waited.

"Wouldn't want to see nothing happen to you." Coop's words were clipped and his eyes darted as if he were afraid of being overheard.

"What do you mean?"

"Things happen around here."

"Things?"

"You'll see. Frank Lawson went and got hisself killed because he stuck his nose in where the town council said he shouldn't."

"The town council had him killed?" Tully asked.

"I ain't saying that. Nobody knows who killed him but the killer, far as I know. The thing is, if the council tells you to steer clear of something, listen. That's the best way to stay healthy, doing what they say. It's not smart to cross the lifers, not even the ones who ain't on the council."

That was the term that Chief Ladd had been so mysterious about. "What are 'lifers'?"

"Why, those are the folks who've been here forever, a'course."

"People who were born here?"

Coop shook his head. "You mean to tell me you don't know about Icehouse Circle—Little Stonehenge?"

"I know there's a lot of mythology attached to it. And it's where they found Frank Lawson's body."

"Wait right there." The old man disappeared into the store and came back a moment later with a red-covered booklet. "You read this." He held out the book. "And keep an open mind."

Tully took it, inwardly groaning as he read the title. *The Occult Secrets of Icehouse Mountain.* There was a line drawing of the mountain with a UFO hovering above it and a silhouette of Bigfoot before it. More of Coop's art, no doubt. "Thanks. This will tell me everything I need to know?" He dug in his pocket for his wallet.

"No charge. You need it. It won't tell you everything you need to know, it's just a tourist book, but you read it and after you've been here a piece and maybe have a reason to wonder at something, you consider what it says. Then, you come to me." He grinned, then spat tobacco juice. "By then, you won't think I'm as crazy as you do right now."

"Thanks for the book," Tully said for lack of anything better.

"Don't go to nobody else, and don't let 'em catch you coming to me. Frank Lawson came to me, but he didn't make no secret of it. That was a mistake."

Tully studied him briefly. "I'll keep it in mind." He headed for his car.

"Good luck, Sheriff," Jackson Coop called after him.

"Christ." Tully glanced at the lurid cover on the thin book, then tossed it on the floor behind his seat. Unerringly, he'd sought out the craziest person in the area, something he'd always been good at. He pulled out and headed back toward the center of town, thinking that Mendoza would love this.

Five

When Tully returned to town, he located Abbott's Bookshop, where he had expected to meet with Mayor Ambrose Abbott. He was annoyed and rather insulted to find the shop closed and a note on the door informing him that Abbott, as Coop had warned, was out for the afternoon. The note directed him to see a councilman, one Harlan King, who was expecting him and would give him the keys to his new home. He was slightly happier once he saw King's address: It was the King's Tart, the bakery with the heavenly fragrance that had nearly seduced him earlier.

Outside the Tart, Tully nodded at several old men who were whiling away the day on a liar's bench, talking, smoking cigars, and drinking coffee. An empty pink bakery box rested on the ground in front of them. It was a tableau worthy of Norman Rockwell.

Inside, the shop was small but neat and spotlessly clean with half a dozen small tables and chairs lining the floor in front of its picture window. Ceiling fans lazily stirred the air and the aromas of freshly baked breads and pastries were irresistible. There were no customers and no one behind the spotless glass counter, but cheerful whistling came from the kitchen beyond a pair of white saloon-style half-doors. Tully hit a silver bell on the counter and immediately, a pleasant voice called, ''Just a moment.'' Then a man in white came out bearing a tray of fresh glazed donuts.

Tully's mouth started watering. Pastry, donuts in particular, were his downfall, a vice he took care to hide because any cop who liked donuts was doomed to nonstop harassment.

"May I help you?" The baker was a hearty broad-shouldered man in his fifties and he obviously enjoyed sampling his own wares: there was a hint of Pillsbury Doughboy about him. He pulled an empty tray out of the case beneath the counter and slid the fresh one in, then folded his arms and smiled at Tully. Dimples appeared in his rosy cheeks and his light blue eyes twinkled beneath thinning sandy blond hair.

"Are you Harlan King?"

"At your service. Would you be Zachary Tully?"

Tully nodded.

King's smile broadened and he came around the counter to shake hands. "We've been looking forward to your arrival. Coffee?"

"Please."

King went back behind the counter and poured two paper cups of coffee and handed them to Tully. "Hope you're not on a diet," he said, bending to snag some donuts. He brought them around and Tully followed him to a corner table.

"I must apologize for Ambrose," King said between sips of coffee. "And for the rest of the council. We'd planned on something of a hero's welcome for you, and then everyone except me ended up saddled with things they couldn't avoid. Since we didn't know exactly when you'd be arriving, Ambrose left for his afternoon constitutional." His words trailed off and he bit into the donut, a contented smile on his face.

"It's no problem," Tully told him. Sugar coursed through his veins and his taste buds vibrated in delight, obliterating his lingering annoyance with the mayor.

"It occurred to us that you might like a day to get settled before you meet the entire council and officially assume your duties as sheriff, so we've planned a meeting and the official swearing in for tomorrow at noon at the courthouse. Luncheon to follow. Will that suit you?''

"Perfectly. I'd like to go over to the station and meet my staff today, though.''

"Of course." The baker dimpled up. "By the way, I must thank you for attracting my favorite reporter to our fair town. I love her program.''

Tully didn't suppress the groan. "Reporter?" he asked, the bottom dropping out of his stomach.

"Not to worry. Ambrose made sure Ms. Rios understands that nothing may come out until you've resolved our current problems.''

Tully decided not to go there. Instead, he studied the smiley man a long moment. "Mr. King.''

"Harlan.''

"Harlan. I have a few questions.''

King watched him expectantly.

"When I spoke with Mr. Abbott, he told me your last sheriff died accidentally, but the CHP chief at Horse Junction tells me he was murdered. And that there was a prior killing as well.'' Tully looked at him sharply. "Why the lies?''

Harlan King blushed and shook his head. "I told them it wasn't a good idea to keep it under our hats, but I was outvoted. Frankly, the council was afraid you wouldn't come if you knew how many of our sheriffs have been killed.''

"I was referring to the man found on the mountain, but now that you mention it, I heard something about the previous sheriff, too. Shot in a bank robbery?''

"So he was. Frankly, for the last century or so, we've had very few sheriffs reach retirement age and we didn't know how superstitious you might be about such things.''

Tully finished his doughnut. "I'm not superstitious. But you're seriously telling me your sheriffs were all murdered?''

"Seems like it. I found one of them once. Terrible thing. It was Reno Mullins, and he was one tough old bird, let me tell you. He was especially fond of my cinnamon rolls and early one morning, before opening time, I took a few over to him at the station. I did that frequently. I walked into the station—that was before the remodel and his desk was out front—and there he was. What a mess. Turned my taste for cinnamon rolls right off.''

Tully nodded, and decided to let that alone for now. "Can you tell me who the acting sheriff is right now?"

"Ron Settles, your senior deputy. He's sort of a sour puss, but he's experienced and reliable.''

"Why wasn't he named sheriff?"

"He doesn't have the personality to deal with the tourists."

"Why was I contacted? I never applied for the job."

"You came highly recommended. We had your résumé." King paused. "You didn't apply? You didn't mail it to Ambrose?"

"No."

"A mystery indeed," King said thoughtfully. "Someone must have sent it to him. I'll ask him for you if you'd like.''

"I'll take care of it. Do you have any idea when he'll be back?"

"Ambrose usually returns before the daylight is gone." There was a slight hint of nervousness in his voice. "I can tell you that you have three deputies—Settles, Albert Stoker, and Tim Hapscomb. Tim's fairly new here. You also have a day dispatcher and an all-night answering service in case no one's in the office."

"Chief Ladd says Eternity's crime rate is pretty high."

"He certainly sang our praises, didn't he?" King's laugh sounded forced. "It's not as low as we might like, but . . . Eternity is actually quite peaceful. Except that we've had problems with that damnable serial killer." He shook his head, a trace of a smile on his lips. "We've never been able to catch up with him, not this century or last, and now he's at it again. That was a terrible thing to do to Frank. Another donut?"

Tully took one without thinking, bit into it, tasted nothing. "Wait a minute. Hold it." He pointed the pastry at King. "You've had killings like Lawson's for over a century and you think it's all been done by the *same* perpetrator?"

King shrugged, smiled enigmatically, and sampled another doughnut.

"Do you mean that other serial crimes in Eternity's past have had the same modus operandi? Dismemberment?" The notion of a series of legacy copycats intrigued him.

King chewed and swallowed. "No, no. Not at all. They're all different. Our killer is, shall we say, playful? Imaginative? Yes. That sums it up, I believe."

"Mr. King—"

"Harlan."

"Harlan. I don't understand. Surely you don't believe this killer has been operating for over a century."

King looked Tully up and down. "No, no. We can talk about that tomorrow." A timer bell rang and King nearly leapt from his chair. "Excuse me. I have to take some bread out of the oven."

The baker disappeared into the kitchen and Tully rose and went to the counter to await his return. The more questions he'd asked, the more anxious Harlan King had become. Maybe there really was something to Jackson Coop's ominous warnings about the workings of the town council.

"Here are the keys to your cabin," King said as he returned with a key chain and a folded piece of paper. "Our sheriffs have always lived there and it's fully furnished. Very comfortable. Sheriff Lawson's clothing and most personal effects were sent to his family, but everything else is there—linens, pots and pans, furniture, appliances. The pantry's partially stocked. I think you'll find everything you'll need, but call me if there's a problem." He smiled apologetically and unfolded the sheet of paper, revealing a hand-drawn map to the cabin. "I wish I could take you over there myself, but my help is out sick today."

"No problem," Tully said. The bell over the entry door jingled as an elderly woman walked in.

"Hello, Miss Quince." Harlan King gave her a twinkling smile. "I'd like to introduce you to our new sheriff. Lizzie Quince, Zach Tully."

Her delicate features spread into a thousand wrinkles as she smiled at him, all faded rosebud lips and cheeks, silvery hair, beauty-parlor perfect, and bright, startlingly green eyes. "Pleased to meet you." She extended her gloved hand.

"It's a pleasure," Tully said, wondering if she expected him to kiss it. Instead he took it in both of his and pressed it lightly. "If you'll excuse me," he said. "I have to run." He took the key chain and map and headed for the door.

Six

The cabin turned out to be nicer than he had dared hope, and Zach Tully spent a pleasant two hours exploring and moving in. The latter didn't take much time. A dozen cartons of possessions had been delivered the day before, but he didn't bother with those. He only unpacked what he'd brought along in the Camaro and as he carried the clothing, box of toiletries, and weapons into the house, he marveled at the meagerness of his belongings. He had divested himself of nearly everything after Linda and Kevin were murdered; since then he'd lived in a furnished apartment and his entire life had revolved around work, around his desire to catch the monster who murdered his family.

Though the identity of the Backdoor Killer remained a mystery he was determined to solve, as Tully stood under the hot shower spray, he reassured himself again that it was time to get on with his life. He toweled off and dressed. Linda would be happy he was making a fresh start. As much as she had hated the hours he put in, she had always made it clear that she understood his devotion to his career.

He knew now that he must have been a real trial for her when they were first married: a gung-ho, by-the-book cop. By the time he made detective he'd mellowed and matured, but at the same time the job demanded even more of his time and attention.

He and Linda had sometimes talked about getting out of the city to begin a new life someplace like this. He dearly wished she and Kevin were with him now; they'd love the town, the mountain, the cabin.

It was situated about a mile's worth of winding roads north of the downtown area and was very secluded and idyllic from the little pond to the big rustic fireplace. Redwood-framed and trimmed in white, the cabin was two stories plus a carport and a small, triangular attic. Upstairs was a large bedroom, two small ones, and a bath. The master bedroom contained a large cherrywood poster bed and matching furniture, and the bath was stocked with towels, cleaning supplies, toilet paper, soap, and Kleenex. He knew the half-empty Kleenex box must have belonged to Frank Lawson. The thought was slightly unnerving.

He took the stairs down to the first floor. One wall of the cozy, oak-paneled living room was taken up entirely by a raised flagstone fireplace. A cord of wood lay in a brass basket near the fire tools, and logs were already arranged in the hearth. A wooden mantelpiece held several duck decoys and a polished brass spittoon. The room reeked of testosterone, but that was fine by Tully.

The floor, wide-planked golden oak, was covered by a braided oval rug, and the furniture, tweedy and overstuffed, went with it perfectly. The heavy pine coffee table was meant to hold tired feet and the walls were decorated with hotel-quality landscapes. Around the corner was a dining area and kitchen, which contained everything from spoons and forks to spices and cans of soup. Tully glanced in the refrigerator. A six-pack of Bud, one can missing, awaited him.

The most interesting room in the house was behind the living room. It had obviously been Sheriff Lawson's study, and the man had been a reader, big time. It looked like a lending library, with shelves full of books lining the walls. A large desk and chair were the only furniture. A turquoise case-glass lamp and a dark blotter decorated the desk.

Tully glanced at the Regulator clock on the wall, but it had stopped running. He wound it and started the pendulum's movement, then set it by his watch. It was seven in the evening. His stomach was growling again, and he wanted to visit the sheriff's office.

Returning to the kitchen, he heated a can of chicken noodle soup and found some slightly stale crackers. Fifteen minutes later, he locked up and drove to the station.

Two black-and-whites were in the lot when he pulled in and parked. The sedan was gone, replaced by a second Explorer, a year or two older than the one he'd already seen. He paused to glance in both. The newer was spotless and he suspected that it was what he would be inheriting from Frank Lawson. The older model had a few country-western tapes and a bottle of cough syrup on the seat.

The one-story log station had modern double glass doors and he pushed on one and found it locked. "What the hell?" Then he spotted a small placard just right of the door instructing visitors to ring the bell after six P.M.

After two rings, he saw a door open behind the reception area. A gangly young man in a tan uniform walked out. He stared suspiciously at Tully, then sneezed into a handkerchief before continuing to the front doors where he studied Tully a moment longer, before deciding to unlock the door.

"May I help you, sir?" he asked in a raspy slightly nasal voice. His nose was red and he looked absolutely miserable.

"I'm Zach Tully."

The young man's face spread in a grin. "Am I glad to see you, sir! Come on in." He stood back as Tully entered, proffering his hand. The deputy started to put his out, then drew it back. "I've got a cold. I sure don't want to give *you* my germs. I'm Tim Hapscomb." He relocked the door. "Come on back." He sneezed twice, apologized, and led Tully past the reception area and behind a door into a corridor leading to offices and restrooms. Tim left to wash his hands.

There were four desks in the office, three smaller ones up front with name placards reading, DEPUTY TIM HAPSCOMB, DEP-

UTY AL STOKER and DEPUTY RON SETTLES. A large desk at the rear of the twenty-foot-long room sported a brand-new nameplate reading, SHERIFF ZACHARY TULLY. At the sight of it, his stomach did a pleasurable little flip: The new title hadn't seemed real until now.

He walked around the desk and tried out the large leather chair. It had seen lots of use and was broken in just to his liking. Tilting back, he put his feet up, careful to avoid the small computer terminal to one side and the file tray and Rolodex to the other.

Staring around the room, he took in the wanted posters, file cabinets, bulletin boards, and a haphazardly stuffed bookcase and decided he felt right at home in the moderate clutter. He noticed that Hapscomb's desk held, in addition to Kleenex, a large paper Coke cup, a bag of cough drops, and mounds of paperwork piled up in his in-and-out boxes. Stoker's was moderately neat but Settles' work area was spotlessly clean. Judging by the evidence, he'd get along with Hapscomb and Stoker just fine.

"Sorry about that." Hapscomb halted in the doorway, staring in surprise at Tully's elevated feet.

Feeling a little sheepish, he took his feet off the desk and gestured at a chair across the desk. "Sit down, Deputy."

Hapscomb paused to grab his box of Kleenex then half collapsed into the chair. "I didn't mean to stare, but you reminded me of Sheriff Lawson with your feet up like that. He looked a lot like you."

Tully nodded, then they gazed at each other an uncomfortable moment. The deputy blew his nose again. Finally, Tully cleared his throat. "Tell me about yourself, Tim."

"I'm twenty-three, I've been in the department for almost two years—" A fit of coughing interrupted him. "Sorry," he managed finally. His forehead sheered with sweat. "Summer cold."

"How long are you on duty tonight?"

"Until six A.M."

"You should be home in bed, Deputy."

"I know, but the night's pretty quiet."

"I'll take your shift."

"But—"

"What can I expect?"

"Sir, you're not official yet."

Tully grinned. "You want to arrest me for impersonating an officer?"

Hapscomb returned the smile. "No, sir."

"Is there a map of the town here somewhere?"

"There's one on the wall in the next room, and there's probably another one in your desk drawer."

Tully opened the top drawer and found a Xerox of a hand-drawn map of Eternity, the town on one side, the county on the other. "This will do fine." He paused. "Does much happen around here at night?"

"Usually, week nights are pretty quiet unless the UFOs are out." He said it with a straight face.

"The what?"

"UFOs. We get them up over Icehouse, and sometimes the New Agers get in accidents hurrying to get up there."

"Hold it." Tully put up his hands. "This afternoon I got an earful about Bigfoot, but that was from a crazy old codger who's probably senile. Now you're talking about flying saucers. What's next? Spontaneous human combustion?"

"Not flying saucers, sir." Hapscomb said, insulted. "Just unidentified flying objects." He sneezed and blew his nose. "The New Agers think they're flying saucers. I don't know what the heck they are."

"You've actually seen them?"

"Everybody has."

Heaven help me. "Deputy. Tim. Are you a native of Eternity?"

Hapscomb eyed him, then sat up straight. "No, sir," he said proudly. "I'm from Bakersfield."

"When you feel better, I'd like to discuss the town with you."

"Sure." He paused to wipe his nose. "The lifers are pretty

touchy about things, so it would be best if we had our discussion when Ron and Al aren't around.''

"They've been here a long time?"

"Al was born here and Ron's been here just about forever, the way he talks.'' He hesitated. ''When he talks. He doesn't talk a lot.''

"You don't get along with him too well, I take it?"

"I didn't mean anything by that, sir. He's just hard to get to know. He's acting sheriff, you know.''

"I know.''

"He's not so bad when he's a deputy. I'm sorry, I don't mean anything by that. Everything's coming out wrong.''

"It's okay, Deputy,'' Tully told him, glancing at Settles' spotless desk. ''I think I understand.''

"He's a good cop,'' Hapscomb said, coughing.

"I'm sure he is. You get on home now. Call in tomorrow afternoon, and let me know if you're up to working.''

"Thanks, Sheriff,'' he said, rising. ''Uh, Sheriff Lawson let us take our vehicles home . . .''

"Of course.''

"Thanks.'' He gave Tully the keys to the building, then pointed at a file cabinet by the desk. ''The keys to Sheriff Lawson's vehicle—*your* vehicle—are in the top drawer. So's his weapon. The ammo's in the next drawer down. Call me at home if you need to know anything else tonight.'' He jotted his number on a scrap of paper.

"Thanks.'' Tully followed the deputy to the front door and locked him out, then returned to the office, loaded Lawson's .38, and studied the Xeroxed map. Just in case. Then he began exploring the file cabinets, hoping to find the report on Frank Lawson's death.

Seven

"Is your homework all done?" Kate McPherson asked as her son skipped down the stairs.

Josh nodded. "Done. Can I have some ice cream?"

Kate smiled. "You had some already."

"Please?"

"Tomorrow."

"Can I watch TV?"

Kate set aside the Patricia Cornwell novel she'd been reading and glanced at her wristwatch. "Do you know what time it is, Josh?"

"No, Mom," the boy said far too innocently. "Eight?"

Kate smiled. "It's nine-thirty and you have school tomorrow."

Another wide-eyed look. "I do?" One side of his mouth was trying to curl upward, but he fought it down valiantly.

"Come here, you." Kate held out her arms to her son, who hesitated briefly before falling into them and burying his face against her neck. Kate hugged him, tousling the thick golden hair. Even a year ago, Josh would never have joked and teased about going to bed. Nor would he have accepted Kate's affection, let alone returned it.

Don't you know that every time you indulge in those bouts of physical affection, you're doing your son irreparable harm?

Carl's voice interrupted. He had actively discouraged hugging and kissing and other displays of emotion between parent and child, always implying that Kate would be smarter to give *him* her excess affection in the form of sex. *You sonofabitch.*

"I love you," she whispered to her son.

Josh squeezed her harder, and mumbled against her neck. He still couldn't say the words; his father had knocked them out of him. Kate knew that hugging remained difficult, too, that he only managed it because it had become part of the evening ritual, something as routine as brushing his teeth. His spontaneity had been crushed under the weight of insecurities Carl had carefully planted. Though he still had far to go, Josh had already come a long way.

Josh pulled away and smiled at his mother. "Do you have to work tomorrow?"

"Afraid so. Have the bus driver take you to Miss Quince's house. I'll pick you up there by five-thirty, okay?"

"Okay." Josh paused. "When are you going to take me to work with you, to see Little Stonehenge, like you said?"

Kate studied him. The only time she had ever taken him up the mountain was last month, on the day she found Frank Lawson. At the time, thank God, Josh didn't realize a murder had occurred. When Kate told him, he barely reacted, though he hadn't asked to see Little Stonehenge again, either. Until now. Probably, Kate told herself, this was a very good sign. "Soon," she finally said. "I'll take you soon. Now, you get on up to bed, young man. Lights out by ten."

"G'night, Mom."

Kate watched him run up the stairs. This was working, really working, being up here on their own, far from Carl's reach. Both she and Josh were healing.

Even the note she found on her doorstep didn't seem so ominous now. She picked up her book, smiling to herself. Ambrose Abbott was probably right about it being a prank; after all, he was right about the intruder in her garage being of the furry persuasion.

The phone rang. Startled, she reached across the end table and snagged it up. "Hello?"

Faintly, she heard someone breathing.

"Hello? Who is this?"

There was no reply, only the slow, steady breathing. Then the connection broke.

Kate's hand trembled as she replaced the receiver. Before she moved here and made peace with Carl, back when she tried to hide from him, he had repeatedly made harassing phone calls. At least she assumed it was him; it was the kind of thing he would do, scaring her instead of coming out and admitting he'd found out her latest unlisted number. Could he be doing it again, just for the fun of it?

Could he have left the note? That was exactly the sort of disturbing thing he specialized in. That would mean he hadn't phoned her from Los Angeles today but from here . . .

Stop it! It was coincidence. Nothing but coincidence. *One hang-up caller and you flip. But the note . . .*

What if it's the murderer calling you?

No. She wouldn't think that way. Resolutely, she opened her novel and tried to concentrate, but she couldn't retain a word so she rose and double checked all the door and window locks. Yawning, exhausted, but knowing she wouldn't sleep, she went into the kitchen and poured herself a small brandy. She swallowed it quickly, not caring for the taste, but enjoying the warmth that spread quickly though her. After rinsing the glass, she started up the stairs.

The phone rang again.

She turned and stared at it, waiting for the machine to pick up but she hadn't switched it on. On the sixth ring she grabbed the receiver and listened.

Again, there was only the sound of slow, steady breathing. Slamming it down, she flipped the machine on then turned and marched up the stairs.

She was determined not to let this get to her, but her hands shook as she brushed her teeth and washed her face. Her shower would have to wait until morning.

The phone rang once more as she entered her bedroom, but the machine took it on the second ring. She wouldn't give the breather—*probably just a kid playing pranks*—any more of her time. Slipping out of her clothes, she pulled on a thigh-length blue T-shirt and brushed her hair then quickly checked on Josh. He was sound asleep.

Back in her bedroom, Kate went to the small safe she kept hidden in her closet. With shaky hands, she tried the combination twice before getting it right. Finally the door swung open and she removed the .38-caliber revolver and checked to make sure it was fully loaded. Satisfied, she carried it to the bed and slipped it under her pillow.

Then she lay there, tense between the cool sheets, wondering if the phone would ring again.

Eight

At half past midnight, a noise downstairs instantly brought Kate out of a fitful sleep. Heart pounding, she sat up in the dark and listened hard. There was nothing for a long moment and she nearly convinced herself she'd dreamed it before she heard the faint scratching sound again.

Silently, she slipped from the bed and padded to the sliding glass doors in her bedroom. She slid one open just enough to squeeze through onto the narrow balcony and peered below. The brightly lit deck was empty. She craned her head around the corner, trying to see the front door. Nothing. No cars were outside, no movement apparent.

She moved silently across the hall to Josh's room. Her son was fast asleep. She passed his bed and went to the window that overlooked the rear of the cabin, gasped as she spotted a dark figure at her back door.

Swiftly, she returned to her bedroom and picked up the phone. She dialed 911 and almost instantly an operator picked up. The woman tried to keep her on the phone while she contacted the Eternity Sheriff's Office, but Kate refused to cooperate beyond giving her name and address and saying she wasn't going to sit around and wait for the prowler to get inside, and to get a car here, fast.

She hung up and pulled the revolver out from under her

pillow then moved to the landing. She knew how to use a gun—she'd taken lessons when she bought it shortly after leaving Carl—but now she hoped she wouldn't have to use it.

Who's out there? Carl? Not likely, and you know it. The killer? She remembered the feeling she'd had as she stood in Icehouse Circle; the sensation that someone's eyes were upon her. Now, standing in the hall, the gun in her trembling hands, she prayed the door would hold until the police arrived.

Nine

Somehow, Zach Tully managed to get to the address in less than three minutes. It was fortunate he'd taken the Explorer out for a cruise around town after growing restless scanning homicide files at the station.

Serendipity was the word; he'd been at the west end of Eternity, only a half mile from the address when the call came in. Urgently, he'd consulted the map and headed in what he prayed was the right direction.

His prayers were answered and he found the cabin along a precariously narrow road running above the town. His heart pounded; he knew the name Kate McPherson from reading the brief report on Lawson's death. She'd found the body. Was the prowler coincidental? He doubted it.

He pulled up, headlights on bright, light bar flashing. Drawing his pistol, he got out of the truck and crouched low while he looked around. The cabin's outdoor lights were ablaze, and the second floor of the cabin was also lit. As he peered up at the open balcony door on the second floor, a backlit female form moved out. Seeing him, she came out onto the balcony. "The back door!" she called, then disappeared back into the house.

Tully ran to the cabin, his feet slipping on pine needles, but miraculously he kept his balance on the rugged hillside. Once he reached the structure, he edged along the side toward the rear, gun in hand. Halfway there, he heard running footsteps, then spied a man sprinting away from the house and across the clearing behind it.

"Halt! Police!" he yelled as the man disappeared up the hill into the shadows of the forest.

He ran after the prowler into the forest, but halted an instant later, breathing hard in the thin atmosphere, trying to listen for the man's footsteps.

He heard nothing. The towering pines blocked out the moonlight. He could see nothing, not the moon, not even the lights from the cabin and he didn't know the area so continuing the search was useless. And dangerous. Tully knew he could turn from the hunter into the hunted in an instant.

He turned around slowly, hoping he was facing in the right direction, and took a few slow steps. The trees closed in and the silence was astonishing, unlike anything he'd ever experienced in the city. The hairs on his neck were standing on end, and not just from the cold.

Keeping his hands extended to feel for trees, he moved a little to the left and spotted a tiny sliver of yellow light down the hill. Relieved, feeling foolish, he carefully made his way down the mountainside. At last the entire cabin came into view. Reaching it, he headed to the front door, not only to save fingerprints, but to keep from further alarming Ms. McPherson.

He knocked and soon a small rectangle of light gleamed out on him as Kate McPherson opened an old-fashioned viewer. In a shaky voice, she demanded, "Who the hell are you?"

"Zach Tully, ma'am. I'm the new sheriff."

"You're not in uniform."

Christ. He should've known this would happen. "Ms. McPherson, Deputy Hapscomb was ill, so I sent him home. I won't be sworn in until tomorrow."

"Do you have any identification?"

"Uh. How about a driver's license?"

"That won't prove you're a cop. You might be the prowler."

"I think my picture's in this week's paper. Do you have a copy?"

"Just a minute."

The viewer closed, then reopened momentarily. "Stand directly under the light," she ordered.

He did, heard paper rustling, and then the viewer closed again and he heard a key in the deadbolt. The door opened and he saw Kate McPherson for the first time.

She was tall, and the blue sleepshirt she wore did nothing to hide her long legs. Quickly, he brought his gaze up to meet hers and was taken by the dark green eyes, the dark blond hair, high cheekbones, and slightly square jaw. Her face, scrubbed and makeupless, was attractive but very pale.

"May I come in?"

"Yes, of course." She seemed flustered, nervous, which was only natural under the circumstances. Standing back to let him enter, she said, "For a moment, I thought you were a ghost. You look like our last sheriff."

"My deputy mentioned it."

She nodded. "Your hair's darker, you're thinner, but well, he could've been your older brother." She looked down, became aware of her apparel and color blushed into her pale cheeks. "Excuse me a moment."

She trotted up the stairs and reappeared quickly with a pair of jeans under the oversized shirt. Descending the stairs, she put her finger to her lips when he started to speak. "My son's asleep," she told him. "Come this way."

She led him into the kitchen where he immediately examined the back door. "Another minute and your prowler would've been inside," he said. The knob lock and the deadbolt had been jimmied; only a sliding bolt still partially held. He turned to face her. "Did you get a look at him?"

"No," she said apologetically. "He had a dark jacket on with the hood up. I couldn't even see the color of his hair. I think he was probably average-sized."

"Well, that's better than nothing," Tully replied. "All I saw was a running silhouette. He disappeared into the forest." He paused. "You're out here all by yourself?"

"Just my son and me," she told him. "Why?"

"Do you have a weapon?"

She looked at him. "What do you mean, a weapon?"

"Mace, a baseball bat, a rifle, you know, a weapon," he said, knowing she had something, probably a gun, by the way she averted her eyes.

"Yes," she said defensively. "I have a gun and it's registered. Do you want me to show you?"

"No, no. Do you know how to handle it?"

"I've had lessons," she said. "And I'm not afraid to use it."

He believed her.

Ten

"Oh, baby," Larry Fraser crooned as he pulled the Dodge into the turn-out low on Icehouse Mountain. "I need you now!"

Joyce Furillo giggled as she straightened her short black skirt. Her legs stuck to the vinyl upholstery; she'd lost her pantyhose in the back row of the Eternity Duplex halfway through the umpteenth screening of *Jurassic Park*. That was evidently Larry's favorite film—they'd been to it twice in the months since they'd met at Shalimar's, the bar where she worked.

"Larry," she protested mildly as he reached for her. "Why don't we go back to your place and do it on your waterbed?"

"Baby, baby, we'll sail the sheets later, I promise." He began rubbing her breasts, tweaking the nipples through her sweater.

"You promise?" she breathed, becoming excited despite the cold. She fumbled for his fly. "More later?"

"Cross my heart. You smell so good." He sucked her earlobe into his mouth. "You taste good, too." He moved his mouth down her neck.

"No hickeys," she warned, and pulled off her sweater, exposing her pride and joys—perfect, pricey C cups. Her skin turned to gooseflesh, her erect nipples into hard little rocks. Larry homed in on one. With one hand, he pushed her seat lever and the back lowered. Joyce wriggled toward the rear, Larry moving above her.

His mouth left her nipple as he raised up over her and lowered his pants. "Larry Junior needs you to keep him warm," he whispered, pushing her skirt up. His hand found her bare ass and Junior instantly sprang to attention.

"Oh, Larry," she whispered as he began to move. "Oh, *Larry*." The man dressed like a polyester throwback, right down to the gold chain around his neck and the shirt unbuttoned to show chest hair. He was a life insurance salesman, for God's sake, but once you got past that, he was Mr. Everready, and he really knew how to make love to a woman. He made her feel good, and that was more important to Joyce than the fact that he wasn't much to look at.

An orgasm began to build. Suddenly Larry stopped moving.

"What's wrong, babe?" she asked, wriggling to keep Junior's interest up.

"Did you hear something?" He quickly glanced around, but the windows were opaque with vapor.

"Nothing. Come on, Larry," she urged. "Let's do it."

Twigs snapped just outside the car and Larry's back stiffened beneath her hands. "It's probably just a deer," she whispered. "It'll go away in a minute."

"Yeah," Larry whispered, poised above her.

"Are there any other cars parked out there?"

"There weren't when we got here and we would've heard anyone pull in."

They listened intently, but heard nothing more. "I'll bet it was just a pinecone falling," Joyce said softly. She curled her fingers up into Larry's slightly greasy hair. "Let's make love, babe."

He smiled. "You got it." Junior twitched and returned to glorious life.

Something thumped against the car door.

"What the hell?" Larry pulled away, fumbling at his zipper. He rolled off Joyce, back into the driver's seat.

She straightened her skirt and flipped the lever controlling the seat back. It flung her upright and she saw Larry's hand on the door handle.

"No, don't!" she hissed. "It might be a bear or something."

He hesitated then removed his hand. An instant passed, then a dull glow showed through the steamy windows. A flashlight.

Someone tapped on the glass. "You folks mind rolling down your window?"

"It's a cop." Larry sighed with relief and put his hand on the window crank.

"Wait." Quickly, Joyce pulled her black sweater back on. "Okay." As she watched the window go down, she shivered, realizing again that they hadn't heard anyone pull up; if it was a cop where was his car? Well, she decided, maybe she'd had her mind on other things.

The light hit in their faces and Joyce thought she caught the glint of a badge behind it. "You folks have some car trouble?" The voice was nonthreatening and pleasant.

"No, sir," Larry replied. "Just enjoying the view."

Joyce glanced out the windshield knowing that the lights of Eternity were below even though she couldn't see them through the fogged glass. "We were just leaving," she called.

"Sir, would you step out of the vehicle for a moment, please?"

"Like Joyce said, we're leaving," Larry said. There was a nervous edge to his voice.

"This will only take a moment, sir."

Larry rolled his eyes at Joyce then put his hand on the door handle.

"No, wait," she hissed, then tried to see the man behind the flashlight. "Can we see some ID, Officer?"

"Of course." The flashlight winked out and she could hear little noises in the dark.

A black-gloved hand snaked through the window and grabbed Larry by the collar, yanking him halfway out. A millisecond passed. There was a clicking sound, then a muted blast and something whizzed past Joyce's face, followed by a spray of hot, salty liquid.

All this in the beat of a heart.

The flashlight came on, blinding her as Larry fell across her lap. She looked down and saw the dark oozing hole in the middle of his forehead, felt hot mushiness against her lap. Vaguely, she heard herself screaming. She thought it was someone else.

Eleven

"Coffee?" Kate asked.

"Please," Tully replied.

"It's instant."

"What other kind is there?"

She smiled and put water on to boil, then gestured at the tiny table and chairs at the edge of the room.

He sat and waited until she brought the mugs over. "Cream and sugar?"

"Black's fine. Listen, make sure you and your son don't touch the outside of the back door. I'll have someone over here to take prints in the morning." He sipped the coffee. "Ms. McPherson, I'm a little concerned."

"So am I."

"I know you found Sheriff Lawson's body."

"And?" She raised her eyebrows.

"And it's possible your prowler is his killer."

He was amazed that this would make her smile. "Thank you."

"What?"

"Your Deputy Settles told me I was hysterical when I suggested that the killer might have seen me that day. He said I was imagining things."

Tully sat back. "I haven't met Mr. Settles yet, but I have to disagree with him. Do you think the killer might know your identity?''

She nodded. "He was still there. In the meadow."

"Deputy Settles' report says he was long gone."

"That was an hour later," she replied impatiently. "Of course he was long gone." Putting her mug down, she sat forward, her eyes boring into his. "I know he was still there because he wasn't done with the body." Her voice was harsh. "Lawson's neck was severed. And his arms at the shoulders, elbows and wrists, his legs at the thighs, the knees. And one ankle. The other was still attached when I was there. He wasn't finished."

Settles' report hadn't mentioned the ankle. *Good God, what kind of people are working for me?* He couldn't believe the man would leave out such a detail. Worse, telling Kate McPherson that she was imagining things was unforgivable. "Did you tell Deputy Settles your suspicions right away?"

She instantly went on the defensive. "Immediately. You can ask Dr. Katz. He was there."

"I believe you," he said gently. He couldn't get out of those deep green eyes.

"Settles didn't believe me. In essence, he told me, 'There, there, don't worry your pretty little head about it.' "

"I'll speak to him about his conduct tomorrow, right after I ask him why parts of your statement are missing from his report."

She sat up a little straighter. "You're . . . a refreshing change from Deputy Settles." She paused, then looked at her coffee. "So, where are you from?"

He was glad she changed the subject; he'd been uncomfortable discussing the deputy he had yet to meet. "Los Angeles. I worked homicide before taking this job."

"Did your family come with you?"

He tried to hide his feelings. "I'm alone." He paused. "Are you a native of Eternity?"

She laughed, a soft musical sound. "Heavens no! I've been here a year. I'm from LA, too."

"What brought you here?"

"An ex-husband who wouldn't leave me alone." She gave him a wry look. "It worked. Maybe."

"What do you mean?"

"Well, the prowler wasn't the only excitement around here today." She told him about the note Ambrose Abbott had taken and about the hang-up calls she'd received earlier in the evening. When she finished, she added, "I'm glad you came out. I never could have told your Deputy Settles about this. It seems too silly. I mean it's probably coincidence. My husband used to call and hang up when I answered. It's possible it's him. I hope it's him; that would mean it's not the killer."

"It's likely just kids. Ms. Mc—"

"Kate. I hate using last names."

"Listen, Kate. The calls could have been the prowler casing the place; could've been your ex, or a kid, or some guy—" He was going to say "beating off," but caught himself. "Some guy amusing himself at your expense. You're right. Probably it was nothing. But maybe it was something. I don't mean to frighten you."

"You aren't. You're being blunt, and I appreciate that."

"You need to get out of here for the night," he said. "That back door won't hold. The perp probably won't be back, but it's not safe for you to stay here."

"I can't afford to leave. I'm on a tight budget. I'll call a locksmith first thing in the morning. We'll be fine until then."

"You and your son are welcome to come back to the station with me."

"Thanks, but that would frighten Josh. He's been through a lot, and I can't risk upsetting him."

Slightly annoyed, Tully glanced at his watch. It was nearly two in the morning; time had flown by. "I can't force you to leave, but I wish I could."

She shook her head.

"I wish you'd reconsider."

"We'll be fine."

Reluctantly, he rose. "I have to go to the station and check on things, but I'll try to cruise by every hour or so.'' He carried one of the wooden chairs to the back door and shoved it tightly beneath the doorknob. ''Keep all your lights on, and keep this place locked up tight.''

''You don't need to tell me that,'' she said as they approached the front door.

''I know, but it makes me feel better.''

''I will. Good night, Sheriff.''

He stood outside and listened to her lock up then walked to the Explorer.

Fifteen minutes later, he knew he'd made a wrong turn somewhere. He should have consulted the map, but of course he hadn't and now the narrow road had led for several miles up a slight incline, going deeper into the forest instead of toward town. He drove, high beams on, looking for a place wide enough to turn around.

Sometimes he and his family would drive out of town, up to Moonfall or Big Bear Lake for the day and Linda would always tease him about his refusal to look at the map. He'd tell her he liked surprises, but the truth was he took pride in how well he knew Los Angeles. The thought of consulting a map once he was on the road, even out of town, rankled him, resulting in many amazing side trips up dead-end roads. Linda always laughed and called him ''macho man'' when he got them lost.

And now, here he was, lost, with no time for adventures.

He rounded a bend and his lights flashed across a broad turnout on the other side of the road. He slowed and made a wide U-turn, and that's when he saw a big old Dodge, the color of dust, parked at the far edge of the clearing. Curious, he pulled up behind it and saw that the trees parted here to reveal the lights of the town below. It was a beautiful view, and he realized that the car probably contained a pair of horny kids.

But it was awfully late. And near freezing outside.

He put the Explorer in park, grabbed his gun and his flashlight and got out of the truck. Very slowly, he approached the car.

No one moved. Maybe someone was sleeping in it. Maybe it was abandoned.

He walked up to the driver's window, saw it was open. Gun partially raised, he shined the light inside.

"Police," he said, then, "Jesus."

The body in the driver's seat was bathed in blood, and it took him a moment to discern the huge hole in the chest. It looked like the guy had been ripped open. Broken ribs glistened with gore. The face was blood-coated and the mouth hung open. Tully glanced around warily, then stuck his head farther inside and shined the light on the man's face, holding his breath against the sharp metallic smell. There was a bullet hole in the forehead. The mouth dripped with gore and he saw a shiny membrane bulging behind the teeth.

A wave of nausea came and went in the blink of an eye, then Tully played the light across the interior of the car. No one else was within, but a woman's black high-heeled shoe lay on the blood-speckled passenger seat.

Shaking his head, Tully returned to the Explorer. It was going to be a long, long night.

Twelve

August 17

The first requisite for immortality is death.

—Stanislaw J. Lec

"All I can tell you for now is that the bullet killed him before the heart was removed and placed in the mouth." Dr. Phil Katz snapped his bloody surgical gloves off and let them fall into a medical refuse container. He shook his head. "What a welcome. A murder like this on your first day here. You must wonder if taking the job was a mistake."

Tully kept his eyes on Katz's earnest young face to avoid looking at the body on the autopsy table between them. "I haven't taken the job yet. Swearing in isn't until tomorrow—later today," he amended, noticing the faint blush of dawn beyond the miniblinds.

The physician's eyes widened in surprise. "You're not thinking of leaving, are you?"

Tully shrugged. "It's crossed my mind."

"The town needs you."

He waited for the inevitable "We're depending on you"

guilt speech, but it didn't come. Instead Katz looked back at the body and rubbed his chin thoughtfully. "This one doesn't resemble the other two. Much. No dismemberment."

"Doesn't resemble *much?*" Although Tully had read the police report on the Shady Pines runaway, one Bertram Meeks, it provided as little information as the one on Frank Lawson. Written by Ron Settles, it was inept, inaccurate, and nearly illegible. "Tell me about the 'much' part."

"I can't be sure without further tests, but see here, where the aorta is cut?" Katz used a scalpel to point at the heart he'd extracted from Larry Fraser's mouth. It lay in a white enamel basin next to the body. Tully looked, saw little, but nodded. "What about it?"

"That, and this cut over here," Katz pointed at the other side of the heart. "The angles lead me to believe our murderer might be a lefty."

"The same for Lawson and Meeks?" As Katz nodded, Tully continued, "Did you do the post mortems on Lawson and Meeks yourself?"

"Yes. I'm the only MD available to the townspeople. I have a specialty in pathology and I do double duty as the county coroner."

"You must work twenty-four hours a day."

"Well, I'm on call." The young man moved away from the table, took off his blood-splotched smock. "I have a physician's assistant to help handle routine work, and a very efficient nurse," he said over his shoulder as he scrubbed his hands at the sink.

"That's not much medical aid for a town of four hundred."

"Almost five hundred," Katz said. He dried his hands, then ran them through his light brown hair. "It gets busy during ski season. Broken legs, arms. Some of the bigger resorts have private doctors in residence during the season. But our year-round population is surprisingly healthy. In the two years I've practiced here, I've only had to call for three air evacs. All heart attacks, two triple bypasses and one quadruple. We've been able to handle everything else on our own."

"You've only been here two years?"

"Yes. The physician I bought the practice from had intended to stay on part-time, but he passed away before I arrived."

"How did he die?"

Katz cocked an eyebrow. "He wasn't murdered. He died of a stroke. He was eighty-one years old, and had served Eternity for half a century. His shoes were hard to fill. The town trusted Doc Sanderson with their lives, so you can imagine how hard it was for a new doctor, an outsider no less, to gain acceptance, even with the council's support." His smile betrayed a trace of sadness. "But I was the only game in town, and I had Sanderson's seal of approval so they eventually accepted me."

"You're very young to have your own practice."

"Not as young as I look. I'm thirty-six. A youthful appearance is a gift, I suppose, but for a doctor trying to establish himself, it's a curse."

"I can imagine," Tully said, a little taken aback that the physician was only three years his junior. "Where'd you go to school?"

"Oxford, then Johns Hopkins."

"Impressive."

Katz shrugged self-consciously.

"What made you decide to come up here?"

"I could ask you the same thing." Katz smiled. "We're probably here for the same reasons. I was tired of the city and sick of having to do the same thing every day. I wanted to be a small town GP. When I heard about the opening here, I simply sent my résumé. That was that."

"I take it you've dealt with Eternity's town council?"

Katz's wide grin made him look like an adolescent. "You've met our esteemed governors, then?"

"Only Harlan King." He paused, gathering his diplomatic skills despite the hint of sarcasm in Katz's voice. "What do you think of the way the town is run?"

Katz shook his head. "Eternity is almost a company town, but not quite, even though the council would like it. I'm glad you're here. It'll be a relief to have another outsider to work with.''

"By 'outsider,' do you mean the opposite of 'lifer'?''

"You've already heard the term?'' The doctor looked bemused.

"Several times.''

"The lifers run everything. They insist on doing everything their way, and no one else gets to play. There's no room for anything new.''

"The entire town couldn't have been born and bred here,'' Tully said slowly.

"No, but I think you have to be a resident for a century or two before they let you into the business associations or politics, let alone the Brotherhood.'' Katz chuckled. "Lifers are rarely born here. They're made.''

"What's the Brotherhood?''

Katz smiled helplessly. "I suspect it's Eternity's twist on the Masons.''

Tully chuckled, at ease now. "They dress up in funny underwear and bay at the moon? That type of thing?''

Katz laughed. "That would be my first guess.'' The humor left his face. "I should warn you: Don't joke about the Brotherhood, or politics or anything else that the lifers take seriously. Not unless they joke first. That goes double in dealing with the town council. There's a definite social order here, and the council members belong to the highest caste.''

"What the hell am I doing here?'' Tully asked. "And why do you stay?''

"It's not that bad. In fact, it's very good. All societies have rules, after all. Eternity is so small that it's just a little more noticeable.'' His mouth twisted wryly. "Think of Eternity as an eccentric uncle. Strange but harmless and really, rather entertaining.''

"I don't see it.''

"You will. The lifers will tell you the tallest tales you've ever heard, and they'll laugh while they do it. They don't expect you to believe them. It's intriguing.''

"Tall tales?"

"While they won't talk about their Brotherhood or discuss politics, most of them will talk Icehouse lore for hours. Tales of supernatural travels. How they came to live here. Tourists eat it up." He smiled. "Eternity bears a striking resemblance to Disneyland and the lifers play their characters to the hilt." He cleared his throat. "It's fun trying to figure out who's role-playing and who's having delusions. The people of this town are eccentric, but they're also harmless."

"Someone's not harmless," Tully said, eyes drifting toward the autopsy table.

"Yes," Katz agreed. "Although I would think the killer might not be a resident."

"Anything's possible." Tully glanced at his watch. It was approaching six-thirty. He'd been up nearly twenty-four hours, and his brain was turning to oatmeal. "Can you give me copies of your reports on Lawson and Meeks? And on Larry Fraser, when it's ready?"

"Certainly. The Fraser PM might take a few days, but I'll keep you informed. I can send the Meeks and Lawson reports to your office this afternoon."

"That's fine." Tully hesitated. "No. On second thought, I'll come by and pick them up this afternoon, after the swearing-in ceremony."

"I'll have them up front waiting for you." They left the autopsy room, walking down the clinic's hallway to the reception area. There, Katz unlocked the front door and they stepped out into the cold, brilliant morning.

Tully, squinting against the sun, reached under his jacket and took his sunglasses from his shirt pocket. His eyes watered, even with the shades.

"The atmosphere is thin up here," Katz said. "It's a shock to city eyes."

"I'll say."

"The angle of the sunlight changes before noon, but it's a good idea to wear sunblock all year long. And if you experience nausea, headaches, dizziness, that's a result of the thin air, too.

It will pass as your body acclimatizes, but if you have any trouble, I'll give you something to get you through it." He gazed at Tully, his dark brown eyes lively. "Give Eternity a chance, Sheriff Tully. I think you'll like it. This town needs you."

"Thanks. My friends just call me Tully."

"Phil."

As they shook hands, Tully felt exhaustion wash over him. He wanted to ask Phil several hundred more questions, but they would have to wait; sack-time was more important right now. "See you later." He turned to leave.

"Sheriff?"

He turned back to the doctor. The young man looked worried. "Did they tell you about the others?"

"Others? Other whats?"

"Look, if they don't tell you, you can't let on I've mentioned it." Katz glanced around nervously.

"Go on."

"Before Frank, and before Meeks, there were others."

"Other homicides?"

Katz nodded. "The council covered it up. The victims weren't locals. They were . . . You won't talk about this?"

"No. Tell me, then I can dig it up on my own."

"They were tourists. Two women, experienced hikers. They checked in, got campfire permits, the whole thing."

"When was this?"

"Mid-June. They'd been gone a week when their bodies were found a half mile from the trailhead. They were badly mutilated."

"Dismembered?"

"No. Worse, in a way. Are you familiar with Jack the Ripper's crimes in London a century ago?"

Tully nodded slowly. "Somewhat. He mutilated prostitutes, disemboweled them."

"Yes. To put it mildly, he performed very crude surgeries upon them, took souvenirs. A kidney, a portion of vagina. He mutilated the genitalia with particular zest." Katz's expression pinched with distaste. "That's what happened to the two women."

"Who found them? Locals?"

"No. A couple college kids from Colorado. Hikers, too. They called your office. Frank was out of town that weekend so Ron Settles, along with half the council, went up and retrieved the bodies. They told the kids who found them that the women had been attacked by a bear, then sent them down to Mt. Shasta to do their hiking."

"Sent them? You mean they shut them up?"

"Basically. The mayor himself drove them over, saw them off." Katz glanced around again. "This is between you and me—"

"Yes."

"They brought me the bodies. There was a late storm coming up and it was so windy and cold that I was surprised they got them off the mountain that night."

"You autopsied?"

"Yes. They were mutilated and at first glance, it could have been a bear's work. But it wasn't. Bears don't use knives or leave notes."

"What?"

"There was a note wrapped in plastic inside one woman's abdominal cavity. All that was written on it was the name: Jack the Ripper."

"What happened to the note?" Tully asked, reminded of the note Kate McPherson had mentioned, the one signed Jacky.

"It disappeared before I could give it to Sheriff Lawson. Someone took it."

Abbott? "Any idea who?"

"No, but I think it was done on the council's behalf. The bodies were removed, too, supposedly at their families' request. Later, the paper mentioned that the women were killed by a bear. I didn't ask any questions."

"Did you tell Lawson all this?"

"Yes. I think the knowledge might have resulted in his murder. That's why I warned you about watching what you say.

There's nothing worse than feeling responsible for another's death.''

"Yes." A second passed, two. "But you did the right thing, telling Lawson. And telling me. So you believe some of the council members lied repeatedly?"

"Well, they're the only ones with a motive."

"Which is . . ."

Katz looked pained. "Eternity depends on tourism. Murders don't help business and I can't think of anyone who would . . . It's been a pleasure to meet you, Sheriff!" Katz said suddenly and heartily. He took Tully's hand and pumped it. "I'm so glad you came by." He looked past Tully's shoulder and called, "Good morning, Nurse Boyle."

Tully turned and saw a short refrigerator in white trundling rapidly toward them.

"This is my right hand, Sheriff. Edna Boyle, this is our new Sheriff, Zach Tully."

Tully smiled at the woman. She was sixtyish, with short iron-gray hair curling in carefully constructed waves around her frowning, iron-jawed face. She stopped short and looked Tully up and down, appearing to smell something she didn't like. "Pleasure," she grunted, ignoring his extended hand. She turned her steely gaze on Katz. "Time to open up. Dr. Katz, I'd advise you to go home and change into fresh clothing." With that, she barreled past them, into the office.

"Lifer?" Tully asked lightly. Katz was pale, his anxiety obvious.

"Yes. She came with the practice."

"Charming woman," Tully said dryly.

"She scares away the hypochondriacs." The physician glanced at the office door. "I can't talk now."

"I understand. We'll talk later."

Tully climbed into the Explorer, feeling like he'd tumbled down a rabbit hole.

Thirteen

"You remind me of someone I once knew," Jack said to the dark-haired woman who lay bound and gagged on a heavy plastic tarp spread across the center of his woodshed. "A lady of the evening who sold her charms to anyone with a coin or two."

He had been pleased and surprised to find this one still breathing after a night in near-freezing temperatures without the benefit of clothing.

A single lightbulb hung from a cord tacked to the ceiling. As he circled her, he reached up and tapped it. It swung back and forth, casting shadows and light against the cordwood lining the walls, like a scene from *Psycho*. He looked down into her wide terrorized eyes.

Pulling on gloves, he crossed the room and pulled a huge plastic picnic chest out from beneath a worktable. "Plastic," he exclaimed, picking the chest up easily, despite its size— five feet long and deep enough to hold a body. "Marvelous thing, plastic. We didn't have it in the old days. A pity. It's so convenient. And waterproof," he added, setting the chest down next to the woman and unsnapping the latches. "Lightweight and sturdy." He opened the lid, sniffed. "You don't mind a faint breath of Kosher dill, do you? If you do, I can try to get rid of it with a little bleach . . ." He laughed. "You enjoy the odor of pickles, I can see it in your eyes. I do as well. A hint of summer, of picnics, and the Fourth of July. Pickles it shall be, then! Excuse me a moment, my dear.''

He smiled to himself as he opened the door leading to his kitchen. It was old-fashioned but nice, the refrigerator its biggest luxury. He opened the freezer door to reveal shelves stocked with TV dinners, Swanson's Salisbury Steak, Marie Callender's Beef Stroganoff, Stouffer's Swedish Meatballs—lots of those. There were pizzas, corn dogs, and Chinese delicacies. ''I love this century,'' he murmured, lifting a facade of dinner boxes from two of the shelves to reveal several bags of ice. He placed them in a laundry basket, then rearranged the rest of his freezer, moving the real dinners into neat stacks equally portioned out among the shelves. He dismantled the facade of boxes then fed the cardboard, piece by piece, into an old-fashioned wood-stove he'd renovated and installed during a fit of nostalgia.

He closed the grate, then hefted the basket of ice. Pushing the door to the shed open with his foot, he called softly. ''Are you ready to go on our picnic, my dear?''

The dream seeped into his sleep. Tully tossed with it, gritting his teeth, soaking the sheets with cold sweat as the freeway crawled, stopped, crawled some more, hampered by rub-berneckers who were compelled to gawk at every stalled car or flat tire along the roadside. Sniffing for blood, that's what they were doing. It's human nature, he told himself, staving off anger and frustration. He felt around for a roll of Tums. Finally, his fingers closed on it and he dropped three tablets into his mouth.

He was angry at himself for being late, for disappointing Kevin and Linda yet again. ''Damn it,'' he muttered. ''Damn me.'' Linda was almost too understanding about his hours; maybe if she'd get mad at him, he wouldn't feel so bad about breaking his promises. Maybe if he'd tell the watch commander where to stick it, he wouldn't have to break his promises. *Don't blame anyone but yourself. You fucked up again.*

Beating himself up wasn't going to help. He forced his thoughts to return to his current case, the Backdoor Man slayings.

The perp hadn't struck for a month, not since Tully came within a hair's breadth of catching the son of a bitch. All indications were that the killer had moved on, but Tully doubted it; he could still feel him, smell him. The Backdoor Man had moved into his head and stayed there, frustratingly out of reach, agonizingly close.

The killer was waiting, biding his time, and meanwhile, Tully's task force was disbanding, a cop here, a detective there. Tight budgets and the sudden cessation of victims were the reasons. The LAPD couldn't afford to keep men on a cold case on one man's hunch.

The traffic eased up after he passed the 605 interchange. He punched the radio on, searching for classic rock, found it, and put the pedal to the metal as AC/DC screamed about dirty deeds done dirt cheap.

Out of patience, aware of the ticking clock, he swung out around a slow-mo, heroically resisting the urge to give her the finger. He maneuvered like a maniac, sliding through the usual intermittent constipation that marked the San Bernardino Freeway between Euclid and Haven. The road finally opened up and he pushed the car to eighty. He was driving like an idiot, but now he'd make it to Sears before nine to pick up Kevin's birthday present.

Last year, after missing Kevin's fourth birthday, he'd made a conscious effort to cut his hours and spend more time with his family. He did well for a while, then began breaking promises again in September when he canceled plans for Kevin's first fishing trip. That was when the Backdoor Man had made his first kill, right under Rampart's nose. Tully grabbed the gauntlet with a vengeance. *Why?* From the moment of that first kill, he had sensed the magnitude of the Backdoor case.

His hours grew longer but didn't get out of control until November, when the killer struck again and the task force was born, small at first, then enlarging the second week in December when the killer took down another woman.

The three victims were females home alone, but beyond that the perp, now dubbed "Backdoor Man," wasn't picky. The first victim was an elderly Korean grandmother, the next an attractive African-American nurse in her thirties, and the third, a twenty-five-year-old Caucasian graduate student.

With January came a fourth murder, then two in February and two more in March. Tully got used to seeing himself on the news again as the terror spread throughout LA County. Thanks to the press and his own reputation, he remained in charge of the case even though it had gone countywide.

It was hell dealing with the press; he had nothing to give them and they expected everything; he'd forgotten what vultures reporters could be. They made references to his previous claims to fame—the "unsolvable" El Niño murders and the Delmonico atrocities. They wrote about his talent for hunches, playing it to the hilt; one weekly rag had labeled his abilities "supernatural," another called him "telepathic," while the others contented themselves with embarrassing references to Sherlock Holmes and *The Silence of the Lambs*.

During the earlier cases, as now, the media's attention made for constant teasing from his friends and not a little resentment among the ranks. And worst of all, the media had turned him into the equivalent of an old west gunfighter who constantly had to defend his number one status. How could he have forgotten how infuriating and stressful that was?

Now it was all back and so far the Backdoor Killer remained a faceless bogeyman. He wore gloves, raped with a large stainless steel knife, then decapitated his victims. He left the heads prominently displayed, ornamented with a white rose. One victim's head decorated a lamp table, displayed in a picture window for three days before the postman noticed. He hadn't noticed the rose.

The others' heads, fortunately, weren't out for public viewing so Tully was able to withhold the grotesque detail of the rose from the press. Keeping this back was calculated to irritate the killer and cause him to initiate some kind of contact.

The more time Tully spent staring at the photos in his office or standing in a shadowed murder site, the more convinced he was that perpetrator didn't like his nickname, either. Tully himself had seeded the press with the name in his second press meeting, telling reporters, quite truthfully, that, "Some perpetrators are second-story men, some are window men, some roof men. This one's a backdoor man." It was all in the phrasing.

Tully smiled to himself, still pleased with the maneuver, still having faith in its ability to annoy the killer who probably found the epithet insulting. The man, with his white roses, was a romantic at heart. He wouldn't like the tawdriness of "Backdoor Man."

Tully zipped through San Bernardino, his mind racing as fast as the car, his mood lighter when he realized he'd arrive at the store with ten minutes to spare. He drove on.

The Backdoor Man took two more victims between April 2 and 10, both in LA County, but barely, one in the north San Fernando Valley, the other in Pomona, a block from the county line. The perp was getting pissed, Tully could feel it. The county-edge kills were a personal message for Tully that the killer was aware of him and his territory.

On April 10, Tully was first at the Pomona crime scene. He'd been on his way home, determined to have dinner with his family after weeks of absence, when the call came over the radio. He knew the street and the Towne Avenue exit, looming straight ahead, would have him there in two minutes.

Barely hearing the blaring horns of the drivers he cut off, Tully tore across three lanes of traffic to make the exit. Slowing at the bottom of the ramp, he clapped the magnetized flasher to the roof of the unmarked car. Seventy seconds later, he entered the run-down neighborhood and turned off the roof light. He cruised slowly, eyes searching the dusk for movement. There was nothing. Yellow light glowed inside flat-roofed houses, televisions played behind barred windows. Dogs barked. That was all until he reached the address.

There, three Latina women stood huddled together at the edge of the lawn. They looked up at his approach, eyes wide, frightened, as they huddled closer together. Tully opened his wallet ID before he got out of the car, holding it up so that they could see the flash of his badge under the streetlamp.

The women were family, mother and aunts of the victim. The mother was worried because her daughter hadn't come to church the previous day, hadn't answered her phone since Friday. She had come to investigate, bringing her sisters for protection because the neighborhood made her nervous. She had unlocked the door and turned on the lights, only to find her daughter's head blindly staring at her from the center of a small dining room table.

He had the women wait outside for the local police while he entered the house, his .38 drawn and ready. The mother had flipped off the lights as soon as she registered what lay before her. Tully's eyes watered from the odor of decay as he pushed the switch up with the edge of his fingernail.

The murderer was long gone but he could feel him nonetheless, sense the man's pleasure, his glee as he arranged the grotesque centerpiece. A full dozen white rose buds wreathed the neck in a wilted, rotting necklace. The Backdoor Man wanted more attention.

In the distance, he heard sirens. Knowing his plain clothes and plain car—not to mention his gun—would get him a rough search before his ID was considered, he walked across the tiny living/dining room and into the hall. He followed his nose to the back bedroom, switched the light on, saw the headless body on the bed, saw the wounds, and felt the killer's rage. The sensations coursing through him, terrible as they were, were vital to his understanding the enemy.

The sirens were only a block away as he turned out the lights and trotted out to wait with the victim's family. He had a feeling he would finally flush out and catch his prey.

That was a little over a month ago. The killer struck once

more, on April 15, and Tully, playing a broad hunch, had come agonizingly close to catching him. He'd stopped the mutilation, but not the murder. He never even caught sight of the killer.

Tully took the Santo Verde exit and soon pulled up to Sears' customer pickup office. It all happened a month ago. Now the Backdoor Man had disappeared, grown bored or been caught for another crime. Maybe he'd show up in Houston or Seattle or Boston next. Perhaps he'd fled the country. Or maybe he'd simply gone to ground for the time being. Whatever the reason, he was gone. "Hey, maybe you didn't catch him," his captain said, clapping him on the back as he told him the task force was being disbanded, "but hell, Tully, you scared him off."

Tully entered the store office and gave his receipt to a grumpy woman who muttered something then disappeared into the warehouse. To theorize that the Backdoor Man had moved on was logical. It was rational. The rest of the taskforce—except his partner Mendoza—believed it. The LAPD and county sheriff released cautiously worded statements to that effect, lauding him for his work.

It was bullshit.

The dream jumped suddenly. He had the bike safely nestled in his trunk and a slightly limp bouquet of tiny blue daisies lay on the seat beside him.

He headed for home, almost relaxed. The night was dark and quiet and he rolled down the window, enjoying the cool air against his face. He sighed. Here, listening to the crickets chirp and the trill of night birds, nothing seemed so bad. *Maybe your instincts are wrong this time. Maybe the Backdoor Man really has moved on.* He pulled into his driveway, warmed by the lights illuminating his way. He grabbed the daisies then quietly opened the trunk and took the bike in his arms and tiptoed up the walk. Maybe, just maybe, he was confusing his need to win, to catch the killer, with legitimate instinct. He leaned the bike against the house, behind the door so that Kevin wouldn't see it immediately. He studied the bicycle for a moment, realizing just how much he had and how much he took for granted. For the sake of his family, he had to let go of the Backdoor Man, had to accept that he'd lost one.

Tully opened the screen door and inserted his key in the deadbolt. Inside, he could hear the TV babbling out something that sounded like a nighttime soap. He smiled as the lock turned, picturing Linda and Kevin dozing on the couch.

He pushed the door open and thrust the daisies inside. "Don't pay the ransom, honey!" he called. "I escaped!" It was a hoary old joke, but a pleasant fit.

He waited for Linda's reply but it didn't come. It was only nine-thirty, but his wife was an early-riser and liked to go to bed early. Maybe she'd put Kevin to bed, read him a story, and fallen asleep next to him. He found them like that frequently.

Or maybe she was really angry at him. Lord knew she had every reason to be. If so, he'd take it like a man and throw himself on her mercy. "Here we go," he murmured as he pushed the door open and stepped inside.

He smelled roses.

Fourteen

The shrieking alarm clock brought Tully bolt upright, heart pounding, skin damp with sweat. Panting, dazed, he gazed at the unfamiliar room. Not the bungalow in Santo Verde, not his apartment in LA. In another few seconds, his confusion drained away. Eternity, he thought as he turned off the alarm. *My new home. And my old dream.*

He'd only had two hours of sleep, but he wasn't tired. The dream had turned his nerves into surging live wires, vibrating, ready to snap. Usually, he felt the urge to throw the alarm clock across the room; today he looked at it with gratitude. It had saved him from the awful conclusion of the nightmare. *The memory.* He shuddered once then stood up and padded to the shower.

He adusted the water flow from a fine spray to hard pulsations and let it beat the stiffness from his neck and shoulders for fifteen minutes, running the water so hot that it nearly scalded his skin. It felt good as it cleansed him of the nightmare.

For the first six months after his family's death, Tully had been plagued by the dream. Each night he had relived every minute detail, every conversation, every lane change, every thought he'd had on Kevin's fifth birthday. Sometimes it began at the station with a conversation he and Mendoza had had, but more often, as this morning, it commenced with him driving home, feeling guilty and reviewing the Backdoor murders. The rest never varied except that sometimes he heard laughter and felt eyes upon him and sometimes he did not.

During that half year of nightly horrors, his waking thoughts often concerned suicide, but somehow he fought on, slogging through another day, another nightmare, then another and another, driven on by the all-consuming fire to inflict the same pain on the killer as he had on his victims, to mutilate him and enjoy the sounds of his screams. He daydreamed about bashing the perp with a sledgehammer until his bones were nothing but gravel. Then, after making him feel the pain for a very long time, he would let the killer watch him take aim. The last thing the Backdoor Man would see in this life was Tully smiling down at him as he pulled the trigger.

Knowing he was almost over the edge, Tully never spoke of his desires. When he spoke of the Backdoor Man at all, even to his partner, he merely said he wanted the murderer brought to justice. If his superiors had been able to read his thoughts, they would have taken him off active duty. It was bad enough he was off the case; not working at all truly would have killed him.

So he played the game, working on new cases by day, by night pouring over the Backdoor Man's files, studying images of death, trying to get inside the murderer's head, to find out what made him tick.

Time passed, and the dreams came less frequently and lost focus. The details blurred with other nightmare images, until they consisted simply of wandering, lost, in darkness, walking blindly on an unseen floor coated with sticky blood that *squitched* under his shoes with every step. As horrible as they were, these dreams were a relief after the others.

He scrubbed his skin with a rough washcloth. He'd had no nightmares in months, and now this, the original, back full force. Guilt, he thought. Guilt for leaving LA without avenging Linda and Kevin. That had to be the reason for the return.

The spray was losing its warmth. He finished up, shampooing, and shaving in less than five minutes. Even so, the water was freezing by the time he jumped out and wrapped himself in one of the thick blue towels that had been left for him. He used another to rub his hair reasonably dry.

Strapping on his watch, he saw the time; he had fifteen minutes to dress and get to the swearing-in ceremony. He should have skipped the nap.

He sprinted to the bedroom and threw open the closet doors, thankful that he'd carried his suit and a good shirt and tie with him in the car. He looked at the suit then paused, tempted by more comfortable clothing. *Put on the suit, babe. It won't kill you.* He heard the words in Linda's voice, the laughing tone she'd used every time he had to make a public appearance.

She'd always been right, so he grabbed his charcoal suit and in three minutes, despite a false start knotting the silk tie, he was out the door. At five of twelve, he pulled the Camaro out of his driveway and onto the winding paved road that led downtown. He'd just make it.

At noon, he conceded he'd gone in the wrong direction, turned around and headed back, doing forty in a twenty-five zone, swerving to miss a gray squirrel, passing his cabin, and taking a two-foot bough off a pine tree growing too close to the road on the hindside of a hairpin turn.

"Damn it." The branch stuck under the right windshield blade. He turned the wipers on, low, high, intermittent, trying to force it off, gave up before he burned out the wiper motor. There was no time to stop; he was already eight minutes late. *What a wonderful first impression I'm going to make.*

Tully had an infallible sense of direction. He prided himself on being able to sense due north with his eyes closed. And he'd found the cabin easily, twice, following Harlan King's verbal directions. This was mortifying. His internal radar had shorted out. He recognized no landmarks. Cities had landmarks . . . Eternity just had trees. And to a city boy, all trees looked pretty much alike.

At ten past the hour, he recognized something: five potholes zigzagging across the road, spaced so that they were almost impossible to miss. "Hallelujah," he muttered a minute later as he slowed for the last curve. There was a sudden, steep descent into Eternity proper then two more blocks before he emerged at Main Street near Harlan King's bakery. He faced the final hurdle: Main ran one way, counterclockwise, and if his location was at nine o'clock, the courthouse was at twelve. He turned right and began the trip around the square, cursing without conviction at every stinking stop sign. At the final intersection, Tully slowed to a crawl. No pedestrians or traffic were in sight, so he started to make the turn, then slammed on the brakes, barely avoiding a vehicle that shot out of the cross-street without even slowing. The yellow Mustang sped past him and pulled into the courthouse driveway.

"We meet again," he murmured, darkly pleased as he finished his turn and steered the Camaro into the same entrance. He pulled in, seeing a flash of brake lights as the Mustang disappeared behind the building. "You're not going to get away this time, my friend." He stepped on the gas and his tires squealed as he rounded the building too fast. Self-conscious, he slowed. *You're already late. Don't improve on things by cutting down a pedestrian.*

A sea of vehicles filled the lot. Pickups, Outbacks, Jeeps, and SUVs of all makes were obviously the vehicles of choice in snow country. He smiled as he spotted the flash of taillights as the other driver parked at the far end of the lot. *Gotcha.*

Sedately, he drove to the aisle and pulled into the neighboring slot, forcing the Mustang's driver, a slender dark-haired woman in a flapping charcoal trenchcoat, high heels, and sunglasses, to stop in her tracks to avoid being hit.

He killed the engine, pocketed his keys and hopped out of the car.

"Mr. Tully?"

"You cut me off," he said. "Twice in two days."

The dark glasses hid her eyes. One side of her mouth twitched up. She said nothing, but casually lifted his wiper blade and removed the pine branch.

He stared at her. She stared at him. The moment grew excruciatingly long. Finally, she spoke, her voice soft, but strong, with a slight huskiness that made her sound a little like Kathleen Turner. "There's a thousand-dollar fine for damaging the trees in this county."

"And you can go to jail for cutting off the sheriff," he countered. "Twice."

The smile broadened slightly, became symmetrical. "What sort of sheriff does the California rolling stop in his new jurisdiction?"

"The kind who's late on his first day of work," he said in frustration. He was now twenty minutes late. "I don't have time for this right now. Just watch it, okay?" He walked toward the courthouse, intent only on getting to the ceremony. He heard the clack of the woman's heels behind him. He kept moving, using long-legged strides, but somehow she kept up with him, high heels and all.

"Don't worry, they won't start without you," she said as they gained the sidewalk.

"Who the hell are you?" he asked, starting up the broad backstairs to the courthouse.

"You mean you don't remember me?"

He paused, hand on the door, and looked down at her. Flawless skin, cheeks faintly flushed from the rapid walk in the nippy air. Hair the color of dark brown mink, smooth waves curling gently under the jawline, rich and gleaming in the bright sunshine. Full lips colored with a trace of rose. Eyes? Who could tell? *Who cares?* He almost said something rude, thought better of it. "You have the advantage, ma'am."

"Relax," she said. "I'm not one of *them.*" She stuck her hand out. "Arlene Rios. I interviewed you when I worked for KBTV News in Los Angeles."

"That morning show," Tully said. Her handshake was a little too strong. *"Hi There, LA?"*

"Hello Today, LA," she corrected. "Now I'm a special correspondent for *Century 2000* on TCN. You know it?"

"TCN?"

"The Crime Network."

"I never bothered with cable," he said, eager to escape. A reporter was all he needed.

"My camera man, Al Bach, is inside. He's going to film the ceremony." She smiled. "And I wangled an invitation to the luncheon. Do you think you might talk Mayor Abbott into letting Al come, too?"

"No." He could already feel her draining his energy. "Excuse me."

"Please think of me as a friend. And a fan."

She smiled winningly and he thought the accompanying smoky chuckle could probably disarm lesser men at twenty feet. He wasn't buying, but he forced himself to be diplomatic. "I'm not going to countermand the mayor. That wouldn't be wise on my first day—especially since I'm late." He pushed open the door.

"Good point," she said as she scooted past him and inside. "Thank you. You're a gentleman," she added, even though they both knew he hadn't intended it.

Fifteen

Until a freak explosion decimated the Masello Brothers Traveling Carnival back in the seventies, Zach Tully had spent every penny he'd earned mowing lawns to spend a week of his summer vacation hanging out at the fairgrounds when the show came to town. He'd eaten corn dogs and cotton candy until he was sublimely sick, rode the Ferris Wheel and Tilt-A-Whirl, shot metal ducks in a row, and he'd paid half a buck at least once a day to enter the Ten-In-One.

It was one of the last bona fide "oddities" shows traveling the states, an old-fashioned tent holding ten exhibits. In addition to the usual mummies and pickled fetuses, the Masellos' show usually had a bearded lady, an elastic man and a tattooed lady, a family of dwarves, and a cow with six legs. Tully paid the fee and slinked in each day, fascinated and ashamed. It was the sugar, he was the fly.

Throughout the postceremony luncheon he couldn't shake the feeling that he was back in the Ten-In-One, and that this time, he was being adopted by the oddities as one of their own. The sensation was at once intriguing and disturbing.

From the moment he and Arlene Rios entered the courtroom, nothing seemed real. Mayor Ambrose Abbott presided from the judge's bench, descending only briefly to swear Tully in. Arlene Rios sat in the first row with a balding man glued to a minicam. The rest of the row was taken up by an odd mix of people he assumed were the town council. Beside Rios, Harlan King, smiling serenely, delicately plucked chocolate chips from an overgrown muffin, savoring each as if it were the one and only. The next man, in a blue Hawaiian shirt, looked oddly familiar as he slouched back on the hard wooden bench, watching the proceedings beneath eyelids at half-mast.

Tully wished there had been time for introductions before the formalities began, but when he and Rios entered the courtroom, the mayor had propelled him straight to the witness box. Muttering something about hot food taking precedence over etiquette, he ascended to the judicial bench and called the meeting to order.

Next to Hawaiian Shirt sat a fortyish woman, long and lean, with short tousled brown hair. She looked like she belonged outdoors despite her tan linen blazer and white Oxford shirt. Beside her was a compact, if slightly stout, middle-aged man in a neat black pinstripe suit, complete with vest and a bowler hat in his lap. He rarely looked up, but as he scribbled on a steno pad, Tully could see his precisely waxed black mustache move as he rhythmically pursed and relaxed his lips.

The final two appeared to be a couple. The woman was an energetic grandma type, reminding Tully strongly of Ethel Mertz. Her mate had a long cadaverous face, incongruously lively eyes, a madras-plaid shirt, a blue bow tie, and had combed what hair he still possessed across his freckled skull. *A fashion don't.* That's what Linda would have said.

Time passed as Mayor Abbott held forth about nothing in particular, evidently enjoying the sound of his own terse voice. As he continued, the council members dissected Tully with their eyes, glancing at one another whenever he shifted position on the numbingly hard wooden chair. *Sizing me up.*

Despite being on display, Tully had a tough time stifling his yawns. Desperate to wake up, he spent a few minutes studying the ornate old courtroom. The jury box was empty, but the gallery behind the front row was a third filled with an assortment of people, many in business clothing, some casually dressed.

There was a sprinkling of uniforms, including a fire chief and Deputy Tim Hapscomb who sniffed constantly except when he paused to blow his nose.

Some in the audience fit no category, such as a young woman in a pink sweatsuit who had evidently come in for a breather after a five-mile jog. Far more interesting was a thin young man, bare-chested beneath an open denim vest. Long hair, tangled golden brown curls, framed his gaunt, haunted face. His eyes were wide, lips barely shut. The expression was, Tully decided, an affectation meant to convey suppressed anger and confusion—and to increase his resemblance to Jim Morrison. Sensing something wrong, something damaged, in the man, Tully thought he probably believed himself to be the dead singer. Most likely a Shady Pines alumni, he probably needed to return for a refresher course. Something in the eyes—or something *not* in them—revealed an intensity bordering on paranoia.

Even so, the Morrison clone did nothing interesting, so Tully continued to scan the room, but spotted no more dead rock singers, no movie stars, not even a stray Napoleon.

As abruptly as he had begun the meeting, Mayor Abbott ended it. Tully stood and quickly found himself swept along in a small herd of people including Abbott, Rios, King, the probable council, and a clutch of dressed-for-success spectators from the gallery. Like a tidal wave, they crashed into the jury deliberation room. Tully counted twenty-two, including himself, as they were packed together at a rectangular table that would have comfortably held sixteen. Tully sat at his assigned place of honor at one end of the table. For a moment, he caught sight of Arlene Rios as Harlan King made a show of pulling out a chair for her near the mayor's end of the table.

The food was bland but edible, catered by Dimple's Boarding House. Not surprisingly, the Dimples, Martha Ann and Elmer, were the married couple on the council. *Just like everywhere else. Keep it in the family.*

He was introduced to the council members and everyone else at the table, but in the hubbub he caught no names. Every aspect of the luncheon was surreal, from the people and their conversations, to the huge helpings of cafeteria-quality food served to them. A mountain of mashed potatoes dominated each plate, stirring memories of *Close Encounters of the Third Kind*. Amazingly, most of the guests finished them, along with the spiceless Swedish meatballs, canned green beans, gloppy macaroni and cheese and tinny-tasting applesauce. But at last the plates were cleared and coffee was served—good coffee— and just when Tully thought the long, noisy meal was over, it slipped another notch into David Lynch Land. They brought out the entertainment, an Elvis impersonator introduced as Elvis Number Two.

He was no more than twenty-five, but he did Old Fat Elvis well, his plump body shoehorned into the a white spandex jumpsuit. Fringe and glitter jiggled in time with his belly as he stood entirely too close to Tully and belted out "Are You Lonesome Tonight?" with karaoke machine backup.

Elvis Number Two finished, but hovered around Tully, a sweaty hand hot on his shoulder, meatball-breath offending his nose. He basked in the applause, then asked for requests. Tully wanted to request that he leave, but halfway down the table someone called out, "Duet!" and for one brief horrifying moment, Tully thought that they wanted him to sing along with the Elvis, whose deodorant was beginning to fail. Then the councilman in the Hawaiian shirt stood up, pushed by seat-mates' hands. He was fortyish, extremely fit, with a headful of thick black hair peppered with silver at the temples. The silver looked wrong, and Tully couldn't quite figure out why the man looked familiar.

"Elvis Number One!" cried Elvis Number Two. "My man!"

Number One, pushed by Harlan King, looked ill-at-ease, but stepped toward Number Two. "Hey, Harlan, I don't really wanna do this," he said, upper lip twitching. "I haven't been keepin' up, you know?" As he spoke he joined the fat Elvis behind Tully, who took the opportunity to compare them. At a distance, Number One looked remarkably like the real Young

Elvis—which was why the silver temples didn't fit. Up close, he was what Elvis would have been like in his forties if he'd curbed his appetites and worked out regularly.

Number One continued to protest, weakly, that he had retired from the entertainment world. Retirement, Tully realized, meant this aging Young Elvis impersonator didn't need to wash away the gray anymore. The guests cheered him on, heedless of his protests.

When Fat Elvis announced he'd brought the karaoke backup for "Jailhouse Rock" specifically for the occasion, Thin Elvis caved. "Why dint'cha say so? Put 'er on."

One and Two performed, but only after Thin shot Tully an exaggerated wink and herded Fat off to an empty square of space at the far end of the room. Tully decided that, as far as impersonators went, Number One deserved his title. The duet wasn't bad, but would have been better if Number Two had stayed on key. When the music ended, the audience applauded with gusto, continuing as Ambrose Abbott rose and joined the bowing Elvises.

A lift of the mayor's hands ended the applause so abruptly that Tully's last clap echoed through the room, all alone. The mayor raised one wiry gray eyebrow then beckoned Tully to join him. As Tully approached, the fat Elvis in spandex leapt forward and shook his hand with sweaty enthusiasm. "Pleasure," he said in his impersonator's voice. "A real pleasure to perform for you, sir."

"Very enjoyable," Tully said.

Fat Elvis grinned. "Two shows a night weekends at Shalimar's, and Monday through Thursday I play the Early Bird Dinner Theater in the Crystal Room at the Eternity Lodge. I'll have a complimentary pair of tickets waiting for you at the box office—"

"Seymour, if you want to bribe the law," Abbott said dryly, "please don't do it in front of witnesses."

Harlan King's belly laugh was the only indication that the mayor had made a joke. Seymour Smiley, a.k.a. Elvis Two, blushed. "I wasn't trying to bribe you."

"Of course not," Tully said.

The man nodded gratefully, then walked to the back of the room and began disassembling his karaoke equipment as Elvis One, the councilman, shook Tully's hand, wished him luck then handed him a celery-colored business card touting the True Grace All-Natural Market. "Your body's a temple," he said. "Gotta treat it right. No pesticides, no preservatives, no drugs."

Tully pocketed the card and studied the impersonator. "If I didn't know better ..." He let the words trail off, feeling ridiculous.

"To paraphrase a great man, reports of my death have been greatly exaggerated." Elvis One executed a perfect upper lip twitch, then returned to his chair.

"I take it, Sheriff Tully," Ambrose Abbott said, dry as dust, "that you are not yet familiar with the finer points of our town's peculiar customs."

"Peculiar being the key word," King drolled from his place at the table.

"Indeed," Abbott agreed, then cleared his throat and spoke to the room at large. "A man is known by the company that he organizes," he began. "With that in mind, Sheriff Tully, as mayor of Eternity I would like to thank you for accepting our invitation to join this community. And on behalf of the governing body, the business owners and residents of Eternity County, I bid you welcome to our land."

Our land? What is this, Oz? Tully smiled stiffly and endured Abbott's iron handshake. "Thank you, Mayor. I'll do my best."

Arlene Rios shot him an amused smile. He nodded, jolted by her dark eyes. The sunglasses had finally come off. He remembered her from a few years before. The interview came at the end of the Delmonico case and Tully had been overwhelmed by a barrage of reporters by the time Rios came along. It was for an early morning television program, one of those fluffy informal news shows, and it only lasted two or three minutes, but he'd been nervous as hell—he never liked being on TV. He mainly remembered being amazed that she asked about the cannibalism aspects—*What makes people eat other people?*—and that her phrasing had elicited an inappropriate smile. He'd erased the grin and given her a serious answer, but in his head he was singing, *People . . . People who eat people . . .* and having a hell of a time keeping a straight face.

He remembered little else about the interview or the interviewer. Except for her eyes, which possessed a deceptive innocence, wide-open and childlike. Yet not. It was an act, and a good one. Behind the guileless mask, she was examining him, sizing him up.

"Thank you all for attending our welcome party in honor of our esteemed new sheriff," Abbott announced brusquely, the unspoken codicil, *Now get out!* hanging in the air. The guests stood and began a mass migration toward the exit.

"Council members, please stay for a brief meeting," Abbott barked.

It's about time. Tully had begun to wonder if he'd ever get to talk business with the people who had hired him.

"Sheriff," Abbott said. "We'll speak with you sometime within the next twenty-four hours."

"There was another murder last—"

Abbott glared at him. "This is not the time, nor is it the place. Now, I'm sure you'd like to explore your new kingdom, perhaps have a chat with your deputies—"

"You *are* aware of the incident last night, aren't you, Mayor?" Tully asked, his voice low but sharp.

"I received a report." Abbott's eyebrow lifted appraisingly. "Why do you think we made no comment on your tardiness? We are aware of your devotion to duty and we appreciate it. That's why we hired you after all."

Tully simmered. "Mayor Abbott," he said loud enough to cause the stragglers, hungry for a speck of dirt, a hint of scandal, to turn and stare. "This can't wait—"

A hand grabbed the back of his elbow and squeezed it painfully. He looked, saw Arlene Rios. *Who else?*

"Mayor, do you mind if I abscond with your new sheriff

for a while?'' Looking at Tully, she added, ''I have a proposal for you I think you'll like.''

''Take him, take him,'' Abbott said waving them off. ''Just make certain you stick to our agreement, Miss Rios.''

Tully pulled free of the reporter and headed for the door, aware she was on his heels. In the corridor he stopped short. She tried valiantly to avoid running into him, almost succeeded. ''Excuse me,'' she said after a slight grazing. ''I assumed we were going outdoors to talk.''

''You know what happens when you assume, Ms. Rios.'' Tully enjoyed her irritation. *Serves you right.* It took effort, but he kept his voice pleasant and soft. ''I don't make deals with the press.''

Her eyes lost their innocence. ''Just hear me out. I have some information you might find very interesting.''

''As I said, I don't make deals.'' He paused, then spoke his mind. ''Your ploy is unimaginative. Now if you'll excuse me, I have work to do.'' He started threading through small groups of people toward the back entrance.

''Wait! Please!'' he heard as he pushed open the door. Half a dozen other people turned and looked expectantly at Rios as she stepped out. Reluctantly, Tully waited. ''Sheriff, wait a moment, please,'' she said.

He stood still as Rios approached. She didn't speak until the other people went back to milling or moving. ''You don't have a clue,'' she said softly, then raised her voice to eavesdropping level. ''Yes, coffee sounds fine. Let's go.'' Glancing around with a bright smile for all, she stepped confidently forward. Tully considered not playing along, but common sense told him not to humiliate a member of the press.

''Thanks,'' she said when they reached their vehicles. A cool afternoon breeze ruffled through her hair as she unlocked the Mustang and climbed into the driver's seat. ''Let's go.'' The car roared to life.

''Where?''

''To your cabin. You lead.''

He opened his mouth to protest, then stopped, shrugged, and

went to the Camaro. What the hell, he thought. *I'll humor her. Then maybe she'll give me some peace.* He knew from painful experience that people as tenacious as Arlene Rios were usually encouraged by refusals.

He pulled onto Main Street then turned on the winding road to his home, the sight of the yellow Mustang in his rearview mirror—right on his bumper—irritating the hell out of him.

He slowed for a hairpin turn and she almost rear-ended him. Obviously, she delighted in flaunting her power as a reporter— who else would tailgate a cop?

He tapped his brakes at odd moments to force her to back off, but she didn't seem to notice. Maybe she had a death wish, maybe she just didn't care. Most likely, he thought, she was hot-dogging—and in that case, her gender was probably involved. The only thing worse than a young male reporter out to prove he had big balls was a young female out to prove that hers were even bigger.

He was so busy watching her ride his ass, he almost overshot his driveway and ended up making a hard right at the last instant. The drive was wide enough for two vehicles and deep enough for two more, but he purposely zagged the Camaro behind the Explorer to force Rios to park on the side of the road. It's petty, he thought as her brake lights flashed, but a little rebellion is good for the soul.

She edged off the road, stopped, pulled forward then backed up, past his driveway, where the shoulder was wider. Then she exited the Mustang, opened the trunk, and began digging around. Tully leaned against his car and waited, watching and wondering what Linda would have made of her.

Finally, Rios slammed the trunk and walked toward him carrying a knapsack over her shoulder, incongruous with her suit and heels. *She's keeping up with the boys.* Linda's voice. He knew it was true, tried to feel less negatively toward the woman, but it wasn't easy. She wasn't a cop proving her equality to the boys; she was a reporter, out to prove she could expose the boys. So to speak.

"Funny-looking briefcase," he said nodding at the knapsack.

"Let's go." She walked to the front door, turned and tapped her foot impatiently.

He walked slowly toward her, examining his key ring. Finding the right key, he slipped it into the lock but didn't turn it. "I hope your information is good enough to excuse your rudeness."

"Me, too. I get a little too focused sometimes." She paused and he was sure her next words would be, "I'm sorry." Instead, she said, "Is that the right key?"

He opened the door and allowed her into the entryway. "What's in the knapsack?" he asked dryly. "Clues?"

She cocked her head and studied him. "No. Clothes."

"I hope you don't think you're staying here," he said quickly.

She grinned wickedly. "Tully, I'd love to see the look on your face if I said I was moving in, but I have a room at Dimple's Boarding House. Where's your bathroom?' "

"Across the living room, first hall door on the right."

"Thanks." She strode purposefully away.

He saw light come on in the bathroom. It began to narrow as she closed the door, then broadened again, accompanied by her call, "Change your clothes, Tully. We're going for a hike."

Sixteen

"Jack be nimble," he murmured as he sprinted from the shadows of the thick stand of pines forty feet from the McPherson residence. "Jack be discrete." He glanced around, saw silence, then placed the folded note on the doorstep, tucking the edge of it beneath the doormat so it wouldn't blow away.

"Jack jog away, ever so fleet." Nonchalantly, he trotted away from the cabin, breathing easily as he continued along the narrow, potted road. Few of the dwellings this far from downtown Eternity were inhabited year round, and none of the ones directly neighboring Kate McPherson's cabin were currently occupied.

The road ascended a slight rise and curved as it began the descent into town. Jack wore dark green sweats that served as unremarkable camouflage, letting him blend with the forest and with any other health-minded resident he might encounter.

In this same outfit, or any of a number of other dark-hued jogging suits, he had explored the town and the lower reaches of the mountain. He had, at various times, conversed with friends, given tourists directions, made peculiar love to careless young women and thoughtless young men, then killed them, for the sport. At other times, he would choose a victim and spend weeks or months stalking, hunting, learning his or her most intimate secrets before striking, ever so gently.

He took only the best of them captive, and only the *crème de la crème* were eventually used within Icehouse Circle. Over the years he had occasionally been forced to make do with anything available, such as he had with the madman from Shady Pines. It amused him to compare his use of inferior life to that of vampires; Dracula or one of his ridiculous fictional kin reduced to feeding on the hot blood of a galley rat caught scuttling in a ghostship's stores of rotting grain. There was a certain romance to it, he thought as he turned off the road onto a trail that would lead home, as long as it happened only rarely.

In popular parlance, it was slumming. He slowed to a brisk walk, deepening his respirations to feed and relax the tight muscles in his calves and thighs.

Each soul taken donated its energy to him, added to his power, to his magic, wisdom, and understanding. Each bit of life, no matter how insignificant, contained sensation—fear, terror, ecstasy—to feed a starving man.

The madman, Meeks, had been such a kill, taken in the Circle because it was time, then removed to the picnic area at the top of Icehouse Road because he was inferior, a scuttling rat.

Frank Lawson, conversely, had been a chosen one. Jack stalked him for months, planning on taking him in the Circle at the proper time. No kidnapping, no drugs, but a trap, something to lure him to the vortex, to seduce him and bring him, of his own volition, a lamb to the slaughter.

When Jack had killed Lawson at the Circle in July, it was impetuous and satisfying, but the hour was incorrect, as well as the date. It had simply been irrestible and though it saw him through admirably, most of the energy had been unusable, which was a shame considering the personal power inherent in Eternity's last sheriff.

Through the trees, Jack saw the back of his house and the attached shed where his firewood and his latest victim were stored. Her name, she'd told him as she tried to offer up her body to keep the knife away, was Joyce. She was formidably prosaic and unspeakably fatuous, nothing but a little welcoming gift for the new sheriff. A small puzzle to keep him busy. She was no Kate McPherson.

Jack smiled as he approached the kitchen door, able to scent the aroma of coffee, freshly brewed. He let himself in and poured a steaming cup, dropped ten hard little cubes of sugar in and stirred until they dissolved into luxurious sweetness.

The day Kate had wandered into Frank Lawson's death, she had been destined to die. Her courage gave him pause and after ten days of observation, he knew she was right for the autumn ritual. It was the most important one of the year, and it required female energy. Beneath her courage, he smelled raw terror. She was perfect.

As he sipped the coffee, heat burned his tongue and sugar kissed it. If leaving Eternity soon wasn't so imperative, he would happily prolong his stay until the winter moon, a time requiring masculine energy. It was too bad he'd have to waste Zach Tully's energy, but it couldn't be helped.

Jack mourned the lack of time even as he rejoiced over the bounty now laid before him.

There had been no time to arouse fear in Frank Lawson, no time to prolong and savor his pain, to explore the boundaries of his terror. It was a terrible loss, a boundless waste. Frank Lawson had always been a worthy opponent, as worthy as any of his ilk could be. Jack had observed him first in Chicago as a street cop walking a beat, had returned fifteen years later to find him in full flower. He toyed with him, tested and teased him, found him worthy. Then used him up all at once.

"You're a very naughty boy, Jacky," he murmured. He filled his mouth with coffee and held it, letting it scald, analyzing the sensation until it dissipated.

He swallowed. Now he'd been handed Zach Tully, given a second chance with the only man he'd tested in recent history who held greater potential than Lawson—and lacked the time to use him properly.

After refilling his cup, he added more sugar, thirteen cubes, a baker's dozen. Even if he only stalked and killed Tully for the pleasure of the hunt, he could still extract every ounce of fear and rage. Every drop of grief. Tully brimmed, overflowed with it. It would blind him.

Jack knew this beyond all doubt because it had happened before. He glanced at his watch and immediately set the cup down. Time was slipping away. He rushed to shower and change, moving quickly and efficiently as he let his mind drift pleasantly among past and future events in Zachary Tully's life.

Seventeen

Kate McPherson smiled at the group gathered around her in the parking area above Icehouse Circle. It was a big one, five adults, four kids, but unusually pleasant in its makeup: The children behaved and there were no erstwhile know-it-alls, whiners, or Don Juans among the adults. "In a few moments we'll be descending the steps to Icehouse Circle," she told them. "But first there are a few things to keep in mind. We're nearly eleven thousand feet above sea level and the air is very thin. It's not uncommon to experience dizziness or even a little nausea at these heights, so speak up if you have any problems." She patted her large purple shoulder bag. "If you feel you can't get enough air, don't worry. In the Alps, St. Bernards carry casks of brandy. On Icehouse Mountain, the tour guides carry oxygen."

She hated that line even though she'd added it to the spiel herself. Company policy was not to mention the foot-long oxygen bottles unless it was necessary, but she'd found that since you couldn't hide the thin air from tourists' lungs, it was better to be up front. It prevented atmosphere-induced panic attacks and there was nothing worse than a frightened tourist clutching his or her throat and gasping, "I can't breathe!" except for an entire herd of suggestible people all catching the panic. Talk about hell on earth.

"Miss?" A boy about Josh's age raised his hand.

"Yes?"

"Is this where the tour guide found the dead guy?"

"Ryan!" hissed his mother, squeezing his shoulder.

The question had been asked a million times since July, but Kate still had to fight to keep from flinching. "Yes," she said, then took a breath and continued briskly, "Icehouse Circle is often called 'Little Stonehenge'—"

The boy's older sister raised a hand and Kate nodded at her.

"Do you know the lady who found him?"

"Heather!" This time Dad did the shushing.

"It's all right," Kate said, her calm voice never betraying the knots in her stomach. "I found him."

As she hoped, the subject was instantly dropped, as were the eyes of the tourists.

"As I was saying, Icehouse Circle is also known as Little Stonehenge because it resembles that famous structure in some respects. But Icehouse Circle has no henge." She paused. "Does anyone know what a henge is?"

The tourists glanced at one another then back to her, expectantly.

"Think about it and I'll fill you in as soon as we get down to the Circle. The steps are small and the path is steep, so please use the handrail and walk slowly. When we arrive, please stay together." She pitched her voice down into mysterious tones. "As you probably know, you're likely to notice some odd things in the meadow around the standing stones. Some of you might suddenly lose your sense of direction, and if any of you are carrying compasses, you'll see them become totally confused.

"There are other phenomena to watch for," she continued, enjoying the awestruck look in the kids' eyes. "People often report that bird calls sound backward. There have even been a handful of reports from people swearing they heard voices coming from inside the Circle when there's no one there." She paused dramatically. "Ghostly conversations, some say. Others believe the voices are coming through a time vortex . . . from the past or, perhaps, the future." Smiling, she added, "Of course, the sounds might only be those of hikers carrying across the peaks from other parts of the mountain. You can make your own conclusions if you hear them."

"Do you think we will?" asked one of the children.

"It's possible, though it doesn't happen very often. We're dealing with something we don't understand, so we can't predict what will or won't happen, beyond being fairly certain that the geomagnetic properties will mess with compasses and watches."

One man hurriedly pushed his sleeve up and began to unfasten a heavy gold band.

"That's not necessary—" Kate began.

"It's a Rolex."

She nodded. "Your watch won't be damaged. At the worst, you might need to reset it."

The man hesitated then rolled down his sleeve. "Safer on my wrist, I guess."

"Definitely. Now, let's go."

She steeled herself and started down the steps, her anxiety real but milder than it had been during the first month after finding Sheriff Lawson's body. She wondered if it would ever abate entirely. Probably not, she thought as the broad circular meadow came into view. Immediately her gaze shot to the standing stones, scanning for . . . *What? A body? Maybe.* She felt her anxiety begin draining away as her brain registered the lack of a corpse.

"So, Ms. Rios, why?"

"Why what, Sheriff Tully?" As the reporter spoke, she pulled the Mustang onto the road heading for Icehouse Mountain. She seemed intent on two things: examining the Lawson murder site and acting mysterious.

Why should I put up with you? was what he wanted to ask, but controlled the urge. At least she didn't have her cameraman in tow. "Why are you here and how long am I to be blessed with the pleasure of your company?"

"I'm here because I've done my research and I think there's a real story here. A big one. A weird one. And I'm staying until the job's done." She glanced at him, eyes invisible behind her dark sunglasses. "Do you have a problem with that?"

One might be developing. He forced a friendly smile and tone. "No problems, Lois Lane. How about you? Any problems yet?"

"Just you," she said pleasantly, but her downshift roared with irritation.

Tully's smile turned into the real thing as he realized he'd found a chink in her armor: She didn't like to be teased. "How am I a problem?"

She glanced sidelong at him as they began the climb up Icehouse Road. "You're like a porcupine with his quills up. What are you afraid of? You went silent after the Backdoor Man . . ." She let her words trail off. "I promise you I won't bring any of that up. My interest is in Eternity."

A bitter taste filled his mouth, but Tully said nothing for a long moment, just watched the tall trees pass by. "I appreciate that, Ms. Rios. But you have to understand that I can't have a reporter dogging my every move. There's a killer loose, a vicious one, and I need the freedom to do my job."

"Of course."

"So, what's your agreement with Mayor Abbott?"

"I'm not going to do any breaking news. I'm just following the case in order to do a report—a special—after the fact on TCN's *Crimes of Today and Yesterday.* This place has been a hotspot for murder and violence for well over a century. Did you know that when you took the job?"

"I thought I wasn't pertinent to your story." The air was getting cold and thin. He rolled up his window until it was open only a crack.

"Give me a break, Tully. The fact that you, of all people, are here, is a big part of the story. In fact, it's the reason the producers let me come up here. You're famous. El Niño, Delmonico, lots of other lesser known but equally important cases. What I promised was that I won't open up any old wounds. In exchange for your cooperation, of course.''

"I don't make deals, Ms. Rios," he said, anger stirring.

"Look, I have permission to do the story from your boss, the mayor. I told you how it's going to work. A lot of my time is going to be spent in research—which may benefit you. I already have information that will help you. I'll stay in the background. I'm going to do the story, Tully, but I promise not to fuck with you.''

"We'll see," he grunted. He could feel her irritation. It was a physical thing.

"So, tell me. Did you seek out the job or did Eternity seek you out?''

He opened his mouth then hesitated. "You're big on research. I'm sure you already know the answer to that.''

She chuckled, a low, throaty sound. "Mayor Abbott was a little vague about it.''

Tully couldn't resist. He said, "Mayor Abbott seems a little vague about everything. That's off the record," he added, immediately sorry he said it.

"Of course.''

It felt like a truce had been declared. "They called me," he told her.

They rode in silence for a short time, then passed a campground dotted with tents just south of the road. The sight stung him with thoughts of adventures with his son that would never be.

"Sheriff?''

"More questions?''

"No. A handy hint.''

"I'm listening.''

"We're almost to Little Stonehenge. Once we're out of the vehicle, our conversation must remain innocuous.''

"The rocks are bugged, Ms. Rios?''

"Voices carry here," she replied, unamused. "They carry well.''

She definitely didn't like to be teased. He'd remember that for later use.

"Okay. What's the information you promised me after the meeting. What should I know?"

"Later," she said. "Too time-consuming for now." She rounded a hairpin curve then swung across the road and pulled into a large turnout, parking next to a massive purple Jeep.

"Here we are." She undid her seat belt and stepped out of the car. He did the same, taking a deep breath of the mountain air.

It made him dizzy. Steadying himself, he listened, and recognized Kate McPherson's voice drifting up from below. He was surprised at how clearly he could hear her words; she was talking about the composition of the standing stones. Then, just as suddenly, her voice was lost to a mountain breeze.

"The air takes some getting used to," Rios commented as she pulled a pair of black gloves from her jacket pocket and tugged them on. "Are you prone to altitude sickness?"

"No," he said, hoping he wasn't. They crossed to the railing at the top leading down to the meadow and Tully strained to hear Kate's voice again. He caught a word, two, then there was a patch of silence followed by a child's giggles.

Rios read his mind. "Weird, isn't it?"

He nodded. "Got any answers?"

"No. Maybe your friend down there can tell you."

"My friend?"

"Ms. McPherson."

"How do you know—"

A scream ricocheted, so loud it hurt his ears. Instantly he started down the trail, irritated as hell that Arlene Rios was already racing ahead of him.

Kate hadn't noticed when the middle-aged woman in a tan safari outfit wandered away from the group. The Circle's electromagnetic activity was stronger than usual today and virtually all her charges were experiencing just enough of it to be very impressed with the outing. They were treating her as if she were providing the special effects as well as the speech. The tourists were clustered closely around her to hear about the megaliths' history and peer past her into the Circle itself, but as the scream tore the air, the group parted.

The screaming woman stood by a deadfall—the huge timber that Frank Lawson's murderer had probably hidden behind. The woman suddenly dropped out of sight and for a horrible instant, as she sprinted across the meadow, Kate thought she had fallen off the cliff.

She hadn't. Kate reached the Medusan roots of the rotten log and saw the woman lying in the long yellowed grass just behind it. She'd fainted but was already coming out of it. Relieved, Kate swung her bag off her shoulder and whipped out the small oxygen tank, at the same time calling to the rest of the group that everything was fine and to stay put. "What happened?" she asked quietly.

The woman didn't answer but moaned softly while Kate pulled the sterile wrapper off the oxygen mask. "It's okay," she said as the tourist's eyelids fluttered open. "You passed out. We'll have the doctor check you, but for now a little oxygen will help."

The woman stared at her, uncomprehending, then opened her mouth and shrieked again. Startled, Kate moved to kneel beside her and administer the oxygen—the poor thing was probably afraid she was suffocating—then Kate had to bite off her own scream.

A leg, feminine, bent at the knee, rose out of the rangy weeds behind the deadfall as if from a bubble bath. Though the flesh was dead-white and blistered where it wasn't mottled bluish-red, the graceful form was perfect down to the pink-painted toenails. Kate forced herself to step around the tangled roots for a closer look.

She was almost relieved to see that the leg wasn't severed,

but attached to a nude woman stuffed half under the log, hidden in the grass. The corpse lay at an angle, its other leg against the earth. The back was curled, flesh stretched tight over hard bumps of spine and her arms were folded in beneath the legs. Her face, hidden behind limp dark hair, was tucked down toward the chest. The body looked like a huge, deformed fetus.

"Stay back!" Kate ordered, hearing running footsteps behind her. She turned, "Don't come any close—"

"What is it?" asked a small dark-haired woman who had arrived at Kate's side. Kate had never seen her before. The woman saw the body and quickly took Kate's arm, trying to pull her away from the corpse.

Kate twisted free, only to trip over the swooning tourist. She began to fall, then strong hands swooped in and caught her from behind before she hit the corpse. They remained on her waist, helping her get her balance. Finally, she saw their owner's face.

"Sheriff Tully!"

"Are you all right?" he asked.

"Fine."

"And you, ma'am?"

The tourist, still sitting on the ground, nodded. Zach Tully glanced back at the body then returned his gaze to Kate. Despite everything, she felt herself blush, very aware of his hands, now on her upper arm. Quickly, she nodded toward the group waiting by the Circle. Waiting there like sheep, she thought. *Thank heaven.* "You're just in time. I wasn't sure how to handle this."

Tully followed her gaze, then nodded and bent to help the tourist up. He passed her to Kate, then paused looking mildly confused.

"The thin air," Kate told him, "and the Circle. They make it hard to think straight."

"Yeah." Tully turned toward the deadfall and suddenly barked, "Get away from the crime scene." The dark-haired woman, squatting beside the body, began to stand, her face pale and grim above the discolored leg. She opened her mouth to speak, closed it again. Kate knew the electromagnetic anomaly was affecting her.

Then the woman lost her balance. Karma, Kate thought as she watched her thrust out her hands to steady herself on the timber. Her hand bumped the corpse's upraised foot, causing a sound that made Kate suddenly think of fresh, crisp peanut brittle. Her mother always made it around Halloween and the sharp crackle as she snapped off that first piece—that was the sound she heard now.

Kate stared at the woman, who was in turn staring at the corpse's foot, which she held in her hand like a shoe she was thinking of trying on. The foot had snapped off clean at the ankle, no muss, no fuss. Just like peanut brittle.

Realizing that the fainting tourist was going down again, Kate eased her to the ground and told her to put her head between her legs, then turned her attention to the strange woman, who, seemingly calm, set the foot on top of the log then rubbed her gloved hands together briskly. Tully was already beside her, making Kate wonder how he'd moved without her noticing. Perhaps the Circle's powers were even affecting her.

Tully and the woman—who the hell was she, anyway?—spoke in whispers before coming back around the deadfall. The woman stepped around the sheriff to get to Kate first. "Arlene Rios, TCN. I'd like to ask you some questions."

"I have some for you, too." Kate spoke firmly. Despite the shock, despite the horrifying but absurd sight of the foot on the log—or maybe because of it—she felt almost as collected as the other woman looked. "Like, what the hell are you doing here? No, don't answer now. I have to take care of my group." On cue, the fainter moaned and put her hands to her forehead.

Tully moved between the two women. "Ms. Rios, would you take care of this lady while Ms. McPherson and I confer?"

"McPherson?" Rios said, brightening. "Kate McPherson?"

Tully ignored her and that pleased Kate. Under his breath, he told her, "Reporter." They took a few steps toward the flock of tourists before he touched her elbow to indicate they should stop. Kate turned to him. "Thanks," she said as she watched Arlene Rios helping the tourist to her feet, none too gently.

Tully watched, too, and Kate saw him wince. "I haven't figured out how to shake her yet. She's as tenacious as a tick. I'll tell her to apologize to you for her rudeness."

"Don't say anything to her," Kate said. "I can take care of myself. Now, what about my group?"

"Take them up to your vehicle and try not to answer any questions. They probably couldn't see what happened. With the foot. Damned nosy reporter."

Kate nodded. "From that distance, they'll assume it's a shoe." She fought off a little twist of laughter, knowing that if she let it out, she wouldn't be able to stop. "I mean," she managed, "who would ever think that a foot would snap off like that?" She fought back the laughter once more and Tully put a reassuring hand on her shoulder.

"Don't lose it, Kate," he said softly.

"Peanut brittle," she sputtered, almost giggling. "It sounded just like peanut brittle."

He smiled gently. "Later, you'll have to explain that one to me."

"I'll be happy to," she said, a little giddy. *The Circle. It's making me act like an idiot.*

"You're okay," Zach murmured. "You know, I think little Miss Cloak-and-Dagger over there would really enjoy it if you lost your nerve about now."

Sobriety hit instantly. "You know just what to say." She studied him briefly, liking that he'd given her a pep talk instead of the there-there crap she'd endured from other males she'd dealt with.

"Need any help herding them up?

"No. I'll tell them you'll explain things shortly. Okay?"

"That sounds fine."

"What about her?" Kate asked nodding toward the tourist who was fluttering, physically and verbally, at the reporter.

"I'll bring her up before Ms. Rios can drag her life story

from her.'' He stared at them then added, ''I hope.'' He squeezed Kate's shoulder once more then let his hand drop. ''Tell them I'll be right up.''

Kate's smile was genuine. ''Will do.''

Eighteen

"Gets dark quick here," Deputy Ron Settles informed Tully in a peculiar nasal grunt.

"Sure does." They stood outside the station watching shadows seep down the forested hillsides while Settles, wafting surliness like cheap aftershave, puffed shamelessly on an unfiltered Camel.

Tully doubted that Settles liked anyone very much. He had no doubt that the former acting sheriff disliked him in particular, not only for taking the job he obviously thought he deserved, but also for ordering him not to light his butt indoors just as they were about to shake hands. Settles' chilly blue eyes, red-rimmed and narrow, had squinted down into a practiced Clint Eastwood scowl while he silently unflicked his Bic. They skipped the handshake altogether.

Tully, not so fresh after a long afternoon over a cold body with county coroner Phil Katz, had forced himself to be friendly, to get off on the right foot, but the deputy seemed less willing to thaw than Joyce Furillo's body. While still-sniffling Tim Hapscomb watched, not trying very hard to hide his amusement, Tully had tried to ease Settles into some small talk. After a few minutes, the deputy rolled his eyes, muttered, "Come on," and led Tully outside, lighting his cigarette before the door even closed behind them.

Now, Settles lit another Camel off the butt of the old.

"Those things'll kill you," Tully said, wishing he'd worn his jacket. He was shivering while Settles lolled against the Crown Victoria cruiser in shirtsleeves.

Settles shot him a sideways Eastwood. "Uh-huh."

"I thought you might stop by Phil Katz's office after the body was brought in. Thought I might see you there."

"Thought about it."

Tully waited for more, but the man just stood there and smoked.

The sunlight was a bare apricot glow behind the western peaks and overhead, stars were materializing. In LA, it would still be light. And warm. He'd be grabbing a beer with John Mendoza about now. Instead, Tully shivered as a breeze poured through the pine trees, cold as ice water. *What am I doing here?* And why he was putting up with Settles' insubordination? It was time to have a serious talk. "Look, Deputy, we have to get something straight right now."

Settles didn't bother to look, just grunted and blew smoke out his nostrils.

"There are problems with your reports."

"Lawson never complained."

Tully ignored him. "I want to hear what you have to say about your encounter with Kate McPherson the day Sheriff Lawson was murdered—"

The roar of an engine drowned him out. Arlene Rios' yellow Mustang bounced into the lot. "Great," Tully sighed and glanced at Settles. "Has she been poking around here much?"

"Damned if I know. I've never seen her before." The deputy dropped his butt and ground it under his heel. "Gotta go. Council won't pay overtime."

With that, he stretched, opened the sedan's door, and climbed in, acting as if Tully hadn't brought up a thing. The cruiser purred to life. Tully stepped out of its path, his eyes on Rios, who was out of her car now and haloed by the dim glow of a single sodium lamp. She carried a briefcase and had to quickly step back, out of Settles' way. The deputy disappeared in a matter of seconds.

"Sheriff Tully?" Her voice was accompanied by the taps of her heels as she crossed the lot. She was back in her chic reporter clothing and must have been freezing.

"Haven't you had enough of me for one day?" he asked, resigned. He hadn't been able to shake her for a good part of the afternoon, though to her credit, she did stay out of his way. Mostly. When she'd suddenly disappeared a few hours previously, he thought he was off the hook for the day. *I should have known better.*

"Can we talk?" she asked.

Chill wind riffled through Tully's hair. He ignored it, playing the tough guy. "As long as you do the talking."

Rios hugged herself. "Inside?"

"Sure." Tully turned and Rios fell in beside him. He felt a brief twinge of pity. How could she walk in those shoes? He pushed the station door open and let her enter ahead of him.

The reporter set her briefcase on the lobby counter. "I'd hate to be stuck here in the winter if they call this summer weather."

"Yeah." Tully had been thinking the same thing, but he wasn't going to admit it. "Come on. It's warmer in the office. And I think I smell coffee."

"Sounds great."

In the back office, Tim Hapscomb stood beside his desk, shrugging on his brown leather uniform jacket. He eyed Rios with undisguised curiosity but no sign of wariness; obviously, he hadn't been accosted yet. Tully felt relief.

"I'm going to make the rounds," Tim said. "I'll be back in about an hour. I've got my keys."

"You sure you're up to the night shift?" Tully asked. The kid's nose looked raw from all the sniffling and blowing.

"No problem. I'm fine." He paused, eyed Rios, then looked back at Tully. "Phil Katz dropped something off for you. It's on your desk."

The autopsy reports. He'd forgotten all about picking them up. "Thanks, Tim," he said lightly. "And you're sure you're all right on your own tonight?"

"Positive. Al's going to relieve me a little early."

"Okay, then," Tully said. "Maybe I won't stick around. But make sure you call me at home if you need to."

"Thanks, Sheriff. I'll do that." He paused. "But don't worry. I won't have to." He shoved his Smoky hat down over his ears. "There's a fresh pot of coffee there."

"I appreciate it, Tim."

Nodding, his deputy went out the door.

Arlene Rios zeroed in on the coffee as Tully went to his desk and picked up the manila envelope from Phil Katz. Suddenly, he wished he hadn't been so hospitable to the reporter.

"Black?" Rios called over her shoulder as she poured the steaming fluid into two paper cups from the stack next to the machine. "Cream? Sugar?"

"Black." He glanced at her back then down at the envelope, badly wanting to read its contents. Instead, he slipped it under the desk blotter an instant before the woman turned around and brought the mugs over. She set them down then relaxed into the chair facing his desk.

"Thanks." Tully wrapped his hand around one of the steaming cups.

"So, tell me. What's your angle?" Tully sat back but locked his eyes on Rios'.

"For the Eternity program you mean?" Rios' smile was guileless.

The coffee was nice and strong. "Yes. That'll do for a start."

"We're aiming to air in late October," she said, as if that explained everything.

Tully raised an eyebrow.

"For Halloween. It's going to have a supernatural bent. You know, Icehouse Circle and so forth? The paranormal is a special interest of mine and I've been wanting to do this for a long time. Thanks to your staid presence, I finally get the chance."

"Okay. Do you mean this is going to be more of a spooky history of Eternity than a true crime program?"

She nodded. "But this *is* for the True Crime Network so I have to tie your presence and the current victims into everything. But back to the point, I said I wouldn't bring up your personal tragedy, and I meant it."

"Why should I trust you?"

"Simple. Your family has nothing to do with my story. My only interest in you is that you're a cop renowned for his crime-solving abilities and that you're working here, at Murder Central."

"I appreciate your honesty, Ms. Rios. If that's what it is."

She chuckled lightly. "You've had some bad experiences with the press?"

Tully nodded then refilled their coffee mugs. When he sat back down, he said, "Tell me about the supernatural goings-on."

"Eternity is a crystal packer's paradise. They've got everything here from immortality to UFOs to, well, you name it. Everyone knows that."

"Not everyone."

"Come on, Sheriff. You're from the city, and you're telling me you'd come to an isolated place like this *without* an interest in some of the phenomena? At least as it relates to homicide?" She grinned. "You do know Eternity's cut off from civilization half the year? That's part of the reason for the murder rate. Cabin fever. 'Heerrre's Johnny!' Catch my drift?"

"Off the record?"

"Totally."

"Eternity is a tourist town," Tully said. "It has a reputation for tall tales, and those stories help bring in travelers. They're good for the economy." Abbott wouldn't approve of what he said, but he was damned if he was going to play make-believe along with the mayor and his merry band of whatever-they-weres. "Ms. Rios, have you been to *Snakes Alive!?*"

"Arlene." She cocked her head. "The souvenir shop? I checked it out. Pretty crazy."

"I think this entire town is one big *Snakes Alive!*"

She laughed. "You're right, but try to keep an open mind

about the supernatural stuff. It could be important to your homicide problems. And remember, I'm on your side.''

"Why?"

"I'm very interested in what's going on. And maybe you'll grant me a real interview down the line. I already have information for you, after all.''

"I appreciate the offer." As he spoke, he sat up and glanced at his watch. "But I'm short on time. Got a meeting." He was supposed to have a late meeting with the council in twenty minutes.

"Don't sell my research short before you even look at it," Rios persisted. "I have extensive files on the homicidal history of this town, going back well over a century.''

"Uh-huh." Tully didn't hide his sarcasm. He'd already heard this baloney from Harlan King. "Let me guess. You believe the murderer has been active here for that long? Let's see. That would make him, what, about a hundred and fifty, give or take a few decades?''

"I didn't say that. Or imply it." Rios' eyes narrowed. "The locals are getting under your skin already, aren't they, Sheriff?"

He didn't reply.

"The only thing I'm suggesting is that there are patterns that date back that far.''

"Legacy killers?" he asked.

"It's possible," Rios said lightly. She set her briefcase on the desk then withdrew a green folder and slid it to Tully. "Here are copies of my notes on your murderer as well as some of my background research.''

Tully riffled the pages. "You've done a lot of work.''

"I've been interested in Eternity since I was a kid. I saw it on *In Search Of* . . . or something.''

"You talk like you know who the killer is. Want to tell me?"

"You'll think I'm nuts if you don't read the material first. Do that, then we'll talk.''

"Okay."

She studied him. "You're very suspicious. But then I suppose it goes with the territory."

The phone rang, the office number. "I'm afraid that's all the time I have for you, Ms. Rios. Why don't you write down the name and number where you're staying? I'll be in touch."

"It's on the back of my card, which is clipped inside the cover of the folder."

"Thanks."

She didn't stand up like she was supposed to and the phone continued to ring. Reluctantly, he picked it up. "Eternity Sheriff's Station. Tully speaking."

"Ambrose Abbott, Tully," the voice announced gruffly. "I'm afraid we'll have to postpone our meeting. Something's come up."

"You can't just postpone it!" Tully said, infuriated. "How do you expect me to accomplish anything in the dark?" He became aware of Arlene Rios and clamped his mouth shut.

"I'll be in touch," Abbott said and hung up.

Tully slammed down the receiver.

"The mayor giving you a hard time?" Rios asked calmly.

"No. He's not giving me *any* time." Tully cupped his hands around the mug to warm them. He knew he shouldn't bad-mouth Abbott, but he wasn't doing that. Not technically. He had merely stated a fact. Still, it wasn't like him. Something about Arlene Rios brought out the worst in him, and in a perverse way, he enjoyed it. He liked irritating Rios. It was like poking a scorpion.

"There's something I haven't told you," she said. "Something I should have already, but we started talking—"

"Tell me."

"Earlier this evening, I went to Kate McPherson's house—"

"Why?" Fresh irritation flooded into on the old.

She looked annoyed. "It's a free country, isn't it?"

"Your presence could endanger her."

"She gave me something to give to you." She handed across a Ziploc bag containing a folded piece of white paper. "Take a look."

Tully opened it. Carefully keeping his fingertips at the very edge of the paper, he read the spidery scrawl.

My Dear,
* You are a beautiful flower and I shall enjoy plucking*
your petals one by one. I wonder, will your flavor be as
pleasing as your fragrance?
* Jackie*
* P.S. I trust your son is well.*

The hairs on the back of his neck stiffened.

"Kate found it under her doormat when she arrived home this evening," Rios said.

Tully stared at the note. He was furious at Arlene Rios for having managed to do what he hadn't. *You should've been there.* Silently, he counted to ten then looked up from the note. "Ms. McPherson gave this to you?"

"Yes. And she says there's another one."

"The one Ambrose Abbott took?"

"Yes."

Tully was going to have to ask Ms. McPherson to be more discreet.

Rios sat back. "Abbott told her he was going to give it to you."

"I know. He didn't." He wanted to give the mayor a chance to hand it over before going after it himself, and he wanted to play down the importance of the notes to Rios. He studied her. "You've been around Mayor Abbott more than I have. What's your impression of him?"

Rios paused, twisting a piece of shining dark hair around her finger. "We've barely spoken. I think he's hiding something. And I think he's a prick." She smirked. "I could slip into Abbott's apartment and try to find the other note for you."

"That's illegal."

"I'm joking, Tully. Don't you have a sense of humor?"

"No." He studied her. She was young and obnoxious and in love with herself. He doubted she'd even found out she wasn't immortal yet. The thought made him smile in spite of himself.

"Liar," she murmured.

"You told me after the ceremony that you have information for me. You said it again a few minutes ago. Now that I have the time, I'd like to hear it."

"You really should read my notes before we talk, but that note signed 'Jackie' pertains to it." Rios leaned forward, elbows on the desk. "What do you think of the handwriting?"

"Reminds me of an ECG readout."

"Does it look familiar?"

"Should it?"

In reply, she took a piece of sheet of paper from her briefcase and pushed it across the desk. "This is a copy of a famous murderer's letter to the police. Notice any similarities?"

The page was Xeroxed from a book. He examined it, remembering what Dr. Katz had told him about the note found inside the unfortunate tourist. He wasn't about to tell her about that, however. "Why would you show me something over a century old? I can assure you that Jack the Ripper isn't hanging around Eternity."

She sat back and sighed, revealing a trace of exhaustion for the first time. "Look, Tully, you and I are on the same side."

Tully shook his head in disgust but dutifully compared the Ripper's writing to that on the note Kate received. There were some strong similarities, including the signature, but that could be coincidence or the perp's desire to emulate the Ripper. He cleared his throat to speak but Rios beat him to it.

"This place is home to Elvis and Jim Morrison, not to mention a host of others. Why *not* Jack the Ripper?

"The MO is all wrong—wait a minute, hold it right there. There could be a copycat or legacy killer, but that's as far as I go." Tully sat back. Rios had almost pulled him into her whacked-out universe.

"Fair enough. Just keep an open mind."

"You keep saying that. I'll be open within reason."

"That may not be enough."

"Look, Ms. Rios. I've had enough."

The reporter tried to look sheepish.

"I have another question," Tully said. "Off the subject."

"Call TCN and check me out. I'm for real."

"I will, but that's not the question."

"Fine. Ask away."

"You wouldn't happen to have any idea why Abbott stood me up, would you?" He didn't expect an answer, but it didn't hurt to ask.

She nodded. "I think there's a meeting of the Brotherhood tonight."

"Tell me about the Brotherhood." Phil Katz had mentioned it, too.

"It's a secret society. I think it's the big thing amongst the town mucky-mucks. Its full name is the Brotherhood of the Robes."

"Rose?" he asked, alarmed by the word.

"No. *Robes.* I think it's Eternity's version of the Lions or Freemasons. It's a business club."

More old news. "So they dress in ceremonial robes and dance by the light of moon?"

"Probably. I'm going to find out."

Tully remembered his father belonged to something like that. When he was six or seven, he'd gotten into his dad's closet, wanting to see the funny hat he wore to the meetings. It had a long gold tassel hanging from the top. It was irresistible. Tully had cut it off and tied it to the chain on the ceiling fan in his room so that he could reach the control without a stepladder. He'd been inordinately proud of himself until his father discovered it. He was punished far more harshly for that than for putting a softball through the picture window. He'd been shocked by the old man's reaction. And he had disliked secret societies ever since.

"Tully?"

"What?"

"Do you want to go with me tonight?"

"Where?"

"To spy on the Brotherhood."

"Where are they meeting?"

"Up on the mountain. Where we found Joyce Furillo's body. They meet pretty frequently. New moon, full moon, like that. Only Brotherhood members allowed."

So much for preserving the crime scene. "What do you *think* they do up there?"

"Are you asking if their activities may be related to the murders?"

"Sure. Why not?" Maybe Rios' overactive imagination could be useful.

She considered. "Well, I don't know. Some people think they're responsible for the UFOs that appear over the mountain. Those are said to be visible on murder nights, too, but they're also supposedly seen during meetings, before a storm, and so forth. So that pretty much is a dead end."

"Go on."

"The Brotherhood's probably involved with the supernatural aspects of Icehouse Circle."

"Is that the best you can do?"

"Without you thinking I'm nuts, it is."

"I appreciate that."

She killed her coffee, her eyes sparkling with excitement. "You didn't answer my question. Do you want to go up there with me now?"

"It's tempting, but no. I'll do some research of my own first." He also wanted to read the autopsy reports, check on Kate McPherson, and get some sleep. He was so tired now that he was secretly glad that the mayor had postponed their meeting.

"You should talk to a few other locals. Ones who don't belong to the club."

"Yes, I know," he said wearily. "Anyway, I don't think I'd make a very good impression on the people paying my salary if I walked in on them while they're dancing naked by the light of the moon. So if you go up on your own, don't say hello on my account."

She nodded then rose and walked to the door. "See you."

"Keep your head down and your guard up."

"Thanks. I will."

PART TWO

PART TWO

Nineteen

August 18

> The reward of great men is that, long after they
> have died, one is not quite sure that they are dead.

—Jules Renard

In the ranks of God's Secret Service, Billy Godfrey thought
of himself as Agent Double-O Heaven, though like any good
spy, he couldn't reveal his true identity. Only in the privacy
of his snug little cabin could Billy talk freely with the Boss
about the evil rampant in the world, especially the demonic
army within Eternity that God had appointed him to vanquish.

Now Billy, in deep cover, checked his reflection in the display
window of the Crystal Unicorn, where he worked, infiltrating
the clutch of Satan's slaves who ran the store. Like most of
Satan's spawn, they called themselves New Agers.

What he saw in the reflection repelled and excited him. No
suit, no buttondown shirt for Billy, not during his operation.
No clean scent of Aspen cologne, no monthly trip to the barber.
No singing in a proper church choir.

Instead of a silk tie and blue suit, he wore faded jeans, desert boots, and a black long-sleeved T-shirt, with the words "Crystal Unicorn" framing an obscenely large, erect quartz crystal painted from belt-line to sternum for all to see. Worse, the same thing was printed on the back of the shirt.

His soft tangle of jaw-length reddish-blond curls bore no resemblance to the neat style he preferred, but it combined well with wire-rimmed glasses to impart a perfect New Age look. Girls, customers and coworkers both, came on to him constantly, wanting to give him their bodies because he was "sensitive" and "understanding." Several men had given him the look and one had even asked him if he was gay. *Loathsome.*

He knew what they really wanted: to pollute his body and his soul; to make him one with Satan. But Billy kept his resolve and his cover expertly, smiling apologetically, claiming a fiancée in college. He did his clerking just as expertly, selling blasphemous "channeled" books and devil-drenched tarot cards to Satan's adepts and idiot tourists alike. And always, he kept his ears and eyes open, listening for the whispers of demonic conspiracy, even as he slowly, subtly, sabotaged the store in the name of the Lord.

"Billy! Hi!"

He turned with a big goofy grin for the manager of the Unicorn as she walked up behind him. "Hi, Jenny," he said. "Beautiful morning." He hated her; she freely confessed to practicing witchcraft.

She pushed her long straight hair away from her face. "Beautiful," she agreed. "What were you looking at?"

"Looking at?" Mortified, he felt heat flush his cheeks.

"In the window." She was oblivious. "Do you like what you see?"

"I, ah . . ."

"I rearranged the crystal ball display last night after you left. That's what you're checking out, right?"

"Oh, yeah. Right. It looks great."

She studied him, her green eyes made greener by too much eye makeup. *Whore's eyes.* "Are you sure? Don't spare my feelings."

"I'm positive. I like the star shape. It reminds me of Chinese checkers," he added as he stared at the blasphemous pentagram of colorful orbs.

She grinned and boldly took his hand. "You're so funny, Billy." She led him to the door then stood back and waited while he used his key to unlock it. "I'm glad you're here early." She batted her eyelashes at him as soon as they stepped inside. "Trying to make brownie points?"

Whore. He smiled. "I just wanted to get that shipment of crystals unpacked and sorted before we open." That wasn't why he was early and he prayed to God to curse the witch for interfering with His work. Billy had two hundred business-sized cards in his jacket pocket, freshly arrived from a mail-order printer. He'd planned on placing them inside some of the books, deep inside so that they wouldn't fall out. They read, "This store is run by Satan and this product is sinful. Find your way back to the Lord through the Bible and Prayer." Now the cards would have to wait.

"You're a Godsend," Jenny said as she stripped off her jacket. Her jeans and shirt matched Billy's. "I've gotta add up yesterday's receipts and get 'em to the bank," she called, disappearing behind the purple curtains of the fortune-teller's alcove, which in turn led to her small office. "I'll help you when I'm done."

"No need," Billy called after her. After he heard her office door close, he went into the storeroom and stared distastefully at the cartons of crystals and gemstones. *Can't blow the cover.* Sighing, he started to open a box, then noticed a pack of Marlboro Lights on a storage shelf, right by the door to the alley. They belonged to Ted, one of the world's last remaining smoking vegetarians. Ted liked to take his breaks out back in the delivery alley and Billy, a social smoker whose God protected him from addictions, often joined him.

Ted or no Ted, a cigarette break sounded like a good idea. Something to ease his irritation before digging into the boxes of outrageously expensive rocks that would be used to worship the forces of darkness. He shook a cigarette from the pack, patted his pocket to make sure he was carrying a lighter, then unlocked the delivery door and walked outside into the narrow alley, happy to be alone with his cigarette and God in the early morning quiet.

Twenty

"It's bad," Tim Hapscomb warned as Tully squatted beside the sheeted corpse in the alley behind the Crystal Unicorn. The deputy's face was dead-white, his upper lip beaded with sweat despite the morning chill. "It's real bad."

"Why are you still on duty?" he asked absently as he stared at the yellow tarp. "Where's Deputy Stoker?"

"Just as he arrived, there was a two-car head-on in Icehouse Gorge. One went over. I called Ron Settles, but he said he didn't feel well and had an appointment with Doc Katz. So I called you."

Tully nodded. "Next time it's something like this—"

"A homicide?"

"Yeah. Next time, call me first." Tully grasped the top edge of the sheet between his fingers. He could smell how bad it was despite it being a fresh kill. He was glad Hapscomb's call had come before breakfast. "You said this was a call-in?"

"Yes, sir, from the proprietor of the store, Ms. Jenny Lindstrom. She says his name is Billy Godfrey. He was a store employee."

"She's inside?"

Tim nodded.

"Has the coroner been called?"

"Yes, sir. He should be here any minute now."

Tully glanced at the tarp then looked back at Hapscomb. "I guess that means Deputy Settles' appointment has been cancelled. Tim, see if you can reach him on the radio. Tell him that unless he's at death's door, I want him on duty, pronto."

"Yes, sir." Hapscomb, trotted down the alley toward his vehicle and got on the radio.

"You ready?" he asked when Hapscomb returned.

His Adam's apple bobbed as he swallowed. "Do it."

The plastic made a *scritching* sound as it reluctantly pulled free of the corpse's head. The stench of blood and excrement intensified as Tully saw blood-matted hair. Just one shining curl told the true color. Grimly, he peeled the cover down past the face.

"Jesus," Hapscomb whispered. "It's just as bad the second time."

A quarter-inch-wide cut traversed the victim's forehead, a crimson sweatband that disappeared into the hair at the temples. Though the hair was drenched, clotted, with blood, the perp had wiped the face clean, making the blood-encrusted mutilation show starkly against the pallid skin. *Showing it off.* But there was more; the source of the stench. A brown ribbon of feces oozed from the dark red head wound. It looked like frosting in the middle of a layer cake.

"Look at this." Tim Hapscomb pointed at a spot just below the cheekbone. Tully craned to peer at the spot. A small triangle of skin had been carefully excised from the left cheek.

"Maybe we've got a signature," he said with hope but no conviction. Briefly, he lifted the rest of the tarp. There appeared to be no more wounds. He once again examined the triangular wound.

The coroner's reports he'd read last night had been written in detail, but there was no mention of any similar marks to connect this murder to the others. It didn't matter. He knew it was.

As yet, he didn't know more about the hikers who had allegedly been ravaged by bears, but he did know that the vagrant, Bertram Meeks, had been ferociously hacked apart, almost assuredly with a hacksaw, while Frank Lawson's dismemberment had been excruciatingly precise and clean.

Larry Fraser had been shot point-blank with a small caliber bullet, his chest cracked with something metallic, probably a brick chisel driven by a hammer. Then the perp had roughly sliced Fraser's heart free of its moorings, leaving chunks of tissue impaled on the jagged ribs. The tattered organ was subsequently forced into the victim's mouth. Joyce Furillo, on the other hand, showed no outward damage except for having been quick-frozen, probably in liquid nitrogen. But none of them had small triangular wounds, and Tully doubted Katz was the type to miss such a mark. Still he'd ask, maybe go take another look at the Furillo corpse later today.

Hopefully, Phil Katz would have more to report this morning, he thought as he studied the triangular excision. It was less than a quarter inch across, probably closer to an eighth. The cut was shallow and precise. "Exacto knife," Tully said. "Razor blade. Scalpel. What do you think, Deputy Hapscomb?"

"It could even be a filleting knife."

"Could be. Hopefully, Dr. Katz can tell us. You ever see a mark like that before?" Tully pointed at the triangle.

"No. It looks like a trademark."

"We don't know that."

A new voice said, "Jack the Ripper did it to several of his victims. It may be a Masonic sign."

Tully looked up. "Ms. Rios, what the hell are you doing here?" He was embarrassed that neither he nor Hapscomb heard her approach.

"I was just passing by. It's true, what I said about the mark. Some people might believe we're chasing the original Ripper."

"Your ideas are outrageous, Ms. Rios," Tully said as Katz's van pulled up near Hapscomb's cruiser. The door opened and Phil Katz's slender form came into view.

"I'm going to go help the doc," Tim announced. He beat it down the alley.

"You don't have a clue," Rios told Tully. "There's also

the organizational tie—with the triangle. Masons. Brotherhood of the Robes.''

The cult connection wasn't a bad point. "Do you know if the Brotherhood has ties to the Masons?"

"Not as far as I know, but most of these groups are patterned after them and their predecessors or they're spin-offs."

Tully nodded. "Did you get up the mountain last night?"

The van door slammed. They saw Hapscomb and Katz walking slowly toward them. Hapscomb pushed a gurney with equipment stacked on it and the doctor carried a crime-scene case. "I got most of the way up," Rios said.

"Up the mountain?"

She nodded impatiently. "There was a landslide blocking the road just above the campground."

"A landslide? People could be stranded up there."

"I don't think so. Landslide isn't the right word." Her expression turned wry. "It was too artfully done. Some rocks no bigger than a human head, a little dirt and a couple of dead trees. Small enough that if you had come with me we could have moved them."

"So you think the Brotherhood set it up to keep people away from Icehouse Circle?"

"Probably. The blockage was on a hairpin where it was impossible for any vehicle to skirt it."

"Convenient," Tully admitted as he unfolded himself. His muscles ached from squatting. "If you're right. What did you do?"

"I didn't go up there prepared for a hike, so I turned around and drove back down a ways and parked off-road."

"Did they come down?"

"At three in the morning." Katz and Hapscomb were almost within earshot, and she lowered her voice. "I guess that slide just cleared itself up, huh, Sheriff?"

"Okay. You're probably right about it being man-made."

"Thank you."

"So who came down?"

"They were in a school bus," she murmured, nodding at Katz. "I couldn't see a thing."

"Sheriff," Phil Katz said, his pale face turning whiter as he came close enough to see the corpse. "Sorry it took me so long to get here . . . Good God," he added after a pause.

Tully squatted and showed Katz the triangle. "Ever see this before?"

Katz shook his head. "No, I don't think so."

"Damn."

Twenty-one

"God," Zach Tully prayed, "save me from Your followers."

Tim Hapscomb, who'd accompanied him to the victim's home after Al Stoker arrived at the crime scene, said, "Billy Godfrey was a fanatic."

"That's putting it mildly." Tully closed a cabinet door on a two-foot pile of religious literature centering on Satan-spotting and packing for the Rapture. He turned toward Tim. "Find anything useful?"

"Just more of the same. A huge box of those cards about the store being run by Satan, like the ones in his pocket. The guy's crazy." He paused. "Anything for his cause. I'll bet he had plenty of enemies."

" 'I am descending into a nest of vipers,' " Tully read aloud from Godfrey's spiral-bound diary. He had quickly scanned a dozen pages and the phrase, in some form, had graced nearly every one of them. "He might have enemies. Or not. It says here that Billy didn't think anyone knew his 'true purpose.' I think that's unlikely, even if he had his boss and coworkers fooled." He shook his head at the homemade Double-O Heaven sign—two zeros and the word "heaven" written out in psychedelic James Bond-style lettering. "I want you to reinterview Ms. Lindstrom and talk to all of the employees, not just the ones who showed up this morning. Neighbors, too."

"Right."

"I wonder if Billy did any time at Shady Pines."

"I'll check." Tim stood next to Tully and stared at the Double-O Heaven sign, then turned his face up to study the eighteen-inch crucifix hanging above it. Tully followed his gaze. The crucifix was rococo plaster spray-painted gold. The bleeding Jesus draped across its length and breadth wore an expression of goggly-eyed horror that made it look more like Frank Zappa than the Savior.

Tully lifted his hand toward the cross then pulled his fingers back when they were an inch away. "Something," he murmured, then looked at Hapscomb. "Something."

"There's some kind of connection," Tim stated what Tully was thinking.

"Yeah." He hadn't felt it in a long time, but the sensation—like ants crawling around in his skull making his brain itch—had been with him, albeit faint, since they'd entered Godfrey's one-room cabin. He glanced at Tim Hapscomb with new respect. If he could sense something this distant, something too far away to touch, then he was probably good at his job. "It's not this," he added, gesturing at the crucifix, then at the room in general. "Not exactly."

Tim's eyes sparked. "It's *like* this."

"Religious fervor?"

"Insanity? Illogic?"

"Logic hidden by apparent illogic," Tully said with sudden sureness.

"Uh-huh." Tim picked up the Godfrey's diary and handed it to Tully. Tentatively, he asked, "Want to grab some breakfast?"

"Let's go," Tully said, pleased that his shy deputy was finally coming out of his shell.

"I'll put a fiver on old Coop. He's got it coming," said an aging redneck on the old-fashioned park bench in front of the King's Tart. The Liar's Bench. Two more retirees shared the space and three others lolled under the store canopy behind those seated. The man standing in the middle, Abe Beakman, was a bald, aptly hawk-nosed gent in his eighties. He held a steno pad and pen. The man on his right, frail but hairy, clutched a small wad of bills in his fist. The third standee, heavyset and a mere youth in his late sixties, was passing around glazed donuts from the bakery box he guarded. The three on the bench, the redneck plus the Delbert Twins, two watery-eyed former schoolteachers who favored plaid shirts and bow ties, grabbed and munched. "Stark raving Looney Tunes," said one.

"Orson, you're full of shi—beans," said Beakman, cleaning up his language as Kate came up the steps.

"Gentlemen." She managed a smile as she passed them— Eternity's gamblers on death and destruction, natural or not— the Death Squad abided no prejudice in the disaster department. She tried to hurry by. She had seen Sheriff Tully's Explorer parked around the corner and she hoped she would find him at the Tart. She'd been hospitable to Arlene Rios last night, but Tully was the one she trusted, the one she wanted to see. For one thing, she wanted to know what he made of the note she'd given Arlene Rios; for another, she wanted to make sure the reporter had actually given it to him. As soon as the woman left, Kate regretted entrusting the note to her. Her only excuse was that Arlene was so sincere—and she could charm fleas off a dog.

" 'Katie, Katie, Katie,' " sang the old redneck. The Delbert Twins' grins were guileless, but the redneck, named Hooter or Hooker, something like that, packed a leer that made her feel filthy.

"There was another murder this morning." Peter Delbert's words hung in the air.

Kate stopped moving. "Really? Who?"

"Haven't been able to find out for sure, but we think it's somebody from . . ." Beakman clicked his pen and held it to his steno pad. "I shouldn't say until I give you a chance to join the pool. It's closed, but since you didn't know about it I'll let you bet."

"No. No thanks." Nearly everyone she knew put a dollar or two into the death pool, but she didn't find it amusing. "Who do you think was killed?"

"Odds are it's someone who works at the New Age store," said Peter. "The cops and the doc were all bunched up behind it."

"The Horny Horse," supplied the redneck. "Sheriff's in there," he said jerking his head toward the Tart. "He wouldn't tell us anything, but I bet you can charm it out of him, at least if you can get him away from that little brunette babe long enough. You got her beat to hell in the hooter department, and you can take *that* to the bank."

"Orson Hooker," said a Delbert. "don't you ever speak like that to this lady again." He turned to Kate. "We apologize for our friend's crudity."

"Yes," echoed the other Delbert.

Kate ignored Hooker, smiled at the Delberts. "Excuse me, gentlemen, but I'm in a bit of a hurry. Everyone at Bigfoot is counting on me to bring back donuts before the first tours run."

"I'll put five down on Herb Clyster for this morning's unfortunate incident," Beakman said, jotting on his pad.

As Kate opened the bakery door, she heard Hooker ask, "Who the hell's Herb Clyster?"

"Traveling salesman, Orson," came Beakman's voice. "Purveyor of crystals and books on enlightenment to the New Age establishments."

"Why him?"

"Salesmen deserve to die."

The door closed behind her, cutting off the conversation.

Harlan King, dapper in his bakery whites, beamed at her from over the counter. "The usual?"

"Yes, please, Harlan. Plus two extra maple bars. The boss brought his brother in today."

"Still trying to get him to take a *real* job?" King's eyes twinkled.

Kate smiled. "He's an optimist."

She waited while the baker began placing twenty-six pastries in pink and white striped bags. Out of the corner of her eye she could see Zach Tully sitting at a corner table with Arlene Rios and the nice deputy, the young one. As she watched, the deputy stood and left, nodding at her as he walked by. Tully and Rios remained drinking coffee. They looked absorbed in conversation. Kate turned back to the counter, and gathering the bags, she pivoted toward the door, catching Tully's gaze, head-on. He looked tired but his smile was real. "Please," he said, indicating the chair the deputy had vacated.

"I don't want to intrude," Kate said. Of their own volition, her feet stepped toward the table. Toward Tully.

"Please. Intrude." He sounded a little desperate.

She set the bags on the table and sat down between the cop and the reporter. "I've only got a minute," she said as she turned to Tully. "What did you make of the new note?"

For an instant, he looked like he wouldn't answer and Kate thought Arlene Rios hadn't given it to him. Then he glanced at Rios and she realized he was deciding whether or not to talk in front of her. "This is not to be repeated," he said to the reporter.

"My lips are sealed, of course."

"I think it's likely to be a real threat." His somberness gave her a chill. "Take it seriously. Your son—"

"Josh is never out of sight," Kate said quickly. "I already warned his teachers and sitter, and I've seen to it that he goes nowhere alone."

"Does he know he's in possible danger?" the reporter asked. Tully threw her a dirty look.

Kate answered anyway. "I don't want to frighten him." Rios hit a sore spot; Kate had been torn about what she should tell her son. He already knew all about avoiding strangers, after all. "I haven't said anything yet." She turned to Tully. "Do you think I should tell him?"

"Tell him," Rios said as Tully opened his mouth. "Scare the hell out of him. It might help keep him alive."

Tully looked annoyed, but said, "Ms. Rios is probably right. But how much you need to tell him depends on his own nature."

Her hands trembled and she hid them under the table. Hardly able to think, she nodded.

"Would it help if I spoke to him?" the sheriff asked gently.

"Yes, I think it might. Shall we come by the station this evening?"

"You and I need to talk, too," Tully added. "In private. So, if it's all right with you, I'll stop by your place. That way Josh won't have to sit and wait. I'd also like to take another look around your property. That okay with you?"

"Of course. We'll be home by five-thirty." Kate's voice didn't tremble, though her hands still did. "Sheriff, may I ask a question?"

"Ask away."

"The Death Squad told me there's been another murder."

"Death Squad?" Tully asked, eyebrows lifting.

She smiled. "That's what we call the old guys out front. They have pools on who's going to die next."

"Murdered, you mean?" asked Arlene Rios.

"Any kind of death. But I think murder stakes are higher."

"Gambling's illegal," Rios murmured, glancing at Tully.

"Shooting the breeze with them would be a lot more profitable than busting them," he said dryly. He turned back to Kate. "I'll see you tonight. Meanwhile, don't go off by yourself. Be careful."

"I will." She stood up, then paused. *"Was* there another murder?"

"Yes," he said simply. "Yes, there was."

Kate nodded, knowing he didn't want to say more. "See you later," she called and headed out the door.

"Ms. McPherson?" said Beakman as she tried to hurry past.

"I'm sorry, but I'm running late."

"Just an instant of your time," said a Delbert.

The gentlemanly twins were harder to resist. She paused. "An instant is all I can spare."

"Was there another murder?"

"You fellows told me there was," she said. "Do you mean you don't know for sure?"

"We deduced it. After all, we're professionals." Beakman spoke with complete sincerity. "You spoke to our new sheriff. Are we correct in our deduction?"

"Yes." She took a step.

"Who?"

"Who?" she asked.

"Who died?"

"I have no idea."

"He wouldn't tell you, either?" asked the redneck in a voice that implied she should have seduced the information out of Tully.

"I didn't ask." She started walking, amused by the collective sigh of disappointment behind her.

"Come on," Arlene Rios said after Kate left the Tart. "I have more material for you."

Tully pushed away from the table. "Come on where?"

"My room at Dimples'. The material's there. I didn't want to cart it around with me. There are a few books involved."

Suppressing a groan, Tully said, "You go ahead. I'll be there in an hour or so."

"Okay. Phone if you're delayed."

Tully stayed where he was until she was out the door and out of sight.

"Quite the character, isn't she?" Harlan King observed.

"I'm afraid so." Seeing that the bakery was empty except for himself and King, he moved to the counter, coffee cup in hand.

"Refill?"

"Please."

"Best coffee in town," King told him as he poured. "Grows hair on the male chest and increases a woman's bust by at least an inch."

Tully grinned. "Even Starbucks doesn't make that claim."

"Starbucks?"

"Nationwide chain of coffeehouses," Tully explained,

slightly stunned as he realized just how far Eternity was from the real world. "Mr. King."

"Harlan."

"Harlan. You're a member of the town council."

"Correct."

"As such, you're part of the team that lured me up here."

"An odd choice of words, Sheriff."

"I don't think so. I understood I'd be meeting with Mayor Abbott and the council last night, but the meeting was canceled. I need the meeting, Harlan. Today. Can you help with that, or can you at least tell me why the mayor is avoiding me?"

"You're direct, Sheriff. I like that. I'll be direct as well." The baker dimpled up. "First, Ambrose is a curmudgeon. An unfathomable curmudgeon. As you know, we had a brief meeting yesterday afternoon at the courthouse after you left. Your presence would have been most appropriate. I asked Ambrose why you were excluded, but he would only harumph."

"He what?"

"He harumphed. You know. That sound politicians make when they have nothing to say but want to sound serious and important."

King made the sound in his throat twice in succession, then lifted his eyebrows at Tully, who now understood perfectly. "Mel Brooks," he said. "There was a lot of harumphing in *Blazing Saddles*.

"Yes, yes, that's right," chortled King.

"Harlan—"

"You're a fellow Brooks aficionado, Sheriff?" He shook his head, a faraway look in his eye. "It saddens me to see how jaded audiences have become. Vaudeville is an art form, a dying art form. I hope it revives. Our West End music halls were the birthplaces of vaudeville, though I know it was the Americans who refined the art. When I was in the Queen's service I was fortunate enough to catch a show at the Palace Theater in New York."

"You're British?" Tully asked, thinking King must have

been here a long time. He hadn't noticed an accent. "When were you in the service?"

"Royal Navy. World War Two."

"You're not old enough. You're not old enough for anything but Vietnam. Don't treat me like a tourist."

"I'm not." The baker looked hurt. "I'm older than I look, young man." King's eyes twinkled and he winked one conspiratorially. "This is Eternity, Sheriff Tully. Time has little meaning here. Now then," he continued, steamrolling along, "back to the question at hand. I can only guess at why Ambrose put you off. Probably for no reason whatsoever, but it might be due to some dissension on the council. One of our members wanted to become sheriff, wanted it very badly. Ambrose might not have cared to rub his nose in you, so to speak. But I don't think that's it. I think it was simply Ambrose being Ambrose. Carrying his big stick. He likes to do that. Never let him know when he's irritated you, Tully, because he'll enjoy it so much he'll redouble his efforts. Now, where was I? Ah yes. The reason last evening's meeting was canceled so ungraciously is that we are a pack of boneheads. Boneheads. We momentarily forgot we had a gathering planned, our businessman's—person's—club, you know—"

"The Brotherhood of the Robes?"

King's eyebrow shot north. "The grapevine flourishes. Or you've been busy detecting. Who told you about it, might I ask?"

"Arlene Rios," Tully said without hesitation. It wasn't even a lie and it kept Phil's name out of things. "I might be interested in joining."

"I'll mention it to the His Nibs, but be prepared for a long wait."

"Who is His Nibs?"

King gave a half mile. "Secret society, secret nibs. I'm sorry, Sheriff. Ah, the stories I'd love to tell."

"I understand. Just out of curiosity, which councilperson wanted to be sheriff?"

King seemed surprised by the question. "Why, Elvis, of

course. Who else? He's always wanted to be the sheriff, but he's much too nice to pull it off. You should see his collection of law enforcement equipment, badges and so forth. Ask him. I'm sure he'd be proud to show it to you."

"I see." Tully glanced at his watch. "I have to get to an appointment, but I appreciate your being candid. I'd like to talk more later."

"Certainly. Drop by Ambrose's bookstore if you really want to see him."

"I'll do that."

Exhausted by King's barrage, Tully left the building, ready to brave the Death Squad. But the benches were bare. He'd have to brave Abbott and Rios instead.

Twenty-two

Of uncertain heritage, the building housing Abbott's Bookshop was two-story, red brick, long and narrow, one of a dozen sandwiched along a narrow street behind the courthouse. Within, towering aisles teemed with books, nearly burst with them, and everything smelled comfortably of aging paper, glue, and dust.

Like the King's Tart, Abbott's Bookshop had an old-fashioned entry bell over the door which jingled when Tully entered, but after five minutes, neither Ambrose Abbott nor any employee had appeared. The only sign of life was the music filtering through an elderly sound system. It filled the shop with Franz Liszt's devilish waltzes, which set Tully's teeth on edge and made him want to pace. It did not encourage browsing, which perhaps was exactly what the irascible shopkeeper intended.

An antiquated cash register sat on a counter near the front door. On the wall behind it were shelves full of clear-wrappered rare books, first editions and autographed tomes. In the middle of the center shelf was a yellowed sign that read NEVER TELL THE TRUTH TO PEOPLE WHO ARE NOT WORTHY OF IT. Mark Twain at his pithiest. It seemed an odd quote to hang over a sales counter, but then again, everything about Abbott was odd.

On the dusty wooden counter was a tarnished brass service bell. Tully tapped it and was surprised to hear a distant electric buzz behind the old-fashioned *ching*. It seemed out of place in a building that might have looked exactly the same a century before.

The ceiling creaked as heavy footsteps crossed overhead. A door slammed then the footsteps thumped down a flight of stairs at the rear of the store. Ambrose Abbott appeared at the end of an aisle and paused to eye Tully. He didn't smile as he resumed walking. Tully thought the old man belonged in a Rockwell painting, with his suspendered pants, starched white shirt, and western string tie.

"Better late than before anybody has invited you," Abbott said as he moved into position behind the counter. His eyes, shaded by unruly gray brows, were dark and piercing. "I wondered how long it would take you to show up."

"Mayor Abbott, why are you avoiding me?"

The man gave him a Mona Lisa look. "You already asked Harlan that question and I believe he gave you a satisfactory answer."

"He warned you I was coming?"

"Speak of the devil and he will hear about it." This time the man actually grinned and it gave Tully the creeps.

"You went to a great deal of trouble to lure me up here then you tell me nothing. What's the point?"

"No point, except perhaps that I wondered when you would come to me on your own."

"You broke our appointment last night."

"Unfortunately unavoidable. But you're here now, so ask your questions. But not too many; I have a client arriving at any moment."

"This is a bookstore. Don't you have customers coming and going all day?"

"A waste of a question, Sheriff Tully. Of course I do. But very few of them are prepared to pay nearly a thousand dollars for an autographed copy of *The Cynic's Word Book*." He shook his head. "There's no accounting for some people's taste. Why don't you ask a pertinent question instead of an impertinent one?"

Why don't you go to hell? Tully swallowed his anger. He wanted to ask about the cover-up of the hikers' deaths in June but couldn't broach the subject until he could protect Phil Katz. Fortunately, he had plenty of other things to talk about. "Kate McPherson received a note that's now in your possession. I'd like to take it in as evidence."

"Of course." He opened a drawer and withdrew a folded piece of paper then handed it to Tully. "Here you are. By the way, you need to watch out for Miss Rios. She was just here and tried her damnedest to talk me into giving it to her. And, do you know? I was quite tempted." He cleared his throat. "Watch out for that one, Sheriff. She's competitive and I think it's likely she's trying to solve our little mystery on her own."

"Why do you trust her?"

"She gave her word and one word is as good as another. Except in certain company, of course." He paused, studying Tully. "Interesting. Miss Rios doesn't have your common sense or caution, of course—witness her clumsy attempt at spying last night—but you and she are quite alike in many ways. Tenacious. Competitive. But then those are two of the qualities that made you right for this position. That and your sharp powers of deduction, which if you don't mind my saying so, or even if you do, might benefit with the application of a proper whetstone."

Tully ignored Abbott's bait. "Tell me, Mayor. Do you have any ideas concerning the murderer's identity?"

"If I knew who it was, Sheriff, we wouldn't need you."

"You'd deal with him yourself?" Tully was sick of Abbott already.

"We would. This is Eternity."

He said it as if the town were a sovereign nation. Tully studied him. "I believe you're serious."

"I never jest."

"All right. I realize you don't know who the perpetrator is, but do you have any suspicions?"

Abbott shrugged. "Someone intelligent. Someone with a sense of irony, perhaps even, gods forbid, a sense of humor.

Someone bored. But the only thing I'm relatively certain of is that he or she is one of our own.''

"Why is that?"

"Because," Abbott said, smoothing his mustache as the front doorbell jangled, "there's a certain—I'm not sure how to describe it—a certain panache to the deeds that harks back to other incidents. Good day, Mr. Morrison.''

The man Abbott greeted was the Jim Morrison clone whom Tully had noticed in the courtroom. He still wore the Morrison poster outfit: the vest over bare skin. Up close he still bore a striking resemblance to the dead rocker.

"Hey, Ambrose," the newcomer mumbled. "How they hanging?"

"Square to the jib, my friend. I have your *Cynic's Word Book* right here." He brought an old leatherbound volume out from behind the counter and placed it in Morrison's hands. "First edition as you can see, with the original title, not the latter *Devil's Dictionary*. As you requested, the autograph is personalized to you.''

"Cash okay?" Morrison glanced suspiciously at Tully.

"Cash is quite delightful. I take it you have yet to meet our new hanger of rogues?''

"Huh?"

"Our new sheriff. Zachary Tully, Jim Morrison.''

Morrison made a peace sign instead of offering a hand. Then he dug into his pants pocket. He checked all four before speaking. "Be right back. Must've left my stash in the car.''

The man walked outside, opened the trunk of a '66 Mustang parked out front, and began rooting around. "Curious fellow," said Abbott.

"Does he really think he's *the* Jim Morrison?"

"I don't know. I've never asked. He is, however, formerly of Shady Pines and has very wealthy relatives, so we take care of our boy Jim.''

"You said the book was personalized. You had whoever wrote it autograph it just for him? It looks a hundred years old.''

Abbott looked amused. "Not quite. First publication was in 1906, and, for your edification, Ambrose Bierce, for whom I am proud to be named, was the author. He was last seen in Mexico in 1913."

"Then how did he manage to personalize this copy?" Tully asked as Morrison found his cash and slammed the trunk.

Abbott smiled, showing square teeth. "This is Eternity."

"Got it," Morrison announced as he came back in.

"Good day, Sheriff. We'll speak again soon."

Jack had watched them all scurry around their new prize, excited, afraid and greedy, like the colony of ants he had once observed as they tried to figure out what to do with the corpse of a hummingbird that he placed in their path.

The humans had amused him for a time, especially the seriousness of the sheriff and reporter. It occurred to him that, given a chance, Arlene Rios might find the sheriff an attractive diversion in a notch-on-the-bedpost sort of way, and if Tully could see beyond Kate McPherson, the fiery little journalist might interest him as well.

For himself, Arlene might be as interesting a toy as he expected Kate to be. He sensed she was too curious to be fearful or terribly cautious. Danger probably excited her and that excited him.

Sipping coffee thick with sugar, he mused on his next move. Should he wait or should he strike again? Either way, stirring up the ants' nest, making them puzzle over similarities or lack of them, was most definitely in order.

Tully and Arlene Rios sat at a dinette table in her room at the boardinghouse. The faded room looked like it hadn't been decorated since 1965. "I don't think you need a graphologist to see that those notes to Kate were written by the same person," Rios said as she handed him a magnifying glass.

He'd been eager to look at the new note and saw no reason

not to examine it in front of Rios since Kate had already told her of its existence and contents. Briefly, he studied the angular writing then set the glass down. "I don't think there's any question about that. What I'd like to establish is a link between them and the perp."

"Could there be more than one killer?" she asked. "I mean, do you have a definite link between Lawson's murder and the three new ones?"

He studied her, thinking Abbott was right about being careful around her. "No comment."

"Come on, Tully. Off the record?"

"I'll give you this answer: I haven't discounted the idea."

"Can't you give me a break?"

"I can't endanger the case. I'm here to listen to your theories. Don't ask for mine. Any more coffee in that pot?"

"Yeah." Rios took their empty cups across to the dresser where a battered avocado-green percolator was plugged into one of the room's few electrical outlets. "Okay. At least you're agreeing to listen."

"For a short time," he said, taking the fresh cup.

"Okay. You agree that the two notes Kate received were written by the same person," she said as she seated herself. "Now humor me and compare those two to the sample from the original Jack the Ripper."

Tully reluctantly picked up the Xeroxed page she had tried to push at him the night before. "Yes, they're similar. This guy has a hard-on for the Ripper. Off the record."

"You don't have to keep saying that."

"I want to make sure you know it."

"Trust me."

He laughed. "Trust a reporter?"

She gave him a dirty look. "What can I do to make you trust me?"

"Nothing." He smiled weakly. "I'm sorry, Ms.—Arlene, but there are some things we can't talk about. It's nothing personal." Eyeing her, he sat back. "So what did you think you were doing, trying to get that note from Ambrose Abbott yourself?''

"I wanted to see it and I didn't think you'd share."

"I probably shouldn't have."

Rios switched subjects before he could say more. "Did Abbott tell you anything about the Brotherhood?"

"I hoped he'd extend an invitation, but he brushed me off. Politely."

"Of course."

"What do you mean, 'Of course'?"

"They don't know you, and no matter what they're really doing on the mountain, the Brotherhood's no simple business-man's association. They obviously have arcane roots—all their Icehouse Circle activity tells us that. Whether or not their club is a load of bullshit, they take their secret rituals and oaths very seriously. I think you have to be a lifer to be a member."

That was probably true. Phil Katz thought the same thing. "Do you know for a fact that all the members are lifers?" Tully asked.

"No, but most of them are. I think. I think most, if not all of the council members are in it, but frankly, everybody's so closemouthed about it that I've only tricked a few people into giving themselves away. But there's enough of them to fill a small school bus."

"Abbott knows you were there, by the way."

She looked surprised. "You're kidding."

"He mentioned it, not me. Has anybody given you any insight into the Brotherhood's purpose?"

She shook her head. "No, but what's any organization's purpose? A common interest."

"To satisfy a need to belong," Tully added.

She studied him. "Yeah. That's the bottom line, isn't it?"

Tully nodded. "Why do you think the Brotherhood is involved in the homicides?"

"I'm not saying it is. I'm just a sucker for conspiracy theories. What about you? You're showing a lot of interest in the Brother-hood yourself."

He saw no reason not to answer. "Just a hunch. But it might not be a good hunch—maybe it's just their secretiveness setting off the alarm bells."

"Maybe, but . . ." Arlene pushed a stray lock of hair from her cheek. "Suppose the Brotherhood is connected to the killer? Is he a member?"

"And they're covering for him?" Tully suggested. "Of course, that would mean the council is covering for him as well."

"Why would they hire the cop most likely to solve the case if they're covering up?" Rios asked.

"I don't know." Tully found Rios to be a good sounding board, so he told her, "Abbott did say he thinks the killer is a local. I believe he said, 'One of our own.' "

She stared into her coffee cup before turning her eyes back to Tully. "Okay. Maybe the Brotherhood is similar to the Freemasons. A Mason can't rat on one of their own under penalty of death, which brings me to—"

Tully cut in. "Abbott also said that if they knew who it was they wouldn't need me; they'd take care of the problem themselves."

"Did he say how?"

Tully shook his head. "He just said, 'This is Eternity.' I think it's the town motto. Whenever one of them doesn't want to answer a question, they say, 'This is Eternity.' " He paused. "By the way, guess who came into the bookstore while I was there?"

"Who?"

"Jim Morrison. From the courtroom. And Shady Pines. He had about a thousand cash for a personalized first edition of an Ambrose Bierce book that was published in 1906. I asked Abbott how a book published ninety years ago could be personalized. Can you guess what he said?"

" 'This is Eternity.' That brings me to something I want to show you—"

"Of course," Tully interrupted, "the lack of cooperation is

astounding. In fact, I don't understand how you ever got Abbott's blessing.''

"I do." She paused before adding, "I flirted with him."

"What about your cameraman? I haven't seen him around. Did Abbott banish him?"

"How'd you guess? He's coming back later, though. If he had been a woman, he'd still be here. Abbott likes women. He visits Kate McPherson frequently. Did you know that?"

"No."

"She says he stops by pretty regularly when he's out walking." While Tully digested the information, she grabbed a book from a stack on the floor beside her chair and opened it to a dog-eared page. "After you look at this, you might be more willing to talk about Jack the Ripper." She pushed the book across the small table. "It's an encyclopedia of literature."

"Literature?" Tully looked down at a page bearing a grainy photograph of Ambrose Abbott. It was framed by a biography of the writer Ambrose Bierce. Tully stared. Then stared some more. At last he read the bio, then looked at Rios. "Abbott said he was named for Bierce. He must be a son or grandson. The similarity is uncanny."

She gazed back. "That's how you get a personalized signature ninety years later."

"Hold it. You *can't* believe Abbott's the original? The man in the photo?"

"This is Eternity," she said dryly. She took the book, closed it, then exchanged it for another, a small general encyclopedia. It had a folded down page as well. "Recognize her?" she asked as she smoothed the page and handed over the book.

Tully studied the photo of Amelia Earhart. "No," he said, relieved. He started to push the book back, but Rios stopped him.

"Look harder. The hair's different, but look at the chin and nose."

Recognition came with a dull thud. "She looks a little like that outdoorsey councilwoman—I can't remember her name."

Arlene raised an eyebrow. "A *little?* Her name is Amelia

Noonan. She's the postmaster here and she's married to a guy named Fred Noonan. He's a mechanic. Read the bio.''

Tully did, his gut clenching at the sight of Earhart's navigator's name. ''Frederick J. Noonan,'' he said dully. ''This is absurd. You know that, don't you?''

''Yes,'' she replied immediately, some of her cool veneer disappearing in her obvious frustration. ''Yes. I know. Assuming they're not the real people, that they've taken on their personas—for tourist trade, or whatever—it still implies it's possible there may be a real link between the historic Ripper and the man you're after.''

''A thin link,'' Tully said quickly. ''One suggesting he's secretly taking on the Ripper persona to some extent. After all, the crimes aren't copies of the originals.'' He didn't mention the hikers who did suffer copycat crimes.

''I think it's more than that.'' She leaned forward, put her elbows on the table and rested her chin on her hands. ''Look. I don't understand this any more than you do. It's illogical. Forget the Ripper for a minute. No one knows his identity. But the similarities between Bierce and Abbott and Earhart and Noonan are amazing. I tried to run checks on some of these people last night, including Abbott and the Noonans. They don't exist. The Social Security numbers seem real, but I've seen fakes that good before.''

''Where have you seen fake numbers before?''

She smiled smugly. ''I'm an investigative reporter, not the society columnist for Podunk, Arkansas. Anyway, there aren't any birth records or histories for them. Nothing.''

''How about Elvis Number One? Did you check him out too?''

She nodded. ''Same story on Elvis One. I also checked out Jim Morrison. His real name is Marvin Flournoy. Paranoid schizophrenic, on medication, considered stable enough to be set loose from Shady Pines.''

''Abbott said his family is wealthy.'' Tully finished his second cup of coffee, pleased that she'd come up with something he knew to be true. "So Jim is welcomed with open arms by the money-grubbing town fathers."

"You've got a lot of suspects."

"Not to imply that I buy the notion that any of these people are originals," Tully said as Rios refilled their cups again, "but I'm particularly curious about Harlan King. He tried to tell me he was in the Royal Navy in the Second World War."

"I checked on him, too," Arlene said as she slid back into her chair and passed Tully his refill. "Harlan King existed. He died in 1945, aged fifty-two."

"The current Harlan's father? It would make some sense if, in the spirit of this insane place, Harlan Junior is pretending to be his own father."

"That's the logical guess, although there's no record of this Harlan's existence, except for a Social Security number which is probably bogus."

"How did the first King die? Casualty of war?"

"Sort of. His ship went missing in the Atlantic."

"Let me guess. His body was never recovered."

"Neither was his ship. Communication was lost in the vicinity of the Merino Triangle. It was never seen or heard from again."

"Christ," Tully said in disgust. "What's that?"

"It's like the Bermuda Triangle but in the north Atlantic below Britain."

"That's just what I need. Another Bermuda Triangle. This place has Bigfoot, UFOs, the living dead, Little Stonehenge. What else? Ghosts? Bogeymen? There's probably a Nessie living in the pond behind my cabin."

Arlene smiled through the diatribe. Finally Tully sighed and asked, "What about your landlords, the Dimples? Do they exist?"

"The Dimples are equally questionable. A couple by that name lived in the Midwest until the twenties and this pair claim to be them. I got chatty with them and they told me a tale about losing their Kansas farm in a tornado and landing here."

"*Landing* here?"

"*Wizard of Oz* time. They 'landed' in Icehouse Circle and settled right in. Elmer said that once they got used to the winters, they found Eternity much more pleasant than Kansas." She paused. "They did do their homework; their tornado matches with meteorological activity at the time."

"That means nothing."

"True. And it's all beginning to sound ridiculous to me, too. Every person who's told me one of these stories claims to have arrived here via the Circle."

"I'm not surprised. The first person I met told me he came through the Circle." He told her about Jackson Coop and the booklet, *Occult Secrets of Icehouse Mountain.* "The Lemurians built it and it's a time portal or something," he finished derisively. "Do you have anything on Coop?"

"I haven't checked Coop, but I will. Listen, it's more of a time and space portal. Nobody claims to have come here from the past or future—they claim to have been living here since their own time. The time aspect involves instantaneous travel from one point to another—"

"Beam me up, Scotty."

"Sort of. Even if you—we—think the Circle is nonsense, you need to understand how it supposedly works. Kate's stalker may believe in the Circle. It may be the only piece of logic, however twisted, you have to work from."

"It could be important, but what's logic have to do with it?" He'd had just about enough.

She lifted another book onto the table titled *Sacred Vortices.* "This explains something about the Circle and what it's supposed to do."

"Enlighten me. I don't have time to read the book."

"Okay. Basically, there are fluctuations in the earth's gravitational and magnetic fields. Some have to do with external sources like tides and sunspots, but others, like the Circle, are caused by internal forces. There are vectors—the Brits call them ley lines—where there are power surges. The rows of standing stones on the British Isles follow the ley lines and

Stonehenge, along with other sites around the world, are built at vector points.''

"Is this New Age bullshit or is there some basis in fact?"

"There seems to be fact behind it. It's certainly not a New Age concept; they've only adopted it. It goes back to the beginning of history. What's certain is that some of these holy places—as well as some places that aren't considered sacred any more, like the Mystery Spot in Santa Cruz—are *really* peculiar. I'm not saying there's anything supernatural going on. It just *seems* supernatural because it's hard to understand. It probably has to do with magnetic ores, tectonic plates, and subterranean volcanic activity. All very scientific."

"Okay. That I can buy. After all, you can feel the effects at Icehouse Circle. Like dizziness. But what does that have to do with people dropping into the Circle out of thin air?" The stories were nothing but the usual New Age psychobabble about magic and faith. In other words, hooey.

"That's where it gets difficult," Rios said. "This book goes into more detail; try to read chapter twelve tonight." She hesitated then said, "I've seen something like it."

"A tour guide materialized in the crazy shack at a mystery spot?"

"Don't be sarcastic, Tully. It doesn't suit you. What I experienced was in New Mexico last year and it was very, very weird."

"People appeared out of nowhere, huh?"

"No." Irritation flashed in her eyes. "It was more along the lines of a haunting."

"Oh, great, you believe in ghosts."

"Tully, shut up and listen. First of all, I'm not talking about the common chain-clinking 'boo!'-crying ghosts you tell stories about around the campfire. A haunting is nowhere near as interesting. Most hauntings are basically the same thing as a sachet you discover in an old trunk of clothes. It's just leftovers, memories embedded in an object or place. Those ghosts don't think—unless sometimes they aren't ghosts but different realities crossing over into ours. The Circle could be the same thing, but maybe it's stronger. Maybe things get through.''

''Well, that's a relief.''

''Do you want to hear about New Mexico?''

Tully resisted an urge to roll his eyes. ''What? Were you at another circle?''

''No. It's a place that the Native Americans considered cursed, though. Up behind Los Alamos, in the mountains, there's a piece of land with a lot of geological anomalies. Not nearly the scope of Eternity's, but enough to give it a reputation. There were some very fierce battles fought in the region between wagon trains and natives and it's always had a reputation for violence, before and after the attacks on wagon trains. Something to do with what the geomagnetic anomalies can do to the brain.''

''If geomagnetics can do more than make you dizzy, or mess with your mind, that explains why this place is full of lunatics. I can buy that part.''

''Me, too. Anyway, I was curious, so I drove up there one afternoon in late summer. The place has a creepy feel, even before the asphalt ends. Something's not right. It had the same kind of feel the Circle does in that it puts you on alert. I hit the dirt road and continued on for ten miles, until I was in the middle of the haunted area. I set up camp there and waited. And you know what, Tully?''

''What?''

''I heard a war. Horses neighing, people yelling, screaming, gun shots. I even heard an arrow whiz past my head and I think I felt the wind of it on my cheek. The wagon noises got louder until I thought I actually saw one coming right at me just like in those stories about ghost trains.''

''Do you seriously expect me to believe all this? It was probably a trick of the moonlight.''

''Probably. Believe what you want, but if you want proof, I'll tell you exactly how to get there and you can see or hear for yourself.'' She was silent a moment. ''Look at it like other people look at your work. Basically, you're a profiler. Plenty of people think you're psychic."

Tully shook his head. "It's all knowledge, an eye for details, and the ability to listen to your instincts."

"Doesn't matter. You'll never convince some people that you're *not* psychic. I'm just saying there's a rational explanation for what you do and that there's a rational explanation, however hidden it is to science, for what happens in New Mexico. And for what's happening here."

"Okay. I'll buy some of that, too." Tully cleared his throat. "I've noticed that until something is explained, science pretends it doesn't exist."

"Exactly."

"How does all this tie in with live people dropping in?"

She shrugged. "Maybe geomagnetics can cause weaknesses in the space-time continuum. Earthly wormholes. Maybe instead of just images or sounds, material things occasionally slip through them. Taking that a step further, maybe it's possible that in some places, like Icehouse Circle, the anomalies are occasionally powerful enough to suck living people in or spit them out." She sipped her coffee.

"Twilight Zone."

"True. But a century ago, you would have said the same thing about lasers, space missions, and for that matter, central air conditioning."

She made a valid point, though he hated to admit it.

"Okay, just to speed things up, let's pretend that Abbott is Bierce and Elvis is Elvis. How do they end up here? Through a wormhole?"

"Yes, if they stop aging."

Tully nodded reluctantly. According to Coop's booklet, arriving through Icehouse Circle conferred immortality of a sort: Though one could be killed, aging often discontinued.

"And if they continue to age?"

"Then they probably arrived by automobile." She half smiled. "If you wanted to disappear, this place would be a great place to do it. It's absolutely loony. Look at Councilman

Elvis. If he's not the real thing, he's the closest I've ever seen. But even people who know about Elvis sightings up here think he's a fake since it's all so outrageous.''

"And probably *is* a fake."

She nodded.

Tully glanced at his watch. It was almost noon and Phil might have something more on Joyce Furillo, maybe Billy Godfrey by now. "I don't have time to argue; just give me a thumbnail about Jack the Ripper."

"Okay. First, Eternity has been plagued by serial murders off and on for years. There was a string of them around nineteen hundred. Since then there is still an occasional Ripper-style murder—and they usually happen at the beginning of a new spate of serial killings."

"Go on."

"That's the pattern. Maybe it's happened already and we haven't found the body yet. Unless you know something I don't."

Tully remained silent, knowing the hikers allegedly killed by a bear must have marked the beginning of the current murder series.

"There are also records of other Ripper notes. Only a few in an entire century, but I expect there could be more. Maybe you should check the files at the station."

"I did. They're in bad shape, very incomplete. There were no pieces of actual written evidence, no notes of any sort."

"Maybe that's a cover-up. Maybe that's a pattern you could look for in the files: that the record-keeping is scanty and inaccurate when it comes to serial killings."

"Maybe, but it's probably just sloppiness. It appears to be scanty across the board." He tapped his watch. "Gotta go."

"Wait. One more thing. Jack the Ripper was never caught. There were a number of suspects, but the important thing is that some experts believe the murders were the work of the Freemasons, who were protecting the Crown from blackmail.''

"Why do they think the Masons were involved?"

"There are a couple reasons. In Masonic culture, a traitor's throat is cut left to right and the entrails are removed and placed over the right shoulder. The other reason is this.'' She passed him a page bearing an image of the famous Ripper graffiti.

'' 'The Juwes are not The men That Will be Blamed for nothing,' '' he read.

''Commonly, it's believed that 'Juwes' is a misspelling of Jews, but that's unlikely. In early Masonic tradition, Juwes was a collective word for Jubela, Jubelo, and Jubelum, the alleged murderers of the master-mason of Solomon's Temple.'' She paused. ''It's probably all myth, but that doesn't matter. What does is that while many people believe the Freemasons were behind Jack the Ripper, it was more likely a plot to make them appear to be involved. The intestines of the women were thrown over the *left* shoulder, for one thing. For another, by 1888, only scholars of Masonry would know about the term 'Juwes.' In Britain, they were always called 'The Three Ruffians.' Also, the Juwes were dropped from Masonic rites years earlier and would have been virtually unknown to the Victorian Masons of that time.''

''And your point is?''

''If Jack wasn't a Mason himself, then he disliked Freemasons and possessed arcane knowledge, probably stemming from previous Masonic experience or activities in some other association.''

''Such as the Brotherhood of the Robes.''

Arlene nodded. ''It's certainly something to look into.'' She bent down and picked up the half dozen books and folders left on the floor and stacked them on the table. ''These are all for you. There's so much Ripper data that just dipping into these will curl your hair. You know, I've never understood the big interest in this guy.''

''Power of the press and the mystery of the unknown,'' Tully said, rising. ''I was starting to run into it a lot on the El Niño case. It wasn't such a big deal, but the press built it into a spectacle.''

''It was pretty unusual,'' Arlene said. ''It read like *Arsenic and Old Lace Meets the Manson Family.*''

Tully chuckled. "You studied the case?"

"Yes. Investigative reporter, remember? I like the way you worked." She hesitated before going on. "I studied the Delmonico case, too, and a number of your lesser known ones. Your style's impressive."

"Thanks," he said. "I thought your interest was in the occult, not police work."

"Sherlock Holmes was my childhood hero."

Tully rose. "Time to go. Thanks for the coffee."

Rios thrust the stack of books into his hands "Take these with you. Try to look through them."

He accepted the books. "I'll try."

She looked pleased. "Thanks for coming. Let's talk again soon." She accompanied him to the door and opened it. He stepped out into the hall.

"Hey there, folks! How are you doing?"

Elvis Number Two, young and plump, had just opened the door across the hall. He stood there grinning idiotically at them, then blurted, "Hey, wait right there just one second!" He disappeared into his room, leaving his door open to reveal walls covered with posters of the King.

Tully and Rios exchanged glances, then Elvis Two returned, thrusting a pair of hot pink tickets at Tully. "I hope you enjoyed the show yesterday at the luncheon, Sheriff, ma'am." He didn't wait for them to reply. "I was wanting to give you these. They're guest passes for dinner and my show at the Crystal Room at the Eternity Lodge."

"Thanks," Tully said, "but that's not necessary."

" 'Course it isn't. Look, I'm not trying to bribe you or anything like that. It's just my way of welcoming you to Eternity."

Tully accepted the tickets. "I look forward to it," he said as he tucked them in his jacket.

"Sheriff?" Elvis Two asked. "Word's around that Billy Godfrey was murdered. Is it true?"

"Word gets around fast. Did you know him?"

"Just slightly. I buy my aromatherapy supplies at the Crystal Unicorn and he waited on me sometimes."

"Are you working at Shalimar's tonight?" Tully asked.

Elvis Two nodded. "Sure am."

"Did you know a waitress there—"

"Joyce?" the impersonator interrupted.

"Furillo. Yes."

"Not too well." He paused. "I asked her out once, but she turned me down."

"I'd like to ask you a few questions about her. I'll stop by the bar later, okay?"

"No problem, Sheriff. I'm glad to help any way I can."

Twenty-three

"Vicious," Phil Katz said as he turned away from the table bearing Billy Godfrey's corpse. He stripped off his latex gloves and put them in the trash.

Tully stood near the doorway of the exam room. The reek of death and fecal matter was almost too much for him.

"Godfrey was killed by a blow to the back of the head. Something blunt and hard. By the shape of the wound, I'd guess a small sledgehammer. After he was killed, the perpetrator used something similar to this . . ." Katz turned and picked up a tool. It had a broad grip handle and the business end held a circular blade. "This is a bone saw. I would have used it to open the skull if it hadn't already been done for me."

"It's electric?"

"This one is. I don't think it was precisely this tool that he used. The cut is rougher. I'll have to get the samples to the lab to see what the blade was made of, but I'm going to guess it was the kind of power tool you'd buy at a home center. Maybe a rechargeable minicircular saw."

"I know what you're talking about," Tully said, nodding. "What about the, ah, contents of the skull?"

"Let's get out of here," Katz said as he tossed his stained white coat into a hamper.

Tully followed him into his office where they sat in comfortable leather chairs. The doctor folded his hands on his desk. "The brain was removed," he said. "I saw traces of tissue, but the bulk of it had been scooped out and taken away."

"Where's your lab?"

"There's a small one on the premises, but it's not equipped to handle this. The council won't allot any funds for more lab equipment and I can't in good conscience raise my office rates. Mayor Abbott suggested overcharging my wealthy patients." The doctor looked disgusted.

"I'll speak to him about upgrading the lab in conjunction with the sheriff's office's needs."

"Thanks," Katz said. "About Godfrey's skull. It was, as you surmised, filled with fecal matter."

"Human?"

"Animal, probably canine."

Tully was disappointed. He'd hoped the murderer had been arrogant enough—or stupid enough—to use his own excrement. That would have provided more clues to his identity. "Was there only the one triangular patch of skin missing?"

"No. There was a second one on the opposite side, at the jawline, hidden by the hair."

"You didn't find similar marks on any of the other victims?" Tully had to ask.

"No, there was nothing like that on any of the others."

"What about the ones in June? The hikers?"

Katz's eyes widened. "No. Please be cautious in speaking of it."

"No one else, including my deputies, will ever know you were the one who put me onto this."

"Thanks for your discretion," the doctor said.

"About Godfrey. How long had he been in the alley before he was found?"

"His core temperature was only a few degrees down when I arrived on scene. There was no sign of rigor. He'd been dead less than an hour." Katz sat back. "I'll have more on Godfrey later. It's Joyce Furillo that fascinates me. Liquid nitrogen. You don't see that very often. It's the only thing that would cause the foot to snap off like that.''

"Is liquid nitrogen what killed her?''

"She died of hypothermia before the nitrogen was applied. I believe she was slowly chilled to death, partly by exposure then with ice packs of some sort. There's evidence of simple frostbite on the hands, feet, ears and nose. I'll give you a copy of the report for the details.''

"What about the liquid nitrogen?'' Tully asked.

"Perhaps you can figure out the why—I certainly can't— but the what is pretty clear. She died in a container—maybe a large footlocker or trunk, maybe an old-fashioned cooler, I don't know, but it was airtight. After her death the ice packs were removed and liquid nitrogen was piped in.''

"Piped?'' asked Tully.

"Liquid nitrogen is kept in tanks. Like oxygen tanks. You spray it.''

"It's used in medicine?''

"Yes. Cryosurgery. It's usually used to freeze off suspicious moles, things of that nature. I have a small canister if you'd like to see it.''

"That's all right. How much nitrogen would be needed to freeze someone as solidly as Furillo?''

"A great deal more than what my tank holds. That's what fascinates me. Who would have enough of the stuff to pull this off? It doesn't make any sense—I can't think of anyone else who would have any, even in small quantities. But while I was working on Godfrey, it struck me. There is a supply of it in town.''

"Don't keep me in suspense, Phil.''

"Uranus 3000.''

"I'm still in suspense,'' Tully told him. "What's that?''

"It's a cryonautic business.''

"Explain, please.''

"You've heard the rumors about Walt Disney being frozen when he died?'' Phil asked.

"Of course.'' Understanding came instantly. "People have

themselves frozen so that when medicine catches up with whatever is killing them, they can be thawed out and cured.''

"That's right," Katz said. "A scam, a way to fleece the gullible legally. The wealthiest people have their entire bodies frozen. The rest just have their heads done."

"May I use your phone?"

"Certainly." Katz pushed it across the desk.

Tully called the station. There had been no reports of stolen liquid nitrogen, in the recent or far past. He plunked the handset back in its cradle. "I think I'll pay a visit to Uranus 3000. Would it be possible for you to come along, Doctor?"

Katz consulted a daily calendar. "I'm booked straight through until four-thirty," he said regretfully. "I don't know how much help I'd be anyway."

"You have medical training. That's a help."

"Barely, since I've never seen a cryo setup or read more than a few articles on it. Do you suppose the business is hiding something?"

"We have no reason to think so."

"They probably don't even know it's missing," Katz agreed. "Assuming I'm correct about their being the source."

"You're right, Doc," Tully answered. "I'll go take a quick peek."

Shalimar's was a throwback to the Playboy era, with a red-quilted entry door and similarly upholstered stools, chairs, and booths. The ceiling was claustrophobically low, the atmosphere dark and defiantly smoky. The red and black indoor-outdoor carpeting had seen better days. Tully mused that Arlene Rios would say Shalimar's was haunted by the fetid ghosts of old spirits.

A waitress clad in gold-glittered cheek-revealing shorts and a red scoop-necked T-shirt a couple sizes too small arrived at Tully's small table near the stage. Her platinum-blond hair was teased and sprayed within an inch of its life, but beneath that and the heavy makeup she was probably an attractive young woman. She placed a platter with a pastrami sandwich and a mound of greasy fries in front of him. "Want more iced tea?"

"Yes, please."

Pouring, she managed to keep her pushed-up breasts fairly close to his face, just like in the city. He'd changed into civies before coming here and he wondered if she would have been as forward if he'd worn his sheriff's badge. "When does the show start?"

"Any minute now. Elvis Two is very prompt. He's just a sweetie pie."

Overhead, suddenly discernible over the clink of glasses and murmuring voices, there was a sound like bedsprings moving. The waitress glanced up and rolled her eyes.

"What's that?" Tully asked, smiling harmlessly.

She giggled. "Just customers up in the special lounge. You can ask at the front desk about membership."

Tully nodded, almost relieved to find out that something as normal as prostitution thrived in Eternity. After his visit to Uranus 3000, he'd wondered if anything was normal. He'd renamed it Corpsicle 3000 the moment he walked into the place. It was surreally housed in a tall modern triangle of a building, faintly churchlike. Within, the faint scent of funereal flowers hung in the air so evenly that it had to be a scent added to the air-conditioning system.

No one was aware of missing nitrogen, so an inventory was conducted. At last, an employee reported that he was "pretty sure" a tank of liquid nitrogen was missing. Ms. Hoff, the director, smiled and said that it wasn't the sort of thing that thieves normally sought out and when Tully began asking questions about the building's security measures he was amazed that there was virtually no protection for the cryonauts. The video cameras were fake except for one that monitored the corpse room, and there was no real guard on duty. No one had noticed anything suspicious, which by that point didn't surprise the sheriff in the least.

After, at the station, he tried unsuccessfully to thaw out Ron

Settles. Talk about a stiff. Resentment oozed from the man like the sweat from his pores.

Tully had returned to the files, but had little success finding relevant police reports. He ordered Settles to start making sense of the filing system and, at five, took a fender-bender call before traveling on to Kate McPherson's cabin. The first half hour was spent talking over coffee, which was pleasant but unfruitful. Then she called Josh into the room. Tully asked a few questions and was soon satisfied that the boy had not been approached by the note-writer thus far. After that, he settled down to have the talk with Josh he'd promised Kate.

The conversation was painful because the boy reminded him so much of his own son—not only was he the age Kevin would have been had he lived, he resembled him in coloring and appearance. Tully forced himself to carefully explain things to the boy and to answer his questions.

Kate was shocked to find out that Josh was aware of her terror, but it didn't surprise Tully in the least. Explaining about the notes and hang-up calls helped Josh understand her fears and calmed him. After Josh had gone upstairs to do his homework, Kate thanked Tully profusely then invited him to dinner in the near future.

That was the big shock for Tully. He found he really wanted to have dinner with Kate McPherson. She was the most normal person he'd met here. He liked her and her son, even though he tried to feel nothing. So he said yes. And now, sitting in Shalimar's, that troubled him almost as much as the unsolved murders.

"Ladies and gentlemen, guys and gals, listen up!" The robust lounge-lizard voice bounded through the sound system and brought Tully out of his reverie. "Here's the man you've been waiting for, the man with a voice that'll melt your wives and heat up your girlfriends—isn't that right, ladies? Mr. Vegas himself, our own Elvis Presley Number Two!"

Spotlights played over the small stage as red brocade curtains opened to reveal Elvis Two in silhouette, head down, white cape fluttering. Canned music came up and the entertainer launched directly into the most unlikely song of all, "In the Ghetto," though Tully thought, it was appropriate to the surroundings.

Tully picked at his soggy pastrami. Obviously this was a place to come and drink, not eat. Elvis, however, wasn't bad. Once he got into real rock and roll, Tully found he could ignore the booze stink, stale cigarettes, and the lousy food and just enjoy the music.

After twenty minutes, the impersonator did an excellent rendition of "Teddy Bear" then bowed. "Folks, I'll be back for another set in half an hour and I'll be taking requests." He let his lip do a curl then made a gun-cocking motion and winked at Tully. "Before I give up the stage, I wantcha all to meet a special visitor."

Tully shook his head no.

Elvis didn't notice. "Well, folks, he's not really a visitor, he's our newest resident. Our new sheriff, Zach Tully. Stand up and take a bow, Sheriff!"

Tully cringed. The place was silent except for squeaking bedsprings overhead.

"Don't be shy now, Sheriff. Take a bow!"

Tully half stood. Elvis Two began applauding and the customers added anemic clapping of their own. Quickly, Tully seated himself. A hand rested lightly on his shoulder and he looked up into the breasts of his waitress. "You should've told me who you were, Sheriff," she purred.

"Why? I'm off-duty," he said lightly.

She lifted her eyes toward the squeaking ceiling. "It just would've been nice."

"Don't worry about it," he said. "But maybe you can answer a question for me."

"It's just a members-only lounge. Nothing but drinks and sometimes lap dances."

"Not about that. Did you know Joyce Furillo very well?"

"Oh!" She glanced around then perched on the chair opposite Tully. "Joyce. That's why you're here."

"Were you friends?"

"Not really. I haven't worked here long and she was an old-timer."

"A lifer?"

"What's that?"

"Never mind. Go on."

"She was really old, like in her thirties, and she was kind of a quiet type. She never hung out with us girls. Her boyfriend, Larry, he always picked her up after work. That was sweet."

"Had they dated long?"

"I've only been here for four months, so at least that long."

"When did you last see her?"

"Ooh, I thought about that. We all talked about it already. We saw her the night she got killed. Larry picked her up like always. And then . . ." She made a slicing motion across her neck. "She and Larry were dead. Isn't it awful? Do you know who did it?"

"That's what I'm trying to find out. Did Joyce have any enemies?"

The girl shrugged. "I don't think so. She was quiet and polite. She didn't let men pinch her butt or nothing, so her tips weren't real big, so maybe that pissed off some customers, but probably not. Lots of the girls don't allow that."

"Sheriff Tully, I was really glad to see you in the audience!" Elvis Two, swabbing his face with a towel, came up to the table and smiled broadly. "Didja enjoy the show so far?"

"Very much."

The waitress stood up. "You sit, E-Two. You want your usual?"

"Yeah, thanks, Alice."

She left and was back with a brimming glass of orange juice and an airplane-sized bottle of vodka before Elvis Two had finished squirreling compliments out of Tully. "Thanks, hon," the impersonator drawled. He gave her a lip-curl and winked. She giggled then wiggled off into the smoke. Elvis drank down half the juice in one gulp then added the vodka to the rest.

Tully didn't find out much. Furillo and Fraser had been going out for six months and were evidently seeing one another

exclusively. Elvis backed up everything the waitress had said
about Joyce and told him a little about Larry Fraser, but it was
all secondhand info. "I gotta get back to work. You sticking
around for the next set?"

"I'm sorry, but not tonight. I've had several very long days
and I have to be up early."

After Elvis left the table, Tully paid the check and prowled
around a little, talking to the bartenders and the servers and
finally, the manager. There was nothing new and Tim Hapscomb's search of Furillo's apartment had yielded nothing infor-
mative, nor had Settles' search of Larry Fraser's condo. Fraser's
neighbors weren't crazy about him because he kept late hours
and played his stereo too loud, but Settles said nothing suspicious came up. Tully figured he'd double check on the neighbors.

Finished at Shalimar's, he walked outside. The air blew cold
and fresh and cut into his lungs, removing the stink of the bar.
After taking several deep breaths, he walked to his car and
went by the station, found Hapscomb was having a quiet night,
then drove home, fighting back yawns all the way. Sleep had
never sounded so good.

Despite his exhaustion, Tully's sleep was marred by nightmares. Finally, he fell into the grip of the death dream and
couldn't wake up.

The scent of roses. Instantly, his flesh prickled up in goose
bumps and Tully stopped in his tracks, one hand grasping the
doorknob of his neat little house in Santo Verde, the other
ready to drop the bouquet of daisies in favor of his .38. In
another instant, he forced himself to relax. He'd had roses on
the brain ever since the Backdoor Man began killing and now
smelling them in his own house had produced the same reaction.

He smelled roses because they were in bloom. The backyard
was overrun with them and Linda must have filled the vases
in the house with the fragrant flowers. Chiding himself, he
pulled the front door closed and turned the deadbolt. "Linda?"

he called softly, poking his head into the living room. She wasn't there. He glanced up the staircase and saw that the hall light wasn't lit on the second floor. Linda was probably righteously irritated and had put their son to bed after having to make up excuses for his father's not being home for the birthday party. With any luck, she would be reading to Kevin in his room, giving Tully a few more minutes of grace.

He raised his voice, called again, "Don't pay the ransom, honey, I got away!" Linda always laughed at that, even when she was trying to be angry.

There was no reply. Before going upstairs to apologize to them, he walked through the small dining room to the kitchen. Light shone beneath the heavy swinging door. Kevin might be asleep already and, if he was, Linda was likely to be fuming in the kitchen. He pushed the door open. "Honey?"

The room was empty. A frosted chocolate cake with virgin candles waited on the counter along with gaily printed paper plates and party hats. In the sink were two dinner plates, silverware, and glasses. He was glad they'd eaten dinner without him; it eased the guilt a little. Quickly, he opened the refrigerator and breathed a sigh of relief as he spotted a plastic-wrapped plate containing a thick corned beef sandwich with a cluster of grapes on the side. That meant he wasn't in too much trouble. Or at least he wasn't when she'd made the sandwich.

He let the refrigerator door fall shut and turned, ready to go upstairs and throw himself on his family's mercy.

Then he saw it. The chain guard hung off the back door and the mounting square had been pulled out of the plaster wall. The door wasn't quite shut.

"Damn." He whispered the word, turning, scanning, in cop mode as he pulled his .38 from the shoulder holster beneath his windbreaker. Approaching the door, he saw a small smear of red on the knob. *Blood.*

Quickly he moved back through the house, alert to every sound, every shadow, his senses heightened, the raw fear pumping through his veins.

Nothing. He moved to the stairs, letting his gun lead the way. The roses smelled stronger now.

The staircase seemed to telescope in length as he took the steps. An eternity passed before he gained the landing. Flattening himself against the wall, smelling roses, he edged along the hallway to the first room, the bath. He waited a few seconds, listening, then reached around the corner and snapped on the light. Immediately, he plunged into the room, gun ready, and threw back the shower curtain.

No one was there.

He saw the sink, then the floor, and stifled a moan. Bloody footprints crossed the pink tile and watery blood puddled in the basin. He'd seen this and far worse many times, but for the first time in years, he felt the shockwaves.

Someone's watching you!

Get a grip! He forced himself to think like a cop, ordered himself to forget that this was his own house, his own family at stake. It worked well enough to get him back out into the hall. He couldn't shake the sensation of eyes upon him, but he had to go on.

Cold sweat dripped into his eyes as he approached the bedroom he and Linda shared. *Please let them be all right. Please.*

Swallowing hard, he flipped the bedroom light switch and rushed the room, turning left and right, yanking the closet open before he focused on the bed.

"Linda?" She was under the covers. He could see her closed eyes and the tip of her nose above the hunter-green bedspread, which was barely visible beneath the bowers of white roses thrown across it. His heart sank and now he acknowledged another scent—blood—which had been there all along. "Linda, honey? Are you asleep?" He heard his slight, cracked voice as if someone else had spoken. Desperate hope filled him as he pulled back the covers.

And drained away as he saw what had been done to her.

The world reeled, black spots formed in front of his eyes. "No!" he growled as he turned and ran out the door, then down the hall, vaguely hearing himself scream, "Kevin!" over and over as he ran for his son's room, not caring if the murderer was waiting there, hoping he was because he would tear him apart with his bare hands. He could feel the monster's eyes on him as he ran, but he didn't care. His son might still be alive.

He pushed open the door and saw the pitiful little body sprawled across the blood-soaked rag rug that Linda had sewn while she was pregnant. White roses ringed the horrible tableau. His son had suffered even worse humiliation and horror than Linda had and Tully, dying inside, dropped to his knees, sick, in shock, tears streaming down his cheeks. He would have recognized the work without the roses.

He had no idea how long he remained by the body of his son or how long he stared at a single spatter of blood on the floor in front of him. He only knew that his wife and son were dead and that Kevin would never blow out the candles on his cake. And it was his fault. *His fault.*

At last, unwilling to look upon his son's body again, Tully turned slightly on his aching knees before he looked up from the floor and across the small bedroom to the little desk they'd bought Kevin last Christmas. On top of the desk was a cup of pencils, a 64-Crayola box, and the small blackboard mounted on the wall.

He stared at the words scrawled on the board for several seconds before his brain processed them. "Now we're even, hero. The Backdoor Man."

Tully rose, steady, in control, cold as ice. "You'll pay for this, you son of a bitch."

Somewhere below, a door might have slammed.

Twenty-four

August 19

> Death is not the greatest loss in life. The greatest
> loss is what dies inside us while we live.

—Norman Cousins

His view of the dinner party in the McPherson residence
was excellent. Jack, infinitely patient, was comfortably hidden
among the branches of a dignified old fir across the road from
Kate's cabin. Having arrived a full hour before Zach Tully, he
had now been in the tree for three hours.

Dinner theater, he thought, amused. Kate had opened the
drapes—*the stage curtains*—twenty minutes before the sheriff's arrival. She had been excited, he could see that in the way
she kept bustling back and forth between the kitchen and the
living room stage.

She wanted Tully, Jack thought with mild disgust, and she
wanted him badly.

He couldn't see into the kitchen, but he could smell the
spaghetti sauce. Or lasagna, or something else Italian and so
delectable that he ended up eating his own meal—three candy

bars stashed in the pockets of his dark green jacket—before Tully had even arrived. He envied the sheriff the meal and the company, although the boy was certainly excess baggage. Young Josh was worthless, except as bait.

The boy had set the small dining table ten minutes before Tully arrived. At the same time, Kate had scurried upstairs. The blinds over her bedroom windows were turned to let the dying sun into the room, and in turn, that allowed Jack to watch Kate as she changed from a peach sweater and blue jeans to a red buttondown shirt and black pants and finally back into indigo jeans and a tantalizing black V-neck pullover that clung more closely to her body than her first choice. Women might be prey, but they knew how to bring their hunters to their knees.

Tully arrived while she was upstairs. Jack saw her peer between the blinds, and with his binoculars, noted the smile lighting up her face as the cop climbed out of his Camaro. He was definitely not here on police business.

Kate ran her fingers through her hair, fluffing it, then disappeared from sight. A moment later she reappeared, opening her front door to Tully and his bottle of wine. The hunter entered the lair.

For the next half hour, Kate zipped in and out of the kitchen, smiling, animated, and undoubtedly wafting sweet perfume over Tully. He was made to remain on the couch—when he tried to follow her into the kitchen, she reached out and touched his chest in a mock push, then led him back to the sofa. Tully would be allowed no woman's work. Instead he was entertained by her son. He was shy at first and Jack watched as the boy warmed up. Man and child were soon in animated discussion, their hands and chins wagging away, undoubtedly talking about sports of some sort. That's what they all did.

Dinner soon commenced. The three sat at the table, a neat little family. They had a good time, the adults each drinking only one glass of wine, the boy downing his spaghetti—Jack's first guess had been correct—with several glasses of milk.

Dinner ended in dessert and coffee an hour and a half after Tully's arrival. The boy was sent upstairs and the couple repaired to the sofa with the remainder of the wine. They were still there now, and although they had finished the wine some time ago, there was no move to fetch more. Jack was surprised they were so moderate in their libations; he had expected them to get drunk and fall into bed quickly. But this was more intriguing. More challenging.

The couple was talking, seated a pristine two feet apart. Tully had made none of the usual masculine moves, had not even draped his arm over the back of the couch. It was curious especially since Jack was fairly sure Tully wasn't fucking the reporter. Maybe he preferred boys. Or, Jack reluctantly admitted, perhaps he had a modicum of self-control.

Three hours in the tree and Jack's own limbs felt as stiff as the fir's. He reached in his pocket and felt the candy wrappers and the small envelope behind them with his gloved fingers. Slowly he began stretching his muscles in preparation for the climb down.

The dinner had gone well, and Kate, sitting on the overstuffed sofa, talking with Zach Tully, was pleased with everything. Josh had behaved and Zach, no, Tully—he didn't like to be called by his first name—Tully had seemed to truly enjoy her son's company. And hers.

She wasn't looking for a new father for Josh any more than she wanted to find a new husband; she valued her freedom too much. But it was nice to think Josh might find a male friend in the sheriff. She'd been overjoyed—and more than a little startled—when Josh ran into the kitchen before dinner and asked if he could go fishing with Tully in his pond. She asked him if he'd invited himself and he'd said no. Tully backed it up and invited her along as well, suggesting they have a picnic while the weather remained fair.

She surprised herself by nearly turning him down. There was something frightening in his eyes, something that she knew was in hers as well. No involvement, she told herself. She could have Tully for a friend just as Josh could. There was nothing dangerous in that.

Now, the wine long gone, they shared easy conversation. She talked far too much about Carl, telling Tully about her dread of his upcoming visit. Tully seemed honestly interested and asked questions that led toward the possibility that the hang-up caller and the note writer might be related to her ex-husband. But underneath, she didn't believe it any more than Tully did. "I wish I could blame those things on Carl," she said, "but he's on a book tour and he isn't the type to hire people to harass me." She couldn't help chuckling. "He'd want to do that himself."

Tully smiled briefly. "I know it's unlikely, especially under the circumstances—"

"You mean my finding the body?"

"Yes. However, if you hadn't found it, your ex would be suspect for the calls and notes, so I had to make sure you don't feel Carl's up to something."

"No," she said. "Not that he isn't capable of it. And he was my first suspect, but I realized it was wishful thinking. Carl is a master manipulator and it was perversely satisfying to think he might be guilty." She gazed into Tully's eyes and her stomach did a little flip as he returned the look. "But," she forced herself to continue, "Carl's very subtle. Image is everything and he wouldn't do anything so pedestrian. He's more of a gaslighter."

Tully nodded.

"May I ask you a question?"

"Of course."

"The person who wrote the note signed his name with different spellings. 'Jackie' with an I-E and 'Jacky' with a Y. That makes it seem like a prankster, doesn't it?"

"Under other circumstances, I might agree, but in this case, I think it's an attempt to mess with our minds."

"You mean he's doing it for fun?"

"It's likely." Tully leaned toward her. "Kate."

Her stomach tilted again. "Yes?"

"I want you to be extremely cautious. You and Josh both."

Those weren't the words she'd expected when he'd said her name so earnestly. She was both relieved and disappointed. "We'll be careful."

"Is there any chance I can talk you into staying in town or with friends for a few days? This place is too isolated."

"No." She paused. "You're really worried, aren't you?"

"Yes."

"Why?"

"It's a feeling."

"A hunch?"

"Yes. A strong one. Maybe it's something about the notes. Maybe it's . . . something else. I don't know." His eyes bored into hers, searching. "It's a feeling that's been with me since the first night, but right now it's so strong that it's all I can do to sit still instead of taking a look around."

"You think someone's spying on us?"

"I don't think it. I feel it." He glanced at the forest silhouetted by moonlight beyond the glass doors to the deck. "It's been a long time. I'm out of practice and I'm probably overreacting because of the notes."

"The guy would have to be nuts to be out there tonight, with your car parked in my driveway."

"Yeah." Tully studied her a moment longer then stood up. "You make a good point. Stay put."

She watched, heart pounding, as he crossed to the sliding doors, checked the lock and drew the drapes. Moving to the front door, he looked out the peephole. "Stay put," he murmured as he opened the door and peered into the darkness beyond the porch light. Finally, he began to pull the door closed then grunted, "Huh," and bent down.

Rising, he closed and locked the door, then turned to face her, a small envelope dangling from his fingertips.

She looked at the white square, then at Tully, then back at the envelope. "Under the welcome mat?"

"Yes. It's addressed to you," he said quietly.

"It looks like an invitation," she said lamely.

"It's the same handwriting."

She swallowed, feeling ill. "You open it."

He nodded. "I'm going into the kitchen to get a knife to slit it and a plastic bag to put it in."

She watched him go, heard him rattling the locks on the doors, then drawers being opened and finally a clatter of utensils when he found the right one. He reappeared, the envelope and a note visible within the Ziploc bag.

"What does it say?" Her voice trembled.

" 'My Dear,' " he read tonelessly. " *'You make a lovely family, but I feel it my duty to remind you that Zachary Tully couldn't save the lives of his own wife and son. What makes you think he can save you and your offspring? Your Friend, Jacky.'* "

"Dear God," she murmured, feeling his humiliation. Standing up, she crossed to him, not speaking as he stared at the note. Gently, she touched his hand. He jumped and stared at her, eyes slightly unfocused. "I'm sorry," she whispered, beginning to pull her hand away.

He focused on her and caught her hand in his, held it. His was warm but his voice sounded numb with cold. "It's not your fault."

Twenty-five

It was nearly nine o'clock, but the Eternity Ragtime Band showed no signs of wrapping up their Wednesday Night Concert in the Park. Dressed in red uniforms with gold and black braid, the twenty-piece orchestra performed in the old-fashioned bandshell as families and couples looked on. The nearby fountain bubbled a counterpoint to "The Man on the Flying Trapeze" and children up past their bedtimes played tag while dogs chased Frisbees and teenagers necked in the shadows beneath the trees. It looked and sounded like a Norman Rockwell painting come to life.

On top of all that, the weather was perfect, at least by Eternity's chilly standards. Many of the locals wore shirtsleeves but Arlene Rios was cold despite her jeans, sweater, and windbreaker.

The whole place seemed unreal as she strolled the winding walk looking at the people, looking for a faceless killer. Was he here? The park was a good meeting spot; with all the music and noise and people it was unlikely anyone would overhear anything they shouldn't. Like a friendly pickup line or a request for directions. How would the murderer approach? Buy something from the pretty young woman working the popcorn machine? Follow someone silently into the shadows? Some of the dark areas could even mask a murder in progress.

She realized she had wandered into just such an area. As she stood beneath a shadowy umbrella of oak limbs, she forced herself to remain calm.

Where was he now? She could be staring right at him and not know it. Or maybe he was staring at her and she didn't know it.

"Spare a dollar, miss?"

The man dressed in layers of shabby clothes sat crosslegged between the roots of the oak tree, hidden further in the darkness cast by a garbage receptacle. He stared up at her, his face nearly hidden by a knit cap and several days' worth of dark stubble. His eyes were unreadable in the darkness, but she felt them on her.

Almost panic-stricken—not quite—she reached in her pocket and pulled out some change. He held his hand up and she let the coins drop from too high so that they bounced off his filthy hand and scattered on the grass around him. He started to rise and a British voice from behind her asked, "Are you in need of help?"

"No, no thank you." The bum had risen to his knees, the better to search for change. She turned toward the voice, but all she saw was a man's receding form silhouetted against the bandshell lights. She fled toward the lights and people, hoping to meet the Englishman, but he was gone like a phantom in the night.

There was a pause in the music as she neared the bandstand. The courtly old bandleader accepted a microphone from a young boy. "And now, for your listening and viewing pleasure, we shall conclude our evening with our own Stars and Stripes Spectacular."

As the band struck up a Sousa march, a blaze of fireworks hit the sky, shooting stars rising from behind the bandshell.

At nine-thirty, Valerie Saylor, former cocktail waitress, entered Shalimar's where she ordered a gin and tonic from

Jake. She took it to a dark corner to survey the market here, away from the fireworks.

Jake was a nice guy. Since she'd been fired from this dive— the manager caught her indulging in the wrong kind of crack— she was no longer welcome anymore, but Jake ignored the rule, serving her and letting her make a living as long as she did it without calling attention to herself in any way. Valerie appreciated that because hooking in Eternity wasn't the easiest way to make a living, not unless you worked the club upstairs at Shalimar's. The girls called it the Almost Mile High Club. She used to call it that, too. Now she called it competition.

This place—not just Shalimar's, but all of Eternity—was such a pig hole she could hardly stand it anymore. The loonies ran wild, the whores at Shalimar's were condoned and boned by the oh-so-perfect male council members—nearly all the males except for the one and only who would have been welcome. Even if Elvis One was a loony like the rest of the lookalikes, he was one hunka-hunka burning love. Or he might be if he ever took it out, which he didn't, at least as far as she knew.

She sipped her drink, her eyes still adjusting to the darkness. The park song-and-dance fest would be ending soon—she could just hear the occasional booms of the fireworks—and then the half-empty lounge would fill up with more than enough beef for her and the girls upstairs.

Elvis Two was between sets and she saw him relaxing with his orange juice and vodka at another dark table nearby. He saw her looking his way and raised his eyebrows. That meant he wouldn't be adverse to a quickie if she had the time. She raised hers back and smiled slightly, telling him she was sorry, not tonight. Elvis Two was a nice guy, but it took him too long to get off, considering the money he could pay. And that meant having to brush her teeth, her hair, which he'd mess up with his hands, and most of her makeup, all for twenty dollars and the same number of minutes, at least. And if her luck was really bad, like last time, he'd take even longer and the manager would barge in to see why he wasn't back on stage and she'd be busted, and Jake wouldn't be so good about overlooking her presence.

A waitress she didn't recognize, young, too blond and too made up, approached and offered her a refill. She accepted, scanning the room, hearing the rumble of more voices as the quilted door opened and closed, opened and closed. The fireworks were over.

The girl brought her drink and Valerie gave her a hefty tip, even if she might be the competition. Then she waited. She was bait and a fish would bite eventually.

It only took ten minutes, which would have pleased Jake, were he watching. The man approached her table politely. "Hello."

"Hi," she said breezily.

"Are you alone, miss?"

"Maybe," she replied coyly as she tried to get a good look at the fellow, which was hard because of the dim light and his facial fur, a well-groomed short beard and mustache. She couldn't see what he was wearing beneath the black trench coat, but that, at least, looked pricey. "You couldn't be local," she said. "You must be a visitor?"

"Touring."

That was pretty much what she expected him to say. "Are you waiting for someone? Your wife?"

"No. I'm not married." His voice was rich and pleasant and veddy veddy British. She loved that so much that if she hadn't had to make a living, she might pick him up just for the accent. "And I'm quite alone."

"Me, too," she said. "Have a seat."

"Thank you. What's your name, if I might be so bold as to ask?"

"Valerie."

"May I refresh your drink, Valerie?" he asked as the blond waitress approached.

"Sure. One more," she told the waitress. Normally, she would have stopped at two, but the drinks were weak and Valerie knew she was going to have a great time. She loved it when she liked her work and this one was just about in the bag. She smiled to herself. In the sack was more accurate.

"You, sir?" the girl asked.

"A brandy. The best you have."

"Be right back."

When the girl was gone, the Brit turned to Valerie. "Are you a working woman, Valerie?"

He had great eyes, vaguely familiar eyes, but she knew she would have recognized the accent if she'd run into him before. "You mean, do I have to earn my rent?" she asked coyly.

He nodded.

"Yes I do."

"You're a very attractive woman, Valerie."

"You're not so bad yourself . . . Tell me what to call you."

He reached across the table and slowly brushed his manicured fingers across the back of her hand. "Call me Jack."

Twenty-six

"Thanks, Deputy," said Tully, crossing the road to join Ron Settles, who was climbing out of the black and white Crown Vic parked across from the McPherson residence. "The stalker was here tonight, so I'd like you to stick around until I get back."

"Inside or out?"

"Out," Tully told him. Kate had only agreed to allow Ron Settles on the premises on the condition that she didn't have to let him in her house. "Just keep an eye out. I don't want to destroy any evidence the perp might have left, so don't poke around unless it's absolutely necessary. I'll be back within the hour. Let Hapscomb take any calls that come in. If it gets busier, page me. Don't leave here. If it's a matter of life and death, take the McPhersons with you. They aren't to be left alone."

Settles, leaning against the Crown Vic, lit a cigarette. It glowed red in the darkness. "You spending the night here?"

None of your fucking business, Tully stopped himself from saying. "Someone needs to, and a four-man force is too small to take care of it officially, so yes. I'm going to stick around."

The deputy leered at him. "Good-looking woman."

"Listen, Settles." Tully was ready to blow. "If Kate McPherson were an eighty-year-old hermaphrodite with fifty cats, I'd be doing the same thing, so you keep your goddamned smart mouth shut." He took a deep calming breath. "You're on very thin ice already, my friend, so just follow orders. You got that?"

Settles blew a smoke ring. "Thin ice. That's funny. I like that."

"I said, you got that?"

"Yeah, I got it."

"Deputy, I don't know what the hell you're doing on a police force in the first place and, frankly, I'd just as soon fire you on the spot. I don't think much of your attitude and if I hear one word about your being rude to Ms. McPherson, you'll be out on your ass by morning."

"You can't fire me."

"The hell I can't."

"Only the mayor can fire me."

"Don't count on it." Tully stalked across the road to his own car and drove off into the darkness.

He was barely able to think. He'd nearly been a basket case since he'd read the note about his family, and although he wanted to remain with Kate and Josh, he had to have some time alone to think. To feel. That was why he announced he had to pick up the Explorer. It was a valid excuse. He might need the radio.

Why didn't I listen to my instincts? He drove the winding road, vaguely aware he'd gotten lost again. *Why didn't I listen?* What he'd told Kate was true; he hadn't listened because he knew he was getting too personally involved.

He drove on, wire-tight. His stomach hurt and his head ached and he wished he'd never come to this goddamned town, a town where the dead were resurrected and buried memories clawed their way out of graves that should have remained untouched and undesecrated. A town where dreams were reborn.

He approached a curve, driving too fast, not caring. *You don't want to be responsible for Kate and Josh. What'll you do if they die, too?*

Oh, God, I want to die. Tears, four years late, streamed down his face. He clung desperately to the steering wheel as his tires squealed and tried to hold the road.

You die, they die! "Shit!" he yelled as the Camaro's wheels edged onto the shoulder, spitting gravel. He couldn't let it happen, not again. "Come on, come on, come on," he urged, trying to keep all four tires on the ground. He couldn't let it roll. He hadn't fastened his seat belt. He'd be roadkill. "Come on!"

The right tires hit the road again and he concentrated on driving. In an instant, it was over, the car straight on the road, safely out of the long curve. The trees thinned, providing a view of Icehouse's southern side. Weird greenish-blue light fanned below the peak.

"What the—" He almost lost control again, but corrected the steering and slowed, turning left across the road to stop in the turnout where Larry Fraser had been mutilated.

There, he put the car in park, the engine idling, and watched the phenomena. It was beautiful, like the Northern Lights, and it made him think of Linda and Kevin and how much they would enjoy seeing it.

The tears came again and wouldn't stop. Years and years worth, hidden in all the anger and rage that had seen him through since his family's murder, hidden in a heart he thought had turned to stone.

When, at last, he ran out of tears and raised his head, the skies were dark and dead. But Zach Tully had finally been resurrected.

Twenty-seven

August 20

> Logic, n. The art of thinking and reasoning in strict
> accordance with the limitations and incapacities of
> human misunderstanding.
>
> —Ambrose Bierce

Reginald "Call me Reggie" Skelton, councilman, publisher and editor-in-chief of *The Eternity Weekly Herald,* was a dapper little man with a waxed mustache who looked like he ought to take tea at four and say "Cheerio, old chap" at the slightest provocation. Despite his Victorian appearance—he wore a prim and proper black pinstripe suit and maroon silk vest—he claimed to be from New, not old, England. Except for the fastidiousness, Reggie seemed relatively normal, though Tully thought the bowler hat hanging on an oak clothes tree in the corner was pushing it.

But even if he was somewhat eccentric, when Tully arrived at the newspaper offices and asked to go through the morgue, Reggie Skelton had been gracious and helpful, even bringing him several cups of coffee over the next two hours.

It was now noon and Tully's stomach wasn't happy. It wasn't hunger, but worry. At dawn, he'd begun searching the woods outside Kate's cabin. It had yielded two Snickers wrappers hidden under a rock at the base of a large pine directly across the road from the residence. Though Tully carefully bagged them, along with some broken twigs and bark scuffed from the tree trunk, he doubted any of it would yield much in the way of useful evidence.

Tully settled into the oak captain's chair across from Reggie Skelton and nursed a fresh cup of coffee while Reggie stirred sugar cubes into his own fine china cup. Worry ate at him; worry over the murders, the lack of cooperation from the town government, worries for Kate and Josh's safety, and worry about the questions Kate would ask him concerning his past. He felt ready to burst. He needed to do something, to act. Spending two hours reading through old newspapers had given him a way to bring up the bogus bear attack, but it hadn't satisfied any other need.

Skelton took a dainty sip. "Did you find everything you needed?" He eyed the Xeroxed articles in Tully's hand.

"Everything I need at the moment."

"Sally showed you how to operate the microfilm machine for the older stories?"

"Yes, but I'm only interested in newer articles for now."

"Is there any other way I might be of service?"

"I hope so." Tully gave him his friendliest smile. "Can you answer a few questions?"

"I'll do my best."

"I'm trying to familiarize myself with Eternity. With the patterns of life here. One thing that I've heard is that we have an usually high homicide rate. As the editor of the *Herald*, you're the expert. Is it true?"

"Unfortunately, yes."

"Any idea why?"

"Perhaps, but it will sound ridiculous."

"Try me."

"It might have to do with Icehouse Circle."

"How so?" Tully waited for the inevitable spiel about evil time travelers.

"Maybe it has something to do with the earth itself," Skelton said, surprising Tully completely. "Something in the makeup of the mountain, of the Circle in particular, that interferes with machinery and animals. If you've been up there, Sheriff, you may have noticed the rather upsetting physical sensations or loss of your own directional sense. The feeling that something isn't right. An unidentifiable sensation that speaks to your more primitive aspects. Something that makes gooseflesh stand alert and causes your body to engage the fight-or-flight response."

"I've experienced some of that, yes."

"If the earth can do such things, might it not also be able to interfere with other aspects of behavior? Eternity—Icehouse Mountain in particular—attracts eccentrics, my dear Sheriff. Most of the people who tell you they've come from another time or place are upstanding citizens. They don't cheat, steal, or lie. They believe what they tell you and you'll never convince them otherwise. Thus, the earth here can cause aberrations in many, but merely exacerbate psychopathic behavior in a few. That's my theory, for what it's worth." He paused. "Not many agree with it. They prefer the more supernatural explanations."

"I've heard it from two other people, so you're not alone." Tully studied him, thinking that the publisher preferred this explanation, too; he'd blinked and looked away too much while talking. "It's an interesting theory. Would it explain the behavior of the town council?"

Skelton looked confused. "How so?"

"They go to all the trouble of getting me up here then refuse to cooperate," he said ingenuously. "As a whole, I'd have to say that the council has actually avoided me."

Skelton blushed. "I've thought about that, Sheriff Tully, and I might have an answer for that as well."

"Go on."

"Individually, men are rational, reasoning creatures, for the most part. But put them together in a group and their less attractive traits surface, from a tendency toward jealous self-protectiveness to mass hysteria in the extreme. And even a group as small as the council isn't immune. We want you to solve our crimes, but we are also jealous with our meager secrets. We're a very small society here, unused to newcomers."

Smooth talker. " I have the impression that the mayor runs a tight ship."

"Ambrose? Yes, yes, he does. But under that crust of his, he's no different from the rest of us. If anything, he's the most fragile. It's a natural consequence of his arrogance. He can't tolerate being crossed, but he's also a good man. These things make him protective, perhaps even when he ought not be."

"Rumor has it he's Ambrose Bierce."

"Rumor has it."

"Do you believe it?"

"Do you?"

"I'd appreciate an honest answer," Tully said, low-key and friendly.

"Logic flies in the face of honesty, Sheriff. I wish I *could* tell you what I believe."

Tully believed him. "Why can't you? Because of the Brotherhood?"

Skelton stared at him for a long moment then chuckled. "There's nothing like a good conspiracy, eh, Sheriff?"

"What do you mean?"

"No one used to be interested in our version of the Lions Club," Reggie said glibly. "Nowadays, any group maintaining any hint of secrecy is assumed to be cloaking some weird conspiracy. It's another unsettling aspect of humanity, don't you think?"

"You tell me."

"As a journalist, I must say it is. We reporters try to do our work in an unbiased way, but even so, people pick up on simple facts and twist them in whichever way they wish the story to go." Reggie returned his gaze to the Xeroxed pages. "Tell me about the patterns you're pursuing. Perhaps I can be more helpful."

"I'm looking for evidence that the murderer was active prior to July."

"There was the homeless man, Bertram Meeks. I assume you know about him."

"Yes, I do." Tully paused, thinking Reggie just didn't have a good poker face.

"That's the only murder I know of in recent months that shares the, ah ... gruesome qualities. There were two other murders, but they were both results of bar brawls."

"Yes. Those were in the station's files, though we're missing most of our reports. Reggie, I need your help." Skelton didn't ask why the police files were skimpy, making Tully pretty sure the council was responsible for all the missing material. "I'm looking at accidental deaths with the thought that they may only *appear* accidental. Like these." He pushed one of the pages across the desk to Skelton who donned a pair of wire-rimmed reading glasses and frowned as he read it.

" 'The bodies of Loretta Horowitz, 21, and Jessica Findhorn, 24, were discovered today not far from the southern trailhead on Icehouse Mountain. The two women had taken out camping permits on June 10 and filed plans to hike to Icehouse Summit. Both were experienced hikers.

" 'The women are believed to have been attacked by a rogue bear which has previously been sighted in the region. The bodies were badly decomposed. It is believed they had been dead for at least a week.

" 'The women, from Dayton, Ohio, were on vacation. At their families' request, the bodies were cremated and shipped to Ohio for internment.

" 'Asked about further danger from the bear, Mayor Ambrose Abbott has promised that capturing the animal is Eternity's first priority.' "

Reggie Skelton set the article down. "Surely, you don't think it *wasn't* a bear?"

"Just a thought."

"Did you find the article about the capture of the bear? That confirms it, doesn't it?"

"I found it. Jackson Coop shot it?"

"Jackson may be slightly cracked, but he's also a crack shot." Reggie chuckled. "Have you met him yet?"

"I met him briefly." Coop liked talking about hunting so it seemed odd he wouldn't have mentioned such a recent shoot to Tully. Maybe he only bragged about bagging a Bigfoot. He manufactured a smile. "I'll bet he took the skin to make a new Bigfoot."

Skelton looked pleased. "Now that you mention it, I'll bet that's exactly what he did."

"I'm surprised the paper didn't run a photo of the hunter and his prize."

"We would have if he'd given us the chance, but he hauled it away too quickly." He chuckled. "He made it into a Bigfoot. Ambrose will get a kick out of that. It's obvious, but it had never occurred to me, I'm ashamed to say."

"Did anyone other than Coop see the bear?"

"Not after its demise, but there were sightings before that."

"Are you acquainted with any of the witnesses?"

"No." Skelton smoothed his mustache with one dainty finger. "Ask your deputies, perhaps they'll have some information." Fidgety, the editor smoothed his mustache again. "Do you really think the women might have been murdered, not attacked by a bear?"

Tully hesitated. "Not really," he lied. "I just want to be thorough. Did you write the articles?"

"Yes, I did."

"Did you go to the site?"

"Yes, but the bodies had been removed by the time I arrived."

"Well, thanks for your time," Tully said, rising. "And for the use of your copier." He gathered up the articles.

"I hope I've been of some help?"

Tully shook Skelton's hand. "You've been a great deal of help."

Twenty-eight

"We'll be fine," Kate said firmly. She leaned against her Jeep in the Bigfoot Tours lot and looked at Tully. "You have a car coming by at least every hour tonight, right?"

"Yes, but it would be better if you and Josh would spend the night in town. At a motel or a friend's."

"Can't afford the motel and you're the closest thing I have to a friend."

"You can stay with me—"

"Don't even say it. I'm staying home. I won't be driven out of my own home by the bastard."

"Don't get mad at me. I'm just concerned about you and Josh."

Her anger subsided. "We were without any special protection for a month and nothing happened. We'll be fine."

Tully gazed steadily back at her. "I'm speaking strictly as a cop. You're taking an unnecessary risk."

"Look, if he wants to get me, he's going to get me wherever I am. I know my own home. I know the sounds it makes. We're as safe there as anywhere, especially with the patrol car cruising by so frequently."

"Okay. Okay." He held up his hands. "I know when I'm licked. But I'm going to insist on two things."

"What?" Lord, he was protective. She resented it, but in a

way, she liked it. Carl had been protective, too, but it felt different. Her ex-husband's protectiveness was smothering, nothing but jealousy, thinly disguised.

"I want to check the house before you and Josh go in at night."

"You, yourself?"

"If it's not me, one of my deputies. Hapscomb or Stoker. Not, I promise you, Deputy Settles."

"Cross your heart?" she asked. Before he could reply, she added, "That's a good idea."

He smiled. "Thank you."

"What else?"

"Call me every hour tonight until, say, midnight. Then call me again by seven A.M. If I don't hear from you, I'll be on your doorstep within fifteen minutes."

"Is that a threat or a promise?" she asked, returning his smile.

"A promise." Tentatively, he reached out and took her hand. "Last night. That note . . ."

"It upset you." She liked the feel of his hand over hers and was sorry when he let it go.

"Yes. It did."

"You don't have to explain."

"Not today." His eyes searched hers. "I do have to explain, though. Soon."

Twenty-nine

At a quarter to midnight, Zach Tully closed the green note-book Arlene Rios had given him. His eyes were bleary from the six hours of reading he'd done since leaving the station in the hands of Ron Settles and Tim Hapscomb, who came on early at Tully's request. "I'll speak to the mayor and make them give you overtime pay," he'd told the young man.

"I've had lots of overtime pay," Tim said. "So has Al."

"Deputy Settles told me the council won't okay it."

Hapscomb grinned. "Ron always says that because he doesn't like to work it."

Tully, sitting on his couch at home, papers and books spread around him, thought it would be satisfying to force Settles to work overtime if he weren't so awful to be around.

Since coming home, all he'd done was read and talk to Kate and Hapscomb on the phone. All was quiet around the McPherson residence. Tim had last called in a half hour ago and promised that he would faithfully make the rounds the rest of the night and call Tully at any inkling of trouble.

He sat up and started stacking books on the coffee table. He had first gone through the material Rios had lent him then, after a paltry meal of Campbell's tomato soup and a tube of Ritz crackers, he reread Jackson Coop's *The Occult Secrets of Icehouse Mountain* before returning to Rios' notes.

He wasn't sure why he'd devoted a whole evening to such outrageous research. Maybe he was already turning into an Eternity eccentric, or maybe something was clicking into place, jogged by tales of vortices or long-dead murderers.

To be honest, some of his motivation came from his curiousity about the perp. His obsessive desire to catch him made him feel crazy and turned his instincts to shit. He knew the killer was trying to push him into emotional reactions. Playing on emotions was part of this killer's MO; he did it to Kate with every note and hang-up call.

Tully set the notes on the table with the books then stood up and yawned. Twelve on the nose and Kate was nothing if not punctual; the phone rang.

"Tully."

"Everything's fine, Sheriff." Kate's voice sounded warm and sleepy. "Can I go to bed now?"

"Have you got my number on your speed dial?"

"Yes, Father."

"Sorry. I just want to be sure you call me for any reason— or no reason if you want to. Don't hesitate, okay?"

"Okay."

He couldn't help himself. He had to say, "Call me in the morning."

"I will. Good night, Zach."

He froze. No one except his mother and Linda ever used his first name.

"Are you there?"

"I'm here. Good night, Kate."

"Good night."

In the shower, Tully let the water beat his neck and shoulders. He wanted to fight his desire to think about Jack or Kate— *Good night, Zach*—so he forced himself to consider the Ripper material he'd gone through tonight.

In 1888, "Jack" had murdered five women, mutilating them, cutting out organs and taking souvenirs, even festooning bed-posts with one of his victim's intestines. He had written notes to the police, sometimes signing them "Jacky." The handwriting was extremely similar to the current murderer's—he'd need a graphologist to tell them apart.

After the last murder, the Ripper disappeared and was never identified. Tully had read about the suspects, from royals to butchers to lawyers to veterinary students. His reaction to it all was to sympathize with the Scotland Yard officers embroiled in the sensational crime. And the end result? Tully didn't know what he believed. How could he? All he was sure of was that the original Ripper was long dead.

He turned his thoughts to Coop's *The Occult Secrets of Icehouse Mountain* where he'd read about the Amazing Timeslip that allowed so many alleged residents of Eternity to arrive from other places. It all sounded like hooey. But when he read Rios' science-oriented notes and book on the same subject, it was almost believable, maybe because the scientific jargon dazzled the modern mind better than magical nonsense ever could.

He wanted to dismiss all of it—the Ripper background, the mountain oddities—as irrelevant to the trouble at hand, but he couldn't. Not quite. His instincts were up; he felt like a hound catching a scent he couldn't identify. Something so familiar . . .

Tully dried off, tossed the towel on the floor. At that moment the phone rang—*Kate*—and he ran for it, catching it in the middle of the second ring. "Tully."

"You better come down to the park," Ron Settles said, sounding bored.

"You're not working overtime, are you?"

"No," he replied, irritation in his voice.

"So what's up?"

"We got another murder."

"Who?" he asked, thinking of the Death Pool.

"Just a hooker."

"I'll be right down. Call Phil Katz."

"Already did."

"Keep the area cordoned off and don't let anyone mess up the ground around the victim."

"I know what to do, Sheriff." Settles sneered the last word.

Thirty

At three A.M., Tully sat in Phil Katz's waiting room, half dozing as he waited for the doctor to finish his preliminary exam.

When Tully had arrived on the murder scene, Settles was hunkered down over the body with a camera. That was fine except that he was ignoring Tully's admonition to be careful not to destroy evidence around the body, Settles was dropping film crap everywhere and grinding his heels into the ground as he jockeyed for good shots.

"Back off a minute, Deputy," Tully said and, slowly, Settles gave up his position over the body, which was sprawled at the edge of a mass of low junipers bordering the band shell.

The woman was nude, legs spread obscenely, one knee bent over a rock as if she were reclining after sex. Tully glanced at Settles and realized that the man was relishing this, enjoying his chance to take photographs.

"Deputy, what were you doing here at this time of night?"

"Couldn't sleep, so I took a walk and found Valerie."

Tully eyed him. "You know her?"

"Everybody knows her. Valerie Saylor, the town pump."

The body was unmarked, at least at first glance; Tully soon noted a tiny triangle of skin excised on Saylor's neck. It was barely visible, mostly covered by her hair. The killer wanted to make sure he got credit; otherwise, this one could be mistaken for a rape gone wrong.

The corpse's left hand was fisted tightly around something that looked feathery. Tully pointed this out to Settles and told him to take pictures of it. Settles grumpily did as asked, then pointed. "That ain't the only place she's got feathers. Look at her snatch."

"I see," Tully said. Fluffy gray-brown tufts mixed with the woman's thick pubic hair.

"I already took pictures of that," Settles told him. "I can take more if you want. Or you can take them."

Tully ignored him—*fucking freak*—but mentally put him up a notch on his suspect list. Phil Katz arrived at that moment, eyes still heavy with sleep. As soon as he saw the body, he came to full alert; Ron Settles wasn't the only one who recognized the victim. Valerie Saylor was known to Katz as well—he'd treated her for venereal diseases several times. He said she was a barmaid at Shalimar's—another link to the bar. Settles confirmed this but thought she'd been fired some time ago.

Tully followed Katz back to his office and watched as the doctor gently pried open the dead woman's hand. A small dead bird was revealed.

There were two more birds in her vagina. After that, Tully had retreated to the waiting room while Katz finished up.

Now Katz emerged from his autopsy room and cleared his throat, bringing Tully out of his thoughts.

"We have a cause of death," the doctor announced.

Tully was fully awake. "Tell me."

"An awl or icepick shoved into the brain at the base of the skull. Very clean and neat. About twenty-four to thirty-six hours ago, give or take. What's odd is there is no sign of sexual molestation other than the birds inserted in her vagina."

"It's not too odd," Tully told Phil. "It looks like our man either can't or chooses not to indulge."

Katz nodded. "I don't have any more to tell you except that she was killed somewhere else then moved to the park."

"When will you know more?"

"I'll do a full PM in the morning, so I might have something by noon. I'll have some lab results, too, though I'll have to send most samples to the big lab in Eureka."

Tully nodded.

"I'll call you when I have something."

"Thanks. I appreciate it." Tully followed him to the door. "You hanging around, Phil?" he asked as the doctor unlocked the front door.

"Not unless you want the lab work right this minute. I'm ready to drop."

"Go shut down, then," Tully said. "I'll see you to your car. It's not a good night to be out alone."

"Fine. I'll be right back."

Tully stood waiting in the cold night air. The silence lay so heavily on the land that it felt suffocating. He drew a deep breath and the chill cut his lungs like a knife. It would probably snow here before another month was up. *What the hell am I doing here? If it's this cold in August, how will I stand December?*

The stars twinkled silver-white overhead. He suddenly remembered the lights hovering around the mountaintop the previous night. Could they really have something to do with the murders? *Could I really be considering such an idiotic notion?*

A car door opened nearby, then a feminine voice said, "Hi."

Startled, Tully turned toward the voice. "What are you doing here?"

Arlene Rios joined him. Shivering, she stuck her gloved hands in her pocket. "I hope you solve things before the snow comes."

"Me, too. What are you doing here?"

"I couldn't sleep so I turned on the police band a little while ago and heard your deputies talking. A prostitute was killed?"

"Yes. A local woman, but that's all I can tell you at this point."

"Was she mutilated?"

He shrugged. "Sorry. Can't talk about it." He made a mental note to tell his deputies to watch the radio jabber.

"There were lights on the mountain last night."

"I saw them."

"I drove up there," Rios said "But they were gone by the time I arrived."

"You went to the Circle by yourself in the middle of the night? Are you insane?"

She ignored the question. "For your information, I didn't walk down the Circle in the dark—I just got out of the car and looked down."

"Oh, well, that's different then."

"Don't be sarcastic, Tully. I wasn't sure where the lights had come from so I drove up to the trailhead, too. No one was there."

"Kate McPherson says the lights are some kind of weather phenomena. They probably originate in the air, not on the mountain."

"Whatever. I'm going to try to match up the murders to the appearance of the lights. Can I get some exact times from you?"

"In the morning," Tully said as Katz returned. "For now, I suggest we all go visit our respective beds."

Thirty-one

August 21

> Superstitions are, for the most part, but the shadows
> of great truths.
>
> —Tyrone Edwards

The word was *preternatural* and it was one Tully had never used before, but it described Little Stonehenge perfectly. At seven A.M., the sun shot rays between the peaks of Icehouse to bathe the tips and edges of the lintels and megaliths in glowing yellow light that prismed against the dew.

A lone eagle's cry echoed eerily across the round meadow. Tully scanned the sky, then turned his attention back to the ground. The area outside the Circle was as pristine as that within it. Except for the scuffed footprints on the trail and the trash bin near the bottom of the stairs, the place looked and felt as if it had been deserted for centuries. If there were such a thing as a haunted place, Tully thought, this was it.

The previous night's conversation with Arlene Rios had inspired him to come up here. He didn't expect to find lights or UFOs, but he thought he might find some trace of ritualistic activity. It was also quite possible that Valerie Saylor had been brought here before her death.

Carrying his evidence case, Tully tried to ignore his uneasiness as he searched the ground for anything that might prove useful. The place was clean. Ridiculously clean. On his knees, he examined the stone-hard ground in the very center of the circle.

"Saying a prayer, Sheriff Tully?"

Tully was on his feet, gun drawn, before he even saw Ambrose Abbott at the edge of the Circle. The old man, leaning on a sturdy polished walking stick, wore tweeds and a bemused expression.

Tully, working hard to control his breathing in the thin atmosphere, holstered his weapon. The last time he was up here, he'd heard Kate's voice clearly from the rise above the meadow, yet Abbott had come upon him without making a sound. More of that preternatural bullshit, he thought.

"Don't look so amazed, Sheriff." Abbott could evidently read minds, too. "Inside the Circle, the real world often ceases to exist. Or perhaps it merely has difficulty penetrating the shield. Either way, I assure you, your senses aren't failing. It's one of the tricks of this place."

Tully joined the mayor outside the standing stones. "What are you doing up here at this hour?"

The smile was enigmatic. "Speak of the devil and he will hear about it."

Tully stared at him.

"Morning constitutional."

"Do you know about last night's murder?"

Abbott nodded. "In the park? A working girl, I believe?"

"Former employee of Shalimar's. Valerie Saylor. What can you tell me about Shalimar's, Mayor? Joyce Furillo worked there and Larry Fraser hung out there."

"Billy Godfrey?" Abbott asked.

"Actually, he does have a tenuous connection. We have reason to believe he left some of his extremist literature at the club, though we can't verify it."

"Shalimar's," Abbott said, "is where we house all our crime. At least that of a less violent nature. I assume you know about the private club upstairs?"

"Yes."

"And I trust you will turn a blind eye?"

"It's the least of my concerns, unless it has something to do with the murders."

"If Miss Saylor had confined her activities to the club, she would probably be alive today." Abbott paused. "In a resort town like Eternity, there is a definite call for, ah, companionship, but we have a reputation to uphold; we can't have prostitutes walking Main Street—"

"But murderers are okay?"

"Don't be snide, Sheriff. It's unbecoming."

"Did you come up here to tell me to leave your whorehouse alone?"

Abbott laughed. "Indeed not, Sheriff. You brought up the subject. I came up here to commune with nature. Instead, I seem to be communing with you." He nodded toward the inner circle of stones. "What are you looking for?"

"Saylor's body was transported after her death. I figured it was worth a look since Joyce Furillo was found here. And lights were seen up here the night of her murder. Maybe that means there's evidence of her presence or of rituals being performed."

Abbott nodded. "The lights occur regularly. I don't know if they've been active during the killings, but I can assure you they've been active without murders."

"What are they? UFOs?"

"A large contingent believe so. If you're fortunate enough to actually be here during the activity, it's quite impressive. Did you see the objects the New Agers call 'saucers'?"

"No. I was low on the road. I saw borealis effects."

"When one is on top of the lights, you'll see swooping and diving bursts dashing all over the sky above Icehouse Circle and sometimes around the peak of the mountain."

"What's the cause?"

"Something to do with high and low air pressure colliding. It also causes reticular clouds which can be seen at dusk. They look like huge flying saucers. The tourists love them."

Kate had said essentially the same thing. "I've seen the clouds on postcards. That's not what I saw."

"No. You saw something similar. Next time, drive up and watch the real show. The alleged saucers. It's quite a pastime around here."

"If there were people up here last night, I see no signs of them."

"They usually don't come down the stairs at night. Fortunately, something about the Circle scares them off. They usually go another quarter mile up to the end of the road and watch from the old Ski Bowl."

Tully cleared his throat. "I wanted to talk to you about Deputy Settles."

"Go right ahead."

"Why is he on the force?"

"He's always been on the force."

" 'Always.' What do you mean, 'always'?"

"Law enforcement is all he knows and when he came here he asked to be a deputy. He's quite good at his job as long as you ignore his attitude."

"The attitude is a real problem. I can't imagine Sheriff Lawson liked it any better than I do. He has no respect for authority or for civilians."

"He has respect for a firm hand."

"He told me I couldn't fire him."

"That's true. The council oversees employment of county servants."

"Then I suggest you fire him. He's inappropriate."

"He leaves the tourists alone, Sheriff, and the locals are used to him. As I said, he's always been on the force. We can't just fire him."

"I asked you before, and I'll ask you again; what's the definition of 'always'?"

"A very long time."

"The man isn't over forty. Do you mean he's been on the force for twenty years?"

"Something to that effect. He's very loyal to Eternity. suggest you make the best of it. Someday, you'll be glad you have him."

"Is Settles a lifer?"

"Yes."

Tully decided not to say he considered the deputy a suspect at least not head on. "The other day you told me that you believe the killer is a local. Do you have any idea who it might be?"

"You already asked me that."

"I'm asking again."

"How tenacious of you. I know no more than I've told you already."

"Then tell me why you think the killer is a lifer."

"Patterns repeat."

"The patterns I've seen—and I've been doing my home work, Mayor—are too far apart to count. There were the mur ders in the forties."

"Which set are you referring to?"

"Two at a time, the body parts exchanged."

Abbott smiled at that. "Particularly curious, don't you think Our killer does have a sense of humor, at least we know tha much."

"Come on. You're not claiming the ones in the forties ar related to the current ones, are you?"

Abbott shrugged. "Look at the ones in 1927. Each bod dressed in an outlandish outfit, each of the victims whimsicall forced to swallow rubber balls, screws, and metal nuts."

"If I'm to believe the killer was active that far back, then have to believe that you're Ambrose Bierce, correct?"

"Don't spread it around. I dislike notoriety."

"When did you come here?"

"Before you were born, quite by accident. One minute I wa in Mexico enjoying the Revolution, the next! . . Icehouse. M biggest regret is that I can't collect royalties on my books."

"You do all right with the autograph business."

"*Caveat emptor.*"

This was going nowhere. "Is the killer a member of the Brotherhood?"

Abbott's eyebrows shot up with glee. "I wondered when you'd get around to asking me about our group. You've asked everyone else."

"Look, Mayor. You want the guy caught, I want to catch him. If he is a member, it would be against the rules to rat him out, right?"

"This is true."

"So am I going on a goose chase and are innocent people being killed to protect a sacred vow?"

"I have no idea. I don't know who the killer is. Though I hope not, he might be a member; after all he's been around for a long time."

"Since the twenties."

"Before that."

"I have one more question."

"As they say, shoot."

"What really happened to those women hikers in June?"

"A bear happened to them. Reggie told me about your impromptu investigation of the newspaper morgue. You'd be better off looking for the current criminal than reading about the large, furry dead one. Anything else?"

"I guess that's about it." The sun was well above the peaks now.

"Snow's coming," the old man said, shielding his eyes as he stared up at Icehouse Summit.

"Thanks for your time, Mayor." Tully barely hid his disgust. "I'll see you around."

"Have a nice day."

The words and Abbott's biting chuckle followed Tully as he headed for the stairs.

Thirty-two

"Well, I was wondering when I'd see you again, Sheriff. Come on in! Come on in!" Jackson Coop gave Tully a gristled grin as he held the door of Snakes Alive! wide open. "See you been to Harlan's," he added as the aroma from the King's Tart bag in Tully's hand caught his attention.

"Bear claws," Tully said.

"In Eternity, we call 'em Bigfoot claws."

"Okay." That's how they'd been listed on Harlan King's menu, but Tully hadn't been able to bring himself to utter the words.

"Got some coffee on," Coop said. "Want some?"

"You bet." Tully watched as Coop snagged two I-Saw-Bigfoot-and-Lived! mugs from a counter display, blew the dust out of them, then poured from an aging Mr. Coffee behind the cash register.

"Sugar?"

"Black," Tully said.

"Hear you have a nasty murder on your hands."

"A few."

Coop carried the mugs around the counter. "Let's go in back where we can sit a spell."

Tully smiled—he'd never heard anybody but Jed Clampett use that expression before. He followed Coop into the faintly rancid museum, grateful at least that they didn't have to sit by the two-headed snakes. They reached Coop's office—a card table and file cabinet in a corner—and Tully tore the pink bag open and placed it on the table. "Help yourself," he said, taking the coffee cup from Coop's gnarled hand.

"Thank you kindly." Coop took a big bite and slurped his coffee. "Hope you been watching what you say to the town council."

Tully shrugged. "You said a lot of things the other day that make more sense now. Or maybe less sense."

"Eternity don't make a lot of sense, all in all."

"I noticed. That's why I'm here."

Coop licked icing off his lip. "You think I can make sense of it for you, son?"

"I doubt it."

Coop cackled gleefully. "Well, you gotcher feet on the ground, that's for sure."

"The council and the mayor won't explain why they seem to think the murderer has been at work for a hundred years."

"You read that book I gave you?"

"Yes."

"Buy any of it?"

"Frankly, no, but I'm ready to grasp at straws."

"Buy what it says, Tully, at least the stuff at the core." He grinned again. "There's a lot of tourist crap coating it, just like the frosting on this Bigfoot claw."

Tully fought back his frustration. What did he expect, that the old man would spout science that would clarify everything? "For starters, tell me about yourself. Are you a lifer?"

"Guess I am, though they don't look too kindly on me. Ain't much of a conformist, you see."

"I don't see."

"I came here by accident. In 1875. Now, I know what you're thinking, and you just keep your mind wide open and your mouth hard shut. Deal?"

Tully nodded.

"I worked for the Circle Bar T outfit down in Arizona. I

was a cowboy, can you beat that? A cowboy. That year, the drive was done and I heard tell about a little vein of gold up in Oak Creek Canyon. That's near Sedona. You heard of Sedona?"

"Yes." Tully had read about it in one of the books Arlene Rios gave him. It was a New Age mecca not so different from Eternity but with better weather.

"There weren't no gold, at least not that I could find, but one night I was camping among those red rocks, along the west fork of the river. I had a fire lit, and I'd had a real good dinner, pan-fried fish straight from the river. Remember it like it was yesterday, yessiree. Like it was yesterday.

"So it got real quiet after a while—too quiet, you know?— and suddenly it didn't feel so good to be there. Weirdest thing I'd ever felt up till then. Hairs fried up all over my body, I got tingly like I was gettin' a little shock and then my ears started gettin' full of rushy sounds. I thought I was having a heart attack or something because everything started swirling around and feeling heavy. I swear on a stack of Bibles that I heard voices yelling and horses runnin' and all sorts of crap like that. And then I passed out.

"Later, when I woke up, it was daylight, but I was freezin' my tail off. The river was gone, that was the first thing I noticed. Weren't no sign of my campfire nor my mule. I was just layin' in the middle of this big meadow practically frozen solid. I noticed the circle of stones about then. And you know what I thought?"

"What?"

"I thought some Injuns had dragged me off in my sleep and were gonna use me for a sacrifice to the Great Spirit. But that weren't the case." Coop lowered his voice. *"Something else* dragged me off and it weren't human. It dropped me smackdab in the center of Icehouse Circle. Little Stonehenge."

Keep an open mind. Tully sipped his watery coffee and started on a second pastry. "What happened then?"

"Well, sir, I hiked down the mountain."

"That must've been tough. How old were you?"

"Same as I am now. Seventy-three and fit as a fiddle."

"Wait a minute."

"Don't ask questions. The answers'll just confound you."

"I don't have time for—"

"Fairy tales?" Coop finished. "Stories from a senile old man? What did you come here for? Not the coffee, I'll wager."

"Sorry. Go on."

"Not much more to it. I got off the mountain and found the makings of Eternity. It was a poor excuse for a logging camp, mostly. There were some lifers here already, and most of 'em are still here, far as I know. Me, I went down further and found me the local tribe. After I got 'em to trust me—I'm a quarter Injun myself and they could see the blood—they told me all about the mountain. Of all the crap I ever heard, theirs still makes the most sense."

"What did they tell you?"

"They didn't climb big mountains like Icehouse or Shasta because the power of the Great Spirit was too strong to take. It could drive a body crazy. Maybe even kill you. They believed the Great Spirit sometimes took up residence on the peaks. Only a shaman who was most pure of heart and supremely powerful dared walk up the mountain. Guess they thought I was a little special because I'd come from there."

"What did they tell you about Icehouse Circle?"

"They feared it. And respected it. Big magic. The Circle was ancient in their time and their stories about how it was built centered around a race that fled a volcano on an island in the Pacific. Matches up real good with the stories about Lemurians. Which is why I think there's a lot of truth hidden in the stories."

Tully nodded and kept his mouth shut.

"By eighteen eighty-seven, Eternity was thriving in a dinky sort of way. They'd opened the first resort for wealthy consumptives. Within a few years, Eternity became all the rage." He said those last words in an artificial accent that betrayed disgust. "The Indians stayed away—like I said, they thought it was cursed—but I went and lived with the whites anyway since that seemed like the thing to do, speaking the language and all. Started me up a little carpentry business. Worked on most of the old buildings in this town, putting in the finishing touches like shelves and cupboards. Suited me as long as I could get out and hunt now and then.''

"Speaking of hunting," Tully said, "I'm told you took out the bear that attacked and killed those women hikers back in June."

Coop set his mug down and regarded Tully with sharp eyes. "I did," he said at last.

"What happened to the carcass?"

"Took the pelt, carcass went to the critters. You probably think I'm making a Bigfoot out of it, don'tcha?" he added with a delighted cackle.

"It crossed my mind. More to the point, Coop," Tully said, leaning forward. "Was there *really* a bear?"

"What makes you think there wasn't?"

"Just a hunch."

Another long silence. "I took out a bear, but it was a sickly old thing."

"Aren't sick animals the usual kind that attack humans?"

"Yep. Or a ma bear if you get between her and her cub. That's what I expected. But this bear, it wasn't from around here and it was scrawny and weak and ready to die. Besides that, it was a little black bear, not a grizz."

"If it was so bad off, how did it get here? And how do you know it wasn't local?"

"Wrong kind of dirt in its paws. I'd say it was from the western forests. Didn't see anything human in its belly but there was some fish—and we got no fish up here. Where'd it get the fish? As for getting here, you take a guess, I ain't gonna say."

"Are you implying someone transported it to the mountain and fed it?"

Coop didn't answer the question. Instead, he said, "You got some good instincts."

"Are you a member of the Brotherhood of the Robes?"

Coop slapped his knee. "Me? Do I look like some fool wants to dance around in black robes and worship a heap of rocks?"

"No. No you don't. But you've been there, I take it?"

"At a meeting?"

"Yeah."

"Oh, well, when they first started the meetings here I guess we all went. Feller from England started it up."

"From England?"

"Via the Circle?"

"Yep, 'course."

Tully couldn't help asking. "Was he the alleged Ripper?"

"You're getting in pretty deep. Good for you. But as far as I know, it was some other feller. There was another redcoat early on and I woulda guessed him, but he died pretty quick in some kind of hunting accident."

"You mean lifers aren't immortal?" Tully asked, trying not to smile.

"It's in the book if you done your homework. You pass through the Circle, you stop aging, at least for a time. A long time. Don't mean you can't get killed. That'd be beyond all the laws of nature."

Like stopping aging isn't. "Do you believe the man committing the murders now is the same one who committed the crimes in the twenties and forties?"

"There was a passel of 'em in the nineties, too. The 1890s, I mean, early on. And around 1915 there was a flurry. Yeah, I think it's the same man, but I also think this feller comes and goes. Or maybe he's here all the time. I don't rightly know." He scratched his frizzy beard. "Killer could be that man that started the Brotherhood, come to think of it. Just never considered it before."

"You wouldn't happen to have a photo or drawing of him, would you?"

Coop's eyes twinkled as he stood up and went to a file cabinet behind the table. He inserted a key and the drawer creaked open. "Got something here I can show you but can't give you. It's a picture of the Eternity Brotherhood in eighteen ninety-one. Only one in existence, far's I know. They don't allow no picture-taking now. Ah, yeah, here 'tis.''

Holding the edges carefully, Coop brought the large photo to the table and turned on an old goose-necked lamp. A group of twenty-one persons stood in dark hooded robes before Little Stonehenge. He pushed it farther under the light. ''That's me, there, third on the right, right next to that old pisspot Edna Boyle.''

Tully stared hard at the picture. Only the faces showed and they were shadowed. The person Coop pointed out as himself could easily have been Coop or a hundred others. Nurse Boyle, ditto. ''Where's the Englishman?''

''There, first row, far left.''

The man was hidden by shadows and a large mustache. Again, he could have been anyone. ''Interesting stuff,'' Tully said. ''What does the Brotherhood do?''

''Anymore, you got me. What I do know—and you didn't hear this from me, you understand?—is that they got it in their heads that rituals and such crap were necessary to appease the Circle, so it keeps 'em young. That wouldn't be their words, mind you, they're mine, but it all amounts to the same thing. You know, Sheriff, they probably aren't worth your attention, they just seem like it because they're so secretive. Hell, I don't worship that dang Circle, and I'm just the same as I ever was and I'm one of the longest been here. If aging starts up again, it starts. That's it.''

''They claim to be a businessman's organization.''

''Would *you* tell people you get down on your knees and pray to a pile of rocks?''

''Good point. Do you know if there are any rituals that involve sacrifice?''

''Thought that's where you was headed. Now, I been on the outside since the early part of the twentieth century, but there was talk. I don't think it's a common thing. I ain't even so sure the Brotherhood's involved, or ever was. But there's stories about the Circle. I mean, take the real Stonehenge. It has what folks call a 'slaughter stone' and it seems to me there was

probably one of them in our circle here. I mean, that's what
people did, was kill one another for power or to make one god
or another happy. Don't see why it should be any different
now."

"Tell me the stories about the Circle."

"Well, it's big magic." Coop chomped into another bear-
claw. "Just like them other mounds and stones and pyramids
and such. It's all connected. Sorcery and magic and all that
stuff's connected. Heard one story once about how the Circle
can be worked instead of it working you."

"I don't understand."

"Now, normally, the Circle's in control, it and all its relatives—the other places a body can slip in and out of, like I
did up in the red rocks. If it decides to suck you up and spit
you out somewhere's else, that's it. Supposedly, though, some
magicians are powerful enough to use it to travel when they
want to. Most of the stories I heard were handed down from
the tribe I stayed with when I first got here. They believed the
island people were great shamans who could do whatever they
pleased with the Circle's power. Don't see no reason that if it
was true then it wouldn't be true now."

"But you don't think that's what the Brotherhood's doing?"

"Frankly, Sheriff, I don't think they're bright enough. That
Brotherhood of the Robes, it claims to go way back, way way
back, past the Masons, some say to the Knights Templar, or
maybe even older. Now, those men way back when, they probably knew some magic. But I don't think the current pack of
Brothers—even the women are called brothers, you know—
in this hick place have a whole lot of power or smarts." He
paused. "Except maybe for Jack."

"Then you do think he's a member?"

"Like as not, I guess. Remember, I'm not a member, and
some of the ones who come via the Circle aren't invited to
join. You get a bad seed up here, they just disappear. The lifers
don't want some pervert running around loose."

"How do you mean, disappear?"

Coop eyed Tully then broadly winked at him. "You know.

Maybe a bear'll get 'em. That happened early on with a feller known as Liver-Eating Johnson. That man and his appetite was making a real pest of himself.''

Tully nodded. Ambrose Abbott had said the same. "Coop, what if the killer was in the Brotherhood before they ever found out he was doing the killing? How would they handle it?"

"That's sticky. See, there's vows of secrecy, like in the Masons and other such societies.'' He studied Tully a long moment. "I ain't supposed to be telling you none of this, on pain of death, but you know that already, don'tcha?"

"Somehow, that doesn't surprise me. Are you concerned for your safety?"

"No, least not as long as you don't advertise our talk. Even then, that'd put you in more danger than me."

Tully raised his eyebrows.

"Like your predecessor."

"I see. Tell me, Coop, what would the Brotherhood do if they knew that Jack belonged to their club?"

"I don't rightly know what they'd do. Your Jack, now, he hasn't been killing none of them. Not to sound chilly or nothing, but he's done away with some annoying people. That lady of the evening, she had a habit of bragging about her conquests. Naming names. And then there was that young pill at that New Age store."

"Billy Godfrey? What about him?"

"Not much. Just that he was a nutty closet preacher who thought he was some sort of spy or something."

"Where'd you hear that?'' Tully asked, wondering if any secret was safe in Eternity.

"My landlady, Cordelia. She knows everybody. She's better than the newspaper, if maybe a little less truthful."

In talking with people who knew Joyce Furillo and Larry Fraser, Tully had found out that both were considered annoyances by their neighbors, so he found Coop's words intriguing. "What about Meeks and the hikers?"

"Meeks was a bum, an aggressive one, and that's an annoyance for sure. And the hikers, well . . .'' He paused. "You got a bug up your wazoo about them hikers, don'tcha? As far as I know, they was killed by a bear." There it was, fear, faint but clear, in Coop's eyes. "If it was murder, maybe they was just in the wrong place at the wrong time."

"Coop, I appreciate your honesty and nothing you tell me will go any further. I have one more question."

"Fire away."

"What can you tell me about Ron Settles?"

"He's a bully, always has been."

"Is he a lifer?"

"That he is. And been here almost as long as me. Being alive so long didn't sour him, though. He came that way."

"Does he belong to the Brotherhood?"

"Sure does." Coop hesitated briefly. "He's right here in this photo."

"Which one is he?"

"I already pointed him out."

"You mean he's the *Englishman?*" He stared at the yellowed photograph but couldn't identify the man behind the mustache and cowl.

"You said it, I didn't."

"So Settles founded the Brotherhood?"

"You said it—"

"I didn't," Tully finished. He stared at the man in the photo searching for recognition, aware that he was clutching at ridiculous straws, even vaguely amused by it. It was easier than he'd thought to get caught up in Eternity's lunacy. He turned to Coop. "The mayor said law enforcement is the only job Settles knows."

"He was a cop in England," Coop told him conspiratorially. "A bobby. Maybe he even worked on the Ripper case. You oughta ask him about it."

"Why isn't he sheriff?"

"The council's got a soft spot for him for sure, but they're not stupid. 'Officious prick' don't begin to describe his nature if he's let off his tether. But you probably know that already."

Tully glanced at his watch and stood up. "I need to head out. I appreciate the conversation and the coffee."

"Likewise. But if anybody asks, we was talking about fishing."

"Fishing . . ." Tully paused. "You said there were no fish up here but that the bear had fish in its stomach. The pond behind my cabin is supposed to have fish."

"True. It was stocked. Guess I meant natural river fish." Coop walked Tully to the entrance. "Guess the critter could've fed himself at your pond then hiked up the mountain, but that's a mighty big space to cover so fast for such a puny animal."

"Settles, Ronald Matthias," Arlene Rios read as the words appeared on her laptop screen. "Born April 15, 1958, in Red Cay, California to . . . yada, yada, yada." She silently scanned the material then turned to Tully. "Settles appears real. Social Security number, medical records, it's all here. It doesn't mean he *is* real. It just means they did a good job on him . ."

"He could've assumed the identity of a dead child."

"True." She studied him. "You're sure doing a one-eighty here."

"No. Well, in a way. If Settles uses the story that he was a policeman a century ago in England, then he's into the Ripper lore, almost undoubtedly."

"And there's the fact that it was always thought the Ripper might be a cop," Rios added thoughtfully.

"Yeah." Tully said it to appease her; he still wasn't buying into the stories about Icehouse Circle's powers. He'd come to Rios despite misgivings because he needed to get the information on Settles without taking a chance on anyone noticing. Settles looked okay, but red flags were waving in Tully's mind.

"I'm not finding anything more on Settles," Rios said at last. "Do you really think he's suspect?"

"None of this, *absolutely* none of this is to be repeated."

"Of course."

"Okay." Ordinarily, he'd never bounce ideas around with

a journalist, but these weren't ordinary circumstances. "We don't have anything but Settles' word on his whereabouts during any of the murders. The perp is leaving no evidence—except what he wants us to find."

"Do you think Settles could've been the bearded man that people saw Valerie Saylor with at Shalimar's?"

"Yeah. Why not? But it could be almost anyone."

"I might have seen him that night."

"What?" Tully barked the word.

"He might be British," she said and told him about the encounter in the park.

"No one heard the man with Saylor speak—I'll have it double-checked. It's probably coincidence. If it's not, the accent must be fake."

"Or it's real and he uses a fake American accent." Tully stood up and paced across Arlene's room, stopping at the percolator. "The trouble is, there are too many suspects."

"You're telling me? I've been doing all the whereabouts cross-checking for murder times and there are very few people we can rule out."

"That's not your job." Tully returned to the table as coffee began to gurgle in the background. In the last few hours, he and Rios—he let her do virtually all the talking—had gone over motives, patterns, and people, but he hadn't learned much. She liked the idea that everyone who had been killed somehow irritated the killer, but that was very nearly ludicrous in its simplicity.

Ron Settles was his only new interest, but by no stretch of the imagination was it a strong one. At least it wouldn't be until Tully heard the story again, from a source other than Jackson Coop.

Thirty-three

August 22

> The world is governed more by appearances than
> by realities, so that it is fully as necessary to seem
> to know something as to know it.
>
> —Daniel Webster

The Crystal Room of the Eternity Icehouse Lodge was family-oriented for the early-bird dinner show, which eased Tully's mind since he and Kate had brought Josh along to see Elvis Two perform.

It was a strange place to be, sitting at a table with a woman and child he barely knew in a room full of tourists waiting for a cheap dinner and a fake Elvis. Tully had made the decision to call Kate and use the tickets Elvis Two had given him only a few hours previously, after a long morning of interviews and snooping that had only served to further irritate the council, Abbott in particular.

Ambrose Abbott hadn't taken too kindly to being questioned about anything having to do with Ron Settles or himself, or the other council members but, oozing annoyance, he allowed it.

At one point, Tully asked, "How do you explain yourself?"

Abbott chuckled. "What do you mean?"

"Your Social Security number is fake. There's no record of your birth."

"Then turn me in to the FBI or the IRS, my good man."

Tully eyed him, trying to cover up the fact that he felt like an idiot. "Maybe if you or your council members would stop talking in circles and explain just what the hell you're trying to do, I wouldn't have to waste my time with all this crap."

"Someone once stole my number," Abbott said at last. "It's been in something of a state of flux ever since. As for a birth certificate, I was born at home a very long time ago. Midwives didn't make out certificates as a general rule." He leaned back. "Anything else?"

"The government of Eternity is run by a man with an uncanny resemblance to Ambrose Bierce, one who also sells personalized autographs."

"As the saying goes, if you've got it, flaunt it," Abbott said. "Do you know how difficult it is to keep a bookstore afloat, especially in a place like this where skiing, crystal gazing, and carnal desires, not necessarily in that order, are far more important than the ability to read a book?"

"On the council, you have a woman who looks exactly like Amelia Earhart who, like Mr. Bierce, disappeared without a trace."

"Amelia works hard to attain that look. Though she doesn't flaunt her chosen identity, it's a source of income and pleasure for our town."

"Tell me about Elvis Number One."

"He runs a grocery store. Health foods. The prices are steep, but up here that's to be expected."

"Who is he really?"

"A man who wants to live quietly and peacefully."

"Is he Elvis?" Tully felt his face redden as he asked the question.

"Oh dear, Sheriff. Has it come to this?"

"Is he?" Tully persisted.

"Elvis died of a drug overdose in the seventies. Surely you know that."

"Just a reality check."

"Any more questions?"

"Tell me more about Ron Settles. What's his story?"

Abbott told him a modest version of the same tale Coop had, without reference to the Brotherhood. Tully nodded. "Why do you coddle him? He's not cop material."

"He's been very good to us."

"Is he the leader of your Brotherhood?"

"What on earth would give you an idea like that?"

"I'm just trying to figure out why you're willing to kiss his ass."

That had made Abbott laugh, but with little humor. "We take turns, just as in any other service organization."

"Sheriff Tully?"

Startled from his reverie by Josh's voice, Tully looked at Kate's son. "Just call me Tully, Josh."

"Is that your first name, too? Tully Tully?" He giggled.

"Honey," Kate began, "Don't bother Sheriff Tully."

"It's okay," he said, looking into her eyes. A shiver, simultaneously pleasurable and frightening, washed over him. "It's Zach." He turned to Josh. "You and your mom can call me Zach."

"Can I go to the bathroom?" Josh asked as the waiters began rolling out trays of food for the audience.

"I'll go with you, sport," Tully said, rising.

"It's right there," Josh protested as he pointed across the room at the restroom sign. "I can go by myself."

Kate hesitated, and Tully gave her an almost imperceptible nod. "Go ahead, Josh, but if you're not back in five minutes, we're coming to look for you."

"No problem." The boy slipped away.

Tully glanced at his watch. "I'm giving him three minutes."

"Thanks," Kate said. "For everything." She gestured around. "This is such a treat for Josh."

"Elvis Two gave me the tickets," he admitted. He didn't want her to think it was a real date. "Your son's great."

"Thanks." Kate's smile lit up her face. "It's so nice of you to do this, and to ask him to go fishing. He's never had any kind of friendship with a normal man. Carl was always out to get him."

"What do you mean?"

"Trip him up verbally. Make him feel like a coward. Or a failure."

"And this guy's a shrink?"

"The worst kind. A best-selling one." She shook her head. "Carl was—is—just one big balloon, an ego balloon, always ready to pop."

"Why'd you marry him?"

"He reminded me of my father, but I didn't see that at the time. I hated my father," she added. "He was just like Carl."

"So you fell for the familiarity."

"Yes. Carl took care of everything. I was at his beck and call. It wasn't until I saw what he was doing to Josh that I really recognized what was going on." She twirled a piece of golden hair. "By the way, I tried to call him today. He hadn't registered at his hotel."

Tully raised his eyebrows, but remained silent, not knowing where she was headed.

"I told you he's coming Labor Day weekend, right?"

"Yes."

"Josh has been invited to go to Hansen's Beach with his friend Billy and his parents. He really wants to go. I wanted to make sure Carl remembered Josh wouldn't be here every day, so I called St. Louis. That's where he's supposed to be. But he's not."

"Do you think he might be here in Eternity already?"

"I'm wondering. I mean, it's easy to check and see if he's making his publicity stops."

"What's he look like?"

"Tall, thin, receding hairline that he hides. He might have transplants or a toupee by now. Brown hair, fair skin."

"Maybe he just changed hotels." He nodded at Josh as the boy returned. "I'll do some checking."

"Thanks."

Dinner was served a moment later, a beef stroganoff that was passable to Kate and Tully but disgusting to Josh, who ate everything else on his plate, picking it away from the creamy beef with the skill of a surgeon. Tully watched, amused; at Josh's age, he would have done the same thing.

"Ladies and gentlemen, may I have your attention?"

A little man in a rumpled suit stood on the dining room's stage and waited for silence before continuing. "Thank you. Our featured act, Elvis: The Vegas Years will be replaced by Sheila and her Magic Baboons, due to unforeseen problems. We hope this substitution won't displease you, but if it does, we'll be glad to give you a raincheck for the Elvis show."

"Oh wow," Josh breathed. "Baboons. Cool."

"Sheriff?"

Tully looked up to see a waiter at his shoulder. "Yes?"

"This was left for you at the front desk." He handed his a plain white envelope.

"Who left it?"

"I don't know, sir. The desk was unattended at the time."

"Thank you."

Tully waited for the man to leave then opened the envelope. The message was written in Jack's unmistakable spiky hand.

My Dear Tully,
Sorry I had to kill the act and spoil your evening. I'm sure you'll understand.
Yours truly,
Jack the Ripper

"Christ," Tully said.

"What's wrong?" Kate asked.

He stood up. "I have to leave. I'm sorry. I'll be back before the show is over, though, to pick you up."

Tully left the dining room and stopped at the front desk to ask about Elvis Two. "He just hasn't shown up," the man behind the counter said. "We've tried to phone him, but there's no answer. This isn't like him at all. You don't think there's something wrong, do you?"

Tully didn't answer.

Thirty-four

"Elvis? Mr. Smiley? Elvis?" Tully rapped on the door to Elvis Number Two's room at Dimple's Boarding House. "It's Sheriff Tully. You there?" Silence. He rapped again then tried the door. It was locked.

The hairs on his neck were at attention; he had known Elvis Two wouldn't—couldn't—answer. He glanced across the hall at Arlene Rios' room, considered knocking; she might know if Elvis kept a key and involving her would be preferable to dealing with the Dimples. He doubted she was in—she would be breathing down his neck by now if she were—but he went over and knocked anyway.

"Sheriff Tully!"

Speak of the devil. Rios' door remained closed, but Martha Ann Dimple appeared on the landing. "May I help you? I saw Miss Rios leave just a bit ago."

"How about Elvis Two?" Tully asked.

"You know, I was just coming to check on him. His car's still here and he should be at the Icehouse Lodge right now, you know, doing his show."

"He never showed," Tully said, "Do you have a passkey?"

"Right here." Martha Ann reached in a pocket on her house-dress and brought forth the key. "Ordinarily, I'd never enter a guest's room without permission."

Yeah, right. "Of course."

"Elvis Two is such a good boy," she continued as she inserted the key. "I like to keep an eye out for him." She fell silent.

Tully stepped in front of her. First, he saw the brash pinks, whites, and blacks of the walls and furniture, then posters of Elvis. These were framed by white running lights, on and twinkling. There were hot-pink vinyl throw pillows on the white fake fur bedspread. An acoustical guitar gleamed on its stand near the head of the bed.

Elvis Two lay in the middle of a pink oval area rug near the bed. Dressed in black spandex, bejeweled and tasseled, a black cape spread around him like batwings. With his arms crossed over the chest, and eyes hidden beneath wraparound shades, Elvis Two looked like Dracula at rest.

Tully stepped into the room and Mrs. Dimple moved with him. "Is he alive?" she whispered.

"Stay where you are, ma'am. I'm going to check. Don't touch anything." Tully walked carefully into the room and squatted next to Elvis Number Two, the late Seymour Smiley. Seeing bloody darkness beneath the folded hands, he didn't bother removing the sunglasses.

"Mrs. Dimple, would you do me a favor?" he asked quietly.

"Anything. Is he . . . ?"

"Yes, he is and this is officially a crime scene. I need you to call the station and say that I'd like either Deputy Hapscomb or Stoker to bring the camera here on the double. Then I need you to call Dr. Katz and ask him to come as soon as he can. Can you do that?"

"Certainly." She looked excited as she turned to leave.

"Mrs. Dimple," he called.

"Yes?"

"Please don't mention this for the time being. We don't want a crowd here while we're investigating."

"Of course not. My lips are sealed." She made a tsking sound in her throat. "Of all the nerve."

"What do you mean?"

"It's one thing to find bodies here and there. Outdoors, you know. In public places." She put her hands on her hips. "But the nerve! That killer shouldn't be breaking into people's homes and doing this." She gestured at the body. "This is just going too far."

Tully closed his mouth, staring at her retreating form. Murder was okay by Martha Ann, except in her house. Then it was rude.

Using his pen, he lifted the glasses off Elvis Two's face to reveal dark eyes dulled by death. The killer apparently hadn't bothered with any triangles this time. Except for the large wound covered by the folded hands, the body appeared undefiled.

Cautiously, he nudged the hands. There was no rigor yet and he was careful not to disturb the position. Checking the wound, he saw that it was similar to Larry Fraser's: there was a hole where the heart should have been, though this one was cleaner. Obviously done after death, there was little blood spilled. The cause of death wasn't apparent and he'd have to wait for Katz's pronouncement to satisfy his curiosity.

He saw a few minuscule drops of blood on the floor trailing toward the bathroom door. Rising, Tully drew his gun and moved. "Police! Open up!" he barked.

Only silence answered. As he held the gun ready in one hand he clasped the doorknob with the other, his sense of déjà vu strong. He turned the knob and the door yawned open. Light from a small window illuminated what lay in the sink.

Elvis Two's heart, neatly cleaved in half.

Thirty-five

"Shit," said Tim Hapscomb.

"Couldn't have said it better myself," Tully said as they stood in the station's parking lot. A half hour earlier, Phil Katz had removed Elvis Two's body and Tully had sealed the singer's room. The only hitch had been Arlene Rios, who arrived halfway through procedures and immediately decided Tully should answer all her questions. Instead, he answered very little. It was good now to be out in the fresh evening air, with only his favorite deputy for company.

"Unless he's got a helper, our boy was also at the Eternity Lodge tonight," Tully told Tim. "This was choreographed. If Phil's right about time of death, the perp killed Elvis Two then immediately came to the Crystal Room lodge and left the note for me. He's keeping track of people."

Hapscomb nodded. "It's not hard to find things out in this town."

"I know. I told Martha Dimple to keep quiet, but I think she called everyone she knew within the hour. She's an interesting old bird. She wasn't as upset about the murder as she was about the rudeness of the killer."

"Yeah, she gave me the same speech. And Elmer's the same way. The murder doesn't matter, just the trespassing."

Tully shook his head. "So what have we learned from this?"

"That Elvis Two knew his killer," Hapscomb said promptly. "There's no sign of a break-in."

"We need to find out who his friends were."

"That's going to be tough. He knew everybody in town."

"Offhand, do you know if he had any enemies?"

Tim shrugged. "As far as I know, everybody liked him."

"Even Elvis Number One?"

"When I stopped by his store for a smoothie, he'd heard it from Martha Ann and wanted to know if it was true. When I said yes, he broke down in tears. I forgot to get my smoothie."

"Well." Tully paused. "Some Elvis purists would find Seymour obnoxious, but I have a feeling he was targeted because it was convenient. Jack knew I'd be at the show."

"The perp's showing you how smart he is," Hapscomb said. "Maybe that big ego will help us catch him."

"The Dimples said they never saw anyone coming or going," Tim said after a momentary silence.

"But Martha Ann noticed Elvis Two's car in his parking space, and she saw me arrive," Tully replied. "I find it hard to believe anyone slipped past her."

"Maybe she was in the bathroom?" Tim paused. "By the way, the info on Carl Leland is here. It's inside."

"Let's go."

Indoors, Ron Settles, at his spotless desk, rose and walked out, saying something about making rounds. That reminded Tully that he'd left Kate and Josh high and dry at the Crystal Room. "Shit," he said. "Hang on a minute, Tim." He punched in Kate's number. She answered on the second ring.

"I'm sorry," Tully said without preamble. "I am so sorry. I forgot—"

"The Wilsons were there. They took us home." She didn't sound angry, just a little formal. "We heard about Elvis Two. It's terrible."

"You heard? Already? How?"

"The employees were talking about it after the show. I asked if you had told them—I thought you might have left a message for me—"

"I'm sorry."

"Forget about it. I understand. They said Mrs. Dimple called to tell the manager."

Tully half groaned, apologized again, then told her to stay locked inside her cabin and that one someone would be driving by again tonight. Hanging up, he turned to Tim Hapscomb. "It's all over town already."

Hapscomb looked disgusted, then handed Tully several sheets of paper on Carl Leland.

Leland was a reasonably good-looking man with an air of intellectual snobbery about him, at least in the faxed photo, which was from a press release. He wore the requisite tweed jacket with leather elbow patches and held a pipe in one hand and a copy of his book in the other. "Well, he's just like Kate described, but I haven't seen him around here. Have you?"

"No, I haven't."

Tully finished reading the bio. "Well, this doesn't tell us much."

"I talked to his people, kind of put the screws to them, and I found out that Leland spent three days away from his book tour. He broke four engagements, but only one of them was a television appearance. Just a small local station."

"Where'd he go?"

"They said he took a few days retreat at a monastery on an island off the coast of Massachusetts."

"Bullshit," said Tully.

"Exactly." Tim grinned. "But he did retreat to a sleazy motel under an assumed name with a woman he met at one of his booksignings. That, I got secondhand so we shouldn't write him off entirely."

"Almost everybody's a suspect," Tully complained.

Thirty-six

August 23

Eternity is in love with the productions of time.

—William Blake

"The body's in the rear." Deputy Stoker hitched his thumb toward Jackson Coop's curiosity shop. "In the museum. You can't miss it."

Tully nodded then looked at the pale middle-aged woman Stoker had been talking to. "Ma'am? I'm Sheriff Tully."

She put out a clammy, trembling hand. "Evelyn Cordelia Caine."

"Mrs. Caine was Jackson Coop's landlady," Stoker explained. "He rents a room from her."

"He didn't come home last night." The woman fluttered around the edges of shock. "He gave me a key, you know, to feed his snakes when he's gone hunting, so I came down this morning."

"Did you expect to find him here?"

"No. Lots of times he goes off on a hunt without bothering to tell anyone. That's what I thought he'd done. I went in the museum because that's where he keeps the food and that's, that's—''

"Thank you, Mrs. Caine. Excuse me. Deputy Stoker will finish taking your statement."

Steeling himself, Tully crossed the lot and grimly opened the door to Snakes Alive! The lights were on, but the only sound was that of a clanking furnace.

Wired by too much coffee, Tully had spent most of the night mulling things over and finding nothing new. Near dawn, he'd finally dozed fitfully on the couch, caught in nightmares. At eight the phone shrilled, sounding like a scream. It made his heart skip a beat, but he was grateful that the dispatcher had interrupted the dream. Until he heard about Jackon Coop's death.

Tully was dressed and on the road less than fifteen minutes after the phone rang. Now his head ached dully, but he was wide awake as he made his way past the souvenirs and snake cages to enter the museum. It was ablaze with yellowed light.

The smell of blood combined with the museum's other odors to create a nauseating stench that made Tully cover his mouth and nose with one hand. But his hand dropped, the smell forgotten, as he stared at the Bigfoot diorama. The green drapes were drawn wide open and Bigfoot still stood framed between plastic Christmas trees before the mural of Icehouse Mountain. But now the monster held up the splayed body of Jackson Coop like a bloody offering to some nether god.

The corpse was naked, arms pulled high and tied at the wrists to the creature's upstretched hands. Coop's eyes were hazed, his mouth slack. There were no marks on the torso, but blood coated the blanched flesh from the groin down. Scarlet had dripped off Coop's feet to pool darkly on the floor, soaking Bigfoot's feet before spreading out to stain the diorama's ground in all directions. There was a hell of a lot of blood.

Tully put one foot in front of the other, moving numbly until he arrived at the edge of the display, five feet from the body. His gut clenched and a soft moan escaped him as he focused on the source of the blood. Jackson Coop's penis had been severed. The inch that remained looked ragged beneath the clotted blood.

Tully felt like hell as he dropped into the chair behind his desk at the station. Elvis Two wasn't even off the autopsy table and now Jackson Coop was waiting in line.

The first thing Tully had done after turning away from Coop's mutilated body was explore the old man's file cabinet. Carefully, he had opened the drawer that had contained the yellowed photograph of the Brotherhood. But the drawer was empty, cleaned out. Checking the other drawer yielded the same. Nada. Zilch.

"Damn," Tully muttered now. He opened his desk drawer and brought out the burgeoning Eternity murder file.

So far, he had few ideas about the killer's methodology in choosing his victims, but the empty file cabinet had told the story on Coop. The old man knew something that the killer didn't want found out. And Tully himself had probably sounded the alarm.

"Damn," he said again. He had planned to take a partial day off for the promised picnic with Kate and Josh, but there was no way he could go on a picnic when he was up to his neck in bodies. It occurred to him as he looked up Kate's number that it had been years since he'd felt like doing anything for the sheer pleasure of it. *Not since Linda and Kevin.*

"Hello."

"Kate?"

"We're not home now. Please leave your name and number after the beep."

More relieved than annoyed to get her machine, he left more apologies for leaving her hanging at the dinner theater and for having to work instead of picnicking. Optimistically, he suggested rescheduling the outing for the following Sunday. Then he apologized again because he still felt guilty; he had barely thought of her since Elvis Two's murder. He hung up, thinking of Linda and Kevin and how he'd neglected them in his fervor to catch a killer.

"Doctor? What's the prognosis?" Tully asked as he entered Phil Katz's office later in the afternoon.

Katz's pale, somber face belied his smile. "On Seymour Smiley or Jackson Coop?"

Tully sat down. "Let's do them in order."

"Smiley—Elvis Two—was stabbed," Katz said without preamble. "There's little evidence on the flesh since the chest wound was widened after death. But there's a horizontal wound on the left side of the heart inflicted by a smooth-bladed knife. Midsize."

Tully nodded. "Anything else?"

"Yes. Either the murderer was very lucky—I'd say the single wound is the cause of death—or he knew precisely what he was doing. I couldn't find any matching marks on the ribs. He went straight in between them on the first try."

"In your opinion?"

"Yes, that and experience," he replied promptly. "The other killings show that he knows how to use a knife. Elvis Two's wound makes me think the murderer probably has some kind of medical or anatomical training."

"A doctor?"

"The only doctors around here other than myself are privately employed at Shady Pines and Uranus 3000."

"Do you know any of them?" Tully asked.

"Sorry. I've met a couple from the sanitarium, but I'm not really acquainted with any of them."

"What about the big resorts? They don't have doctors?"

"During ski season only."

"I'll run some checks this afternoon," Tully said.

"You're going to run one on me as well, I trust?" Katz asked.

"I checked you out early on." Tully smiled. "Along with everyone else," he added, not wanting the weary doctor to feel picked on. "It's procedure. If we're talking about someone who's an expert cutter, what other fields might he be versed in?"

"Anyone who has studied anatomy. An artist or a veterinarian or a butcher come to mind. Or very possibly someone who's merely taken a premed course or two. Particularly if he's been a resident of Shady Pines. They escape constantly."

Tully could almost hear Arlene Rios pointing out that those professions were under scrutiny when Scotland Yard was after the Ripper.

"What about Coop?" he asked finally.

"His wound is not indicative of specialized knowledge. If it weren't for the bizarre aspects of his murder, I'd almost be tempted to say he wasn't a victim of the same person."

"Why?"

"The lack of precision. The other victims' wounds display the precision. For instance, Larry Fraser. The removal of his heart wasn't as clean as Elvis Two's, but the killer knew where he was going. He didn't have to look around for the heart. I mentioned this in his postmortem, didn't I?"

"Yes, you did," Tully said. Katz was right. "What was the cause of Coop's death?"

"Exsanguination due to severing of the penis. Technically, the blood loss stopped his heart." Katz looked somberly at his folded hands then back up at Tully. "I stand by the observations I made this morning. Coop was tied to the Bigfoot while still alive. His clothes were probably cut off—have you found them yet?"

"No sign so far."

Katz nodded. "After he was bound and his clothing removed, his penis was severed approximately an inch above the corona. He bled to death."

Tully's balls climbed north at Katz's words. "The museum is too isolated for anyone to hear him scream."

"What a horrible way to go," the doctor commiserated. He looked as uncomfortable as Tully felt.

"What kind of weapon was used to sever the penis?"

"A dull serrated blade."

"Kitchen knife?"

"Very likely."

"As far as we can tell," Tully began, "the perp hasn't spent a lot of time torturing his victims before now. That's what he was doing to Coop. Torturing him. Making him pay for something." *For talking to me.* "This was not a random killing."

"I agree," Katz said. "Although it's likely he tortured Joyce Furillo in a very different manner. The freezing process was slow prior to the introduction of liquid nitrogen." Katz paused. "But there's something else about Coop that sets him apart. Something more important."

"He's a lifer," Tully said. "Jack's upped the stakes."

A sharp rap startled them. As the door opened, Tully saw Edna Boyle's gargoyle glare and wondered how long she'd been listening. "Dr. Katz," the woman said in her granite-hard voice, "you have patients waiting."

Katz looked annoyed and slightly embarrassed by his nurse's behavior. "Thank you, Mrs. Boyle. I'll be out shortly."

"I've already put Mr. Settles in exam room 2," she announced.

"Thank you. That will be all."

The woman turned, pulling the door shut in something just short of a slam. "Phil," Tully said as he rose. "Did Deputy Settles have an appointment with you last Tuesday? The morning Billy Godfrey was killed?"

Katz thought a moment. "Yes, but he canceled it. Nurse Boyle rescheduled him for today."

"I won't ask you to violate patient-physician confidentiality, Doctor, but is there any reason for me to be concerned about him?"

"No," he said without hesitation. "Just a minor chronic problem. Surely, it's in his records, Sheriff?"

"Records have a way of disappearing around here."

"Well, he doesn't have anything Tagamet won't help. Does that answer your question?"

"Yes. Thanks." Tully shook Katz's hand, then they left the office, Katz accompanying him to the empty front office. As soon as the doctor walked back up the hall, Tully decided to try to charm Nurse Boyle.

He approached the glass window covering the dragon's den. "Mrs. Boyle?" he asked pleasantly.

She looked up from her paperwork, her expression frosted with annoyance. "Yes, Sheriff. What do you want?"

"You're a lifer."

She didn't answer.

"I'm surprised you're not on the town council." The words popped out unexpectedly, and he was glad he'd let them; her glare showed a modicum of interest now.

"I've been there off and on. Bunch of idiots and fools."

Tully constructed a perfect one-sided smile. "I wish I could speak as freely, but they pay my salary."

"Hmmph." Boyle rustled a couple charts and picked up a pen.

Tully calmly watched her and formed his next words as carefully as he had the smile. "Did you have to serve any time with Mayor Abbott?"

Her sharp bark of a laugh would have made a bulldog proud. " 'Serving time' is what it was, all right. I was on that damned council before he ever was, but once he got on, he just steam-rolled everything, him and his poison tongue."

Tully hid his amusement. "If I had to bet on who'd win in a showdown, you or Abbott, I'd bet on you."

"Don't push your luck, Tully."

"I think you could whip his ass and hang it out to dry."

She cocked her head, studying him, then decided, correctly, that he was serious; he could see it in her face, and in—*Good God*—the tiniest frightening hint of flirtation in her eyes.

"That's true," she rumbled, "and Ambrose knows it. But whipping the man to a pulp isn't allowed in polite society. That's why you have a job."

"I know."

The old battle-ax cracked a smile. It wasn't pretty. "You

promise to look the other way, maybe sometime I'll . . ." She squashed the grotesque smile in favor of a wink. "The mayor's been riding your tail, has he?"

Tully shrugged. "He has a powerful presence."

"He's an opinionated old fart. We both know that. And I know you're not talking to me for my good looks. Spit it out."

"Okay. You've been here a long time—"

"Long enough."

"Can I persuade you to give me your take on a few people?"

"I already told you my opinion of Ambrose."

"Did you leave the council voluntarily or did Abbott force you out?"

"Voluntarily. I was sick of their nonsense. Nothing but a bunch of twittering old hens."

"What do you think of Harlan King?"

"Smiles too much."

"And?"

"And what? You can't trust someone who smiles too much."

"Did you serve on the council with him?"

"Yes. With most all of them. All but Amelia Noonan. She replaced me. She's not bad."

"Reggie Skelton."

"Anal retentive popinjay. Kisses Abbott's ass, but he's all right."

"The Dimples."

"You set them up and I knock them back?"

He held her gaze. "If you say so. What do you think of the Dimples?"

"He's whipped. She's a long-nosed, meddling old bitch. Can't stand that sniveling two-faced old gossip-whore."

Tully let her see his amusement. Evidently, she approved. "You want to know about Elvis Number One?"

"Sure do."

"He's nuts."

"Really? He seemed normal to me. Other than the obvious."

"He hasn't come asking to help you out as a volunteer deputy yet?"

"No."

"Probably afraid of what Ambrose would do. You oughta ask to see his collections sometime."

"Collections?"

"Guns, badges, all that malarkey."

"Is he dangerous?"

She snorted. "He'd be dangerous if you let him wear a badge and carry one of those guns. He'd make Ron Settles look like a real prize."

"I'll keep that in mind. Speaking of Deputy Settles—"

"Asshole of the universe," Boyle announced. "He and Ambrose go way back."

"So I gathered. It's been suggested that my deputy was the original founder of the Eternity Brotherhood."

Boyle's stony face closed up. "You can't possibly believe that claptrap." She glanced down the hall again. "That's all the time I can spare."

"You don't seem to like Dr. Katz very much."

"He's young and needs toughening up. In case you haven't noticed, Sheriff, I don't like anybody very much. That includes you."

Nurse Boyle shuffled her papers significantly and Tully moved to the door, then turned, his hand on the knob. "Mrs. Boyle?"

She put her beady-bright eyes on his face. "What?"

"I just wanted you to know that I do like talking to you." He winked and walked out the door, grinning and feeling her stare until he got in the Explorer and pulled away.

Thirty-seven

August 29

> All is mystery; but he is a slave who will not strug-
> gle to penetrate the dark veil.
>
> —Benjamin Disraeli

The night before, Kate McPherson had tucked Josh into bed
at nine-thirty amid cautious assurances that Zach would keep his
promise of a Sunday picnic as long as work—*more murders*—
didn't interfere. She had then stayed up another hour, hoping
for a call from the sheriff. When the phone finally rang she
picked it up expectantly, but heard only slow breathing on an
open line. Her hang-up caller was back.

She had slammed the phone down, turned off the ringer and
put the machine on, before going upstairs to bed, more irritated
than frightened. The previous week had been quiet and that
was reassuring.

As she'd slipped between the cool sheets, she realized that
even though she had no right and no real reason, she was
irritated with Zach Tully—not for leaving them at the show a
week ago, but for forgetting to pick them up later.

She knew it was irrational to feel that way. She was also irritated—again, without any right whatsoever—because Zach had phoned to reschedule the picnic he'd promised Josh. *Shades of Carl.* But she knew Zach had much better reasons for letting the boy down then Carl ever had. *He's trying to catch a killer, for Christ's sake. Give the guy a break.*

After all, he had phoned several times and had stopped by twice. Also, he'd been honest with Josh, something Carl never managed. When Zach rescheduled the picnic for this coming Sunday, he'd told the boy outright that they might have to change the dates again if work interfered. Josh, who was fascinated by the man—what kid his age wouldn't find a friendly sheriff interesting?—took Zach's words with seeming understanding, maybe even a little empathy. Kate, on the other hand, had forced herself to be gracious, knowing her experiences in the Land of Carl had jaded her.

Perhaps Carl hadn't managed to disillusion their son—his belief in Zach was evidence of that. On the other hand, Josh was good at hiding his feelings; was he putting the armor on again? She hoped not. She hoped Zach would come through. Even so, she wouldn't damn him if he canceled again. *Third time's the charm.*

Now, Kate stretched, basking in the muted gleam of the morning sun that peeked between the slats of the miniblinds. When she glanced at the clock, she sat up with a start she'd forgotten to set the alarm and it was nearly nine A.M. She had to be at work in an hour.

She pulled on her robe and opened the bedroom door just in time to hear the sounds of the *Animaniacs* singing, *"We've got baloney in our slacks!"* drift up from the living room. She smiled to herself as Josh's giggles followed.

Descending the stairs, she found her son sitting crosslegged on the floor in front of the TV, eating a big slopping bowl of Cheerios. "Hi, Mom," he called between bites. "You got a present."

"What?" she asked, moving to turn the volume down on the television.

"You got a present. I put 'em in the vase."

She turned and saw her crystal vase filled with white rosebuds peeking out of green florist's tissue on the dining table. "Did Zach stop by with these?" She lifted the vase and held the flowers to her face.

"I guess."

"Did you see who it was?"

He shook his head.

"Okay. Next time, sweetie, take the wrapper off before you stick them in water, okay?"

"Okay," he said absently, his attention back on the cartoons.

She carried the roses to the kitchen, their delicate scent surrounding her. Lifting them out of the water, she removed the soggy tissue. A tiny florist's envelope fell out of the flowers and she opened it eagerly. Neatly printed inside were the words, "To Kate, with apologies, Zach." Nothing else.

As she arranged the flowers, she felt guilty for ever being annoyed by him. *I'm too selfish.* She returned the bouquet to the table. "In fifteen minutes, turn off the TV and get ready to go to Miss Quince's," she told Josh. Then, a schoolgirlish smile plastered across her face, she went upstairs to shower and get ready for work.

When Tully arrived at the station a little after nine, he found the dispatcher reading *Time,* Al Stoker out on a call, and Arlene Rios making herself at home in the back office. He quelled a smile—she was at Settles' chronically neat desk, tilted back in his chair, her feet up. Tully wished Settles would walk in so he could see his face. He could use a good laugh, especially after finding the letter on his doorstep when he left for work this morning.

He had sat in the Explorer and scanned the missive before pulling out of the driveway. Driving to the station, he thought the most frightening aspect of the letter was finding it on his own porch. The historically inclined contents made him think of Arlene Rios, who hadn't bothered him for a few days. This message was one he could show her and she might well be able to tell him something more about it.

And here she was. "I want to talk to you," he said as he quickly dusted the pages for fingerprints. As expected, he came up with zip. He tapped the powder off the paper into the sink and rinsed it down, grabbed a cup of coffee, and walked over to Rios, who had silently watched the whole procedure.

"I found this on my doorstep this morning." He handed her the letter. "Do me a favor and read it. Read it aloud. I think you'll find it very interesting."

Tully sat on the edge of the desk, taking great pleasure in planting his ass on Settles' territory. It was childish, he knew, but what the hell. Anything that could ease the stress was welcome.

Arlene planted her feet firmly on the ground now as she eagerly glanced over the pages. She looked up, trying not to look too happy. "Are you ready?"

"Ready." He wanted to hear the letter, to see if he could pick up any nuances he'd missed on the first reading.

" 'My Dear Sheriff,' " Arlene began, then interrupted herself, looking up. "Even though he's printed this, it's obviously been written by the same person."

He nodded. "Go on, please."

" 'They wrote a song for me, did you know that? It was 1918 when I first took a fancy to the ax. I struck my victims on the head, then slit their throats with a straight razor. I've always been fond of a fine, sharp razor.' "

"Maybe you should look for people who buy old-fashioned things like razors and shaving cups," Arlene said.

Tully nodded. He'd already thought of that.

Rios went back to reading. " 'I killed some, spared others. A good many of them were of Italian extraction, the majority, grocers. You might be interested to know, dear Tully, that the first murder set the style.

" 'The notes were the most enjoyable aspect. I sent one to

a newspaper in nineteen nineteen and signed it "The Axman." In it, I referred to myself as "a fell demon from the hottest hell." You know how the press is, Tully. You know very well how it is. They ate it up.

" 'What pleased me most resulted from a rather whimsical demand I made. On St. Joseph's night I wrote that no inhabitants of any house where jazz was being played would be attacked, but that people who weren't playing jazz would get the ax, so to speak.

" 'It was marvelous, Tully, how they responded, like school-children obediently reciting lessons for their master. Jazz cloyed the air that March night.

" 'And they played a new song, written just for me. Mind you, "The Mysterious Axman's Jazz" was no masterpiece, but it's the thought that counts, don't you think?

" 'What do you think the good people of Eternity will do for me? More importantly, dearest Sheriff, what will *you* do for me? And what might I do for you?

" 'Yours truly, Jack.' "

"What do you think?" Tully asked.

"The Axman of New Orleans was never caught," Rios said. "I'd have to double-check the facts, but I think this is all true. I know the part about 'The Mysterious Axman's Jazz' is dead-on."

"The story's an easy claim to fame. No need to prove anything. Is it truly unsolved?"

"Yes," Rios said. "He's baiting you."

"Yes, I think so." He stood up and took the letter to the Xerox machine, made a copy, and handed it to the reporter. "Check the facts but don't show this around."

"Haven't I proven myself to you by now?"

"I guess you have." He smiled. "Get back to me ASAP, okay?"

"I'll call you when I have something." She was up and out the door in a flash.

Tully went to his desk and studied the note, then locked it

in a drawer. He sat back. There was something. Something
he'd missed. Maybe in the notes, certainly in the murders
themselves. It was so close. His mind clawed for the missing
clue but he couldn't find it. Not yet.

Thirty-eight

August 30

It is fear that first brought gods into the world.

—Petronius

Sunday dawned clear and surprisingly warm. After sleeping in—it was the first full night's sleep he'd allowed himself for days—Tully spent the morning getting ready for the picnic with Kate and Josh. He spread a blanket on the soft bed of pine needles surrounding the small pond behind his cabin then went inside to make sandwiches. Kate had offered to take care of the food, but he insisted on preparing most of it himself. Looking at the simple ham-on-wheats he'd constructed, gathering the apples and bag of chips to go with them, he wondered if she would be disappointed in his lack of culinary skills.

It was approaching eleven-thirty and he knew the McPhersons would arrive at any moment. Quickly, he moved through the house picking clothes from the backs of chairs, stacking papers and books that were strewn here and there, straightening towels in the bathroom. He'd lived here for two weeks, but the cabin already looked like he'd been there for months.

He'd washed the few dishes and done one load of laundry, but otherwise, he'd done nothing to keep the place neat. He'd spent nearly every waking hour poring over the murders, reading and researching alone, sometimes consulting with Tim Hapscomb and Al Stoker, Arlene Rios, or Phil Katz. In odd moments, he continued to read up on the original Ripper and on long-ago murders in town.

Last night, Rios had told him that what Jack had written in the latest letter was historically accurate—and utterly accessible to anyone who cared to read about the series of assaults and murders. There were no odd details not commonly known to lend it credence. Jack, he'd concluded, had done a very cursory job. In a strange way, Tully was disappointed. But something about it—the very lack of obscurities—also aroused his instincts.

Jack was playing cat-and-mouse, biding his time, teasing Tully in a lazy feline way. No murders for a week after a near bloodbath, only the note. The man was planning something big. He could feel it.

The doorbell rang. Halfway there, he could hear Josh's voice raised in a question and Kate's, quieter, answering. He swallowed and opened the door. "Hi, guys."

"Hi, Zach," Kate said, thrusting a covered plate at him. "Cherry pie. I baked it myself."

"Hi," Josh said, hanging back behind his mother until Tully gestured for them to enter.

"All the food's on the kitchen table," he told the boy. "If you want to start carrying it to the pond, just head straight out the back door."

Josh smiled, said that he was starving, and began carrying. Tully set the pie plate on the kitchen counter. "Let's leave this where it's safe from the ants until we're ready for it."

"Good idea," Kate said. "Thanks for inviting us—and for making lunch," she added, smiling.

"Well, it's not much of a feast. Making potato salad's out of my league and I didn't get to the market to buy any."

Josh trotted in and grabbed the plastic-wrapped plate of sandwiches and the chips. He was gone again in a flash.

"He really *is* hungry." Tully picked up the bowl of apples.

"He's in a growth spurt. He's been wolfing food down for a couple weeks." She paused then touched his hand. "I thought you'd probably have to cancel today. I'm glad it worked out—for Josh's sake."

"Me, too," Tully said, surprised that her touch sent a little thrill through him.

She smiled warmly. "And for my sake, too." She withdrew her hand.

"My motives aren't exactly lacking in selfishness. I've been looking forward to this, too."

Kate hesitated. "I especially wanted to thank you for the flowers."

"Flowers?"

"The roses you sent yesterday. That was very thoughtful. They made my day."

Tully's stomach flipped. His ears began ringing. "Roses? What color were they?"

She laughed. "You ordered them, don't you remember?"

"Kate, I didn't order them."

"You didn't?" Her eyes searched his face. "But the note was from you."

"I wish that I *had* sent you flowers, but I didn't. If I had they would have been daisies, violets or carnations. Anything but roses, Kate." *Roses surrounding a head on a platter, a bower of them around Linda's body, roses strewn across Kevin's bedroom. Roses—a detail not released to the public.* He forced himself to speak. "Were they white?"

"Yes," Kate said, catching the bowl of fruit as his numb fingers let go of it.

"Mom?" Josh asked from the doorway.

"Here, honey. Take the apples outside. We'll be along in a minute."

Wordlessly, the boy took the bowl and went out the door. This time, he didn't run but walked, shoulders rounded.

"Don't worry," Kate said as she stared after her son. "He's very sensitive. The minute he sees us smiling again, he'll perk up."

Tully didn't answer.

"Zach? We *will* be smiling again, won't we?"

White roses twined in Linda's blood-matted hair. White roses and the sound of distant laughter. Could Jack really be the Backdoor Man? He'd thought of it fleetingly several times, but dismissed it quickly. *No use getting paranoid.*

Tully forced himself to shut out the images in his head and look at Kate. He took her hand. "We'll smile, don't worry. But later, we need to talk."

"About the roses?"

He nodded.

Only minutes after Kate and her brat arrived at Tully's cabin, Jack saw that the three of them were making family-style noises by the sheriff's pathetic excuse for a pond. Tully seemed slightly subdued at first, but that meant very little. Surely, Jack thought, Kate had mentioned the bouquet by now. *Surely.*

He watched for another fifteen minutes, growing more and more irritated, then pocketed his small binoculars and took a few deep, cleansing breaths. The roses would leave their mark, one way or another. Meanwhile, he would go about his real job for the day: birdwatching.

"So, Josh, are you looking forward to seeing your dad next week?"

Josh took a last bite of apple then rolled over on the pine-needle carpet and propped his chin up on his hands. That gave him a good look at the pond. He briefly glanced back at Zach's cabin to make sure his mom wasn't coming back yet, then he turned his gaze on Tully. "Can I ask you something?"

The man met his gaze with somber eyes. "Sure. Ask away."

"Have you ever shot anybody?"

He was surprised when Zach didn't look away. "Yes, I have."

"How come?"

Tully hesitated. "Once, a bad guy was going to shoot my partner. Another time a man ... well, Josh, he was going to kill somebody, too."

"Who?"

"Josh, I don't think your mother would want me to—"

"Come on, she doesn't care, and I won't tell her. Who was the man gonna kill?"

"His own son."

"How old was he?"

"The son?"

"Yeah."

"Twelve."

"Wow. Why was he gonna do that?"

"Because he was drunk and because his brain wasn't healthy."

"You mean he was nuts?"

Zach smiled slightly. "Yeah. Pretty nuts."

"Would he *really* have killed his son?"

"Yes. I think he would have. That's why I shot him."

"Did you kill him?"

"No. I shot him in the shoulder to make him drop the gun."

"Have you ever killed anybody?"

"No."

"How come you look sad? Aren't you glad you didn't kill anybody?"

"Yes, I'm glad."

"Then what makes you sad?"

"It's hard being a man, Josh. You want to protect people. Like you want to make sure your mom's safe, right?"

"Right. But why—"

"Well, it's a little harder being a cop, too, because you feel responsible for protecting lots and lots of people and sometimes you can't save them."

"My mom says you're the best though. She said you're even famous."

Zach smiled. "Everybody's famous at one time or another."

Josh sat up, staring hard at the sheriff. With Zach around, he'd been feeling like he and his mom were safe from the guy who killed Sheriff Lawson and even from having to be around his father. With Zach around he didn't have to wonder if his mother was okay all the time. But Zach wasn't acting the way a sheriff should.

"Josh?"

"You're not going to let anything happen to my mom, are you?" He fought back embarrassing tears. His throat felt thick and hot. "You won't let her get killed!" The hot silent tears overflowed.

Zach closed the space between them and folded him in his arms before he could protest, before he could say he was just joking, just pretending to cry, that he wasn't a coward, he wasn't.

But the sheriff didn't call him a coward or a crybaby, he just held him and promised that he'd never let anybody hurt him or his mom, never ever. Josh burrowed his face into Zach's shoulder and let the tears come, hot and hard and when he finally stopped shaking he gently pushed back from Zach and looked at the sheriff's face to see if he was looking at him like he was a crybaby.

He wasn't. Tears stained Zach Tully's cheeks, but as their eyes met, he smiled slightly and Josh knew beyond all doubt that even though the man had cried, he wasn't a crybaby or a coward. He knew Zach meant it when he promised to keep them safe. Josh smiled back at him. "Don't tell my mom, okay?"

"Are you kidding? This is just between you and me."

"Guy stuff?" Josh asked, delighted.

"Guy stuff."

* * *

"Lynette and Jerry Robbins," Jack said from his hiding place among the pines a hundred feet from the cabin. "Birds of a feather defiling together." He settled in with his binoculars to watch the couple's front yard antics.

It wasn't precisely a front yard of course, and the Robbins' cabin wasn't really a cabin, but a faded white and green single-wide mobile home with a corrugated metal steeple constructed over it to deflect the snow. The domicile was particularly ugly this time of year, when the lack of snow revealed the amateurish murals of blue and white doves and peace symbols the couple painted on the makeshift roof three decades ago. The entire disaster was fronted by a strip of ground littered with plaster dwarves, pink flamingos, whirligigs, and trash. Jack could see stacks of magazines, a few dozen paper cups, Twinkie wrappers, and the occasional blackening banana peel. The land was dotted with pine trees. On the left side of the property, a twelve-foot boulder, phallic in appearance, stood sentry among a smattering of smaller stones. The couple used its shadow as a place to picnic, drink, smoke, and have sexual intercourse, unconcerned with who might see them.

The Robbins were lifers, old hippies who didn't look old; Jack knew their history. They had arrived in Icehouse Circle one summer night in 1968, evidently transported from a little-known vortex on San Franciso's Mount Sutro. The Robbins weren't really sure how they'd got there, which wasn't surprising considering how much LSD they had taken.

The couple hadn't changed over the years; rather they even more exuberantly embraced their fringed and tie-dyed lifestyle, most likely because their brains were so disarrayed that they were incapable of anything else. They were, in short, reprehensible. And they were about to have a picnic, just as Jack had expected. It was a Sunday tradition.

Both Robbins were dressed in denim shorts and nothing else. Though there was a hint of a chill in the air, Jerry's scrawny, hairy body glistened with sweat as he carried a laundry basket to the shady spot under the giant phallus. He plunked himself down. Although the Circle could stop aging, it couldn't stop gravity, and Lynette, her pendulous breasts hanging obscenely unfettered, followed, a bottle of wine in one hand, a marijuana cigarette in the other. She giggled as she tumbled down next to her miscreant mate.

Jack watched, his hand on a small black control box, as they took bags of chips and cookies, bananas, and half a ham out of the basket and placed it all on an old towel between them.

He watched them eat, relishing the knowledge that he'd planted enough explosive beneath the tumescent boulder to squash them flat. Or if he miscalculated, to blow them into tiny bits of human scum that would rain down to oil the earth. As pagans, they might even appreciate such a mode of extermination. Either way, it was a different sort of trick, one that would confound Zachary Tully no end.

The shorts were coming off now even though the culinary feasting continued in fits and starts. The pair began to nibble on one another between bites of ham and Twinkies.

He waited and watched, tempering his disgust with thoughts of the other picnic going on a mile away. But when Jerry peeled a banana and put it into a place that no self-respecting banana ought to go, Jack could take it no longer. After retreating a proper distance, he pressed the button on his controller.

Thirty-nine

Tully noticed the unnatural silence a bare instant before he felt the thud and heard a sound like muffled thunder. Before he could think, the birds began singing again.

"What was that?" Kate pulled Josh to her.

Tully watched the ripples trembling across the surface of the pond. Being from LA, his first thought was earthquake, but he knew it wasn't; it didn't have the rhythm of a natural tremor. "Explosion, I think." He spoke slowly, still trying to get a handle on it.

He stood up and brushed the pine needles from his knees, angry that his picnic with the McPhersons had been interrupted. It just damn figured that something had to cut short the first enjoyable day he'd had in this godforsaken place. He had been enjoying himself despite his concern about the roses and despite the dreaded fact that he was going to tell Kate about his family's death. But he'd been able to forget all that for the last hour. Until now.

Josh was up and scanning the treetops. For smoke? Tully wondered as it came to him that Icehouse was a dormant volcano.

Kate read his mind. "It wasn't the mountain."

* * *

When Tully pulled up at the site of the explosion, he wasn't particularly happy to see at least six dozen miscellaneous gawkers already on the scene.

He was a little surprised there were so many because less than twenty minutes had passed since the explosion. He'd called in immediately, just as the first nebulous reports were coming in. Five more minutes passed before the locale was narrowed down. It took another ten minutes to convince Kate and Josh not to go home. Kate finally said they'd wait for him at his cabin, but he nixed that, too: he didn't want them to be alone anywhere. The white roses had seen to that. At last, he'd talked them into going to the movies by handing Josh a twenty when Kate went to use the facilities. He told the boy he should take his mother to the forever-running matinee of *Jurrasic Park* and *The Lost World.* Josh had eagerly accepted, though he'd said his mom probably wouldn't want to go see the movies *again,* but Tully pointed out that there was plenty of money for popcorn and soda and candy bars. The instant Kate returned, Josh was all over her. She glared daggers at Tully, but she couldn't say no. As they left the cabin Tully made her promise to stay downtown until they reconnected.

Now, at the disaster site, he climbed out of the Explorer just as Phil Katz pulled up in his coroner's van. They exchanged nods then the doctor followed as Tully elbowed a trail through the crust of onlookers. He was relieved to see yellow police tape already barring the scene of whatever the hell had happened. Outside the barrier stood Reggie Skelton and the Dimples. Inside were Ron Settles, Al Stoker, and Ambrose Abbott. Tully was surprised to see Settles; it was his day off.

"What happened?" Phil Katz asked as Tully's gaze fell on human legs—three of them—and one arm protruding from beneath a huge stone. The hand clutched an unbroken beer bottle. One foot wore an old brown sandal, the other two sported blue toenail polish. Except for the blood, the scene looked like something out of a Roadrunner cartoon.

"I'd say somebody blew the hippies to kingdom come," Ron Settles drawled sourly.

"The hippies?" Tully asked. "Who are the hippies?"

"It's only an educated guess," Ambrose Abbott said dryly. "But I would imagine those limbs akimbo belong to the tenants of that rather unfortunate structure." He nodded toward the triangulated mobile home. "Jerry and Lynette Robbins. Not our most illustrious citizens."

"Goddamned hippies," Settles grunted.

"Who found them?"

"Mayor Abbott," Settles replied.

"I am able to speak for myself, Deputy," Abbott said haughtily. "I was out for a stroll."

"Did you see what happened?"

"No," said Abbott. "But you might say I was within a stone's throw when everything went up."

"Tell me about it, Mayor," Tully said, drawing the older man out of earshot. "What happened?"

"The stone covering the bodies stood upright until the explosion. It was a well-known landmark," he added distastefully.

"Not one you cared for?"

"The least offensive common epithet for it was 'dickrock.' I hate to imagine the new twists on the verb 'ejaculate' that common tongues will be refining."

"What did you see?"

"I was walking along the next street up the hill from here. I heard the explosion and saw dirt and rock fly into the air. It was quite spectaclar. It's fortunate no falling debris hit me."

"Then what happened?"

"I proceeded here, of course."

"Was there anyone else here before you?"

"Of course not. I told you I was the first."

"When did all those other people show up?"

"The first neighbors showed up almost immediately after I did. The rest wandered in over the next few minutes. You know how people gather around gore. Like flies to excrement."

Tully nodded then turned and approached Phil Katz who stood before the bodies. Katz glanced up. "I don't know how we're going to get them out from under all this mess."

"After we finish the preliminaries, try to ascertain if there are just the two people under there. Then we need to establish positive ID. Were the Robbins your patients?"

"Yes, I knew them. They were both in last winter with the flu."

Uneasy, Tully left the murder site at dusk. Kate hadn't called the station, so he cruised downtown, looking for her car, his concern growing when he didn't spot it by the theater. He toured all the adjacent streets and parking areas in vain.

The theater ticket-taker confirmed that Kate and Josh had been there, but as Tully drove toward her cabin, the knowledge didn't help much. Soon, he pulled up in front of her closed and locked garage door. He trotted to the front door, the evening air chill in his lungs.

The drapes were closed and the upstairs was dark, but dim light glowed downstairs.

He knocked.

"Kate? It's Tully. Open up."

Impatient, he hammered on the door again, waited ten seconds then tried the knob. Locked. "Kate?" He took his wallet from his inside jacket pocket and extracted a credit card; she had lousy locks.

As he pushed the card into the gap, he heard footsteps inside. Quickly he pulled the card out and pocketed it just as the door opened.

"Zach!" Kate said.

"Why didn't you phone the station or beep me?" he demanded as she stepped back and let him enter.

"Hello to you, too. I didn't want to bother you."

He glanced around. "Where's Josh?"

"He spilled ice cream down his shirtfront. He's upstairs taking a shower."

"Why didn't you call?"

"Calm down, will you?" Her eyes flashed. "We've only

been here a few minutes. I was about to beep when you started pounding on the door. You scared me half to death.''

''Good. You shouldn't be here. I told you not to come back here alone.''

''We had to. Josh was a sticky mess. He was drenched in chocolate. Even ten-year-old boys can be too embarrassed to want to be seen by other people.'' She looked at him with narrowed eyes. ''And what gives you the right to talk to me like this?''

The first rush of adrenaline had died and with it his anger. He looked down at his hands, then back up into Kate's eyes. ''Nothing gives me that right. I'm sorry. I truly am.''

''Sit down,'' she said, her words still clipped. He moved to the couch and sat. Kate crossed her arms and looked down at him.

He felt decidedly sheepish. ''My reaction to the roses—I'm ready to tell you about it.''

Her arms dropped to her sides then she sat down a cushion away. ''Tell me about the roses.''

At a little after six, after the excitement in town had died down, Arlene Rios had stashed her Mustang in a copse of young pines in the Panther Meadows Campground. The camping area was located an eighth of a mile below the place where the Brotherhood had blocked the road during their last meeting, so she figured she'd be able to return to her car and then to town without attracting attention—assuming there was any attention to attract.

She wasn't positive the Brotherhood was meeting tonight, but she had overheard a few references among the council members today at the explosion site that led her to believe there might be. And if they did meet, it would be well worth spending a few half-frozen hours in hiding to find out what they were up to. In the dark, odiferous restroom, she changed clothes, slipping into dark gray hiking clothes that would blend with the shadows and the night. She wanted to be invisible.

After a long hike in the chilly evening air, she had finally arrived at Little Stonehenge. There were no vehicles in the parking area but she edged down the steep trail, keeping to the brush, out of sight in case anyone was down there. She finally reached the round meadow, where she hunkered down to wait and watch for any sign of movement before venturing closer to the Icehouse Circle.

Arlene had spoken briefly to Tully at the Robbins murder site around four P.M. Hours after the explosion, it had still been a zoo and the sheriff seemed more harried than usual. As a precaution, she'd mentioned her destination to him, but in the confusion she wasn't sure he heard her—she'd spoken quietly, not wanting to be overheard. Anyway, it didn't matter now. She was here and she had plenty of time to pick a good hiding place.

She looked up as a large bird cried and she saw it soaring in a wide arc, avoiding the megalithic circle. Tully had acted oddly the entire afternoon. Though she had watched him throw himself into the investigation, showing the fire and flare she imagined he had before the Backdoor Man got his family, there was something off about his manner. It was nothing she could define, much to her annoyance. An air of distraction, perhaps of worry. He gave off tension like he was ready to explode and she wished she knew what was going on with him. Had something else happened? Something she didn't know about yet? Maybe, she thought as she tugged her jacket around her and zipped it against the chill, Maybe even he couldn't say, perhaps he didn't know. But she doubted it.

Something was off about the town, too. All afternoon, it had felt like Eternity was holding its collective breath, waiting, waiting. *Waiting for what?*

The last salmon-tinted sunlight still showed behind the mountains to the southwest, but it would be full dark soon. She scanned the entire meadow and up the trail from the parking area one last time before tugging on thin gray gloves, wishing she'd brought a warmer pair, wishing too that her shoes, pants, and jacket were lined. Quickly, she checked her miniature tape recorder and tiny camera. She hoped she'd be close enough to use both. When she was through here, maybe she would have something important. Maybe she would have some answers.

Preternatural silence surrounded her as she made her way closer to the megalithic circle. She scanned around constantly for signs of movement as she approached a natural crop of gray granite boulders standing silhouetted against the darkening sky. They were no more than a hundred feet from the Circle. She had checked them out on previous visits and knew that there was a grotto in the middle of them, a place she could climb into easily and be reasonably comfortable—except for the cold—as she watched the performance she hoped would come.

She had to pass through open land to get to the rocks, and after a short pause, she moved swiftly across the unprotected area. Reaching the mound of stones, she stepped up onto one that was three feet tall then, just as she heard a heavy vehicle grinding its way up the mountain, slipped smoothly into the dark hollow.

Before she could take a breath, a hand covered her mouth and her head was snapped roughly back. Something cold and sharp pressed into the back of her neck just at the base of her skull.

Forty

"So the Backdoor Man used roses as his calling card," Kate said when Tully stopped talking. The story so far had horrified her and she was trying not to tremble.

"Yes. White roses." Tully looked at his hands.

"I'm sorry, Zach," she said softly. "I understand. I wish you'd explained earlier, though."

"So do I, especially in light of the roses. I'd intended to tell you about my family today when Josh was out of earshot, but the explosion changed everything."

"What happened out there?"

"Someone—Jack, I assume—set an explosion to knock over a huge rock. He killed a couple named Robbins."

"The Robbins?"

Tully looked surprised. "Yes. Can you tell me anything about them?"

"Not really. They're supposed to be lifers. Newish ones. They're not favorites among the others, though. You saw their place?"

"Yeah. They're the people everyone hopes won't move in next door. But do you think they're so disliked that someone would kill them?"

"I don't know, but I doubt it. Mostly, people just ignored

them. You know how they are around here. The Robbins weren't that bad compared to some of the Shady Pines types.''

"How did the Robbins make a living?''

"Arts and crafts. They sell to the tourist shops. They're not bad at what they do. Did.''

"Hi, Zach!'' Josh said, coming down the stairs. "Are you going to stay for dinner?''

"Please do,'' Kate said immediately. "All we've got are leftovers, but—''

"Leftovers sound great.'' He smiled at Josh. "Think you could do me a favor, kiddo?''

"Sure.'' Josh's face lit up.

"Would you mind giving your mom and me a few more minutes to talk about some business?''

"You mean wait upstairs?'' His smile faded.

"Just for a few minutes. Then I'll come up and see that T-Bird model you told me about, okay?''

The smile returned. "It's almost done. I've just gotta put the decals on. Can you be like half an hour or something?''

Zach grinned. "I'll be up in half an hour, Josh.''

Kate watched her son bound up the stairs then turned to look at Zach. He wasn't smiling now, in fact he looked desolate. "What's wrong?''

"I need to finish telling you about the roses.''

She took his hand. "This part is about your family, isn't it?''

He nodded.

"You don't have to.''

He gazed into her eyes. "Yes. I do have to. It's amazing there were no witnesses the night he broke into our house because he brought armfuls of roses, maybe two hundred flowers, with him. Linda . . . She was on the bed and he covered her with them. And Kevin's room was strewn with them.''

"My God, Zach. I'm sorry.''

His eyes burned. "I really hate the smell of roses.''

She held his hand and waited for him to speak again, but he

didn't. Finally, she did. "You're worried because Jack found out about the roses and he sent them to me to scare you."

"Maybe there was a leak," he replied, his eyes on hers. "Maybe that's all it is, but I doubt it. I think that Jack is reminding me that he can kill you and Josh, just like he did Linda and Kevin."

"Zach! My God! Do you mean Jack *is* the Backdoor Man?"

"I think so, but I don't have proof. One, he was never caught and two, someone sent a résumé purported to be mine to Ambrose Abbott. I didn't ask to come up here. I was invited out of the blue."

"The killer lured you here?"

"If Jack is the Backdoor Man, it makes sense. So far, he hasn't done anything to convince me that he is. Everything he said is common knowledge if you know where to look. Even the roses. We suppressed that information but it easily could've been leaked."

"What could he do to convince you?"

Tully shuddered. "Let's not go there."

"Okay." Goose bumps crawled up Kate's arms, but she tried not to let him see her fear. "Why would the Backdoor Man want to lure you up here?"

He gave her a twisted smile. "I interrupted his work, and almost caught him. He killed my family for revenge. He's an arrogant son of a bitch. What better place to bring me for a showdown? Make me the sheriff of an extremely isolated town, make me responsible for others' lives, then begin killing. He's smart, whoever he is. Isolate, threaten, then go in for the kill."

"He wants to kill you?"

"It's likely. But, Kate, listen to me. He'll kill you first. You and Josh."

"To hurt you."

"Yes, in part—if I'm right. I think you're on his list anyway; he was after you before I even arrived because you interrupted Lawson's murder. You and I have, uh—a thing—"

"An attraction?" There, she'd said it.

"Yes. Our mutual attraction just makes it more fun for him."

"I understand. So what do we do now?"

"We don't leave you or Josh alone."

"You're not going to talk me into going to a motel are you? It won't help. Elvis Two was killed at the boardinghouse."

He shook his head. "No. You'd still be alone. You can spend the nights at my house, but I can't be there twenty-four hours a day."

"I can't stay with you. It wouldn't look right. I have to consider Josh."

He nodded. "Okay. For tonight, how about I sleep here on the couch? We can work out other arrangements later."

"Sure. Remember, I still have to go to work and Josh has school."

"As long as neither of you are alone it'll be okay. The only thing certain about Jack is that he doesn't strike in front of witnesses. Josh has to be picked up at school. We can't trust anyone else except Tim Hapscomb and Al Stoker to help. I know they're clean. We have to remember that Jack could be anyone."

"Can Lizzie Quince pick him up? We know it's not her, too, and she normally baby-sits him at her house—"

"She's old and frail. It would be in her best interest as well as yours and Josh's to keep her out of this as much as possible." He rubbed his chin. "There's Arlene Rios. She might be able to stay here with you."

"Do you really trust her?"

He was silent a long moment. "Where you and Josh are concerned, yes. I do. I'll call her tomorrow. She's up on the mountain spying on the Brotherhood by now. At least I think that's what she said. But back to Josh. He can come to the station with me until you're off work."

"Okay, but what about Ambrose? Josh likes him. Maybe he could stay at the bookstore?"

"No," he said firmly.

"Why? Surely he's not a suspect?"

"Virtually everyone is at this point, Kate."

She almost argued, then decided that whatever Tully's reasons were, they were probably good ones. "This Friday school's out and Josh was invited to go to the beach with the Wilsons. It's in Oregon. Their son Billy is his best friend. Is that all right?"

"I'll run a quick check, but yes, I think that's okay."

"He'd be back Tuesday afternoon."

"He'll be safer away with them than here with us." He paused. "In fact, Kate, you might consider going along."

"No." She spoke firmly. "If Jack's after me, he might follow them to the coast if I go along."

Tully nodded.

"What are you going to do?"

"Catch the bastard."

"Zach?" Josh's voice echoed down the stairwell. "I'm done."

"Coming," he called. "Try not to worry too much, Kate. We'll get him."

"But will you get him soon enough?" she murmured as Zach disappeared up the stairway.

The hand stayed clamped hard against Arlene Rios' mouth, and the cold sharpness at the base of her skull caused icy pain. Whoever it was had been waiting for her, she was sure. Had she been overheard telling Tully where she was going?

"I thought you would like to know, Miss Rios, that I admire your ability to look beyond the everyday for answers. You've been a good influence on our dear sheriff."

The voice was male, cultured, and British, maybe vaguely familiar without the accent; she couldn't be sure. His grip was iron. She could smell his clean cologne and the dust on his gloves, plus campfire smoke and pine on the wind. Most of all, she picked up the scent of her own fear.

"Don't struggle, Miss Rios. It's quite impossible for you to escape and you might drive the icepick into your skull prematurely." As he spoke, the accent faded to plain American and then slid into a slow southern accent. "I'm quite versatile," he added, now with an unmistakable German accent. The timbre of his voice changed with the accents, too. He was a master. "I spent time in Germany in the late thirties," he explained.

Then the southern accent returned, slow and syrupy, like a snake hypnotizing its victim before a strike. "Listen to this," he said and began humming an unfamiliar tune. "That's 'The Mysterious Axman's Jazz.' It's not well known anymore. A pity."

The voice smoothed to the mild British accent. "It's unfortunate I can't allow you to speak, Miss Rios. Or might I call you Arlene? Do you know that I was beginning to think that you and Sheriff Tully might fuck? Fuck. It's an eloquent word in its way. I was wrong, though. Our Tully is interested in Kate McPherson and he's not the sort to fuck two women at the same time."

The icepick stung her flesh. He was slowly twirling it in his fingers. She tried to yank free, but the rocks didn't leave her enough room to move, not with *him* in there.

"I want you to know that you were right, Arlene. That's a comfort in your time of need, is it not? I was Jack the Ripper many years ago. And the Axman, among many more lesser known affectations, all of them amusing in their own ways. If I were to allow you to go free, you could even confirm my identity as the Backdoor Man to Sheriff Tully. Poor Tully. I don't envy him what's to come." He paused. "The Brotherhood will be arriving soon, so I'm afraid our time together runs short." Silence punctuated only by the sound of Jack's breathing and the pounding of her own heart filled the darkness. "I'm going to move my hand to let you ask a question. If you scream, you'll be dead before you can finish." He lifted his hand.

She sucked in cold air. Finally, she spoke. "Who are you?"

He chuckled softly as he recovered her mouth. "Don't you know me by now? Are you so naive?" He paused. "My dear lady, I am Death."

A sharp pain shot into her head. And then there was nothing.

Forty-one

Tully, sprawled uncomfortably on Kate's sofa, was only slightly more asleep than awake and he sensed that the long, fateful walk he was taking up the stairs in his Santo Verde house was only a nightmare. He vaguely knew that the cloying scent of roses was really the clean fragrance of an orange-scented potpourri and that the gun in his hand was really the edge of a cushion. Still, the dream continued to play out. He told himself to wake up, knowing that if he could, he would avoid the worst of it.

But the dream went on and he entered the upstairs bath and saw the bloody water in the sink. It occurred to him that even if he couldn't wake himself up, he might be able to control the dream. It was worth a shot. He veered out of the pattern by telling himself to turn the cold water handle. At first it wouldn't work, but he tried again and this time he watched as his hand obeyed. He saw the bloody drops swirl down the drain.

Stubbornly, the dream tried to return to its normal pattern, forcing him to move cautiously out of the bathroom and into the hall, toward the bedroom where he would find Linda's tortured body. Stubbornly, he changed the dream, making himself turn in the other direction, back toward the staircase.

Distant laughter, queued forward from the end of the dream, drifted up from the first floor. Tully fought and won, forcing the dream to go his way, and he moved down the stairs, down toward the phantom laughter.

He took the last steps two at a time then ran toward the kitchen, following the laugh. Just as he shoved through the swinging door he glimpsed the silhouette of a man exiting the back door, the flapping tails of his dark overcoat disappearing into the night, taunting laughter echoing behind.

"No!" Tully screamed as he raced to the door. He pulled the knob, twisted it, pounded it. "No!"

In one swift motion, he grabbed his pistol from beneath the couch and sat bolt upright. He brought the gun up, aiming it at the stairs, at the puddling shadows.

"Zach!"

Kate's urgent whisper brought him to full wakefulness. He lowered the gun.

"Zach?" she said again. Her voiced drifted down the staircase. "Zach, are you all right?"

"Nothing's wrong," he said softly. Embarrassed, he quickly slid the gun back into its hiding place and turned on the table lamp.

Kate descended the stairs and now came to the couch and stood before him. "What happened?"

"Is Josh asleep?" he asked.

"Yes. He sleeps through anything."

"Was I that loud?"

"Pretty loud. Did something happen?" she asked impatiently.

What could he say? That he was about to ID the killer in his dream? That would go over real well. "Nothing happened," he managed. "Just a nightmare."

Kate nodded. "That must've been some nightmare."

"Yeah. It always is." What the hell, he thought. "Sit down," he told her, gesturing at the couch. "I'll tell you about it."

He was surprised at how little time it took to tell, and how easy it was to tell it. When he finished the story, he looked at her. "I really thought I was going to ID the guy. Pretty stupid, but that's what made me yell."

"Not stupid at all. Your instincts are talking to you. There's something you might subconsciously know about him that you haven't realized yet."

"It was the damnedest thing, that dream tonight."

"You haven't gone lucid before?"

"Huh?"

"Taken control of your dreams. Guided them."

"No. I didn't know that was possible."

"It just takes practice. Some cultures teach it to their kids so that they can get rid of their dream monsters. Jeez, Zach. Didn't you ever see *Nightmare on Elm Street?*"

"Yeah. I saw it a long time ago. *That's* what you're talking about?"

"The basics are there, all duded up for Hollywood, of course. The thing is, you can arm yourself and stop your nightmare if you want. Kill the dream, kill the bogeyman."

"Not until I get him in real life."

She studied him. "Maybe. Maybe the dream can help."

"I don't rely on dreams."

"No, but they give your instincts a medium to relay messages you might be missing."

He didn't want to agree, but he couldn't argue the sense of what she was saying. He'd been thinking it himself, after all.

"Maybe you actually saw the Backdoor Man previous to your family's murder and your subconscious is trying to make you realize it. After all," she added, "now would be a good time to recognize him."

"It would be, yes," he said dryly.

"What did he look like?"

"He wasn't much more than a phantom. Tall—well, he, didn't look tall, necessarily. He just *seemed* tall. He seemed big. He wore an overcoat, a trenchcoat, maybe. Everything was dark."

"The man seen with that murdered prostitute was wearing a long coat, according to the paper."

"We're pretty sure it was a trench."

"I think your instincts are telling you something. Maybe you subconsciously—"

"Know he's tall?" Tully interrupted. "Maybe. Or maybe it's just my particular metaphor for someone who's a tall order, you know, dangerous. And, for that matter, trenchcoats stir up images of mysterious people, spies and murderers, that kind of thing."

"What do you *feel* it meant?"

"Kate, I don't know."

"You're too close, maybe. Just let it simmer." She paused. "You said you started having the dream again when you came up here. Does the laugh sound like someone's laugh you've heard recently?"

He thought. "Actually, it sounded a little like Harlan King's."

"Do you know where he was when the Backdoor Man was active?"

"I did look into that on a few people. King was allegedly backpacking across Europe. I haven't asked him for any proof. Chances are, he won't have any and I don't want to arouse his suspicions right now by asking."

"So he could be the Backdoor Man," Kate said. "But I hope not. He seems so nice."

"Don't jump to any conclusions."

"I'm not. I'm just wondering what your instincts are about him."

"The man laughs all the time and he's full of the same crap everybody else is around here." He shook his head. "No. I think plain old guilt for leaving LA without catching the killer set off the dream. Who knows?"

"You know," she said somberly.

He rolled his eyes. "Hey, maybe next weekend when your ex arrives, he can hypnotize me and we'll have all the answers."

"Damn it, Tully, you sarcastic bastard, I'm just trying to help."

Her eyes filled with fire and he felt instant remorse. "Kate, I'm sorry for saying that. I have no excuse."

"You don't?" She took his hand and squeezed it briefly. "I don't know how you stay sane under all the pressure." She gave him the eye. "Just don't take your frustration out on me. Save it for someone who deserves it. Like Ron Settles."

He covered her hand with both of his. "I promise," he said, as sincere as he'd ever been in his life. "You're right about my being frustrated. Trying to analyze dreams is more frustration than I can handle at this point."

"Don't think about it anymore. It's going to come."

"How many more people will die before it comes?" He blinked back threatening tears. The final humiliation, he thought. She'd heard the worst. She didn't need to see it, too. He needed to change the subject, and quickly. "Do you really believe in all that dream interpretation stuff?"

She smiled. "I don't believe skyscrapers are always penises. But I used to have nightmares about Carl breaking in. I bought a book on lucid dreaming and taught myself. After about a month of trying, I changed the dream."

"How?"

"Every night before I fell asleep I told myself that if Carl knocked on my dream door, I'd throw a dream dart at him. You know, to get rid of him and his hot air."

"So what happened?" he asked, fascinated.

"He came, I threw the dart, and he flew away like a balloon with a slow leak." She laughed and her eyes were merry, too. "What I didn't expect was the sound. As he blew away, he sounded like a big, long, squeaky fart."

He laughed, too. "Talk about dream imagery. Sights *and* sounds."

"Thank God my dream nose wasn't working!" She wiped her eyes and looked at him. "I can't remember the last time I laughed like this."

"Me, either."

Forty-two

September 2

> Everyone is a moon, and has a dark side which he
> never shows to anybody.
>
> —Mark Twain

"Good morning, Sheriff. This is for you." Sally the dispatcher entered the back office and handed Tully a white envelope then headed for the coffee.

"Who delivered it?"

"I just got here. It was in the in-box."

His stomach knotted as he brushed the crumbs from a maple bar off the desk then swallowed the dregs of his coffee. He felt like he was being eaten alive, that soon he'd be nothing but a sorry pile of scraps. He had no new leads and his tension mounted with each passing hour. Adding to his problems was the disappearance of Arlene Rios, whom he had hoped to persuade to stay with Kate and Josh. Instead, Al Stoker had volunteered while his wife was visiting her sister in Crescent City. He was eight inches shorter and a couple inches narrower than Tully and claimed the McPherson couch was a comfortable fit.

Meanwhile, nothing had happened for a couple days—no notes, no phone calls, no bodies. Arlene's disappearance worried him, however. He'd gone days at a time without seeing her before this, but when he checked with the Dimples he found that she evidently hadn't returned to the boardinghouse at all.

He remembered her saying that she was going up the mountain to spy on the Brotherhood, but when he'd checked with Ambrose Abbott, the mayor swore there had been no meeting. That night the council had met at his office in the courthouse to decide what to do about the fallen stone and the Robbins' property in general, but that was all. He claimed he hadn't seen Rios since the explosion.

Tully intended to go up to the Circle today and look around, although it might be a long shot since no one had reported seeing her car in the vicinity. As soon as Sally left his office, he got up and refilled his mug. Returning to his desk, he sat down, picked up the envelope, and turned it over.

And saw his name written in Jack's spiked cursive.

It was only eight in the morning. Tully had walked in at six-thirty. The in-box had been empty then and it was empty at seven, when Tim Hapscomb went home. He'd locked the door behind the deputy himself, so whoever left it had to have a key or be an incredibly accomplished lock-picker. He wondered how many people in town had keys, other than his deputies. He thought the council members might and he mused again about Ron Settles.

The thing was, however it had been done, someone came in and he hadn't heard them, and that was scary. Silently, he retrieved a fingerprint kit and put it to use, but a short time later he'd found only his and Sally's prints on the smooth envelope and paper. He resisted reading the words. Settles, he thought as he opened the envelope. Settles really could be the one.

Or not. Maybe he was just hoping for a quick resolution. He thought about putting the man on leave for a few days, but with such a small force, it would be too hard on himself, Hapscomb, and Stoker. Besides, if Settles was the killer, his not working would just make him harder to track. It would give him more time to kill. He decided to try to ascertain Settles' whereabouts during each killing.

He glanced at the note then picked up the phone and punched in Kate's number. The machine answered, as he expected. After the beep, he said, "This is Tully," and the machine clicked off as the receiver was picked up.

"Hi," came a male voice. "It's Al. I was just getting ready to come to the station."

"Are Kate and Josh safely wherever they're supposed to be?"

"Yes. I escorted them and then came back here for a quick recheck. Doors. Windows."

"Do me a favor?"

"Sure."

"Try to find Arlene Rios, or at least her car. The yellow Mustang. Try hard. Check up the mountain in the vicinity of the Circle."

"You got it, boss."

"While you're driving around, check and see if Ron Settles is home. If he's not, try to find him, but don't let him catch on. Let me know what you find out."

"No problem. What's up?"

"Just covering all the bases. By the way, you didn't stop by the station earlier, did you?"

"No. Why?"

"A new letter from Jack has appeared."

There was a pause. "What's it say?"

"I haven't read it yet, but it means somebody came in here without my knowledge. While I was here and the front door was locked."

"Is that possible?"

"My office door was closed. It's very possible."

"Christ. I'll report in later."

"Thanks." Tully hung up and turned to the letter. He dreaded reading it.

*   *   *

In his car on the way to work, one of Reggie Skelton's underclothing straps dropped down over his shoulder. The feel of it had nearly driven him mad by the time he'd finally finished with the morning editorial meeting and all the usual bits of business the editor-in-chief of the *Herald* had to contend with. When he'd finally made it into his private office and shut the door, he'd briefly scanned the While-You-Were-Out notes his secretary had left, then decided all the callbacks could wait for another five minutes while he fixed the offending strap. Glancing back once more at Betty's empty office, he entered his private restroom, which was only accessible through his office. A man needed his privacy.

Reggie loved the feel of fine silks and satins against his body. Beneath his dapper three-piece suits he dressed in the very finest lingerie available in specialty catalogs.

Today, he wore a pink stretch satin bikini and a complementary pink satin teddy trimmed with white piping. The garter belt was also pink, but the hose hidden under his gray pinstripe trousers and black socks were a subtle shade of taupe.

Reggie adjusted the teddy's strap then rebuttoned his crisp white shirt, retied his bow tie, and buttoned his vest.

He quickly combed his thin dark hair then slipped his jacket back on and inspected himself in the mirror. Satisfied, he unlocked the restroom and reentered his office. He opened the office door and poked his head into Betty's office, intending to ask her to check with the printshop and make sure the ink supplier had shown up on schedule. But she still hadn't returned to her desk. He left his own door ajar so that when she returned she'd know he wanted to see her. It was a longtime signal.

Before sitting down to make the phone calls, he opened a large closet door opposite the one to the restroom and removed a whisk broom and dust pan. He bent to sweep up a few pieces of foam popcorn packing material he'd spied beneath his desk. The task done, he turned back to the supply closet. As he hung up the whisk broom, he heard someone step into the office.

"I'm glad you're back, Betty," he said, neatly replacing the dustpan on its hook.

He felt a pain in the back of his neck before the world ended. His visitor left unseen and unheard.

Tully forced himself to read the letter a second time. He hadn't wanted to read it even once, but now it was easier because numbness had set in.

My Dear Sheriff,

I cut a woman in half in 1947. Perhaps you heard about it. It was before your time but in your old stomping grounds. Los Angeles.

The City of Angels, an ironically apt name for such an amoral city.

I tortured her before I killed her and it was quite delightful, really. She was a rather attractive woman, though she couldn't compare to your wife, Tully.

Your wife, your wife. Linda, wasn't it? She proved quite a prize. I would have loved to have heard her screams, but unfortunately the neighbors might have heard as well.

Linda was a fighter, I assure you, and this new interest of yours, Kate McPherson, puts me in mind of her. I have no doubt that Kate will fight to protect the fruit of her loins just as your wife did to protect hers.

Your wife was very feminine; I examined a simple heart-shaped gold locket in her jewelry box. That impressed me with her good taste, or was it yours? Did you give it to her? Your picture—so young, Tully, so young—and your son's baby picture were within the locket, denoting a sentimental woman.

You can tell so much about a woman by her accoutrements, her bangles and baubles. Did you also give her the filigree silver earrings, the oval ones? They weren't right for her, you know, and I doubt she wore them often.

She was a woman made for gold, just as Kate McPherson does best with that metal. Silver is too cold.

In with her underthings, I found a fascinating stack of Post-it Note love letters that you wrote to her. Did you leave them on the refrigerator for her to find some mornings? Perhaps after a night of fucking? ''You're the greatest, Love, Zach,'' was rather prosaic but you favored it. There were at least ten of those alone.

As I said, a sentimental woman. And a woman with nerves of steel. Did you know that about her, my dear sheriff? She refused to cry, no matter what I did to her. I wonder if Kate will be so strong and proud?

Let me assure you, Sheriff Tully, I did many things to Linda. Many, many things. In fact, I would venture to say that in some ways, I came to know her far more intimately than you ever did.

Your son went much too easily, as most children do. Their terror, at least, is pure. They hold little interest for me otherwise. Your son kept trying to lose consciousness. That is what I most remember about him, trying to keep him alert. Trying to make sure he was aware of what he was experiencing, reminding him of what he watched me do to his mother. After all, it was a once-in-a-lifetime experience. For him, that is.

I thought you were an excellent foil, my friend, but I am disappointed in your inability to discern my presence now. Perhaps you need less subtle clues.

Your friend,
Jack

There was no longer a shred of doubt that Jack was the Backdoor Man. The truth was in the details and that fact coursed through Tully's veins. Jack wanted a fight and he would have it. A fight to the death.

Forty-three

The day moved along slowly for Tully, who was immersed in paperwork. He hated spending time on such mundane matters, but it had to be done—he'd let things stack up as much as he dared. Any more and he'd drown in paper, but it gave him something to do besides dwell on the letter.

Al Stoker was busy too, running minor calls all morning. Around ten, he'd driven past Ron Settles' house and reported that the Crown Vic was in the driveway, right where it was supposed to be. Tully was relieved to hear it.

Shortly before noon, Al found Arlene Rios' yellow Mustang parked in the rear of Panther Meadows Campground. There were no signs of trouble except, of course, for the absence of Arlene Rios. Right after that, a call came in about a bar brawl. Tully sent Stoker to the Oktober Fest and headed up Icehouse himself.

He stopped at the campground to check the Mustang and found only that the lock was as easy to jimmy as Stoker had said it was. With a gloved hand, he searched for a note or anything else that might be helpful. There was nothing so he headed up to the Circle and parked in the turnout near one of the ever-present purple Jeeps. He wondered if Kate was here.

It was much cooler up here in the thin air and Tully shivered in his shirtsleeves as he made his way down the trail. Voices carried across the meadow, happy voices.

He felt a rush of dizziness as he reached the bottom of the stairs. Circle effects, he thought. That much, he could believe. In his years in law enforcement, certain places seemed to attract violence—and not because of the neighborhood. There was a square block in Burbank that looked like the rest of the neighborhood—upper middle class—that constantly had murders, suicides, violence of all sorts. The people seemed normal enough, maybe a little edgy, but they had every right to be. That was a strange place, one where Tully never felt comfortable. Icehouse Circle was like that.

The tour—guided by someone other than Kate—was wrapping up, so Tully, as yet unnoticed, quietly walked along the mountainside, putting distance between himself and the stairs. He searched the brush, a couple hillside deadfalls, and looked around some mounds of boulders but found nothing. He turned back to search the hillside on other side of the stairs.

His timing was deplorable. The tour guide, with his tourists in tow, was fast approaching. The guide waved and Tully nodded and, quelling his urge to move on, stood his ground until they reached him.

The guide introduced him to the group. They looked at him and at each other and ultimately at their guide.

He said, a little uneasily, "On a case, Sheriff?"

"No, no. Like all of you, I find this a fascinating place. I'm visiting just like you are." He plastered a smile on his face to go with the aw-shucks speech he'd delivered.

The guide looked very relieved. "Please join us on a tour sometime."

"I'll do that."

The guide led his pack away and within a few minutes, Tully heard the Jeep pull out. He finished checking the mountainside then started across the meadow toward the Circle. In places, the grass was long enough to hide a body and Tully zigzagged back and forth, scanning. He stopped at a three-foot-high crop of stones, found nothing, and moved on. He had a feeling

something was wrong, very wrong, but he didn't trust his
instincts here, where the land confused everything.

Nearing the Circle, he moved to a taller stand of stones,
boulders really. The hairs on his neck rose as he caught a very
faint whiff of death. "Damn," he whispered, catching the odor
again, stronger now. You couldn't mistake the smell of human
putrefaction for that of other animals; nature saw to that.

He wanted to turn and walk away from what he knew was
there in the darkness between the stones. He wanted to, but he
couldn't. Instead, he took a penlight from his pocket and shined
it into the darkness.

Peering inside, he forced back a wave of nausea. Arlene
Rios was there, sitting propped against the rocks. There was a
prominent triangle of raw flesh on her cheek. And there was
the place where her nose was supposed to be. It had been sliced
cleanly off. Dried blood masked the lower part of her face.
"Damn. Damn it."

A lead weight in his stomach, Tully went to call for help.

When Phil Katz finally called, Tully had just seen off Kate
and Josh, who traveled home with Al Stoker picking up the
rear. Al had brought the boy to the station since Tully was tied
up, and now the deputy was going to spend another night at
Kate's cabin. Tully wished he was the one going home with
her.

Instead, he'd just found out from Phil that the severed nose
was not tucked into some other part of Arlene Rios' body. It
was a souvenir, the doctor theorized. The reporter had been
killed cleanly with a well-placed icepick. That and the triangle
of missing skin were the only signs of trauma. Death, at least,
had probably been quick and painless—the nose had been
removed after. Tully couldn't help feeling that Rios' murder
was somehow his fault.

The intercom buzzed. "Sheriff?"

"Yes, Sally? What are you still doing here?"

"I'm about to leave," the dispatcher said hurriedly. "Someone from the *Herald* is on line one. All she'd say is that she wants to talk to you."

"Okay." The paper already wanted a statement about the Rios murder. "I'll take it in here. See you tomorrow."

"Good night."

Sally clicked off and Tully took the call. The woman didn't want a statement. Another body had been found. Reggie Skelton, editor, councilman, and lifer, was dead.

Settles came in just as Tully was heading out. Briefly he told him the latest and asked him to call Tim Hapscomb and offer him some overtime to come in early tonight. Settles grunted acknowledgment and headed for the office.

Ten mintes later, he arrived at the *Herald* and he pulled around back. Only two cars were parked in the newspaper's potholed lot. Obviously, the paper wasn't going to press tonight.

Entering the unlocked backdoor, he found himself in the press room, where the air was filled with the fresh smell of ink and the old black-iron presses were practically antiques. Nothing seemed wrong or out of place in the deserted room, but he drew his .38 before walking through the cavernous space and into the main corridor.

Tully passed the camera and typesetting rooms then surprised a heavyset man in janitor's greens as he entered the editorial pool. His eyes on the gun, he backed away, hands raised.

"Where's Betty?"

"The boss's office." The custodian hitched his thumb toward the front of the building.

"Stay put," Tully ordered as he moved on, the light spilling from the doorway to the office of Reggie Skelton's secretary. The room protected Reggie's private office from the rest of the world. Betty sat at her desk, softly sobbing. He holstered his gun and entered.

"Ms. Sanderson?" he called softly. "Sheriff Tully."

Betty Sanderson turned and looked up. She was deadly pale as he shook her trembling, clammy hand.

"I found Reggie's—Mr. Skelton's—body right before I called. It's in his office closet."

Tully nodded and entered the editor's office. The man sitting in the supply closet was impeccably neat. Skelton's eyes were open, his features slack. His clothing unmussed, he looked as if he were merely resting. There was no blood visible and Tully thought odds were Jack had used his icepick again.

Tully stood and rejoined Betty in the doorway. "I'm calling in the coroner and another officer to help me take photos and gather evidence. The office is off-limits otherwise. Why don't you wait in the office across the way?"

She nodded. "What about Rocky?"

"Who?"

"The janitor. Shall I tell him?"

"Please. Tell him not to do any more cleaning. Bring him back up here. But first, I have a couple questions for you."

"Of course."

Reggie had been dead a while. "When did you last see Mr. Skelton?"

"I saw him this morning before he went to the editorial meeting. I was down to the bakery getting donuts for the office when the meeting ended. He wasn't in his office when I returned, but I knew he'd been there because he'd left the door ajar. He does that when he wants to see me. So he doesn't have to leave a note or anything, I mean."

"And you entered at that time?"

"Yes, but he wasn't there."

"The closet door was closed?"

"Yes. Nothing looked out of place. I just went back to my office. Things got busy. About lunchtime, I realized I still hadn't seen him. He was getting lots of calls, so I started asking around the shop. Reggie—Mr. Skelton—he spends a lot of time in the press-room. He's often out of his office for hours at a time."

"To your knowledge, had anyone seen him?"

"No. I called his house, but there wasn't any answer."

"Did you leave a message?"

"He doesn't have a machine, Sheriff. He always answers himself if he's home. He didn't answer, and when he didn't come in after lunch I was a little concerned, but there were a million things to do and time just flew away. We go to press tomorrow night and it's always hectic this time of the week. I didn't have time to think anymore about it. People started going home between four and five—that's because we all work late tomorrow—but I stayed late. I remember hearing Rocky come in a little while before I . . . Before I opened the closet.''

"Why did you open the closet?" Tess asked.

"To get a box of paperclips. I was out of them. I—I opened the door and Reggie was just sitting there." Tears started to flow. "I said his name. He didn't answer. I saw his eyes were open and I touched his hand." She shuddered. "It was cold as ice.''

"During business hours, how likely is it that someone would enter the building through the front door without being seen?''

"Oh, not at all," she said as she dabbed at her eyes with a damp Kleenex. "We have a receptionist and if she isn't here, there's a bell. And no one could get past me. Oh dear.''

"What?''

"Myrna wasn't out front this morning. She had an appointment.''

"And you were away from your desk for how long?''

"Twenty minutes. Maybe thirty. Oh dear." The secretary glanced toward Skelton's door. "Oh dear.''

"It's not your fault, Ms. Sanderson," Tully said gently. "Tell me, did you see Harlan King when you were at the bakery?''

Sally shook her head. "No. He wasn't in this morning. He has an assistant. She waited on me.''

"Did you happen to see Deputy Settles any time this morning before Mr. Skelton disappeared?''

She thought then brightened slightly. "Yes, actually, I did. He came into the bakery just as I was leaving.''

Tully nodded. Unfortunately, neither Settles nor King was off the list. "Thank you, Ms. Sanderson. That's all for now. Why don't you go get Rocky?''

Nodding, she left. Tully thought she looked grateful to have something to do.

* * *

It was approaching midnight when Tully turned onto the dark road leading to his cabin. Now, he was glad that Al Stoker was spending another night on Kate's sofa. Tully was too exhausted, physically and mentally, to do it himself.

Scanning for his driveway, he slowed. The porchlight had burned out days ago and no matter how many times he was reminded—coming home in the dark this way—he hadn't gotten around to replacing it. Tomorrow morning he promised himself, he'd do it. If he lived in this place for twenty years— *Lord, no!*—he'd never be able to find the cabin in the thick and unrelenting mountain darkness.

He saw the driveway at the last possible instant and turned in, pulling up to the carport and thinking that if he'd at least leave a second-story light on it would be much easier to find the house. *If, if, if.* Yawning, he got out and stretched, then walked slowly up the path to the cabin, shuffling his feet to make sure he didn't trip in the dark. *Been there, done that.* He found the lowest porch step with his toe and stepped up, keys in hand, ready to open the door as soon as he found the lock.

His foot came down on something as he took a final step onto his doormat. It surprised him, but it felt like nothing but a piece of brush or a rolled-up flyer. He unlocked the door and stepped inside, shaking his foot as he realized that whatever he'd stepped on was stuck to his shoe. Balancing on one foot, he felt for the light switch and flicked it on.

A white rose clung to his sole by a single sharp thorn. There was only that and nothing more.

PART THREE

Forty-four

> Sorcerer, n. The ancient prototype and forerunner
> of political influence.
>
> —Ambrose Bierce

"I'm going to call a town meeting." Ambrose Abbott puffed
is pipe and paced the length of his office. "Shut the door,"
e barked. "Shut the damn door and sit down."

Tully pulled the door closed but made no move to sit. Rather,
e leaned against a file cabinet, crossed his arms, and silently
vatched as Abbott stalked the room like a caged lion. When
he mayor called him at the station and requested his presence,
'ully had been intrigued, thinking that maybe he was finally
oing to get some answers, or at least, some cooperation.

This was his first visit to Abbott's office, which was pretty
veird considering that the man was his employer. It was located
a the courthouse building along with most of the other town
nd county offices.

Abbott's office was as dust-dry as the mayor himself. Fur-
ished with dark reddish Mission-style furniture, the room's

Navajo white walls were decorated with aging photos of Eter
nity and Icehouse Mountain. Nowhere was there any relie
from the monochromatics; the entire room looked like a sepia
tone print. The mayor, in brown tweeds, was perfectly suite
to his office.

Abbott stared at the framed photo of the park hanging at th
far end of the room. It depicted the bandshell, complete wit
orchestra, picnickers, and strolling couples. It looked like
modern picture except for the turn-of-the-century clothing; me
in light suits and boaters, women in long Gibsonesque summe
dresses, some ornamented with delicate parasols. A policema
on a horse kept watch from the shade of an oak tree as childre
skipped along the paths.

The mayor turned to face Tully. "Well?"

"Well what?"

"I'm calling a town meeting."

"So you said. Concerning?"

"The murders, of course," Abbott growled. "Why els
would I call you in?"

"Mayor Abbott, until now, you've been very uncommunica
tive," Tully said. "I can't read your mind."

Abbott eyed him then nodded gruffly. "Noted. I'm tellin
you now. I want your input and I want you to speak at th
meeting."

"Not a problem. What exactly is the purpose of th
meeting?"

"It's time we tell the general populace that things are gettin
out of hand and something must be done."

"I think they know that already. Things have been out o
hand for a long time," Tully said. "Does this decision hav
anything to do with Reggie Skelton's murder?"

"Of course it does. And the others, naturally," he added. I
sounded like an afterthought.

"But Skelton's death is what did it, isn't it? That's why
we're talking now."

Abbott blinked slowly, his expression enigmatic. "Why d
you say that?"

"He was a lifer."

"Jackson Coop was a lifer as well. So were the Robbins."

"But they weren't insiders; they weren't on the council. Or
the Brotherhood. Skelton was."

"I don't see—"

"You don't see?" Tully exploded. "You don't see? Cut the
bullshit, Mayor. It's obvious. Until Skelton died, it was one
big party among you so-called lifers. You joke about the murders, the Death Pool bets on who's going to die next. None of
the victims except Skelton and Coop were lifers."

"You forgot about the Robbins again."

"You people regarded them as unwanted trash. But the
respectable lifers didn't think anything would happen to their
own, did they? At least not to the ones who play along."

Abbott shrugged, but his eyes never wavered.

"You said the killer is one of your own."

"I suspect it, Sheriff. I do not know it."

"This is a game to you, isn't it? A little excitement is fine,
but maybe now there's too much? It might harm the tourist
trade."

"The human race is ghoulish. It takes more than this to
effect tourism negatively. As for my playing a game, that is
incorrect. I would not consider murder a game."

"A diversion, then."

"Oh, please, Tully. Sarcasm doesn't suit you. Leave it to
an expert."

"Just cut the crap." Tully took a deep breath. "You've lied
to me. You've lied to the entire town, you and your goddamned
council."

"I have no idea what you mean."

"You want me to catch the killer, but you lied about the
murders in June."

"June?" Abbott raised his eyebrows.

"The hikers. The two women who were mutilated on the
mountain."

"That was not murder. It was an accident I don't recall even
mentioning to you. A bear—"

"The bear was a cover-up. The women were murdered."

"How did you come to such a conclusion?" Abbott demanded. "Don't you have enough deaths to investigate without going after unrelated incidents?"

"Jackson Coop told me all about it."

"The council hired him to kill the bear. Coop was eccentric. He loved to spin tall tales. Undoubtedly he told you stories about Bigfoot as well?"

"And government conspiracies," Tully said quickly. He wanted to bring up the note that had disappeared from the coroner's office, but Coop wouldn't have known about that and the revelation might endanger Phil Katz. Then he thought of another way.

"Reggie Skelton," he said, gazing steadily at the mayor, "told me about the note in the woman's body. The one that said 'Jack the Ripper.' "

"Did you confirm that with Dr. Katz?"

"He claimed no knowledge," Tully lied.

Abbott sank into his chair. "I can't imagine why Reggie would say such a thing to you. By the way, what was the cause of his death?"

"A small ice pick or awl. One of our killer's favorite tools Arlene Rios was murdered in the same manner. In case you care." Tully crossed to stand before Abbott, anxious to get back to the subject. "Maybe Reggie told me about the Jack the Ripper note because he feared for his life. Maybe he thought telling me the truth about the June incidents would help keep him alive."

"It didn't though, did it?"

Abbott spoke smoothly, but Tully detected a tinge of uneasiness in his voice. "No," he replied. "But the truth might help save others. Including yourself. Why did you lie?"

"You said it yourself," he said simply. "It's one thing if a local waitress or salesman is killed. That doesn't affect the tourist trade. But visitors—the tourists themselves—getting killed, well, that's something else entirely." He chuckled "Killing tourists kills the trade. It takes all the fun out of it for them. The June incident was isolated and we took care of it.''

"And left a killer loose.''

"We investigated. Sheriff Lawson was on it.''

"He knew the truth?''

"Of course he knew.''

"Why aren't there any police reports available?''

Abbott narrowed his eyes and said with finality, "Because, Sheriff Tully, a bear killed the women, not a murderer. And I'll deny I ever told you anything else.''

"I guess you didn't want any reporters finding out the truth.''

"What do you think?''

"I think covering up a crime makes you an accessory to murder.''

"The only proof of murder you have is in stories told by persons now deceased.''

"True.'' Tully decided to back off; there was no point in further alienating the man when he was finally beginning to show some twisted signs of cooperation. He'd play along and worry about ethics later. Pulling up a chair, he sat down in front of Abbott's desk. "Fine. It was a bear. Let's get back to the town meeting. It's a good idea. Perhaps you can give a talk first; I'll want plenty of time to observe the audience. Our man will probably be there.''

Abbott nodded, his craggy face relaxing slightly. "I'll see that you have it.''

"When?''

"As soon as feasible. Monday night. The seventh. Six-thirty. The council and I will meet privately with you at six.''

"Monday's Labor Day. Can't we do this sooner?''

"There's not enough time to get the word out and the holiday doesn't matter. A winter storm is predicted to arrive by Tuesday evening and if it's a bad one, we won't have many attendees.''

"A storm? It's a little early for that, isn't it?''

"Yes, but it's not unheard of. The weather reports are full of it. Remember El Niño? Don't you listen to the news?''

"Sure, but—''

"A storm in Eternity is not the same creature as a storm in Los Angeles. Trust me. It's in the air. It's coming. It's something those of us who have lived here a while can sense. So, we'll get the word out for a Monday night town meeting."

"Before you're inundated with skiers?"

Abbott almost smiled. Almost. "Yes. There's that, isn't there?"

"Fine. Let's do it." Tully paused. "I have one more question."

"Go ahead."

"Ron Settles."

"What about him?"

"Do you have any suspicions about him that you haven't shared with me?"

Abbott's eyebrows raised. "Why? Do you suspect him?"

"I suspect everyone. What about Settles, Mayor?"

"It's possible, I suppose. I hadn't really thought about it." Tully figured that was a lie. "And Harlan King?"

"The same answer as Settles."

"Either of the Dimples?"

"Are you going to list off all the council members, Sheriff?"

"Should I?"

"I think it's a waste of time." Abbott studied him. "What about me? Am I a suspect?"

"Where were you yesterday morning between eight-thirty and nine-thirty?"

"In my bookshop getting ready to open."

"Anyone see you?"

"Not before ten. Mornings are trial enough without enduring the company of my alleged fellow man."

Tully walked to the door and turned the knob before replying, "I suspect everyone, you included. Good day."

Forty-five

September 4

> When we remember we are all mad, the mysteries
> disappear and life stands explained.
>
> —Mark Twain

"Hello, gentlemen," Zach Tully said to the gaggle of old men draped on and around the bench fronting the King's Tart.

"Good morning, Sheriff," the Delbert twins said in chorus.

"Sheriff," said Abe Beakman. "How are you today?"

"Fine."

"Eating donuts instead of chasing the killer?" asked Orson Hooker in his usual sullen tone.

"Need to keep my strength up," Tully said. Then he smiled, but only with his lips. His eyes were cold.

The old men returned tentative, harmless grins. "May we help you?" asked a Delbert.

"You might help by answering a couple questions."

"We can't divulge names under any circumstances," intoned the other twin.

"We're like priests or doctors in that regard," added Beakman, tightly shutting his ever-present notepad.

"Fucking priests," Hooker emphasized.

"I understand," Tully told them in soothing tones as he leaned against the stair railing and crossed his arms. "I don't expect you to reveal nonpertinent information. Okay?"

"All right," said Beakman.

"How long had Jackson Coop been cropping up as a candidate in your death pool?"

"Maybe a hundred years." Hooker laughed heartily.

Tully stared at him until he stopped.

"It's a joke, Sheriff, a joke!" Hooker said, his fat face red, mostly with merriment. "Don't you have jokes in Los Angeles?"

"The man is dead," Tully stated.

"And Orson here would apologize if he knew how," said Beakman. "The answer to your question is that Coop's come up many times over many years."

"But he's a lifer. Isn't it unusual for a lifer's name to come up so often?"

Beakman appeared amused. "Yes, but he's always been a troublemaker."

"A trickster," amended a Delbert twin. "Not malicious."

"Just full of shit," Hooker finished.

"He irritated people?"

"Yes, indeed," Beakman replied. "But not to any serious extent."

"He talked a lot," Tully observed.

"Yes. Yes he did," said Beakman. "That's probably what started the wagering on him. Over the years, betting on Coop became a habit." He rubbed his chin thoughtfully. "Of course, there was more to it: Coop was a careless hunter."

"Yes," said a Delbert. "And he had a penchant for handling snakes."

"So," said the other twin, "there were always good odds on him accidentally killing himself."

"I don't think anyone expected he'd actually be murdered," said Beakman. "At least not by a human being."

"How often did he go hunting?"

"Any time he damn well wanted," said Hooker.

"Very frequently." Beakman gave Hooker a withering but unnoticed look. "Primarily, he hunted squirrel, which he loved to have for supper."

"He always went out loaded for bear," said a Delbert, "Even when it was small game he was after. Of course, he'd take a twenty-two along, too."

"Yeah," chuckled Hooker. "Ain't much meat left on a squirrel that's been blasted with double-ought."

Tully listened as the men eulogized Coop and decided they were telling the truth. He cleared his throat. That produced silence, the desired effect. "Were there many bets on the Robbins?" he asked, peering at each man in turn.

"No. We just tried to pretend they didn't exist. Betting on them would have made them more real," explained Beakman.

"What about Reggie Skelton?"

They replied with a chorus of no's.

"So who's big on the hit list today?"

"The answer may upset you," Beakman said.

"Me?" Tully asked.

"Yes, Sheriff. You're second only to Kate McPherson. Her son doesn't count since we decided it's rude to bet on kids, so Edna Boyle rounds out the top three," Beakman told him.

"Dr. Katz's nurse?"

"Yes."

"She's a lifer. Why her?"

"Wishful thinking, probably," said a Delbert.

"You ever seen that dried-up old heap of bear droppings?" Hooker asked.

"You might be interested to know that we're having a run on all the council members now," Beakman interrupted.

"Fad," claimed a twin.

"It will pass," said the other.

"What about Ron Settles?"

"Well," said Beakman slowly, "He's come up once or twice, but not regularly."

"What about Sheriff Lawson?" Tully asked "Did he make it to your list?"

"A lot of people made a little money upon his demise."

"Sheriff's always on the list," Hooker said, grinning like a pumpkin.

"Naturally. Thank you for your help, gentlemen." Tully smiled then headed for the bakery door.

"Sheriff Tully!" boomed Harlan King, dapper in his baker's whites. "How are you this morning?

Tully let the door shut before answering. "All right. Yourself?"

"Fine." He shook his head. "A shame about Reggie, though," he said in a quieter voice.

"Yes."

"What can I get you?"

"Lemon bar and coffee." He hadn't intended to eat, but the fragrance was irresistible.

King poured black brew into a foam cup then retrieved the pastry. Tully paid and sipped the strong, hot liquid. "When did you hear about Reggie?"

"Last night. How did he die?"

"Sharp instrument to the back of the head."

"How terrible for him. But not as bad as what I heard about poor old Coop. Is the rumor about him true?"

"What rumor?"

King actually blushed. "That his . . . That he . . . Let's just say that he went off half-cocked. Is that true?"

"Uh, yeah," Tully replied after an instant of confusion. "I guess you could say that. Where'd you hear about it?" He had requested that this detail be suppressed and the paper had reported only that Coop had died of blood loss from an abdominal wound.

"Evelyn Cordelia Caine. She's almost as big a gossip as Martha Ann Dimple." King smiled knowingly. "Don't bother reprimanding her, Sheriff. She swore everyone she told to secrecy, I'm certain. She always does. The simple truth is, Mrs. Caine can't be stopped. Her tongue is a force of nature.''

Tully nodded. ''The other day, you mentioned the leader of the Brotherhood.''

''Did I?'' Harlan's eyebrows went up Doughboy-style.

''Yes, you did. I wonder if you might tell me who the leader is?''

''The leader?''

Tully hid his irritation. ''You called him His Nibs. I'd like to speak to him. He's probably in danger.''

''I'll let him know,'' King said, showing no surprise whatsoever.

''Is it Abbott?'' Tully asked. ''Settles? Yourself, perhaps?''

''I took a sworn oath, but I'll give him your message.''

''Then keep this in mind, Mr. King. You're all in danger.''

''We all are,'' King amended, including Tully in the mix. ''We all are.''

''Can you tell me where you were between eight-thirty and nine-thirty Tuesday morning?''

King looked abashed. ''I felt a bit under the weather so I had my assistant open for me. As you undoubtedly already know, I have no witnesses, but I was at home.''

''Any idea who might have it in for Reggie Skelton?''

King only shrugged. ''If it weren't for all the other murders, I'd be more willing to guess. As it is, I couldn't make a logical guess with what little I know. How does his death compare to the others?''

It was Tully's turn to shrug. ''Let's not even consider that for now. Just tell me what you think—without thinking about it first. Who would have it in for Reggie? Just for Reggie?''

''Homophobes,'' Harlan said promptly.

''He was gay, not just a transvestite?''

''Maybe. I only say that because he never kept the company of women, at least not in public view. Whether he was or wasn't gay doesn't matter to a homophobe.''

Tully nodded. ''They usually don't know the difference. Was

his proclivity for women's underthings common knowledge around here?''

''Oh my, no. Reggie stayed in the closet. But his oldest, dearest friends knew, of course. We never spoke of it because Reggie never spoke of it.''

''Then how did you know?''

King chuckled softly. ''There were no women around his house, but there was always plus-size lingerie hanging over the shower curtain. He also kept Victoria's Secret and Frederick's catalogs in the bathroom, but I doubt he used them in the way most men would.''

''Who were Reggie's oldest friends?''

''Myself, Ambrose, Elmer Dimple, Coop.'' He paused meaningfully. ''There were only a few others he ever socialized with. I don't know of anyone ever invited to his home that I haven't mentioned by name. He was a private man.''

''Who are the local homophobes?'' Tully's mind had again drifted in Ron Settles' direction—he gave off bigotry like shitty cologne.

''Offhand, I can't think of anyone.''

''Hooker?'' Tully prompted.

''Hooker?''

''Out there on your bench.''

''He's harmless.''

''Is he homophobic?''

''Probably, but he's all hot air and feathers. I wouldn't count him a suspect.'' King smiled. ''Let me think about it, Sheriff.''

''What about people who read the newspaper?''

''Reggie kept his pleasures private.''

''That's not what I meant. Did he ever rile up the readership? Make someone angry?''

''That's possible. Reggie was a good man. A fair man. But the simple act of reporting can make enemies. Let me think about that as well. Offhand, I don't remember his mentioning problems with anyone. Perhaps,'' he added, ''he wasn't entertaining the killer adequately? Not paying enough homage via the written word. Could that be why he was killed?''

"Could be," Tully said, annoyed he hadn't thought of that himself.

"Tell you what, Sheriff," King said. "I'll come and see you Monday, before the town meeting. I'm closing early, five or five-thirty, and I'll be over directly after that. Meanwhile, I'll jot down anything I can come up with that might help you."

"I appreciate that. See you Monday."

Many years ago she had been certified insane, but that was during a dark time in the annals of psychiatry, during Freudian times, when every tower was a masculine symbol and each tunnel, a feminine one. She had never been mad, but was dosed with drugs that made her insane to prove her family's assertion that she was not a creature of lucidity.

It happened because she did not conform to society's vision of wife and mother; it happened because she was assertive in a time when ambition in a woman meant insanity.

They put her in an one asylum then another, dark dank places overrun with patients, and for each patient there were a dozen rats and five times that in cockroaches. She had lain chained to iron beds, fouled with her own excrement and vomitus, and listened to the screams of the true madwomen in the ward.

She wondered still how many of them had been as sane as she, how many were victims of their own ambitions and desires, of their own families. Of their own bodies.

Only one of her many children cared enough about her to arrange her release. He replaced her at the asylum with a true madwoman from Spitalfields. There was only a passing resemblance between them, but in those days, it was enough. Her son had then taken her along on an amazing journey, one she never quite understood. It had ended in Eternity, California.

He was a dutiful son, but she dreaded the nights when the blood ran and the lights on the mountain went wild.

She knew. She had always known. Sometimes he would talk about his deeds back in London and his eyes would glow with the bright enthusiasm of a child. She had been declared insane, but it was her son, her poor loyal son, who was mad.

Lately, he'd begun to speak of foul crimes he had committed in other places. She did not want to hear any of it, but he insisted on telling her the most minute of details. Soon, she feared, he would brag of his current activities. If he did, she would be torn in two. She loved her son and he loved her, but could she live with such knowledge?

She stared momentarily at the knife on her kitchen counter, a sharp paring knife that she might take to the bath and use to drain herself of blood in the warm, soothing water. She had thought of it many times over the years, but it would have disappointed the son who had gone to such lengths to ensure her life continued. She put the knife back in the drawer. Her son, she reminded herself, had a tremendous imagination and he loved to tell tales. He even wrote them for a time and had them published under another name. They were good tales, but very grim. Perhaps, she told herself for the thousandth time, perhaps he was only telling stories, embroidering little fictions on the reality of others' lives.

Kate's stomach dropped as she watched Carl climb from a silver Lexus he'd parked in her driveway. *Son of a bitch. You son of a bitch.* He was a day early. Not only that, but he hadn't even had the courtesy to let her know. If he had, she would have made sure she wasn't home.

He knocked and knocked again. After about five minutes, she went to the door and opened it. She looked at Carl, who was holding a Saks shopping bag in one hand and a small bouquet of red roses in the other. The roses gave her the creeps. "You were supposed to arrive tomorrow," she said, blocking the doorway with her body. It wasn't very subtle, but who cared.

"Yes. Isn't it nice? I caught an earlier flight so we'd have time to all go out to dinner together tonight, you, me, and Joshua."

"I see."

"You said he was going somewhere tomorrow?"

"Out of town with friends."

"It would have been thoughtful of you to cancel those plans since I rarely get to see my own son."

"Thoughtful for you, not for him."

"I've got presents for you both." He bent down and retrieved a shopping bag. "Including copies of my new book for both of you." He tried unsuccessfully to step inside.

Kate made no move to take the proffered gifts. "You can come in for a few minutes." She stepped aside and he slithered in, going immediately to the dining table to deposit the presents. Then he turned to her, quickly approaching. He tried to put his arms around her.

She flinched away. "Keep your distance."

"Don't worry. I won't bite."

That smile. That smarmy smile.

"You're the last thing that worries me, Carl." She wanted to kick his teeth in, but she kept it to herself. Instead, she said, "You should go to your cabin." She crossed to the kitchen and took a map and a key from the drawer then handed them to him. She was ready for the bastard. "If you stay here, the police are going to get very excited unless I tell them otherwise."

"What? What do you mean, sweetheart?"

"Don't call me that. I witnessed a murder. Josh was with me. We have reason to believe we're being stalked."

"Katherine," Carl oozed, his eyes popping. "What are you doing? You and Joshua must come and stay with me in Beverly Hills. This is too dangerous."

"We're not going anywhere, Carl. I have a job. Josh has school and friends. We have a life."

Carl smiled sympathetically. "Darling, are you sure this killer is really after you? In the past, you've exhibited a tendency to overreact. You possess quite an active imagination."

"I'm not your darling and I won't allow you to mindfuck

me again.'' She used coarse words to shock him and it appeared to work, if briefly.

"Dinner?" he asked in a falsely meek tone.

"Yes." She looked at Carl. "Josh and I will go to dinner with you tonight, but if you pull any more of your headgames, we're leaving." Turning toward the stairs, she raised her voice. "Josh? Come on down here."

"In a minute, Mom," he called.

"We're going out to dinner, honey. Wash up."

" 'Kay."

"Just the three of us," Carl said. "Just like old times."

Ignoring him, she picked up the phone and dialed the sheriff's station. "Sheriff Tully, please. Yes, I'll hold."

"Do you have to report your every move?" Carl asked. "Is it that serious?"

She glanced at him. "*I'm* that serious. Yes, Zach?" Emphasis on *Zach.* "This is me." She saw Carl's eyebrow arch at the familiarities. After indulging in a moment of small talk she told Zach that Carl had arrived early. "He's asked us out to dinner," she said.

"Where?" Tully asked.

"I thought Carlo's. That's a nice, safe place. You *will* come with us, won't you?" She watched Carl's expression turn sour and she suppressed a secret smile.

"I think I can arrange that," Tully said. "Seven o'clock?"

"See you there." Kate hung up. "Just the four of us."

"I can't believe you need to have a guard with you to have dinner in a public place."

"Carl," Kate said softly. "Let's get one thing straight. "I'm only going to dinner with you for Josh's sake. You're his father, he should see you, and dinner in a family restaurant seems like a good idea."

"But we don't need the cop."

"I do. So does Josh."

"But I want to talk to you privately."

"You want to talk me into moving back into your house."

"*Our* home."

"*Your* home, Carl. This is *my* home. I won't have you trying
o con me back to LA in front of Josh. Is that clear?"

"Of course. But you don't need someone else there to make
ne keep my word."

"Yes, I do."

At that moment Kate heard Josh coming downstairs.

"Your father's here," Kate said, for lack of anything better.

"Hi, Joshua, my boy."

"Hi," he replied, studying his shoes.

"You dad's going to take us to dinner."

"I'm not hungry."

"Come on. It'll be fun. Zach's coming, too."

"Zach? Cool!" Josh raised his gaze, a smile threatening.

"He'll meet us there," Kate said. She was perversely
njoying the boy's reaction to his father, but she also felt guilty
or the enjoyment. She hadn't realized that Josh would behave
o negatively. Kate tried hard to be neutral about Carl in front
f their son. Had she failed? She knocked the thought away.
Carl had alienated him all by his lonesome. "This will be fun,
osh," she said, feeling a little sorry for the pompous windbag
vho was trying hard—too hard—to smile like Robert Young
n *Father Knows Best*. "This way we all get to spend a little
ime together."

"I'm still going to the beach tomorrow with Billy," he
lurted defensively.

"Of course you are. And tonight we'll go to Carlo's and
ou can have spaghetti or anything else you want."

"I've got presents for you, sport," Carl said. He went to the
able and retrieved the books and the wrapped boxes. "Here's
 copy of *Healing Through Manipulation* for each of you," he
aid as he handed them out. "I autographed them so you can
how everybody that you're related to a celebrity."

Kate suppressed a groan.

"And this is for you." He handed her a small box. She set
 on top of the book, ready to return both to the table.

"Open it, Katharine. Please."

"Okay." She made herself smile for Josh's sake as she

removed the wrapper, revealing a bottle of Opium perfume. "Thanks, Carl." Underneath, she was furious. She hated the stuff, always had. It gave her migraines. She had told Carl that much on a half-dozen occasions. She set the items on the table.

"You can wear it tonight," he said.

She wasn't about to bother reminding him she was hypersensitive; that would just elicit a condescending lecture on the power of negative thinking. "We'll see," she said instead. "Josh, why don't you open your gift?"

The boy tore into the foot-square box and pulled out a white volley ball. He looked at it oddly, then up at his father. "Thanks."

Kate said nothing. Josh had written him a letter a few months ago (at her insistence) and he said that he liked softball and basketball. He hadn't mentioned volleyball. She doubted there was even a court in town. The man's thoughtlessness astounded her. "I'm going to change clothes," she announced.

She moved swiftly up the stairs, frazzled but pleased. She hadn't let Carl push her around. She'd taken charge. And if he still tried to get her to wear the perfume, she'd just say no.

Forty-six

Carl Leland was, Tully thought, a fatuous dickhead. He could think of no better word. He felt sorry for Josh, who kept cringing away from the man, especially when he went on a braggadocio binge. Kate looked embarrassed and disgusted by turns and had rolled her eyes in Tully's direction several times.

Tully spent most of his time watching the other diners and studying the people walking by on the sidewalk. Doing those things were infinitely more interesting than listening to Carl Leland expound on everything from the psychology of truculent ten-year-old boys to that of serial killers threatening ex-wives. None of it made good dinner conversation and none of it bore any relevancy to reality.

Now they were having spumoni and while Carl had the spoon in his mouth, Josh finally spoke up. "Zach and Mom and I had a picnic by Zach's pond last Sunday. It was really cool."

Carl threw Tully a studied, deprecating glance then looked at Josh. "Son, if you want to bypass your trip tomorrow, I'll be happy to take you on the *best* picnic you've ever been on in your entire life."

Josh shook his head. "Huh-uh. Zach already did that and I'm going to the beach tomorrow. Mom said."

Carl chuckled. "I'm sorry you don't realize that you should

spend time with me, but you're only a child. When you're older, you'll remember this. When you do, try not to feel guilty, won't you, son? Remember, even when you're wrong, I love you. While you're gone, perhaps your mother would like to accompany me—''

"I have plans," Kate interrupted. "But thanks anyway."

"Surely you'll have one day free while I'm here."

"Sorry, no. Between work and previous plans I have no time whatsoever." She looked hard at her ex-husband and Tully saw she was exploring new territory. "You and I have nothing in common but our son, Carl, so enjoy his company while you can."

After a few more minutes of awkward banter, Tully cleared his throat. "I have some work to finish. Dr. Leland, if you'd like to follow me I can show you the way to your cabin. Kate, I'll see you and Josh home after that."

"Kate already gave me a map," Carl protested. "I'll take them home then find the cabin myself."

"I'm sorry," Tully said, not sorry at all, "but because of the threats, I or one of my deputies always accompany Kate and Josh home."

Kate asked brightly, "Who's spending the night? You or Al?"

Leland's mouth worked before anything came out. "What? Katherine, what is the meaning of this?"

"Zach doesn't want us home alone at night," Kate said, a little too smugly.

"Al is my deputy," Tully said out of pity. "He's been good enough to guard Kate and Josh at night." He said to Kate, "Al will be there tonight."

He rose, basking in Kate's smile.

"Why don't I join you?" Carl asked.

"We've got an early day tomorrow," Kate said.

"I'll call you tomorrow, Katherine."

"If you like." She rose.

As they made their way to the door, Tully thought that Kate had done an admirable job of keeping her temper the entire evening. He traded quick glances with her; they were going to spend the evening alone together tomorrow night. Kate smiled sideways at him and he wondered what she was thinking.

Forty-seven

September 5

> Faith, n. Belief without evidence in what is told
> by one who speaks, without knowledge, of things
> without parallel.

> —Ambrose Bierce

"That was an incredible meal," Tully said as he and Kate cleared the dishes from his dining table. "What did I do to deserve such a feast?"

Kate set the plates in the sink then turned on the hot water. "Lots of things. For instance, you sat through that interminable dinner last night. You've bent over backward to keep us safe." She smiled. "Besides, I promised to cook you dinner again. You wash. I'll dry."

"Don't bother with the dishes. They'll keep." Tully reached over and turned off the water.

"You sure you want to let this stuff get hardened on?"

"Positive. That's why God invented dishwashers. Come on."

A few minutes later they were settled on the sofa sipping a

smooth Chardonnay and enjoying the warmth of the flames that licked the logs in the huge stone fireplace.

"I imagine Josh was happy to leave this morning."

"Very," she replied. "He's always been quiet around his father, but last night, well, I've never seen him act hostile before. I hope I haven't been too transparent about my feelings."

"Maybe he decided it was okay to show *his* true feelings. The man's pretty hard to take."

Kate laughed. "You're much too kind."

"In that case, I'll chance asking the million dollar question."

"How could I live with him?"

"You're a mindreader."

"He's worse now that he's found fame and fortune." She paused. "But I still don't know how I stood him. I guess I was like Josh; I didn't have the nerve to show my true feelings for a long time." She kicked her shoes off and put her feet on the heavy pine coffee table. "Mmmm. The fire feels great. Did you and Carl have any interesting conversation last night while I was in the ladies' room?"

Tully chuckled, then undid his shoes and put his feet up next to hers. Without thinking, he stretched his arms out across the top of the couch.

Kate took it as an invitation and snuggled closer to him. "Well?"

"We had a conversation."

"About what?"

Tully was embarrassed, but what the hell. His belly was full, the wine adding an extra warmth, and he could smell Kate's hair, a fresh light shampoo scent. Her side pressed companionably against his, making him feel safe and at ease. "He, ah, wanted to know my intentions toward you."

"I'll bet you're not paraphrasing what he said."

"No," he said, amused. " 'What are your intentions toward my wife?' is the exact quote. Josh pretended not to be listening."

"His wife." Kate's voice dripped disgust.

"I reminded him of your ex-ness."

"Your intentions are none of his business," Kate said softly.

"That's what I told him."

"Did he say anything else?"

"He said he'd like to be an expert consultant on the Jack case and that he could make me famous."

She set her glass down. "So, what did you tell him?"

He placed his glass next to hers and let his hand drop down around her shoulders then pressed her closer to him. He used his other hand to gently turn her face toward his. "I declined the offers."

"I see." Her voice was soft, her lips slightly open and tremulous. Her eyes searched his.

"Do you want to know what my intentions are, Kate? Toward you?" He heard himself speak the words, could barely believe they were his. But they felt right.

"Yes." She took his hand from her face and held it in hers. "Tell me."

"My intentions are to love you. Kate, I love you already." Softly, chastely, he kissed her.

"I love you," she whispered.

There was nothing chaste about the next kiss.

They were fornicating in front of the fireplace.

From beyond the front window, Jack had watched them smile and laugh as they prepared dinner, playing house like children. He watched them trade looks and conversation as they dined, and then watched them move to the couch, watched Tully's arm encircle her, watched them kiss.

Moments later, she made the first move, pulling Tully to the floor. Together they pushed the coffee table off the round braided rug and took its place in front of the fire, where they rolled around, touching and tasting and undressing, so involved that even Zachary Tully, he of the killer instinct, had no inkling he was there.

Jack was disappointed in them both.

Forty-eight

September 7
Labor Day

As if you could kill time without injuring eternity.

—H.D. Thoreau

"Damn it." Tully slammed his fist against his desk. "Damn it." He'd found another letter this morning, stuck between his cabin's front door and frame.

Ron Settles, who had traded shifts with Hapscomb for some reason Tully didn't remember, stuck his head in the doorway. "Got a problem?"

Tully glowered at him. "No. Go on home, get some rest. I'm going to need you at the courthouse tonight. Earlier if the storm shows up."

"I don't work overtime, but I'm going back on my regular shift tonight, so I'll be there."

"Good." *And I get to keep my eye on you.* "See you later."

Settles grunted and pulled the door shut, leaving Tully alone to stew over the letter. He read it for the third time.

My Dear Tully,

I expected better than to witness you and Kate rutting on the floor like a pair of dogs. I've been aware of your attraction to Miss McPherson, of course, but I thought you would put the good of the town before your baser instincts. I misjudged you both: Fornication should be beneath your morals. One should only have encounters within the sanctity of marriage.

Lest you tell yourself I am merely extrapolating, I will tell you that you have a long scar on your left buttock and that Miss McPherson repeatedly ran her fingers over it. This activity seemed to greatly titillate you both.

Your time runs short, Dear Sheriff, and you had best keep your mind on business. Do not disappoint me again.

Jackie.

"You son of a bitch," Tully muttered. "You goddamned son of a bitch." He reached for the phone, punched in Kate's number.

"Hello?" Kate sounded rushed.

"Kate. I hoped I'd catch you."

"I'm just leaving for work."

"Will I see you tonight?" he asked softly. Memories of the last two nights pervaded his thoughts, Jack or no Jack.

"Yes. I'm coming to the meeting. Then we can have one more night together before Josh gets home."

"I don't want to stop seeing you," he said even as it occurred to him that he should station one of his deputies outside his own cabin tonight. The thought clanged coldly inside him.

"Neither do I. We should talk."

"Yes. Tonight. About us." He paused, not wanting to tell her about the letter, about the fact that Jack had spied on them. But he knew he had to. "I also want to tell you about some other things," he finished, stifling a sudden urge to tell her now. It would do no good. He'd wait.

She was silent a long moment. "All right. After the meeting."

"Will you get off work early if the weather turns ugly?"

"It's unlikely. The boss will want to get in all the tours we can—we've already got a load of tourists here for the holiday. Even a few hopeful skiers. I know it looks ominous out there, but I don't think the storm will arrive before tomorrow night. At least I hope not."

"You're worried about Josh getting home tomorrow?"

"A little. The Wilsons are good people and Ron knows the weather—he drives a snow plow in the winter, after all—so they won't attempt to drive in during a blizzard."

"Any chance they'll come home today?"

Kate paused. "I doubt it. The weatherman still says the storm won't be in until Tuesday night, so I don't think they'll show up before tomorrow afternoon. Listen, I'm going to be late. I'll see you tonight, Zach." There was a brief pause then she added, almost in a whisper, "I love you."

Tully was about to repeat the words back to her but Al Stoker walked in at that moment, aimed at the coffeemaker. "Al's here," he said.

"I'll see you tonight." There was magic in her voice.

"Sheriff Tully?"

"Speaking." Tully set his coffee cup down. "Phil? Is that you?"

"Yes."

Hearing tension in the doctor's voice, his nerves immediately went on alert. "Something wrong?"

"I don't know," Katz said. "Edna—Nurse Boyle—hasn't shown up for work his morning and she's not answering her phone. It's probably nothing, but I can't leave the office and I didn't know who else to call."

"Want me to go check up on her?"

"If you would. She always calls when she's going to be late. This isn't like her."

"I'll go over now and get back to you soon." Edna Boyle,

he thought, a Death Pool favorite. "Don't worry," he added, then quickly got directions to the nurse's home.

He told Sally where he'd be then walked outside for the first time since he'd arrived. The wind was cold now, the bright sky dotted with dark clouds. Even he, city boy that he was, could sense the coming storm. He marveled at the sensation as he buttoned his lamb's wool–lined jacket and trotted to the Explorer. He wondered if it was moving in sooner than the forecasters expected.

Inside the SUV, he searched for a pair of gloves while the engine warmed. Lord, it was cold—but according to the thermometer at the station, it was well above freezing, somewhere around fifty degrees. It had to be the wind, he thought, tugging the gloves on his stiff fingers.

Edna Boyle lived on the east side of town, not too far from Kate, and as Tully drove, his mind was still more on the latter than the former. She was all mixed in with feelings of love, lust, and terror.

He turned onto Evergreen and parked in front of Edna Boyle's cottage. It had white siding and a dark green roof with an old-fashioned iron weathervane on the chimney. The attached garage was closed and locked. Tully removed his gloves and double-checked his gun, then walked to the garage and peered into a small window. An older Blazer was parked inside. His pulse quickened.

The front porch held a single chair and a myriad of potted pines, ranging from a few inches to two feet in height. He never would have guessed Nurse Boyle was into ecology.

Within, he heard music playing, recognized it as Wagner's *The Ring.* He knocked on the door then stood to the side, waiting, his hand hovering near his weapon.

The music continued but Edna wasn't answering.

"Mrs. Boyle, it's Sheriff Tully," he called, pounding the door once more. He tried the doorknob. Locked.

The windows were all covered by wide venetian blinds. Tully walked around the side of the house to the rear. The music was louder and as he stepped up to the back door and knocked, "The Ride of the Valkyries" began.

Edna didn't answer. Again he tried the doorknob and this one turned freely in his hand. The door swung open revealing a tidy kitchen. Behind the music, he could hear water running.

"Mrs. Boyle?" he called, his gun drawn now. "Mrs. Boyle? It's Zach Tully. Mrs. Boyle?"

He stepped inside, silently closing the door behind him, turning the lock to slow down any intruder who might still be inside.

The kitchen was galley-style and three steps took him into a postage-stamp dining room, then a slightly bigger living room, where an old record player was sawing away at Wagner. Nothing looked out of place. He crossed the room and looked carefully into the hall. At one end was a bedroom, at the other, a closed door, the bathroom. The beat of water came from there.

He quickly checked the bedroom. The bed was unmade, a flannel nightgown on the floor next to it. Another puddle of clothes—old lady panties, a torpedo bra that a Valkyrie would approve of, a cotton slip, and a wrinkled white nurse's uniform—lay on the floor next to a laundry hamper.

Tully didn't like what he saw; Edna Boyle didn't strike him as a messy woman and he hadn't seen a speck of dust or anything out of place except for the clothes. He checked the closet and beneath the bed. Then he edged into the hall, passed the living room threshold carefully, and came back to the bathroom door. Water beat so hard within that it seemed to compete with the LP grinding away in the other room.

"Mrs. Boyle?" he called, rapping on the door. "Are you all right? It's Sheriff Tully."

Behind the music and the water, he imagined he heard a groan.

A wave of foggy steam enveloped him as he pushed open the door. For a moment, he could see nothing, but he heard the groan again.

It wasn't a groan, he realized, but Boyle's deep grumbly voice humming along with the Valkyries, "Dum-dum-dum-

DEE-DUM, dum-dum-dum-DEE-DUM.'' The steam sifted and eddied around him, fading away to reveal a small square room with a sink, toilet and an old-fashioned claw-foot tub with a white shower curtain drawn around it. The silver curve of a shower head was just visible above it. The last of the steam dissipated as Tully flashed on the shower scene in *The Shining*, then the one in *Psycho*. The thoughts flared and fled as he made out the silhouette of a fire hydrant body standing behind the curtain. ''Dum dum dum DEE DUM,'' it growled.

He looked away and his gaze fell on an almost empty bottle of Stoli next to the toilet. *Oh God. What have I gotten into?* ''Mrs. Boyle, are you all right?''

The singing broke off and, in an instant, the water, too. ''Who the hell is out there?''

''Zach Tully, ma'am. Dr. Katz asked me to check on you. He was worried—''

''Get the hell out of here. Go wait in the living room and make sure you don't track dirt across my rug.''

''Yes, ma'am,'' he said as he holstered his gun and gratefully left the room.

Edna Boyle appeared five minutes later wrapped in a white robe, scuffs, and a white towel turbaned around her head. She marched to the record player and turned it off.

Her eyes were bloodshot as she glared at him. ''You have no right to just walk into my house.''

''I'm sorry, but Dr. Katz was very worried. Your backdoor was unlocked and with all the problems we've had here—''

''Problems,'' she snorted. ''Prettying it up a little, aren't you, Sheriff? The doctor and I see all those 'problems' laid out and flayed out, so you don't need to mince your words around me. Do you have any idea who you're chasing yet?''

''I can't talk about that, ma'am.''

''You can't, huh?'' She studied him, then her granite face softened, but barely. ''Check out that old fucker, Ambrose.''

''Why?''

''He's nothing but a scribbling old bastard and he'd sell his own mother if it suited his purposes.''

"Does that mean you think he might be capable of murder?"

"I wouldn't be surprised. The doctor sent you?" she asked abruptly.

"Yes."

"I guess it's okay, then. You can tell him I was a little under the weather and forgot to set my alarm last night. I'll be at work in a half hour."

"Sure. May I use your phone?"

"Go ahead," she said as she walked away. "Then get the hell out of here and lock the goddamned door behind you."

The weekend with the Wilsons had been great. They'd driven all the way to a beach in southern Oregon and it had been plenty warm for swimming. They'd played ball and had picnics and a barbecue and Josh McPherson had loved every single minute of it.

But early this morning, really, really early, Billy's dad woke him and Billy up and announced they were going to head for home a day early to make sure they arrived ahead of a storm. They protested that the TV weatherman said it wouldn't be there before Tuesday, but Billy's dad said the weather guy was wrong.

So, at four in the morning they were on the road and by dawn, they were driving into the lower forests, swimming through spooky ground fog. They'd seen lots of deer and Josh had been mesmerized by the saucer eyes of an owl staring down from a tree.

As they passed through the Humbolt Forest and headed east toward Eternity County, vast storm clouds began to gather in the distance. At about two-thirty, when they began the last thirty miles to town, the wind grew so strong that Mr. Wilson had to hang onto the wheel of his Cherokee with both hands just to keep it on the road.

Despite the wind, they made good time. Maybe, Mr. Wilson had said, even better time because of it.

The last twenty miles had been white-knucklers. It was really

windy and Mr. and Mrs. Wilson stopped chatting up front to
stare grimly at the rock-strewn road ahead of them. Even Josh
and Billy had quieted when a big rock came crashing down a
mountainside and Mr. Wilson had swerved almost off the road
to miss it.

At least there was hardly any traffic, which was good because
there probably would have been a bazillion accidents if more
people were out.

At three-forty, they arrived in Eternity. As they drove through
the center of town Billy's parents started talking and laughing
again and Josh saw that all the businesses were open. People
in Eternity didn't like to let the weather interfere with anything.
Suddenly, it was the good kind of exciting again.

"We should have called your mother to tell her we were
coming home early," Billy's mother said all of a sudden.

"That's okay."

"Do you think she's home from work? What with the storm
and all, they're probably closing the tours early today. We can
take you home if you like."

"I'd better go to Lizzie's," Josh said. "Just in case." Zach
wasn't expecting him so if he went to the sheriff's station, he
might not be there. Besides, he liked going to Lizzie's and he
hadn't been there for days. He figured it would be safe since
nobody even knew he was home early, including the bad guy.
She'd make hot chocolate and she always had homemade cookies or cupcakes. They'd watch TV or play Othello or maybe
he'd get her to tell him stories about her childhood in Trinity
County. She told great stories.

"We're real close to Lizzie's house," he said. "Turn on the
next street."

Billy's father nodded and turned. "Are you going to see
your dad tomorrow?" he asked.

"I already saw him," Josh said solemnly. "Turn right at
that green cabin."

In a way, Josh wanted to see him once more, but in another,
he wished he didn't ever have to see him again. He wasn't sure
exactly what he thought of his father. Mostly, he didn't like

him, but he always made that thought go away because he knew it was wrong not to like your dad, or at least to tell other people you didn't. It upset them. Lately, he'd been wishing he had Sheriff Tully for a dad. He'd even told Mom that, but she'd acted weird, turning red and making a funny little laugh, then telling him it was good they had Zach for a friend.

"It's right there," he said as Mr. Wilson pulled even with Lizzie's house. It was a dark red pointy-roofed cabin with white trim. He could see warm light glowing behind the fluffy white curtains. The porch swing was jiggling in the wind even though it was well under the roof and Lizzie's big silver windchimes were going crazy. He could hear them from here, from inside the Cherokee, right over the wind. The front door was hidden behind a vine-covered trellis, but he thought the porch light was probably on. It usually was.

"Does she have any idea that you might show up today?" Mr. Wilson asked as Josh grabbed his backpack and opened the SUV's door.

"Yeah. She said she'd be home just in case." The lie came easily. "She told my mom."

"We'll wait until you're inside," Mrs. Wilson said.

"That's okay, I've got a key." He patted his pocket then got out, slammed the door and ran through the wind to the porch. He glanced back at the Wilsons, waved, then ran out of sight to the front door and waited until they drove away.

Josh wasn't sure why he had lied about the key, but he had. Usually, he was a crappy liar, but not today. Maybe he just wanted to be on his own for even one short minute. Maybe even a little longer.

Now he couldn't get his father off his mind. Mom had told him he should visit him at least once more after he got back. He didn't want to and he could probably talk her out of it. He always felt like a bug under a magnifying glass around him. A stupid bug under a stupid magnifying glass.

He put his hand up to knock on the door, then didn't. Instead, he moved to the window. The tiebacks gave him a view of the whole living room.

Lizzie Quince looked like a sweet little silver-haired grandma as she dozed in her rocking chair across the room, near another window. Her head was against the back of the chair, her mouth slightly open. Josh imagined he could hear her soft snores above the rushing, blowing wind and the clanging, clanging, clanging of the chimes.

Lizzie looked like a sweet old grandma, but when she snored, she sounded like Godzilla. The image made Josh giggle. He watched her for a while, then turned to look at the swaying trees and gathering clouds.

When the first storm had threatened last year, he and Mom sat by their fireplace and roasted marshmallows. It was a big blizzard and he was a little nervous, but Mom loved it. She insisted on keeping the drapes open over the sliding doors so that they could watch the trees and clouds battle it out.

As they sat in front of the fire, his fear diminished. And now, standing on Lizzie's porch, the howling wind didn't bother him much, either. It was scary but fun. He gulped cold air, feeling it fill his lungs, all fresh and piney. A loose branch skittered across the road and he wanted to run after it. Instead, he looked in at Lizzie again. It was five minutes to four. Mom wouldn't get home before five-thirty. That was way more than enough time to walk home. If Mom was there, he'd tell her the Wilsons had just dropped him off, but if she wasn't, he really did have a key to his own house.

Josh slung his backpack and zipped up his coat. He didn't have his gloves or knit cap, but it was only a mile to the house and he wouldn't get that cold. As he headed down the steps and trotted to the edge of the road, the wind slapped him. It felt good. Exhilarated, he began to jog.

Forty-nine

Lizzie Quince nearly jumped from her rocking chair as a pine branch raked across the window. She jumped again as the cuckoo popped out of the clock and called, one, two, three times, then once more.

"Four o'clock," she muttered, her joints creaking as she rose to gaze out the window. "Four o'clock."

The wind chimes on Lizzie's front porch sang in deep harmonic voices that made shivers run down her spine. The music also made her think of Josh. She missed taking care of him and hoped all the problems would be over soon so that they could settle back into their old routine.

The way the wind was whipping outside made her wonder if Ron Wilson, who certainly knew his storms, would wait the storm out or perhaps bring everyone back a day early. If so, she might even see him today; perhaps that was why she woke up with the boy on her mind. But either way, she hoped they were safe, all of them.

Lizzie slipped into a thick sweater before walking to the small foyer. As she opened the heavy door, the wind caught and slammed it against her nearly hard enough to knock her down. "Heavens!"

Beyond the storm door, the tall pines bent and whipped in the wind. Above the trees she could see clouds massing, black-bottomed and ugly, slowly thickening and pressing lower, threatening to engulf the earth. Soon, she thought, the treetops would be devoured.

Lizzie fought with the wind to shut the door again then rested her cheek against the polished door for a moment before going to build a fire. She had intended to attend the town meeting tonight, but now, sitting by a cozy fire and sipping tea seemed a much better idea. Kate would fill her in on the meeting tomorrow. That would be time enough.

Outside, the wind shrieked. The pine branch slammed the window again, ripping the heavy screen off. Lizzie turned from the fire, *tsk-tsking,* and sent a little prayer to heaven that the glass wouldn't go next.

The phone by her rocker rang once. On the second ring, the sound died halfway through, but Lizzie plucked up the receiver anyway. ''Hello?''

Static answered her as the lamplight briefly flickered. She hung up and the phone rang again. This time she snatched it midring. ''Hello.''

Static.

''Hello!'' she said loudly. ''Kate, is that you? I can't hear you.''

Static sang to her.

''Who is this?''

Static, then abrupt, utter silence as the line went dead, a victim of the weather.

''Drat,'' Lizzie muttered and paused to fill her kerosene lantern before returning to the fireplace.

Jack, refreshed and alert, listened to the wind howling down the slopes of the mountain, smelled the crisp cold air, and gazed out at the swirling, pulsing energy that built beyond his window. The power of the coming storm was palpable. He could feel it enhancing his own power. Exhilarated, he embraced the cold. Intoxicated by thoughts of the night to come, he stepped outside, jacketless, and inhaled the energy, let it seep coldly into his pores and invade his lungs.

Standing in the shadows, he watched a Jeep Cherokee come slowly up the street. As it passed, he recognized the driver, Ron Wilson. Jack smiled to himself, knowing that the universe was indeed his own. The Wilsons had returned and that meant young Josh was back in town. And that, as they said, was the icing on the cake.

By the time Josh was halfway home he was half frozen, and when he finally saw the dark silhouette of his house he was just about frozen stiff. He wished he'd stayed at Lizzie's where it would have been warm and snug, where there was hot chocolate and cookies and television.

At least no one was home and he doubted that the bad guy would hang around during the weather. He trudged up to the house, his head bent down against the wind. At the front door, he realized he didn't have a key to the new lock yet, but his mom had given him a new backdoor key.

Turning, he saw the edge of a piece of paper under the doormat. He unfolded it. It was a note from his father inviting his mom to come to his cabin. He made a face then went to the back of the house and unlocked the kitchen door. Inside, he dropped his backpack and the note on the floor then yanked hard with both hands to get the door shut again. Then flipped the light switch. Nothing happened. He tried a couple more times before making his way into the dining room by the dim gray light seeping in the windows. He kept his eyes straight forward, ignoring the darkness that seemed to move by itself. *It's just tree shadows blowing outside.*

The dining room light didn't work, either. Neither did the lamp in the living room or the ceiling light over the entryway. *The power's out.* The realization raised goose bumps all over his body. At least he didn't feel cold anymore.

It was quarter to five and Mom wouldn't be home for at

least a half hour, probably more. He didn't want to be here alone, not in the dark.

He heard a creak upstairs. Was the killer hiding there, waiting for him so he could grab him and slit his throat or cut him into pieces? *It's just house sounds.* That's what his mom called them, and he was pretty sure it was true, but as he heard the creaking again, he couldn't be sure. *What if the killer is up there?*

He told himself it was nothing, ordered himself to be brave, but as he stared into the darkness at the top of the stairs, he knew he couldn't stay here. Maybe outside, he thought. *Mom's gonna be so mad.* He should have gone home with Billy, or gone to Zach's office, or stayed at Lizzie's, anything but this. *Stupid. Stupid.* In his mind, he could hear Mom crying as she discovered his dead body in a pool of blood on the kitchen floor.

Suddenly, he made a decision. He opened the coat closet by the door and traded his light jacket for his heavy parka. Then he exchanged his shoes for winter boots. He kicked all the damp stuff into the closet and shut the door.

Tiptoeing back into the kitchen, he pulled his gloves from a parka pocket then raised the fleecey hood over his head. If he took a shortcut down the hill, he could get to the sheriff's station pretty fast.

He locked the kitchen door behind him and started back down the hill. It was almost full dark now and so cold that even the winter parka couldn't keep him very warm. Briefly, he thought about going back to the house, but one look back at the darkened cabin, its windows staring at him like blind eyes, convinced him to stick to his plan.

Bundled in black, warm if not toasty, Jack stood outside the rental cabin inhabited by Dr. Carl Leland. It had been a short but strenuous hike from his house to Leland's, a jaunt that he thought would be well worth the effort.

Dim yellow light flickered and glowed beyond the front

window and smoke whipped above the chimney. Undoubtedly, the good doctor was enjoying a pipe and a bit of brandy as he daydreamed before the fire.

As Jack, knowledgeable of the nature of Leland's daydreams, knocked on the door, a first flurry of snowflakes danced about his head.

Fifty

Tully had been closeted in his office at the station for two hours trying to pare down the suspect list, which was much too long, especially considering the distinct possibility that the killer wasn't even on the list. Now it was an hour and a half until the town meeting and he was running out of time. If Harlan King kept his word, he'd be showing up any minute. But, suddenly, he didn't think the baker would be coming.

"He went off half-cocked." Tully sat up straight and stared at Tim Hapscomb.

"What?" Tim sat down in the chair next to Tully's desk. He'd come to work early because of the problems the storm would inevitably cause.

"That's what Harlan King said about Jackson Coop. 'He went off half-cocked.' " His stomach did a roller coaster swoop and rise. He stared at Hapscomb, a sick grin stealing over his face. *I've got it.*

"Half-cocked?" the young man asked.

"The pattern."

"I don't understand."

"That's the goddamned pattern. It's been there all along." Tully studied the page listing the murder victims, amazed that he could have missed it. "We have it," he told Tim again.

Maybe. No, in his gut he knew it was true. "It's something a little nuts, but then what else is new?"

Tim nodded, watching him.

"Tim, think about what Jack does to the bodies. Do you think he's doing that stuff just for his own amusement?"

Tim's eyes sparkled with anticipation. "He wants to confuse the investigators."

"Of course. That's the primary source of amusement. Jack's been toying with us."

"But we already know that," Tim said. "What about the pattern?"

"Have you double-checked Harlan King's alibis for the current murders?"

"Harlan?" Tim asked, surprise fleeting across his face. "He's short on alibis in the strictest sense. We have people who claim to have been with him. Why?"

"Think he's capable of committing murder?"

"Most people are," Hapscomb said impatiently. "How does his remark about Coop fit in?"

"It fits, Coop would say, as smooth as owl shit." Tully tried to control his growing excitement. "It doesn't mean King's our man, but if he isn't, he gave us the clue we needed." He shook his head. "I can't believe I didn't see this before."

The deputy sat forward as Tully pushed the victim list over to him. He stared at it then at Tully. "I'm still in the dark."

"King said Jackson Coop went off 'half-cocked.' What did Katz's report name as the cause of death?"

"Blood loss due to severing the penis." Tim shook his head slowly. "I can't believe I didn't know what you meant."

"Still," Tully had to say, "it might not be King. Everyone in town knew what happened to Coop."

"Can't keep a secret in this place," Tim said as he studied the list, then looked up at Tully. "Elvis Two's heart was removed and cut in half in his room at the Dimples' boarding-house."

"Heartbreak Hotel?" Tully suggested.

Tim grinned. "So that would make Joyce Furillo chilled to the bone."

"Or a frozen stiff. I believe King said that, too."

Hapscomb nodded. "What about Larry Fraser?"

"He had his heart in his mouth."

"Mouth or throat?"

"Maybe it's throat. It doesn't matter, it's the same cliché."

"What about Sheriff Lawson?"

"Assuming he was part of the pattern, maybe he went to pieces."

"Or fell apart."

"Came undone at the seams." Tully couldn't stop the grin anymore, grisly as it was. "Resting in pieces. Look at this, though," he said pointing at Billy Godfrey's name. "Dog feces replaced the contents of the skull."

Tim chuckled softly. "Shit for brains!"

"Yeah. Here's one I can't quite place. The prostitute, Valerie Saylor. Three dead birds. Two in her vagina. One in her fist."

"That's easy," Hapscomb said after scratching his chin. "A bird in the hand is worth two in the bush."

Tully nodded. "You're good at this, Tim."

"Thanks."

"Okay. Jack likes birds. The Robbins. He killed two birds with one stone."

Tim tapped the list. "And Reggie Skelton. Skeleton in the closet."

"That works, but he also came out of the closet."

"And you suspect King because . . . ?"

"Other than his inability to verify his whereabouts during various crimes? The man's a walking pun. Maybe he dropped a clue or two out of impatience."

"And he's way too jolly." Tim paused. "But none of that means he's Jack. May I?"

Tully nodded and Tim grabbed the Jack file and thumbed through the dog-eared pages, stopping halfway through the stack.

"What have you got?"

"His whereabouts during the Backdoor killings."

"Remind me," Tully said.

"There's no proof, but he was supposed to be on an extended vacation, bicycling across country." Tim blushed. "Maybe I forgot to show this to you." He displayed a Xeroxed page with a short newspaper story on it. "I found it in the *Eternity. Herald.*" He replaced the article in the file. "You know, though, if Harlan's the perp, he's being awfully obvious."

"I know. The only thing we can be sure of is that we're looking for someone with a sense of humor. Or an understanding of how humor works."

"Sheriff, did you ever have any info on the appearance of the Backdoor Man?"

"No one ever lived to tell. But you know the profile as well as I do. The usual. White male, twenty-five to thirty-five, well-dressed, fits in with society."

"Typical Ted Bundy."

"Yes."

"What about you?" Tim asked. "Do you think that's accurate? If you're considering Harlan, he doesn't fit the profile perfectly. He's older and kind of heavy."

"I think it's a mistake to assume anything," Tully replied. "I don't think the Backdoor Man was less than thirty years old. I'm inclined to think he was at least thirty-five. There was a flair that spoke of maturity." He looked at Tim. "Jack—the Backdoor Man—is having a good time. Hopefully we'll stop his fun tonight. "I . . ."" He let the word trail off.

"What?" Tim asked eagerly.

What the hell. "I'm reasonably sure the Backdoor Man was still in my house when I came home the night my family was murdered."

Hapscomb remained silent.

"I thought I heard laughter and a door shut, but I had just found my son and I was distraught."

Tim looked down at the desk. "That's only natural."

"I didn't tell anyone at the time; I don't know if it was embarrassment because the guy was in my house and I missed him, or because I thought I imagined it. Either way, I wasn't exactly professional." Fury built beneath the external calm and he clipped his words to control it. "I think the son of a bitch watched me find them. I think his plan is to do it again. With the McPhersons."

"Tonight?"

"If not tonight, then as soon as Josh is home. He wants to treat me to a repeat performance." Speaking his fears aloud made them gel; he felt both relieved and terrified.

"Then we have to stop him."

"This stays between us for the moment. I'll tell Al tonight, but I want Settles kept in the dark."

They were silent for a moment then Tully glanced at the wall clock. "King ought to be here by now." He picked up the phone then dropped it back in the cradle. "Still out."

"It's usually out until the storm's over."

"Let's try the radio." Tully rose and went out to the lobby. The dispatcher was long gone, so he worked it himself. Settles didn't reply, Al Stoker's voice, mixed with strong static, came through instead. He reported scattered power outages and said he was currently overseeing the removal of a downed tree near the Dimples'.

Tully and Tim walked to the thick glass door. "Listen to the wind howling out there." As Tully spoke, the wind changed direction and he saw tiny white specks flying at the doors, like stars at warp speed. Fascinated, he said, "It's starting to snow."

"Anything you want me to do before it gets really bad?"

Tully nodded. "Go check up on Settles and King. Let me know their whereabouts. And be careful." He stared outside as Hapscomb put on his parka and flipped up the hood. "I hate snow."

"Why's that?"

"It's too white."

* * *

Sleet bit into Josh's face and wind fought his every step. At least half an hour had passed since he'd left home and he didn't think he was even halfway to town.

At least he wasn't lost. He had followed the road because he couldn't even find the shortcut after he left his house. In the barage of snowflakes, he couldn't see more than a few feet in any direction.

His teeth clattered together and his feet felt icy cold. Josh wished a car would come along—any car. He was beyond caring about his mom being mad at him. He just wanted to be with her, warm and safe.

On his right, he spotted the dim outline of a dark cabin near the road. Without pause, he went to the porch then cupped his hands, trying to see inside.

It was an A-frame vacation cabin, uninhabited. He tried the door, but it was locked. Barely realizing what he was doing, he took an empty clay flower pot, a big heavy one, and threw it through the window.

The glass broke, tinkling like windchimes and the wind howled into the opening as he cleared off the sill. A moment passed and Josh was inside the tiny building. It was all murky darkness but he didn't care—he was more afraid of the storm than the dark.

He moved away from the broken window, feeling his way in the sparsely furnished cabin. He felt a bedframe and eagerly reached down to grab a blanket, but found nothing except a stripped mattress.

Sighing, he passed the window again and found the door. He unlocked it so that when a car came along he'd be able to run out fast enough to flag it down. Then he hunkered down in the corner to listen and to wait.

The streetlamps were out all around the Main Street square and most of the businesses were dark as well. The quarter or so that were open for business were usir.g lanterns or backup generators.

Tim Hapscomb had expected his to be the only vehicle moving on Main, but traffic trickled around the square as people stocked up on necessities. He cruised past the courthouse. It was well-lit with flickering backup power—a message from the town elders that the meeting would go on as planned.

He turned toward the King's Tart. The bakery was open and doing landslide business. *That's why King's late for his appointment with Tully.* Tim eased into a parking space right in front of the shop. If King was here, he told himself, it didn't mean he was or wasn't the killer. He would tell Harlan the sheriff was still expecting him and pick up a few donuts if any were to be had. Dinnerless, he was starving.

There were at least a dozen people milling around inside and the smell of sugar and coffee made his mouth water and stomach growl. He moved to the front of the line only to find King's assistant behind the counter. "Where's Harlan?"

"He went home around three-thirty."

"Did he give a reason?"

"He just had some things to do."

"Are you expecting him to return soon?"

"No, not this late. He said he was going to be busy after five. I'm going to close up in a few minutes, as soon as we're out of stock."

First, Tim decided, he'd check up on Settles, who lived nearby, then he'd go on to King's house to see what he was up to. He pulled out his wallet and bought two glazed donuts, then hurried out into the night.

Kate had left her car at Bigfoot Tours and driven home in one of the big purple Jeeps. *Thank you, God,* she thought as she turned into the driveway. Her little car would have been blown off the road before she was halfway home.

The power's out. The house was dark, like all the others she'd passed. She hadn't planned to go home before the meeting but she needed to clean up. She hesitated before getting out of the vehicle, scanning, listening, unable to hear anything over the shriek of the wind and, suddenly, she missed her bodyguard very much.

Damn it. It was an hour until the meeting and she had to shower and change her clothes before she could go; she'd slipped in a mud puddle in the parking lot. Her clothing and hair were wet and clotted with dirt.

Grabbing a flashlight, she left the Jeep. The wind tried to knock her over, but she persevered and made it to the front door and inside. Locking the door, she turned on the flashlight and shined it around the living room, then up the stairs. Everything looked normal.

She trotted upstairs and showered quickly by the light of a battery-operated lantern. She finished just as the water cooled and in ten minutes she was clean and dressed in a sleek but very warm black ski outfit.

The light guided her downstairs and to the coat closet near the front door. She opened it and stepped slightly inside to grab her warmest parka. Drawing it out, she shined the light on the closet floor, looking for her snow boots.

"What?" she whispered, bending down to pick up Josh's squall jacket. *Wasn't he wearing it when he left with the Wilsons? I must be losing my mind.* She turned it, intending to hang it up, then realized it was damp. Her heart jumped as she shined the light directly on it and saw the dark patches of moisture.

Dear God. Josh was here. "Josh?" she yelled. "Josh?" Dropping the coat she turned and went back upstairs. She shined the trembling light everywhere. Back downstairs again, she quickly examined the rest of the house. Entering the kitchen, she opened the door to the garage and shined the light around. There was no sign of her son, and even as she searched she knew he wasn't there.

She returned to the living room and tried the phone. Dead, as expected. Then she paused, forcing herself to think. Where would he be?

Jack. The name leapt into her mind, but she pushed it away. Josh was with the Wilsons or with Tully. One of them had brought him by for warmer clothes. *But what if he's alone?* Could the Wilsons have dropped him off without seeing him inside? Yes, she decided, they might. They didn't know the details of the problem with Jack; Josh had talked her into being vague with them since they were going to be out of town anyway. *Idiot, Kate. You knew better than that.*

Jack. She forced the name away once more and thought about Tully and the Wilsons. *A note. There's got to be a note around here someplace. Unless there's a message I can't get off the answering machine.* Steeling herself, she checked all the tables for notes, then went into the kitchen and examined the little chalkboard on the wall. "Milk, bread, peanut butter, tinfoil, Mountain Dew," she read. Nothing but a shopping list in her own handwriting. She checked the counters in vain, then her gaze fell on Josh's knapsack on the floor by the back door.

She picked it up. It was damp and stuffed full. Quickly, she dumped its contents on the table. A jumble of dirty clothes fell out, then beach thongs and a plastic bag full of seashells. "Damn it." There was nothing. She picked up the light and the ray beamed across something white on the floor. *Paper. A note!*

Relieved, she snatched it up and read it.

Dear Katherine,

For Josh's sake, won't you join me tonight at my cabin? I'll cook you dinner and I promise I won't try to talk you into coming back to me. Josh is our son and we should discuss his future. It's our duty as parents.

Your Carl

"Christ," she muttered, relief and outrage mingling as she dropped the note on the table. "Carl, you bastard, you took him to your godforsaken cabin."

Fifty-one

Kate blessed the Bigfoot Jeep as she drove the narrow winding road toward Carl's cabin. "Road" was being too kind, she thought; "trail" was more like it. Her car would have stalled at the mere sight of it.

Not that it was easy to see. Even in good weather, the dirt track was a pathetic excuse for a road. Now her glee at making it hard for Carl to get in and out had come back to haunt her. With sleet, rain, and snow hurtling all around, she was driving the path more by memory than sight.

It was less than a mile from her house to the cabin, and although she had plenty of practice driving under hazardous conditions, her teeth were gritted and her knuckles were white on the wheel.

Easing over a patch of black ice, she kept the Jeep close to the hill side of the road as she crawled around a hairpin turn. She would fetch Josh and get out while she still could; almost nothing would be worse than being snowed-in with Carl. She wouldn't let him slow her down. "Therapeutic," he would say. "Good for our little family unit."

"Bastard," she muttered. How could Josh refuse to go with him? She couldn't be angry with her son. But Carl was another matter. He knew about the danger, but he took the boy and didn't even bother saying so in his note.

To be fair, she would offer Carl a ride to a hotel in town. She was going in for the meeting anyway. Whether her ex-husband chose that or to be snowed in by himself, she didn't care. She only cared about getting her son back.

She ground down into first gear on the last steep rise and scanned for the cabin. *How dare he take Josh?* she thought, then, *There it is.* Relieved, she looked at the dim reddish glow of lamplight behind the cabin's front window. She pulled to a halt in the middle of the road and set the flashers to blink just in case some other idiot was on this road from hell.

She fought the wind to open the door, then had to hang on to the Jeep to steady herself in the harsh gale. The cabin was fifty feet up a steep staircase. *What if Carl didn't take him? Of course he did.* It was just the kind of power play he liked.

Pulling the hood of the parka tight, she took the wooden staircase to the cabin, hanging on to the rickety railings to keep from being thrown by the wind. Finally she made the porch and pounded on the door. "Carl! Josh! Open up!"

When no one answered, she tried the door. It opened easily. Inside, a Coleman lantern provided light for the cozy but deserted living room. The remains of a fire glowed red behind a black mesh fireplace screen.

"Carl?" she called. Entering the tiny kitchen, she shined her flashlight around. There were dishes in the sink and the backdoor wasn't locked, but both were typical of Carl.

Nervous now, she reentered the living room and crossed to the hall. There was one bedroom and a bath. She checked the bedroom first; it yielded nothing but an unmade bed.

They probably went into town, She hadn't thought to check for Carl's car, which would be garaged nearby in a carport. He probably couldn't get the Lexus back up the dirt road. She should have thought of that already.

Relieved, she glanced at the bathroom door and turned away. Then she turned back, thinking she might as well be thorough. She shined the light on the door as she opened it.

Carl was naked and sitting on the toilet. He held a white rose between his teeth like Gomez on *The Addams Family*. She stared at him for an instant, unable to comprehend what she saw. It registered that he was dead first, then that his legs had been cut off. He was tied to the toilet tank so that he wouldn't tip over. The entire floor was covered in dark congealing blood and a yard beyond the body she saw the top of a thigh poking above the bathtub rim like a big raw pot roast. Bone in, she thought, then the world spun into darkness.

Tim Hapscomb hadn't returned to the station yet, but Al Stoker had, so Tully left for the courthouse after instructing Stoker to send Hapscomb over as soon as he arrived.

It took twenty minutes to cross downtown instead of the usual five, but he'd expected and allowed time for it. He wasn't about to give up that half hour of private meeting time with the council.

As he walked toward the mayor's office, he wondered if Harlan King would be there. Or if he'd slipped town. Or maybe, he thought, the baker was lying dead somewhere, not the killer, but another victim.

Light glowed from beneath Abbott's office door. Tully hesitated then skipped knocking and just walked in.

Abbott sat behind his desk. Chairs, all but two occupied, were arranged in a half circle around it. Both Dimples were in attendance, as was the postmistress and Elvis Number One. Tully took one of the chairs, all eyes upon him. "Where's Harlan?" he asked.

"We hoped you might know," Abbott said dryly.

"Deputy Hapscomb is looking for him. Ron Settles hasn't shown up for work."

"Settles is missing?"

"Unlikely, but it's impossible to know. Even our radios are out now. We'll know more when Deputy Hapscomb arrives." Tully rose and paced around the desk to stand next to Abbott. "While we're waiting, I'd like some answers."

"Answers?" Martha Ann Dimple asked. "To what, dear?"

"Why the hell are you people protecting the killer?"

"We're not doing that," protested Elvis One.

"You covered up the first murders, the ones back in June," Tully said, his eyes traveling over the group. "You actually imported a bear to hide what happened to those women. Your mayor, who speaks for you, implied that Sheriff Lawson met with an accident, but the man was chopped up like a side of beef. You claim your Brotherhood has nothing to do with the killings, but you won't divulge anything to dissuade me. What are you hiding, Abbott?"

"Sit down, Sheriff Tully."

Tully eyed him a moment then took a seat. "I can't do my job this way."

"Sheriff Lawson was much like you, Tully," Abbott began. "He dug very deeply. He swam in dangerous waters to find the murderer."

"Then why did he let you cover up the June murders?"

"He didn't let us. He was out of town when they occurred, but he agreed to the cover-up when we explained to him what we're going to explain to you tonight."

"Tell me why he agreed."

"Because if the truth about Eternity and Icehouse Circle came out in a believable way, the town would be overrun with scientists and government types. It would be ruined." Abbott gazed sternly at Tully. "Above all, Eternity must survive intact."

"What has that got to do with the killings?"

"Sheriff, we joke about the powers of the Circle and we tell funny stories that tourists eat up. Some think I'm Ambrose Bierce, others," he gestured at Elvis One, "believe him to be The King. We play that particular one down, though, because we don't want too much tourist activity here. I could go on and on. Of course, many of our citizens are simply mad refugees from Shady Pines that we willingly allow to live here because they serve as proof that our wild tales are just that. Crazy stories concocted to lure tourists to our resorts."

"You really want me to believe all that time travel stuff is for real?"

"Not time travel. Haven't you learned that much by now? It's location travel and it also happens to halt the aging process."

"I'd be gray as a goat by now. Or dead," Elvis One said.

Tully barely glanced at him. "How does it work?"

Abbott shrugged. "As for the aging process, we have no idea. It doesn't matter to us—and those who would care are exactly the ones we do not want here. Location travel is poorly understood; it has something to do with the physical anomalies in the Circle and other places like it. The travel only occurs from one such place to another and we think it happens very rarely. We do know that a few adepts know how to force travel. Jack the Ripper is one of them."

Tully felt himself roll his eyes. "This bastard just recently became Jack. He called himself the Backdoor Man when he murdered my family."

"And he's called himself by many other names as well," Abbott said. "It might be more accurate to say that he has only recently gone back to Jack."

"Who is he?"

"Jack the Ripper."

"Goddammit, Abbott, that's not what I meant and you know it. Who is he when he's not killing people? Does he belong to the Brotherhood? Do you have some sort of warped secrecy pledge that says you have to lie to me even though you want me to catch him?"

"We don't know who he is. We think he only comes here occasionally, perhaps to travel from the Circle or to cool off after one of his sprees. Or, sometimes, he comes to kill; I assume you've looked at our history, Sheriff. We have had more than our share of serial killings."

"And you're telling me he's been here repeatedly but you still don't know who he is?"

"We assume he changes his identity and appearance when he comes to town. And, as I said, he's an adept. A master of sorcery or science, whatever you wish to call it. A preceptor who does not share his knowledge. We don't know what his capabilities are and we don't know who he is."

Tully shot out of his chair. "Look, I'm sick of these stories. What the hell is going on here? Why do you spew this stuff?" He wondered if they believed it themselves.

Abbott chuckled but there was nothing humorous in the sound. "You see how well it works, Sheriff? We tell the truth nearly all the time, yet you assume it's nothing but a joke." Abbott rose and strode forward, his eyes fierce on Tully's. "We are telling you the truth and we expect you to use it to stop the killer. And we expect you to never reveal any of it."

"On the bright side," Martha Ann said, "you can join the Brotherhood now that we've told you."

"Thanks, but I'll pass."

"You won't tell, though, will you." Abbott made the question into a firm statement.

Tully stared at him then looked around at the others. "If I repeated any of this, it would be assumed that I lost my mind."

"Good." Abbott took his coat from a rack near the door. "You may talk amongst yourselves. I have someone coming in a few minutes to put plywood over my display window at the shop. I have to be there, but I'll be back for the meeting."

At that moment, the door opened. Tim Hapscomb, wet and windblown, stepped in.

"Settles is dead," he told them.

"How?" Abbott asked.

"Twelve-inch spike driven through his head."

"In one ear and out the other?" Tully asked.

"You bet."

Abbott looked from Tully to Hapscomb. "You seem pleased with yourselves. You'll have to explain why when I return." Then he was out the door.

Kate fought her way out of darkness, but when she opened her eyes, she wasn't sure where she was. Then she remembered: Carl on the toilet, his legs in the bathtub. At least she'd fallen backward and missed the blood.

"Oh God," she muttered, beginning to retch. As she regained

control, she grabbed the flashlight and turned it away from the carnage. Stumbling to her feet, she made her way down the short hall to the living room. She yanked the front door open and was nearly thrown backward by the wind. Steadfastly, she hunched forward and grabbed the stair railing to make her way down the wobbling, creaking stairs.

It was really snowing now and in the fifteen minutes or so that she was indoors, a layer of white had blanketed the ground, the wind already sweeping snow into small drifts around the steps and tree trunks. Three stairs from the ground, wind tore her hands from the railing and she tumbled to the bottom, the flashlight rolling away. Slightly stunned, she watched as a pine sapling uprooted and sailed into the swirling white night.

She retrieved the flashlight then headed for the Jeep. The wind knocked her down again and she crawled the last ten feet, then yanked the door open and swung herself into the vehicle.

The door snapped off before she could close it. *To hell with it.* The Jeep coughed to life. She was determined to get out of this place and find her son. She let the vehicle roll slowly forward until she found a driveway she could use to turn around. Successful, she switched to first gear and lightly pressed the accelerator. A tremendous crash occurred somewhere behind her and in the rearview mirror she saw something dark thunder across the road. A huge tree had fallen where she'd been only a moment ago. Silently, she gave a prayer of thanks, then edged forward, fighting the buffeting wind and blinding snow. She'd passed Carl's cabin and began to creep down the incline into the hairpin curve when the Jeep's tires hit ice and spun out.

She tried to control it, but she felt the passenger side tires drop off the road. In an instant, the vehicle began tumbling. At the same time, Kate threw herself out the empty doorframe, away from the Jeep. She landed hard but safe at the edge of the road.

She heard the clunkings and crashings behind the sound of the storm as the vehicle toppled down the mountainside. It seemed to go on forever.

You're going to freeze to death if you don't get moving. Stiff and sore, she stood up. The flashlight was still in her pocket, but it would be almost useless under these conditions so, head down, she began walking down the road. After all, she told herself, it wasn't very far and she'd get back to her cabin almost as quickly on foot as in the Jeep. Sleet stung her face. *Please, Zach, be there when I get home. Be there with Josh.*

Ambrose Abbott sat in his rocking chair in his apartment above the bookshop and sipped a quick cup of tea with a healthy dollop of brandy. He had arrived at the store just as the handyman was finishing covering the window. After paying him, he decided to go upstairs and steel himself for the meeting.

Assuming anyone would show. He thought they would; most of the people in Eternity would never admit defeat to mere weather. This one, though, was not a typical early storm. This one reeked of winter at its worst. Snow was already on the ground and it was building fast.

That thought caused him to set down the teacup half finished. He had walked the block and a half from the courthouse to his shop. Unfortunately, he would have to walk back as well, but first he needed his winter boots.

As he stood up, someone knocked on his door. "Damn fool idiot left the shop door unlocked," he muttered, not knowing if he or the handyman was the damned fool responsible. "Coming," he called as the knocking repeated. "Hold your water." Harlan, he thought. Harlan had a key and had come to pick him up, the old softie. Abbott cringed. The only other person who had a key was Edna Boyle, who watered his plants when he was out of town. Edna Gargoyle, he liked to call her. Old Edna, who hated his innards for all to hear, but who also had a bit of a crush on him, which meant it was likely she'd use the weather as an excuse to come by. Harlan or Edna or an uninvited stranger?

He opened the door. "Hello there. Come to give me a ride to the courthouse?"

Fifty-two

Josh was sleepy, so sleepy, and when he heard the rumble of an engine coming down the road, he thought it was a dream. Forcing himself to listen, he realized that a car really was nearing.

It was hard to move, even to open his eyes, but the sound was so loud now that it could be heard easily over the howls of wind and scrapings of trees. He stood up, still groggy, and pulled the door open. Staggering out into the storm, he waved his arms and yelled.

Snow swirled in the headlights of the oncoming vehicle and Josh, barely thinking, ran straight in front of it, trying to flag it down. Suddenly, there was a squeal of brakes and the truck slid sideways until its fender was nudged against the dirt and snow.

Josh ran to the driver's door of the big blue Land Rover and pulled on the handle. He really couldn't see the driver, but it didn't matter as he realized whoever it was trying to open the door from the inside. Josh stood back and waited.

"Josh," said Harlan King. "Josh McPherson. What in the world are you doing out here by yourself? Where's your mother?" He got out of the vehicle and waited for Josh to climb up and scoot across to the passenger side.

King got back in and pulled the door closed. "Here," he

said, reaching into the back seat and pulling a plaid blanket up. "You must be freezing. Wrap yourself up in this. Can you feel your toes?"

Josh wiggled them as he shivered and clutched the blanket. "Uh-huh. They're okay."

"So, what's going on, son?"

Josh told him quickly, not bothering to cover up any part of the story. "So I went in the cabin and waited for somebody to come," he finished.

King nodded. "You didn't get very far. I'm on my way to the town meeting. I'm already late, but let's go check your house and see if your mother is there. She must be worried sick."

"But I told you, she doesn't know I'm home."

"You said you changed coats. She'd probably notice that. It's the kind of thing a mother always notices. Mine did."

"I left my knapsack in the kitchen," Josh said slowly.

"There you go." King put the big SUV in gear and slowly eased off the berm before backing up and slowly turning around. "If she's been home, she knows. We'll go there first. If she's not home, we'll find her."

"Let's come to order folks," Elmer Dimple called. The banging of the gavel reverberated throughout the courthouse. "Come to order. Mayor Abbott should be here shortly, but we're going to start without him so that you folks can all get home before the storm gets any worse. Sheriff Tully? You coming in? The rest of you people out there in the hall pestering that poor man, you come in here if you're intending to come."

Tully heard the words with gratitude. A half-dozen people trying to get him to assure them there would be no more deaths began to move away. Elmer called out again and all but one moved on.

Edna Boyle, the stout little fire hydrant, looked at him with eyes so full of fear that he gently took her arm. "Are you all right?"

She made an effort to put on her stern expression, but didn't do too well. She pulled out a folded note from a pocket and shoved it into his hand. "Here. I have to leave now." She pulled away and trundled down the corridor and out the doors.

"Sheriff Tully? We're waiting on you," Elmer called.

Tully shoved the note in his pocket and entered the courtroom. About thirty people had shown up so far, and they all started yelling questions as he stood at a small podium before the judge's stand. It was going to be hell, he thought. Pure hell.

There were tree branches and even whole trees tumbled across the road Josh had walked down less than two hours ago. Harlan drove really slow, the big Land Rover bumping over branches like it owned the road. Twice they got out of the SUV to move small trees and Harlan said they were really lucky nothing big had come down across the road because then they'd be stuck walking.

King pulled up in Josh's driveway and together, they walked to the back door, their way lit by Harlan's big halogen flashlight. It looked like his mom wasn't home, but Josh was eager to go in and make sure. Almost as eager as he was to change into dry clothes.

Inside, Josh swallowed hard when he saw the contents of his knapsack dumped on the table. "She's been here," he said. "Or somebody has." He looked at the baker, fearful again. "That Jack the Ripper guy? He wants to kill my mom, I think. Maybe he was in here."

"Maybe your father?" King suggested, pointing at the note on the table. "You know what? Maybe your mother thinks you went with him."

Josh considered. "Maybe, but the road to his cabin is no good. We couldn't get there tonight."

Harlan was nodding at him, an odd smile playing around the corners of his mouth. "You sound like a grownup, Josh."

"Well, my mom knows all the weather and road stuff and

she tells me. She's the only one that could maybe drive there, but she'd know I'd way rather go to Zach's.''

"The sheriff's?"

"Yeah, he and my mom and me, we're friends."

"I see. Here, take the light and go upstairs. Change your clothes." A branch snapped outside and wind screamed under the rafters.

Fifty-three

"Wait!" Kate screamed at the dim glow of red taillights leaving her house. "Wait!"

Fresh adrenaline kicked in and she started running, slipping, falling, running and slipping again. "Wait!"

But her voice was lost in the wind. She trudged to the house, using the flashlight now to find her way. As she unlocked the door she tried to figure out who had been there. Her watch read 6:45, so it probably wasn't Zach because the meeting would be in full swing. Maybe he sent someone to check on her.

Inside, she checked the phone—dead as ever—then went in the kitchen, shucking her coat. And stopped. There were two sets of muddy footprints, one small, one large, heading in and out the back door. "Josh," she whispered, relief flooding over her. She raised her voice. "Josh? Are you here?"

No answer, but that was all right, wasn't it? No adult would leave a child home alone in the storm. She sat down and pulled off her boots. Josh was all right. But where was he? And with whom? And how could she find him? She was stranded. *What if those are Jack's footprints?*

"Are there any more questions?" Tully asked the audience in the courtroom. About twenty more people had arrived since he'd come in, but the ones he wanted to see—Abbott, King, and most of all, Kate—were not among them.

Although he'd only met Ron Wilson briefly a week before, he had recognized him when he and his wife and son entered the courtroom halfway through the meeting. *Where are Kate and Josh?*

"Yes," he said to a raised hand.

The Jim Morrison clone stood up. "I just wanted to say that he's supernatural. You can't catch the Ripper unless you're supernatural, too."

"I'll take that under consideration," Tully said, not wanting that particular subject to start up again. He'd squashed it twice already. "I'm going to adjourn the meeting for Mayor Abbott—"

"You can't," Elmer Dimple said, rising. "I have to."

"Fine." *Let me out of this place!* "One more thing, folks. As you know, we're without power and phones. I'm told that we have downed electrical lines and roads blocked by trees. It may not be possible for you all to get home. Don't even try it if you live on the outskirts of town. Elmer," he said turning to the old man, "can we arrange some kind of emergency shelter here? Or maybe you can take some folks to your boardinghouse?"

"We could take twenty on the parlor floor," Martha Ann announced. "There'd just be a small fee."

Tully raised his hands to quell the sudden murmurs. "Martha, this is an emergency situation."

The woman sniffed. "Very well. As long as the town covers the cost of food."

"Anyone who'd like to spend the night at the Dimples' may meet with them by the jury box," Tully said.

"I'll stick around here if some of them want to bunk in the courtroom," Elvis One offered.

"You're on." Tully looked at the crowd. "The rest of you, drive slowly. Stay out of the square; Deputy Hapscomb tells me it's impassable. Everyone who's leaving, meet with Deputy

Hapscomb. We'll arrange some kind of caravan system. Thanks for your attention.''

"Meeting adjourned," Elmer called.

Tully strode across the courtroom to the Wilsons. "Mr. Wilson?"

"Yes, Sheriff?"

"I thought you weren't coming back until tomorrow."

The man smiled. "I knew better than to believe the weatherman. We got back this afternoon."

"Where's Josh?"

Wilson looked surprised. "We dropped him at Lizzie Quince's."

Damn. "Why did you do that?"

"His mom wouldn't be off work for a couple hours."

"And he told us to," added Mrs. Wilson.

"Did you see Miss Quince?"

"No. We just waited until he had time to go in. She was obviously home." Wilson started going pale under his tan.

"What's wrong?" asked his wife. "What happened?"

"Probably nothing," Tully said without conviction. "He didn't tell you he was supposed to be in my or my deputies' care?"

Both shook their heads.

"He told me about how the killer was still bugging them, but it was a secret," Billy volunteered.

"Why didn't you tell me?" his mother asked.

" 'Cause he said it was a secret swear."

"Mrs. McPherson didn't tell you, either?"

"She said there was some concern, but she didn't give us any details," Wilson said. "She was glad Josh was going out of town."

"We didn't know. We never would have—" Mrs. Wilson was starting to hyperventilate. "Dear God, we didn't even make sure he got inside Lizzie's house."

Tully didn't feel like saying it wasn't her fault, but he did try to hide his frustration. "Ms. McPherson was supposed to be here tonight. Have you been in contact with her at all today?"

"No."

"Are you staying here tonight?"

"No," Wilson said, all the life gone from his eyes. "We only live three blocks away."

Tim Hapscomb arrived at Tully's side as he was telling the Wilsons to go home. Quickly, he explained the problem to Tim. "We need to locate Josh and Kate," he said. "I'll do that. Have you found Harlan King?"

"No, but his Land Rover is gone."

"Okay. We also need to check up on Ambrose Abbott. He didn't make the meeting."

"Hi," Phil Katz said, his face flushed from the cold outside. "Sorry I was so late." He looked from Tully to Hapscomb then lowered his voice. "What's going on?"

"We have some missing people." Quickly, Tully filled him in.

"I have to go check on a pregnant patient," Phil said, his voice betraying worry. "I'll keep an eye out for them."

"It's not safe out there," Tim said.

"I've got an Explorer and it's not that far. I'm going to try to talk her and her husband into staying at my house for the duration of the storm. She may be in early labor. I have to go."

Tully nodded. "Listen, if you see Harlan King or Ambrose Abbott, or the McPhersons, for that matter, send them here, will you? Tell them I'm looking for them."

"I sure will."

The doctor shrugged into a navy parka and, with a nod, made his exit. "What a job," Tim said, watching the man head into the storm.

"Not as bad as ours," Tully told him.

"Where are you headed first?"

"Kate's, via Lizzie Quince's house. You check on the other two. We'll have to leave messages here for each other until we reconnect."

"Sounds good. What do you want to do about Settles' body?"

Tully grimaced. "Nothing we can do tonight."

"I figured. I made sure the heaters were all shut off in case we get power back, so he'll keep just fine."

"We'll probably end up with another frozen stiff." Tully reached in his pants pocket for his keys and found Edna Boyle's note. "Hang on." He opened it and held it so both of them could read it at the same time:

> Come to my house after your meeting. I know who the murderer is.
>   E. Boyle.

"I'll go there first," Tim said.

"It's going to be a hard drive to get there."

He nodded. "But not impossible."

"See you later."

Tully bundled up and headed out to the parking lot behind the courthouse. The Explorer was up to its hubcaps in snow, which was still falling fast and hard. An aspen had cracked and fallen on someone's Mazda pickup nearby. Shivering, Tully climbed out of his Explorer.

"You're gonna need chains on that puppy if you're going any distance," Elmer Dimple said from a foot away. Tully hadn't even heard him walk up. "You got chains?"

"Yeah."

"Ever put 'em on before?"

"No."

"Okay. I'll talk you through it, then I got to get back inside before Martha Ann starts charging for floor space again."

The drive to Edna Boyle's cottage was long and hard, testing the Explorer's prowess and Tim's instincts for the road.

Settles, Tim mused, had been relatively lucky, as far as Jack's victims went. Probably, he'd been in a hurry. He'd put a bullet through the deputy's forehead before driving the rod through his ears.

Hapscomb braked slowly as he neared Boyle's house. He was rewarded with a clean, nonskidding stop. Twenty yards back from the road he made out a dim flickering glow, barely visible through the sheets of snow.

He stripped off his outer gloves, leaving only black spandex Thinsulate ones on so that he could handle his gun. He killed the lights then climbed out, barely saving the SUV's door from being ripped off by the wind. "Jesus," he whispered. He checked the clip in his gun then shielded it against the freezing wind.

The wind buffeted him as he tramped toward the cottage. That wasn't so bad, but the shrieking and howling irritated the hell out of him. And scared him. At least, he thought, the noise didn't play favorites.

He arrived on the porch and saw that the light in the window came from a lantern, an old-fashioned kerosene type. He knocked. Knocked again.

This isn't good. He checked out the lock and within thirty seconds, he'd forced it open and entered, gun out, pointed at the ground, ready to come up in a heartbeat.

The living room was neat and clean, but he could smell the blood. Quickly, he went through the house, checking each room for signs of life, ignoring momentarily the red wash of death in the bedroom.

The place was deserted, but it hadn't been for long; Edna Boyle had been alive and well before the town meeting. Swallowing hard, turning himself cold inside, he stood on the threshold of the bedroom and played the light over the bed.

No pun here, he thought. Edna Boyle's body was spread across the bed, the torso opened, intestines piled between her legs. Her breasts—at least that's what Tim thought they were— were on the bedside table. No, no puns. This was a throwback to the Ripper murders, a quickie version of the murder of the prostitute Mary Kelly.

He fought the urge to retch and won. Grimly sweeping the light over the dresser, he saw a blood-spattered manila envelope. Tim snagged it by one corner and took it to the kitchen, where he wrapped it in Saran Wrap. Then he headed out to check on King and Abbott.

Trees were down all over the place and it had taken forever for Harlan King to find a way to get anywhere near downtown. Now he and Josh were closing in. They were on a regular two-lane road and the baker kept muttering about stopping to put on chains, then talking himself out of it because they were so close to their destination.

"Holy Moses," King cried as he made out headlights through the snow. Josh held his breath as Harlan slowed and started flashing his brights to make sure the oncoming vehicle saw him. It worked. The big SUV stopped on the road, driver's window to driver's window.

King rolled his down and Josh strained to see the other driver as that window came down, too. It was Dr. Katz. "Have you seen my mom?" he called.

King rubbed his ear. "Sorry," Josh muttered.

"What?" Phil called.

"You coming from the meeting?" Harlan yelled.

"Yeah. I'm going out to check on a patient."

"Stay off of Pinetop. Half a dozen trees are down."

"Thanks."

"Ask him about my mom," Josh said urgently.

"Was Kate McPherson at the meeting?"

Katz paused. "No, I don't think so. Harlan, they were looking for you."

"I'm running late."

Katz nodded. "Sheriff Tully said to go meet him at the courthouse. He needs to talk to you. It's a slow ride but you can make it if you go the back way."

"Thanks, Phil. You be careful now."

Fifty-four

"So Josh was never here?"

Lizzie Quince, alive and well to Tully's relief, shook her head. "I wish I could tell you otherwise. Do you want more chocolate?"

Tully looked down at the mug Lizzie had thrust upon him only five minutes before. Yes, he wanted more. "I would if I could afford the time, ma'am, but every minute counts."

"Yes," Lizzie said briskly. She took the mug and practically pushed him out the door. "I'm praying for Kate and Josh. And for you, Sheriff."

"Thanks."

Head down, Tully raced to the Explorer, shut himself in, and turned the defroster on high. It didn't help much. The snow was falling even harder as he pulled out, heading for Kate's cabin. Between the snow blindness and the wind, it was going to be a slow trip.

Getting to Lizzie's had been tough, but he already knew that Kate's place on that winding road was going to be a real challenge, one he was ill prepared for. He clutched the steering wheel and drove until a drift of snow turned out to have a tree trunk in it.

"Damn it!" he yelled as he got out. At least he hadn't hit it hard enough to do any real damage. "Damn it!" The tree was good-sized but not huge. He figured he could move it out of the way if he tried hard enough.

Kate stood silent sentry at the sliding glass doors. She was dressed in another warm ski suit, white on blue, and she'd traded her soggy parka for another one, just as warm but older and bulkier. It hung by the front door, ready to grab when Zach showed up. *If he shows up.*

Impatient, she began pacing. Surely the meeting was over by now. Surely Zach would come soon, or send someone for her.

Snow hit and clung to the sliding doors, propelled by the relentless wind. Peering out, she could see little but streaks of white and black. Then, she caught sight of headlights and squinted to make sure her eyes weren't playing tricks.

In another minute, the vehicle was close enough that there was no mistaking it. In the stormy darkness she was unable to identify it, but it didn't matter. She was getting out of here, one way or another, at last. At long last.

Quickly, she pulled on her parka and gloves and ran out to meet her savior.

Tully couldn't catch a break. Following a tough, twenty-minute crawl up the road after moving the fallen pine, he came up short at a huge uprooted fir. There was no way to get around it and it obviously couldn't be moved.

Twenty minutes later, he was at the turnoff from town he'd used to get to Lizzie's. He retraced the original drive, intending to try to pick up the road to Kate's from the other side of town.

As he approached the square he turned right and took the street behind the courthouse to avoid the Main Street mess. Realizing he was a block from Abbott's Bookshop, he cut up one more street; he didn't intend to stop, but he could scope things out, maybe even run into Hapscomb or Stoker.

Wind screeched between the old stone buildings. Tully drove

the center of the road to avoid the occasional white lumps of parked vehicles. After he turned onto Abbott's street, he pulled over right behind Tim Hapcomb's Explorer, which was idling, lights on, directly in front of Abbott's bookstore. There was no light in the shop, but a dim glow showed from the apartment above.

As Tully killed his engine, Hapscomb climbed out. He carried something under his arm as he hurried to the recessed entry of the bookshop, gesturing at Tully to follow him.

Tully arrived at the entry. Tim turned on a flashlight and twisted it so that it shed a diffuse lantern-type glow. "Did Edna Boyle pan out?"

"More like bled out." Hapscomb's face was a pale mask. "He did her like that Whitechapel prostitute. No puns, just viciousness. Breasts on the bedstand, the whole bit. Just like in the books."

"Were the intestines roped around the headboard?" Tully heard himself ask. He was embarrassed by the question but he couldn't take it back.

"No. He left them piled between her legs. This was a rush job." Hapscomb pulled a blood-spattered manila envelope encased in plastic wrap from inside his parka. "This was in the bedroom with her. I don't know if it's anything important, but I took it just in case." He pushed damp hair back off his forehead. "After I left there, I checked on King. He wasn't home."

"You sure?"

"His vehicle was missing."

"That's not enough—"

"I also let myself in just to make sure." He glanced at the door. "I was just about to check on Abbott."

"Yeah," he said even though he wanted to rush to Kate's. "I want to take a quick look at the contents of that envelope, see if there's anything to help ID the bastard."

"Here," Hapscomb said, thrusting the envelope at Tully. He turned to the door and after a swift series of movements with a thin strip of metal he swung the door inward, the little bells over the door going wild in the wind.

"I didn't realize you were an expert lock-picker." Tully switched on his own flashlight and shined it inside, saw nothing but shelves of books. They stepped across the threshold and Tully turned to close the door, then stopped. "Hear that?"

"Hear what?"

"I thought I heard an engine—" Tully stepped outside. "Yeah. Headlights. Someone's coming." He stepped out on the sidewalk and used the flashlight to wave the vehicle down.

"It's King's Land Rover," Tim said.

He glanced at Hapscomb. The younger man touched his gun, a question in his eyes. Tully nodded and put his hand on his own gun as the driver's door opened.

"Sheriff?" Harlan King's voice carried over the noise of the storm. "Sheriff Tully, is that you?"

"It's me. Come forward slowly, Harlan, hands in the air."

"What?"

The passenger door opened and Tully brought his gun up. Beside him, Hapscomb had his weapon leveled at King.

"Zach!"

"Josh?"

"Zach!" the boy yelled, running. Tully put his gun away and bent to scoop the boy up as he flung himself into his arms. "Where's my mom?" he cried in Tully's ear, hugging him tightly.

A hug never felt so good. "We're looking for her." Tully carried Josh into the bookshop while Hapscomb took charge of King. "Why were you with Mr. King?" he asked, easing the boy down near the counter.

"He saved me. He was bringing me to the courthouse to see my mom and you." He gulped a big breath. "We had to come this way because the other street was all messed up and then you shined your light at us—"

"Okay, Josh. Slow down. It's okay. How long were you with Harlan?"

"I dunno. A real long time." He looked up as the baker

walked in, hands cuffed, Hapscomb right behind him. "It was around when the meeting was supposed to be 'cause Harlan said he was going to be late."

"I never thought we'd be this late," King said. "We had to backtrack a number of times and try several routes."

Tully was fairly sure the guy was innocent, but he had to be certain. "Deputy, cuff Mr. King to that chair." He pointed at a wooden captain's chair, one of several around a long narrow table across the room from the sales counter.

"Why the cuffs?" Harlan asked. His eyebrows raised in sudden comprehension. "You don't think *I'm* the killer, do you?"

"Josh gives you a good alibi," Tully said. "But we have to be careful."

King sat down and made no protest as Tim attached one wrist to the chair arm. Josh immediately sat down in a chair opposite him.

"We're going up to check on Mayor Abbott," Tully said, turning the inside lock on the front door. "We'll only be a minute or two. You two just sit tight. Josh, don't go near Mr. King."

Tully walked back to the staircase, Hapscomb following. "Sheriff," he said softly. "Shouldn't one of us stay here?"

"By the book, sure. But do you see any need?"

"No, sir. He's not the killer."

Ambrose Abbott's apartment had a separate door on the second floor landing. Tully rapped on it. Either Abbott wasn't in or something had happened to him. Otherwise, Abbott would have heard them in his shop.

"Mayor Abbott?" Hapscomb called.

Tully barely shook his head, then put his hand on the doorknob. It turned easily. He and Hapscomb drew their guns, stood back and pushed the door open.

Tully moved in, sweeping the room with eyes and gun. He could see the top of Abbott's gray head above the back of a rocking chair facing the fireplace. "Mayor?"

Of course, there was no reply. The man's hand was visible on one chair arm. The fingers were limp.

Behind Tully, Tim moved around the room, heading for the rear of the apartment. He took the bedroom and bath, while Tully quickly checked the kitchen.

Satisfied, they turned their attention to Ambrose Abbott.

The man's eyes were half shut, but his mouth was stretched wide, the lower half of his face a wash of dried blood. His shirtfront was sodden. Tully glanced at his deputy then they both moved forward.

A small wooden figure, an exquisitely carved rabbit sitting up on two legs, propped the jaw open. A pool of blood had settled behind the lower teeth. Tully shined his flashlight directly into the gaping mouth and saw the damage. It all clicked into place.

Tully switched the light off and gazed at Hapscomb. "Katz got his tongue."

Fifty-five

"I'm so glad you came along," Kate said to Phil Katz as he piloted his Explorer along the road. Conditions had worsened and they were nearly snow blind now. At least the heavy vehicle was holding up under the fierce gale.

"Sheriff Tully said to keep an eye out for you and I had to come this way, so I thought I'd check and see if you were home."

"Have you seen my son? Josh?"

"No, I'm sorry. He might have been at the meeting, though. I was only there for a few minutes. I was late." He smiled. "I'm glad I could help you out."

"I am, too. I—I thought Josh was at my ex-husband's cabin, but he wasn't."

"You went to your ex-husband's?" he asked with a quick sideways glance.

"Yes. He was dead. Jack got him."

"What makes you think that?"

She shuddered. "His legs. They were cut off."

"The poor man didn't have a leg to stand on?"

Kate looked at Katz. "That's not funny."

"No, it isn't. I'm sorry. I've just seen so much death lately that I indulge a little too much in black humor. It takes the edge off. Was there any sign that Josh had been there?"

"No, thank heaven. But I just missed him at home. He left with somebody in an SUV. I couldn't get their attention." She sighed. "I think that's the turnoff," she said, pointing to the left. "Yes. That's it."

Katz continued on slowly past the barely visible intersection. He said nothing, but stayed on the road as it began to climb.

"Dr. Katz? We're going the wrong way. If you'd prefer, I'll be happy to drive us in. I'm used to these kinds of conditions."

"I'm fine," the doctor said.

"There's a turnaround area coming up on our right in about a quarter of a mile. If you take that, we can turn around pretty easily. We merged with Icehouse Road back there and if we keep going this way, we'll end up on the mountain."

Katz nodded.

There was a good half foot of snow on the road now, but Kate relaxed a little when they finally made the turnout and the doctor pulled onto it. He stopped and set the parking brake.

"The turnout's very deep," Kate said. "I think you can back up a ways and make the turn."

"That's not necessary." As he spoke, his hand shot out and snaked under her parka and darted up to her neck. She felt a painful pinch, then spots of black began to swim in her vision. A *Spock pinch*, she thought as she lost consciousness.

Tully and Hapscomb left Abbott in his rocker and descended the stairs to find Harlan King reading the contents of the blood-spattered envelope. Josh stood behind him, reading over his shoulder.

Tim hurried forward. "That's evidence," he said, snatching it away. "You can't—"

"But I did. Did you know that Edna Boyle was a mother?"

"What?" Tully asked.

"Look at that top page, the handwritten one with the photo clipped to it. She says she's Jack's mother. And she says Jack's real name is John Druitt."

"Katz is the killer." Tully unlocked King.

"You know, we saw Dr. Katz on the way here. That's how I knew you wanted to see me—he told me. What about Ambrose? He's not here?"

"He's dead. You and Josh wait at the courthouse. Deputy Hapscomb will escort you. I'm going after Katz."

"I think I know where he is," King said, rising.

"Up the mountain," Josh said. "It's in the letter. He's gonna do a ceremony to go somewhere."

Tully took the letter and read it quickly. "According to this, he has to have a sacrifice." he said, knowing that Kate was the chosen one. "I'm going to Bigfoot Tours. I'll hotwire a snowmobile and go up to the Circle."

Tully paused to look at the letter again. He flipped to a photograph and studied the young-looking man in the shot. He sat pensively at a desk, chin resting on one hand. He had dark hair parted in the middle and a small mustache that went perfectly with his Victorian suit. Beneath the photo a line read *Montague John Druitt*. He'd seen the photo before, in a book about the Ripper, but he hadn't noticed the resemblance to Phil Katz.

"I see you're awake," Katz said as Kate moaned.

Briefly, she struggled against the ropes securing her wrists and ankles, then she stopped and tried to get her bearings.

They were heading up Icehouse Road in a large Sno-Cat. The one from Bigfoot Tours, she realized. "What the hell is going on?" she muttered, fighting to sit up straight in the passenger seat. There was a dull ache in her neck where Katz had pinched off her blood flow, but other than that she felt uninjured.

"No need for profanity," Katz told her. "This road is difficult to follow. I wish I could take you up on your offer to drive."

"Where's Josh?"

"I don't think that matters anymore."

Kate fought back tears. "Where are you taking me?"

"My, you're full of questions, aren't you?"

"Where?"

"A place you've been many times before. Icehouse Circle."

"Why?"

Katz chuckled. "Why do you think? You're going to help me travel. I'm returning to England tonight. Things are so much more civilized there and it's been quite some time. I miss it." As he spoke, a slight British accent emerged.

"How the hell am I supposed to help you travel from the Circle?"

He glanced at her. "You provide the extra energy I need. It's a special night. There are only a few times each year that controlled travel is possible."

"That's insane."

"Why, Kate, I'm surprised to hear you say such a thing when you spend your days telling tourists all about it."

"Why not take a plane like everyone else?"

"Have you checked the air fares lately?" He laughed again, a sound that made her cringe. "No, my dear Kate, this is the only way to fly."

"Where's Josh?"

He made a *tsk-ing* sound. "I haven't seen him since this afternoon."

"If you've done anything to him I'll kill you."

"Now, now. Don't make empty promises." Katz glanced at her. "At the meeting tonight, your paramour was looking for him. And you. He seemed quite concerned. Did you enjoy fucking him?"

"You bastard."

"I told you," Katz said angrily, "no profanities."

"You sonofabitch. You object to words, but you think it's all right to kill people?"

He reached across the cab and slapped her cheek with the back of his hand. "No profanities," he growled. When he spoke again, his voice was calm and cool. "I admire you, Kate, but you must cooperate."

"You won't get away with this."

He laughed again. "That's what my mother said just before I slit her throat."

"You killed your own mother?" she asked, buying time.

"Yes. Just a bit ago. She used to be so kind to me, but today she told me I had to stop killing. She threatened to tell. You've met her, I'm sure. She calls herself Edna Boyle."

"Your nurse?"

"Yes. It's a pity. I've done so much for her over the years. In 1888, when I decided to leave England, I arranged to take her with me even though my siblings considered her insane. She wasn't. Do you know what was really wrong with her?"

Kate remained silent.

"Diabetes. It went away after we traveled through the vortex. We took the Stonehenge crossing. Soon after, I realized that she still had minor mental problems, so I started giving her an elixir containing St. John's Wort. It lifted her depression and muted her neuroses. Why, she'd even gotten over her fear of electricity." Another laugh. "St. John's Wort. Everything old is new again."

While Katz spoke, Kate worked on the ropes around her wrists. They were looser than they had been a few minutes before. She had to keep him talking. "Did you love your mother?"

"Love? I suppose sons always love their mothers. She loved me. I'd tell her over and over again about the East End prostitutes I killed. She always listened. I don't think she believed me, but you know how mothers are." He fell silent.

"Did you buy sexual favors from them then kill them?"

"Heavens, no. They weren't attractive, you know," he told Kate. "Not at all like you."

Outside, the road was barely visible beyond the sheeting snow. Kate flinched as the vehicle's treads slipped on black ice. It quickly righted itself, but she felt little relief.

"These were coarse women," he told her. "Hard-bitten. Diseased old whores," he added distastefully. "They deserved to die."

"Do I deserve to die?" Kate asked quietly.

"Everyone deserves to die for one reason or another, my dear. Or even for no reason." He downshifted. "You, Kate, are privileged. You have a special purpose. By virtue of your uncommon personality, I have chosen you to fuel my journey." His teeth flashed white in the reflected glare of the headlights. "It's time for me to take my leave."

Back to that again, she thought. The ropes were a little looser now. If she could get them loose enough, they might slip down over her gloves. She'd have a chance. *Zach, where are you?* "You killed them all, didn't you? The prostitutes?"

"The five women in the East End? Yes. There were actually seven but two were never really connected by our bumbling constables. During my term as Jack the Ripper I actually killed many more."

An hour had passed since he'd left Abbott's place, but Tully was finally heading up the mountain. At Bigfoot Tours Tully helped himself to a snowmobile. As an afterthought, he'd broken into the office and took a face mask, snow boots, warmer gloves, and bundled himself in a thick but lightweight parka he found hanging over the back of a chair.

Tully didn't know what time it was now, but it seemed like hours had passed. His rear was numb from the vibrations of the machine and his face felt half frozen despite the knit mask. In reality, he thought, only an hour or so had probably passed. He wasn't even sure where he was, but at least the blinding snow was beginning to let up.

Grimly, he continued his long, hazardous journey up the mountain. The Backdoor Man wouldn't win again. *God, let her be all right.*

Hours had passed and now Kate was being led down the treacherously snowy trail by Phil Katz. It was rough going, but Katz moved slowly. Thank God, the wind had died down to healthy but relatively harmless gusts about the time they'd passed Panther Meadows. Snow still fell, but it was gentle now, coming in light flurries.

When they arrived at the Circle's parking area, Katz had untied her feet so that she could walk. When he finished, Kate was terrified that he would check the bonds on her wrists. Fortunately, he didn't, so he had no idea how loose they were now. She prayed the moment would come soon.

As they reached the bottom of the stairs, Katz's lantern reflected off white crystalline snow blanketing the ground and trees. Here, far from the Circle, it was at least a foot deep. Katz, wearing a backpack, had a gun of some kind trained on her. He nudged it against her ribs. "Walk to the Circle, Kate."

She began moving and as she did a patch of sky cleared, letting the moon shine down upon the scene. Little Stonehenge was eerily beautiful, the stones dark beneath cold white caps. The Circle looked like something out of a dark fairy tale.

She slipped once and Katz waited while she got to her feet unaided. They trudged on and as they approached the standing stones, Kate felt the familiar oddness of the atmosphere wash over her.

For about three feet outside the stones, all the way around, the snow was thinner, perhaps only six inches deep. As she stepped inside the Circle, the gun in her back, she saw that only an inch or two of snow had fallen there. She'd heard of such a thing but had never seen it.

Katz took her to a tall narrow stone in the inner circle near the center where she'd found Lawson's body. He pulled a coil of rope from his backpack. "Stand against the stone," he ordered.

She did as she was told, again afraid that he'd notice the loose ropes on her hands. He bound her to the stone at the waist, two wraps, knotted at her left flank. He ignored her hands; she still had a chance.

Suddenly, she felt dizzy. Icehouse Circle dizzy, not the way she'd felt when she'd fainted in Carl's cabin. The Circle was powerful tonight, she realized. Somewhere in the distance a bird screeched, the sound crashing down in louder and louder echoes. She shivered.

Katz extracted a white robe from the backpack and slipped it over his clothing. With the hood up, he looked like a ghost. He had set the lantern on the ground in front of her. The backpack was there, too. His gun was in the pack; she'd seen him put it there. Now the doctor, standing before her, began speaking in a foreign language, something Latinlike and archaic-sounding. She thought he might be casting a spell.

For a few minutes nothing happened. Light snow swirled and eddied as the man chanted and danced, then suddenly, Kate was nearly overcome by vertigo. She let herself slump against the ropes, waiting to see if Katz would come to her. He didn't. Instead, he continued the chant. It was time to try to make her escape.

As she began to pull her hands free, the air pressure changed, the atmosphere thickening and pounding into her ears like a jet taking off much too fast. She thought she heard high-pitched voices singing, but told herself it was just the wind. She worked at the bonds.

Out of the corners of her eyes, she saw yellow-green light rising from the earth. She'd seen something like it once before, but much paler, when the Circle was particularly active. She wanted to look up, to raise her head and see if there were more colors, but she didn't dare risk making eye contact with Katz. Slowly she slipped off one glove, the ropes with it, careful to keep hold of both. As she slipped off the other one and the rope and gloves nearly fell, but she caught them just in time, holding the rope between her knees while she pulled the gloves back on. After, she wrapped the rope loosely around her wrists and began working on the knot at her waist. As soon as Katz turned away, she planned to go for the gun. It wasn't safe to shoot from a distance here in the Circle where nothing happened the way it should, but if she could get up close, put it right to his heart . . . or his head.

From somewhere above, she thought she heard the whine of a snowmobile, but the sound disappeared into the warm humming wind that was filling the Circle now. The snow began to melt around her shoes.

"What the hell is going on?" Tully muttered as he stood at the top of the stairs. Below, weird light emanated from the ground, bathing the Circle in a glow of colors ranging from a greenish-yellow at ground level to blue and purple twenty feet above the tallest stones.

Jack's getting ready to kill her. As he descended the steps, he prayed that Kate was still alive.

Fifty-six

"Hands in the air!"

Tully's voice broke through the thick atmosphere of the Circle. Kate, the last of her bindings free, looked up and saw him advancing on Katz. Katz must have seen and heard him, but he paid no attention.

The doctor's arms were in the air, hands stretched high, a silvery mist glowing around them. He continued his incantation as if Tully wasn't there.

Kate was sweating in her parka. The snow inside the Circle was completely gone and waves of tingling heat oozed from the center, where Katz stood staring up toward the moon.

"Philip Katz, you are under arrest," Tully yelled. "Stop what you're doing and lay down on the ground!"

Katz looked at him then, his eyes bright and fierce as the hood blew back. He continued his incantation, his eyes still focused on Tully.

A blast of dizzying heat washed over Tully, an explosion of power that sent him flying backward, his gun torn from his hand. He heard Kate cry out as he landed on his back in the thin snow outside the Circle.

Katz continued chanting, acting as if Tully was only a fly

that needed swatting. Dizzy, the sheriff got to his knees then pushed himself up and staggered back toward the Circle. He found his weapon.

Suddenly, he saw Kate drop to the ground in front of Katz. She grabbed the backpack lying near him and dug her hand in. It came out holding a gun.

"Stay down, Kate" Tully screamed as he took aim and pulled the trigger.

"Don't shoot! It's too far!" she cried, too late.

In a blur, the doctor was bending over Kate, wrenching the gun from her hand. Tully realized Katz thought she'd done the shooting.

Tully's bullet ricocheted, missing Katz, banging against one stone, then another. Then it screamed out of the Circle, right past Tully's temple, and disappeared into the darkness beyond.

Kate was still on the ground, but Katz had his gun and it was trained on Kate. Tully watched, his gun on Katz.

"Drop it!" Tully yelled, moving nearer in hopes of shooting Katz.

But the other fired his gun first. Tully hit the earth, rolling away. He stayed down a few seconds in case the bullet ricocheted.

Kate jumped to her feet and leapt on Katz's back, holding tight as he tried to buck her off. He still held the gun. Tully ran into the Circle and moved up behind them. "Get out of here!" he yelled at her as he kicked Katz's legs out from under him. Katz dropped and Kate rolled away as Tully knocked the gun out of Katz's hand. Kate grabbed it and ran to the edge of the Circle.

She watched Tully and Katz fighting in the midst of the colored lights. Even here, at the edge of the Circle, she could feel the weird air pressure and warmth. Disembodied voices seemed to float through her head. She thought she saw bodies undulating in the colors bathing Zach and Katz.

Mesmerized by the lights and sounds, she suddenly realized

that Katz and Zach were edging out of the Circle, locked in close combat. The were headed for the cliff, Katz pushing the sheriff slowly backward.

Katz was strong. Tully was losing the fight, but he had at least thirty pounds and a couple inches on the man. It didn't make sense.

Kate yelled something, but he didn't know what. He was in a fight to the death. Katz's souless eyes bored into his.

"You can't win, Sheriff. Sorcery beats muscle every time."

He was pushed backward, his feet slipping on the icy grass.

"Cliff!" he heard Kate cry.

"You can't win, Tully," Katz said, still driving him steadily backward. "You couldn't stop me from killing your wife and son and you won't stop me from killing your precious Kate. And I'll come back someday for young Josh. But you know that, don't you?"

"Go to hell."

"How does it feel, Tully? You're the first law officer ever to get this close to me. Congratulations. How do you feel? Powerful?"

Katz shoved and Tully's feet slid out from under him. He fell, keenly aware that the earth was slipping away from him. There was a moment of weightlessness, a heart-stopping drop, and then his hands clutched at heavy roots growing out the side of the cliff.

He couldn't hang on long. He found a foothold and began to push himself back up.

"No, no, Sheriff. You can't come back." Katz pulled a knife out from beneath his white robe and flicked it open. He bent toward Tully, the blade aimed at his fingers. "How does it go, Tully, that old rhyme? This little piggy went to market—NO!"

Suddenly, Katz was flying over Tully, tumbling through the air.

Kate's face appeared, pale, above Tully's. She got down on her stomach in the melting snow and reached down, putting her bare hands under his sleeves, grabbing his wrists. She began to pull. Tully dug his feet into the rock and ice.

"I'm slipping," she said after Tully made it six inches up. "Wait'll I get my feet hooked into the branches—There!" She began to pull again, harder now.

It took thirty seconds, maybe a minute, he didn't know exactly, and then he was over the lip of the cliff, sprawled on solid ground. Breathing heavily, he stood up. Kate did the same. She looked at him, panic in her eyes. "Josh is alive and well," he said.

"Thank God." She threw her arms around him in a bear hug. He hugged her just as hard.

At last, they stood together, looking down into the icy crevasse. "It's all glacier down there," Kate said. "No one will ever see him again."

Tully stared into the darkness. "I hope not," he said. "I hope not."

Epilogue

"So much for small mountain towns being havens of peace," Tully said, watching as Josh poked up the fire's red embers. He, Kate, and the boy had spent the day sledding and building snow creatures on Icehouse Mountain—on the side where the resorts were, not in the vicinity of Little Stonehenge. He never wanted to see that place again.

"Time for bed, Josh." Kate held out her arms to her son.

"Do I have to?"

"Yep."

Carefully, he set the poker down then went to Kate and gave her a hug. Without hesitation, he turned and hugged Tully almost as hard. " 'Night."

"Good night," they called as he trotted up the stairs.

Tully settled back on the couch and put his arm around Kate. Her reaction to the events at Icehouse Circle was not as severe as his. In fact, she was talking about the tours frequently now, looking forward to the season when she could do more than drive skiers to and from the resorts and lifts and give an occasional nature talk.

She had wanted to stay in Eternity and he had wanted to leave. Both wanted to remain together, so they had talked and talked. The town wanted him to stay as well, and Mayor Harlan King and his newly restocked city council offered to let him hire not one, but two new deputies that Tully would handpick. They even offered more money; no one wanted to see him go.

Still, he would have gone if it hadn't been for Kate and Josh. But really, he thought, it wasn't so bad here, now that the killer had been stopped. A little cold, a little claustrophobic in the winter, but that just made the hot coffee more delicious and the crackling fire more romantic.

He looked at Kate as she took his hand and caressed it. "Have you made up your mind?" she asked.

He'd lost one family and he wasn't about to lose another. "You're stuck with me," he said.

Then their lips met in a long, warm kiss.

Dear Reader:

I hope you enjoyed *Eternity* as much as I enjoyed writing it. While Icehouse Mountain, Little Stonehenge, and Eternity are fictional, some of the folklore is taken from the lore of Mount Shasta, a famously mysterious mountain in northern California. Whether or not there really are Lemurians living inside Shasta is up for debate, but the mountain itself is a magnificent and awe-inspiring place.

I'd like to tell you about my next book, *Candle Bay*. It's about vampires who run a luxurious hotel on the California coast.

The Darlings are a close-knit family who feed upon their pampered guests with the utmost in civility and panache, but after a mysterious and ancient vampire named Julian Valentyn moves in, they begin to lose their self-control. Hotel manager Natasha Darling can no longer control her lusts and her brother, Stephen, is falling in love with a human, against his will. "Sixteen-year-old" twin vampires, Ivy and Lucy are just plain draining the guests dry, and Uncle Ori thinks he's Don Corleone. Added to their problems are the Dantes, another vampiric family seeking the Darling family fortune.

How will the Darlings overcome their personal problems? Will they vanquish the Dantes and be able to deal with the powerful Julian Valentyn? Will Stephen bite his human love? Will Uncle Ori make you an offer you can't refuse? Come and find out this August!

Tamara Thorne

P.S. I always love hearing from my readers. You can write to me in care of Pinnacle Books. Enclose an SASE if you want a reply.

<u>BOOK YOUR PLACE ON OUR WEBSITE</u> AND MAKE THE <u>READING CONNECTION!</u>

We've created a customized website just for our very special readers, where you can get the inside scoop on everything that's going on with Zebra, Pinnacle and Kensington books.

When you come online, you'll have the exciting opportunity to:

- View covers of upcoming books

- Read sample chapters

- Learn about our future publishing schedule (listed by publication month *and author*)

- Find out when your favorite authors will be visiting a city near you

- Search for and order backlist books from our online catalog

- Check out author bios and background information

- Send e-mail to your favorite authors

- Meet the Kensington staff online

- Join us in weekly chats with authors, readers and other guests

- Get writing guidelines

- AND MUCH MORE!

**Visit our website at
http://www.pinnaclebooks.com**

HORROR FROM PINNACLE . . .